Dead Soil

a zombie novel

Also by Alex Apostol

Earth Angel (Book 1 of The Kamlyn Paige Novels)
Hunted Angel (Book 2 of The Kamlyn Paige Novels)
Girls Like Us
Novel Notes: A Writing Journal

Dead Soil

ISBN 978-1518681943

FOR MY DAD

MAY WE ALWAYS SURVIVE THE ZOMBIE
APOCALYPSE

Prologue

I looked down at the journal in my hands and gave it a squeeze. A smile spread across my weary face. We might not have the key to ending this plague. There's no guarantee we will even make it to Chicago. Some of us could die trying to get there. We could all die. But we're going to try. We have to.

Part One

"The nation that destroys its soil destroys itself."

—Franklin D. Roosevelt

I.

The shooting range where Liam Scott took his fiancée was nothing more than targets set up on a local farmer's home acreage. Tight knit piles of hay sat ten feet high in neat rows. Crudely cut wood with red and white bullseyes were attached to the middle and swayed slightly in the light summer breeze.

There was no one else there to watch as Christine Moore attempted to practice archery for the first time. It was peaceful to be somewhere so remote after five days in the bustle of the Chicago Loop, where the firm she worked at for the last four years was located. Every day she found a reason to be thankful she'd decided to stay in northwest Indiana instead, even if she had to commute an hour and fifteen minutes to work.

Christine closed her eyes and drew in a deep breath of thick, hot air while Liam set up their spot in front of an end target. The scents of freshly cut grass, stale hay, and the water of Lake Michigan wafted up her nostrils. They reminded Christine of her childhood and where she grew up, along the scenic route of highway twelve, which wasn't far from where she stood.

"Arrows used to be made out wood, of course, but now they make them out of aluminum," Liam Scott said in his cool British accent as he dove right into his role of teacher for the day. "Now the bow is made up of this piece here."

He pointed to the curved solid limb. "And the bow string, here."

Christine cocked her head to the side, her big blue eyes glazed over. One minute in and she was bored with the lesson. "I didn't come here to learn the anatomy of a bow. We could've done that at home. I came to shoot."

"How are you supposed to *release* the arrow if you don't even know how the bow works?" Liam's voice was loving with just a hint of condensation.

"It's not rocket science, sweetie," Christine replied back in the same tone. "You pull back and you let go."

"That's Doctor Sweetie to you." Liam gave a coy smile.

Christine let out a huff of laughter. "Doctor of plants. And that doesn't mean you know everything either. I know what I'm doing."

"By all means." Liam Scott grinned and held the bow out to his fiancée.

Christine snatched it from his hands with a confident smile, her chin raised slightly toward the unyielding sun. With her feet planted firmly on the ground, perpendicular to the target, she readied the arrow. She drew back and heard a soft snort from behind her. Ignoring Liam as best she could, she concentrated on her hold. It required more effort than she thought it would. It took all her strength to keep her arms from shaking under the pressure.

Even with the trembling, there was still no doubt in her mind that she would be able to hit the target. She envisioned the arrow piercing the solid red middle of the bullseye. She didn't want Liam to know how much she struggled to hold the arrow steady.

Christine Moore loved Liam Scott unconditionally, but sometimes he treated her like a fragile doll. If he didn't think she could learn to shoot, then why did he bring her there in the first place? She wanted to show him she was just as capable as he was, that he didn't have to protect her all the time. They could protect each other. She shook her head and her long, blonde ponytail swung at her back. It wasn't medieval times. What would they ever use a bow and arrow for aside from practice shooting? What were they practicing for?

Liam Scott stood a ways behind his fiancée with his thin arms folded over his chest. The summer breeze blew his ginger hair freely as the sun beat down on his neck. He could feel his fair skin prickle with the beginnings of a burn.

He watched Christine stare at the target with more dedicated concentration than he'd seen her give anything else in the five years he'd known her, and that included the time he snuck into court and watched her take down the CEO of a fortune five hundred company for embezzlement. A crooked smile spread across his face. It didn't matter if she hit the target or not. They were sharing an honored Scott tradition together and she was actually taking it seriously, even if it was only to prove him wrong.

The longer Christine tried to hold the arrow steady, Liam's mind wandered to his father. He was the one who had started the birthday target practices back when they lived in Liverpool. Even his mother joined them on her birthday. They did it every year until his parents' fatal car accident when Liam was only nine. None of his foster parents had bothered to take him on any of his following birthdays. It warmed his heart to carry the tradition on with the woman who was going to be his wife and the mother of his children.

Christine Moore made one last attempt to pull the arrow further back to ensure it would make it all the way to its target. With a soft exhale, her fingers released the arrow. It seemed to move in slow motion as it cut through the heavy air and landed in the mess of hay beneath the target board.

She immediately turned to look at Liam. Her face was flushed with embarrassment. She silently waited for him to rub her defeat in her face.

"When I first tried I came this close to shooting the man at the target next to us in the foot," he said as he held his thumb and index finger as closely together as possible without touching.

Christine walked over to him and wrapped her arms around his neck with the bow still clutched in her hand.

He laughed into her soft, wavy hair. "Mind you, I *was* only five at the time."

She pulled away and slapped him on the chest. They both gave in to laughter.

"Want me to show you the proper way now?" he asked, but not in a condescending way that said he knew better than her.

It was genuine and Christine knew she could say no to if she wanted to without any hard feelings between them. That was just how Liam was and, after all, it was *her* birthday.

She smiled up at him, her neck bent all the way back to stare into his light green eyes. "Thank you for making me a part of your family today."

Liam Scott smiled back down at her. He took the bow from her hand, picked up an arrow, and drew it back with ease. With the quick release of his fingers, he let it go. The arrow shot straight into the bullseye.

II.

Allison Murphy gallivanted around Christine and Liam's apartment for hours as she hung streamers and balloons from wherever she could reach. Confetti littered the floor in metallic clumps. She wasn't worried about the cleanup the next day, only about making the surprise party amazing for her dearest friend and colleague.

She jumped when someone knocked at the door. The guests had started to arrive and she still hadn't found the wine and Champaign glasses to set up on the buffet table. Quickly, she raced to the kitchen and wrenched open all the cabinets. She should have brought her own glasses. Tupperware and white paper napkins scattered the floor as she swiped them out of the way. In the far back next to the slow cooker there was a box of assorted plastic party glasses. It would have to do.

There was another series of knocks, more impatient and aggressive. "Just a minute!" she yelled. She turned on her heels as she squat on the floor with clear Tupperware gathered in her arms. She shoved them back in the cabinet and shut the door before they could come tumbling back out onto the floor.

Within a half hour the small one bedroom apartment was packed.

"Shh!" Allison Murphy hushed the twenty or so people as she peeked through the blinds at the parking lot below. "They're coming! Hide!"

"Hide where?" Sylvia Goldstein asked in her thick New York accent. "This place is like a sardine can."

Allison rolled her eyes and knelt down beside the couch, still in clear view of the doorway. Her ankles wobbled on her thin high heels. Hushed giggles filled the darkness as Christine Moore's voice echoed through the open hallway outside.

"We're home!" Liam yelled.

Christine looked at him like he was off his rocker. There was tenderness hidden behind her scrunched eyes. She knew what was waiting for her on the other side of the door. They walked into the apartment holding hands. Christine flipped the light switch on in the entryway.

"Surprise!" everyone shouted as they jumped up from their hiding spots.

Christine screamed and smacked her hands over her mouth as her blue eyes bulged. The apartment looked like a wishy washy teenage girl's sweet sixteen party with pink streamers, balloons, vinyl tablecloths, and paper plates covering every surface. Multicolored confetti littered the floor and permeated the carpet. It wasn't Christine's taste in the least. She'd never been the girly girl type. But she genuinely smiled when she saw it, because she knew it was absolutely Allison Murphy.

"Happy birthday, love," Liam said and kissed her forehead.

Christine looked at all her friends with a gaping smile. There were a few people mixed in she'd seen around before, but didn't know personally, a couple she didn't know at all, and then there were her parents. Even though they were involved in her life she was still surprised to see them there. Parties weren't really their thing. Parties weren't really Christine's thing either, but Liam seemed so excited to throw one for her that she kept her mouth shut about it.

Lidia Moore walked over to her daughter and cupped her face in her hands and kissed her on the cheek. "I can't believe you're twenty-eight already," she said with misty eyes. "It's like I blinked and you were all grown up."

Christine's mouth pulled into a smile only a daughter could give her mother when she thought she was being overly sentimental. "Mom…"

"I'm sorry. You're right," Lidia Moore said as she sniffed back her tears and dabbed at her eyes. "It's a party. Your father's here too," she added as if he hadn't been standing right beside to her the entire time.

Thomas Moore leaned in and gave Christine a tight, one-armed hug as she wrapped both her arms around his waist. He smelled faintly of cigar smoke and potting soil. He'd no doubt spent the day working in the backyard garden, a hobby he'd taken to after retirement from the iron-workers union.

"I'm really glad you both came," Christine said.

Lidia Moore leaned in close to her daughter's ear as her eyes lingered on Liam. "He's a good man," she whispered. "Take care of him."

Christine nodded her head and smiled at her fiancé, who was talking to some of the other guests. "I will," she said to her mother. "I'm going to go say hi to everyone—"

Her mother nodded zealously before she finished speaking. "Go, go, mingle. It's your party. We'll be here."

Christine walked over to Liam and looped her arm through his. They were still in their jeans and t-shirts from the range. She felt his warm, burnt skin on her bare arm and felt relaxed.

"Happy birthda-a-a-ay, girl!" Carolyn Bock, the younger woman from upstairs, said with a crooked smile and an almost empty Champaign glass in her hand.

Christine had only met Carolyn once before when Liam suggested they get together because they were both relatively close in age, ignoring the fact that they had absolutely nothing in common except the color of their hair. Carolyn Bock was a twenty-six year old HR office girl at the local steel mill. She was surrounded by good old country boys and loved every minute of it. Christine was a corporate lawyer at a firm in downtown Chicago. She wore a nice suit, carried a briefcase, and didn't say things like "ya'll" or "bitchin'".

"Thanks. Glad you could make it," Christine said as her eyes drifted to the mousy-looking woman standing next to Carolyn.

"This is Debbie Henson. She lives next door to me. I hope it's OK I brought her along. I thought she could use a wild night out," Carolyn said as she nudged the meek woman with scraggly red hair.

Debbie looked around nervously. She let out a hoarse laugh and then cleared her throat. "Nice to meet you.

Happy birthday," she said just above a whisper. Her eyes shifted around the apartment as if she expected the boogeyman to pop out and snatch her away.

Christine only knew Debbie by her last name. She'd heard stories about the fights she and her husband had late at night. She noticed the small, scabbed over split in Debbie's lip and wondered if that was his doing.

"Thank you, both," Christine said politely. "Enjoy!"

Carolyn raised her glass and threw back what little alcohol was left in it, draining it down to the very bottom.

"The look on your face!" Allison Murphy yelled as she wrapped Christine in a tight hug. "It was priceless. We got her!" She shoved Liam playfully on the shoulder.

He gave a quick laugh. "Yes, we did. She didn't have the slightest clue."

Christine smiled and looked away as she sipped from her glass. She'd seen an email from Liam on Allison's computer a week ago that discussed the plans for her surprise party. She was glad her practiced shocked face had fooled them both. She'd hate to disappoint her fiancé.

Liam spotted Zack Kran, his friend and neighbor, from across the room and gestured his head several times toward Allison.

The girls looked at each other through squinted eyes and Christine shrugged her shoulders.

Zack, a thin man with a groomed beard and tight button-down shirt, caught sight of Liam and gave him two thumbs up before he meandered over. "Oh, hey!" he said. "Happy birthday, Chris. Almost thirty!"

"Don't remind me," she huffed.

"Hey, I take offense to that. Thirty's not so bad," Zack said with a hearty chuckle.

Liam jumped in before either of the women could roll their eyes. "Zack this is Allison. Allison…*this* is Zack."

The two shook hands awkwardly as Allison looked to her friend with pleading eyes.

Christine pinched the arm of Liam's shirt and pulled him aside. "What are you doing?" she asked as she tried not to laugh. "You know Allison's married, right?"

"No! Isn't that something you should tell your fiancé about your best friend?"

Christine looked at him hard. "She is *not* my best friend. She's just…my only ally at work."

Allison looked over her shoulder at Christine while Zack laughed at his own joke, her brown eyes wide with animosity. Christine couldn't help giving Allison a thumbs up in mockery. Allison slipped her middle finger up discreetly when Zack wasn't looking. Christine laughed. Then, her face fell. Allison *was* undeniably her best friend.

"Oh, shit. When did that happen?"

"It's only natural," Liam answered in his best therapist voice, which he always used when proving a point. "She was your mother hen when you first arrived at the firm and since then you two have grown accustomed to relying on each other for comfort and familiarity in a place you both despise."

"Yeah? Well your best friend rides a skateboard to the comic book store every day and has a beard like Grizzly Adams," Christine retorted.

"Zack *owns* the store. It's not like he simply hangs out there daily."

They both broke out into laughter simultaneously. Having Allison as a best friend wasn't the worst thing in the world Christine decided. Her short, brown bob always lay perfectly above her shoulders, never a hair out of place. She wore the most expensive high heels Christine had ever seen and never stumbled as she walked flawlessly in them. Her beautiful suits hugged her tight and made it look like she had curves on her thin, straight body. Not only was she Christine's friend…she looked up to her. The last person she'd ever looked up to was her sister and she hadn't seen her since she took off when she was eighteen and Christine was still in the tenth grade.

Christine's mood sobered in the flicker of a heartbeat. "Hey, did you happen to invite my sister?"

Liam's face fell. "I passed the invitation along for her to your parents, but they said she never responded. Last they heard from her, she was in California selling hats on the boardwalk or something. I'm not sure," he said softly.

Christine stared for a moment at the carpet and blinked to clear her eyes. She looked at the small black butterfly tattooed on the underside of her right forearm. The ink of the crooked wings was faded from years of neglect. She touched a finger to it and then looked away. "It's fine," she assured Liam with a contrived smile. "It's fine. I should know better by now."

"She left a long time ago," he said as he put a hand on her shoulder. Liam saw her eyes flicker to her arm again. "How about a drink?" He reached over to the buffet table and grabbed a bottle of wine and a glass. He filled it to the brim.

"Thanks," she said, "I just need to go to the bathroom."

He nodded his head slowly.

Christine shut the door behind her and set the glass of wine on the bathroom counter. As she stared at herself in the mirror, she thought about how different she and her sister had looked from each other as children and what she must look like now. Was she taller, thinner, heavier, tanner? Had her butterfly tattoo faded as much as Christine's had? She shook her head and blinked a few times. None of it mattered. She was probably never going to see her sister again.

She emerged from the cramped bathroom and almost ran right into Sylvia Goldstein, the last person she wanted to see. Why had Liam invited her and her husband after their disastrous double date?

"Great party!" Sylvia said in her loud, nasally voice. "It's quite a group you've put together. So many people here in this tiny apartment!"

"Thanks. It was all Liam's—"

"And you still don't look a day over twenty-one. *What* is your secret?" Sylvia interrupted as she raised a hand to her dark, bouffant hair to make sure it was still in place.

"Actually," Christine said as she nudged her way past Sylvia. "Would you excuse me? I have to say hi to…" she looked around the room for someone available. She spotted an old woman with white hair sitting alone on the bay window seat. Christine pointed to her and walked away without another word. Once Sylvia's back was turned, Christine changed her course for Liam.

"Hey," she leaned in to whisper. "Who brought the Golden Girl?"

Liam stared blankly back.

"*The Golden Girls*? Blanch? Rose…nothing? Let me try again. Who brought the old woman sitting by the window?"

He turned to look and his green eyes lit up with recognition. "Oh, that's Ralph Sherman's mother-in-law. Her flat's on the first floor."

She smiled. Flat. His British accent got her every time. "And who's Ralph Sherman?"

Liam gazed around the room until he spotted Ralph and his wife, Sally, who held their nine month old daughter in her arms while she talked to Ben and Sylvia Goldstein. Liam pointed them out with a slight nod of his head. Sylvia gave an enthusiastic wave before Christine could look away and pretend she hadn't seen her.

"And how do we know him?" she asked.

"He's the kid who installed our cable and internet when we moved in." Liam raised his glass to Ralph when their eyes met.

"Oh." She didn't remember him. How could these people live in the same building as her for a year and she still had no idea who they were? And why did Liam know everyone?

As if Christine's thoughts were written across her face, Liam looked at her with soft eyes. "You've been really stressed with work, staying late at the office…It's hard to get to know people with those hours."

She nodded, but was still lost in thought. Maybe it *was* her fault she didn't have any real friends. She'd always preferred time alone as opposed to being surrounded by people. That was just who she was, until she met Liam during her last semester at law school. Then all she wanted to do was spend time with him when she wasn't working. She didn't have the time for much else.

Liam could tell his fiancée was stuck inside her own head by the glossy, vacant look on her face. He was determined to get her out to enjoy the party, maybe even make some new friends. "Yeah, I feel bad for the whole lot of them actually," he said as he looked back at Ralph. "They don't get out much because his wife is always at home with the baby or taking care of her mother. Seems like she could really use a companion. Someone to expand her horizons a bit, or just to talk to…" He trailed off when he saw the stern look on Christine's face.

"You promised me no more blind friend-dates," she hissed. "Not after *Sylvia Goldstein*." She spat the name out like it was a rancid piece of meat. "You've lost all hook-up privileges."

Liam laughed and threw his arm over her shoulder to reel her in. "How about another drink?" He turned to walk to the buffet table, but his path was blocked.

"Looks like we're going to have to get going," Dr. Ronald Conrad, Liam's colleague, said with his wife at his side. Her cheeks were burning bright red and she kept tugging at the sleeve of his crisp blue shirt.

"Everything alright?" Liam asked.

"Yeah, it's just Gloria, here, installed one of those nanny cams, y'know, to see what Olivia was up to when we're not home. Turns out the minute we left she put the baby to bed and invited her delinquent boyfriend over."

Liam stretched his mouth back and grit his teeth in a show of pained sympathy. "Sorry, mate."

"No matter. It's this one who's all bent out of shape now because she caught this kid plowing her seventeen-year-old niece."

"They weren't having sex!" Gloria Conrad screeched. She turned to Liam and spoke to him directly. "They had their clothes on."

He nodded his head and opened his mouth, but was at a loss for what to say.

"Great party," Gloria said as she touched Liam lightly on the arm and then turned in a flurry to head for the door. Ronald scurried after her.

"She's…" Christine said as the Conrads hurried off, "…passionate."

"Right," Liam laughed. "Well said."

"When is Ronnie being transferred out to Stanford?"

Liam shrugged his shoulders. "He hopes soon. He hates it at the university's lab."

"Why's that?"

"He thinks Dr. Hyde uses him like an errand boy. I mean, the man's got a doctorate in microbiology. He shouldn't be picking up the dry cleaning."

"And Dr. Hyde is your new boss?"

"Correct," Liam said with a nod. "He invited me to join his team to create a vaccine for that new strain of flu everyone's on about."

Christine nodded her head. She tried to remember when Liam had told her all this, but she couldn't. She did, however, remember all the breaking news over the deadly flu. It was hard to miss. If they weren't interrupting shows to update everyone with breaking news, it scrolled slowly across the bottom of the screen on every local channel.

"They project it to wipe out almost forty percent of the population if someone doesn't make a working vaccine soon."

"What's taking so long?" Christine asked with a furrowed brow.

Liam gave a discordant laugh. "It's not that simple. Every time we think we've got it, the flu strand changes and we have to start all over. That's why almost every lab in the country is working around the clock to stop it. They just...can't."

Christine let Liam's word drift in and out of her mind as the wine hit her all at once. Unexpectedly, a ball of panic dropped in her stomach and weighed it down like a bowling ball. Forty percent of the population could be wiped out in one year because of something as common as the flu. Maybe she should consider getting one of those disposable hospital masks, even though it looked creepy when she saw someone walking around in one.

Over the next twenty minutes people said their goodbyes. The crowd dissipated until it was only Liam, Christine, Luke Benson from upstairs, and Carolyn Bock left.

Luke claimed he wanted to help the couple clean up, but it was his anxiety over Carolyn cornering him at his apartment door that kept him there. She had jumped at the chance to offer to help once he had. Her eyes lingered on him whenever he bent over to pick up a dropped plate or napkin. She watched his dark skin tighten over his rounded arm muscles and sighed. Each time, he looked to Liam and Christine with wide, desperate eyes.

"Poor guy," Christine cooed in a whisper to Liam. "We should help him."

Liam nodded and opened his mouth to speak, but was cut off by the muffled sounds of shouting from the floor above. Everyone looked up in silence.

"I better go," Carolyn said immediately and dropped the trash that was in her hand before she darted out the door. She left it open behind her.

The warm breeze from the open hallway wafted up Christine's nose, bringing the scent of the Dunes and Lake Michigan along with it. A vision of her grandmother picking wildflowers along the Calumet bike path swam through her fermented mind. She missed her so much, even though she died almost ten years ago. The woman had practically raised her while her parents immersed themselves in their work.

A faint knock, only heard because of the door that stood ajar, brought Christine out of her reminiscent trance. A new slew of curses from Colt Hansen upstairs was now directed at Carolyn for interfering in the argument with his wife.

"Shit," Liam said and put down the garbage bag he'd been filling. "Think we should help her out?"

Luke didn't stop for a second to think about it. He continued to pick up paper plates with half eaten pieces of vanilla cake on them. "Carolyn's tougher than she looks. She got this. It's not the first time she's stuck her nose in the middle of the Hansen's business. Ever since she called the cops on him last month, he usually checks himself. He mighta learned his lesson if his wife hadn't bailed him out right away. Don't know why she did. She shoulda left him to rot. If I ever did that to my wife…ex-wife…she'da let me rot too. That's for sure."

A heavy silence hung in the room like a storm on the horizon. Christine couldn't imagine what it felt like to be hurt by someone she thought loved her. No matter what she did, she couldn't picture Liam ever raising a hand to her, even as an empty threat. He was a good, gentle man. If a bug got into the apartment, he was the one who cupped it in his hands and set it free out on the patio.

"Well, I'm going to head out while crazy is occupied," Luke said as he looked down at the gold watch on his wrist. It was half past midnight.

"Yeah, we're going to nod off now too." Liam tied the last garbage bag closed and tossed it by the door.

Christine dragged her feet along the beige carpet. Little pieces of shiny confetti stuck in between her toes. She peeled them from her feet, but when she tried to throw them away they stuck to her fingers. No amount of flailing freed them. "Dammit Allison," she mumbled as she shuffled off to the bedroom, still flicking her hands through the air. She sighed and tossed herself back onto the bed.

Liam stopped in the doorway and smiled at her. He'd never been so happy in his life.

III.

Liam's phone beeped relentlessly early Sunday morning. At first he thought it was part of his dream, then a truck backing up in the parking lot outside their bedroom window, and finally the sound of an unread text message on his phone on the bedside table. He groaned and rolled over. It was a struggle to open his eyes as he rubbed the back of his hands over them. Everything was a blur.

He patted the table in search of his red-rimmed glasses and put them on. He blinked a few times to clear the sleep from his eyes and the remnants of his dreams. There was a red light blinking on his phone. When he pushed the button on the side the time flashed. It was six-eighteen in the morning. He threw his head back and sighed. Despite his desires to drop the phone and go back to sleep, he read the message.

```
                    Dr. Hyde

     Please come in to work today, as soon as
you can. I have something important to tell
     you. There's still work to be done.
```

IV.

Liam arrived at Valparaiso University at eight in the morning on the dot, like every work morning, though it was his day off. His legs moved swiftly as he rushed to Dr. Hyde's office, as if he were gliding instead of walking.

Dr. Ronald Conrad joined his side from an adjoining hallway and tried to keep pace with him. "What's this all about?" he asked with perfectly rounded eyes.

"I don't know," Liam said through labored breath as panic rose in his stomach. There couldn't be something wrong with the vaccine. It'd worked. They did the trial. He saw it work.

Liam burst into his boss's darkened office. He stopped with his hand still on the doorknob. Ronald ran into his back, his hands up to brace the impact. The only source of light was a small lamp that gave off a dim orange glow. Behind the desk Dr. Hyde sat hunched, a soft rattle emanated every time he took a breath, the movement of his shoulders almost undetectable.

"Dr. Hyde," Liam said as his chest clenched at the sight of his boss. "Dr. Hyde, are you OK?" He rushed around the desk and bent down at his side.

Ronald stayed where he was with his hands on his hips as he tapped his foot. He did a small circle while he rubbed his hand over his blonde hair to slick it back.

"The vaccine," Dr. Hyde huffed out through slightly parted, cracked lips. They were blue around the edges.

Liam bent in closer, his ear next to the doctor's mouth.

"No…good…" Dr. Hyde gave a hacking cough and struggled to raise his arm to place his hand over his mouth.

Liam looked at the desk and saw drops of blood splattered over the large, paper calendar. He took a deep breath.

"Call nine-one-one. Hurry!" Liam said to Ronald as he reached out to Dr. Hyde. "Just relax. Help is on the way," he said louder than he needed to. His heart beat at twice its normal speed.

Dr. Hyde's breath slowed. It hissed from his chest with every exhale. "The trials...they're all...going..." he gasped. His pale blue eyes were distant.

Liam stood up straight and covered his mouth with one hand. His lips trembled. He turned to look at Ronald, who had taken a few steps out of the office to call the police, his back turned to them.

Dr. Hyde's body shook violently as he coughed again. The sound echoed through the office and down the hall. He threw himself forward, face down, onto the desk as he struggled to breath between fits of coughing. More blood flew from his lips to speckle the surface of the desk with red droplets.

"Oh, God, Dr. Hyde!" Liam said as he turned to him again and bent over him. He lightly touched the man's back to feel his chest wrack with force. "Dr. Hyde! Ronald, help!"

Ronald rushed in, but froze in the doorway. Dr. Hyde strained to take in air as blood oozed from the sides of his ivory lips. A puddle formed slowly under his face and crept outward. Then, all at once, the office fell silent.

Dr. Hyde lay still. He no longer gulped for air like a fish out of water. Blood reached the end of the desk and dripped over the side as Liam still stood bent over him, frozen. He shook his head slowly, his eyes wet.

"My God," Ronald whispered. "Is he...?"

Liam didn't hear him. He couldn't hear anything. All his focus was on the now dead Dr. Hyde who lay across the desk, arms outstretched before him.

"Liam…Liam!" Ronald yelled, finally making his way across the office to put a hand to his friend's shoulder. He shook Liam from his stupor.

"We have to help him!" Liam yelled as he reached out to an inert Dr. Hyde. "We have to save him!"

Ronald pulled at Liam's shoulders as he struggled to grasp Dr. Hyde, sure that there was something he could do to bring him back. He swung his body to try and break free from Ronald's grip

"He's gone, man. He's gone. There's nothing we can do. Look! He's gone." Ronald said as he threw his arms from Liam and gestured to Dr. Hyde, who remained silent and unmoving.

Liam broke down. Death had played an important part in his life, but he'd never seen it up close before. He'd never seen the life of someone he knew extinguished before his eyes. His whole body shook as he tried to pull himself together. His knees wobbled as he stood up straight.

Ronald rested a hand on Liam's shoulder to lead him away from the dead man slumped over the desk.

"Wait," Liam said as he looked over his shoulder. "Do you hear that?"

Both men strained their ears, rooted where they stood, and leaned their bodies forward toward Dr. Hyde. A low rattle followed by a hissing wheeze grew in volume until there was no mistaking what it was.

"He's alive!" Liam yelled and rushed back over to the doctor. "Dr. Hyde, can you hear me? Are you OK?"

The doctor's fingers flexed and released. His nails scratched deeply into the wood of the desk. The rattling subsided and transformed into a low, rumbling growl from the depths of Dr. Hyde's throat.

Liam backed away slowly, hands held out in front of him as if his boss were a possibly rabid dog. The man clearly needed help. He didn't know why he was frightened. He should've given him CPR, but all he could think about was getting as far away from him as possible. He jumped when he felt the solidity of the door frame at his back.

"What the…" Ronald mumbled next to Liam, his head leaned forward as the rest of his body pressed against the wall.

Dr. Hyde's head moved from side to side in a jagged, broken motion, the growling built until it escaped his lips. Blood dripped from between his teeth as he lifted his head slowly. His eyes opened to reveal sickly yellowish-green irises veiled with a milky glaze, sunken in and surrounded by dark circles. As he stood up, his bones cracked like the popping of bubble wrap until he stood, slackened, with the desk in front of him. It was a small barrier between him and the two terrified doctors.

"No…fucking…way," Ronald whispered as his hands reached behind him to feel for the opening of the door.

Neither men wanted to make a move. Liam didn't know what they were looking at, but scrambling in a panic felt wrong, like painful and certain death. Liam wanted to say something to Dr. Hyde, sure that the man was lost and in some sort of pre-death shock, but nothing came out when he opened his mouth.

Dr. Hyde twisted his head slowly to the side like an animal assessing its prey. A moan escaped from between his red teeth. Liam gasped loudly and the doctor's head snapped to focus on the source of the sound. He wretched his mouth open and forced out a high cry as his feet dragged on the floor to move him alongside the desk and then forward. He gave a guttural growl with his arms outstretched, his stiff fingers flexed to grip the first thing they came in contact with.

Liam turned and fell through the doorway at top speed. "Come on!" he called out to Ronald, who ran as fast as he could but still fell behind Liam at lengths.

There was no thought of trying any of the other office doors to take shelter behind. No one had been there to unlock them since it was Sunday. All Liam saw in his mind was the pathway laid before him to the parking lot. He wasn't going to stop until he was in his car, his vision tunneled to the door at the end of the hallway that lead to the reception area.

He looked over his shoulder when he heard Ronald cry out. His friend was spread across the floor and was trying to crawl in a scramble away from Dr. Hyde, who closed in on him. Ronald attempted to stand up, but slipped on the tile and fell back down onto his chest. Liam stopped to face his friend. "Ronnie! Come on!"

Dr. Hyde threw himself down onto Ronald with his mouth wide open.

"No!" Liam screamed, hunched over as his fingers pulled at his ginger hair. "Ronnie!"

Ronald reached out to Liam from down the hall as Dr. Hyde's jaw clenched the back of his neck. There was a blood curdling scream. Ronald's mouth opened and closed with silent gasps. Dr. Hyde tugged at him until he was on his back, face up, to watch the horror he would behold. Nails dug into the helpless doctor's face and shoulders and ripped the skin and muscles from the bones as his body jerked. Dr. Hyde groaned, his glazed eyes rolled back, as he shoved the flesh into his mouth. He chewed at it vigorously.

Liam couldn't move. He sobbed, repeating Ronald's name in a whisper as he watched in disgust and terror. His friend had just been torn apart before his eyes and he'd done nothing to stop it. What could he have done?

Once Ronald fell still, Dr. Hyde no longer dug into him. His head raised as his shark-like, dead eyes stared right at Liam. He pushed himself up off the ground and shambled down the hall towards the only live prey left.

Liam couldn't take his eyes away from what used to be his best friend lying broken and bleeding on the floor. He gurgled blood through his ripped throat and then, against all odds, rose slowly to stand up. Liam squeezed his eyes shut and opened them again. He was sure he had to be seeing things. Ronald stood in a pool of burgundy blood that dripped freshly from his wounds and down his pale blue button up shirt. As he turned his gnarled face up to the ceiling, he let out an appalling shriek.

Ronald started forward and passed Dr. Hyde as Liam ran for the door. He pushed on it and moved the handle up and down to no avail. Somewhere in the depths of his memory he remembered he had to pull the door in order to open it. He shoved his way through just in time to miss the superhuman grip of Ronald's cold, dead hands.

Liam's breathing was labored as he ran at full speed out of the building and to his car. He let out gasping screams to the beat of his pounding feet. He felt his pockets for his keys and pulled them out, but the sweat in his eyes prevented him from seeing which button unlocked the doors. He pushed them all at random until he finally found the right one and heard the click as the locks popped up.

Meanwhile, Ronald and Dr. Hyde were closing in on him at a hauntingly slow pace. Every time Liam looked over his shoulder they were a few paces closer, their mouths open and stained with black, dried blood.

There was no one else around to help Liam. He was far into campus and students weren't permitted to go near the labs unless it was for class. He was all alone. He yanked open the door, shut himself inside, and slammed the palm of his hand down on the locks.

The thing that used to be Dr. Ronald Conrad made it to the car first and pressed itself against the window, pounding its fists into the glass. With each strike the window became streaked with dingy, darkened blood. The corpse of Dr. Hyde made its way over and followed Ronald's relentless attack on the car to get to the meat inside.

Liam's hands shook violently and he struggled to put the key into the ignition while jaws snapped at the air. Putrid eyes locked onto Liam's.

"This can't be happening," he repeated as he sat in the car, his eyes squeezed shut, the sound of dead fists beating against the window a distant sound in the background. Somewhere, he mustered up the strength and courage to step on the gas and drive away from what used to be his boss and friend. He looked over at the blood streaked window and noticed a spidering crack. The sight sent a shiver down his neck and arms. He moved his eyes forward to the road as breathing in became harder for him to do.

V.

Christine heard the front door open and close from the bedroom. "Honey?" she asked, though she knew it was Liam. No one else had access to their apartment and she'd locked the door behind him when he left for the university that morning. "How'd it go? Why'd he call you in so early?" she asked with a fire in her voice over their ruined Sunday morning.

She froze when she saw Liam standing in the middle of the living room, his back turned to her. His shoulders moved up and down intensely as he heaved breaths through his parted mouth. The back of his grey button down shirt had a bloody handprint smeared on it.

"What have I done?" he whispered just loud enough for Christine to hear. He whirled around to look at her, his normally thin eyes wide. "What have I done?"

Christine walked over to him slowly with her mouth agape. She touched his chest lightly with the palms of her hands. "Liam, what happened?" she asked. "Please, tell me."

Liam just stood there, lips trembling, as he explained what happened at the lab with a vacant look in his red-rimmed eyes—Dr. Hyde's hungry expression as he shuffled after Liam, the shreds of flesh hanging from Ronald's throat and Dr. Hyde's teeth, the way Ronald stood back up despite his bloody, torn face and ragged windpipe.

Christine's large, blue eyes welled with tears as she gaped at Liam, who was consumed in what he'd seen, his face frozen in permanent horror. She didn't know what to say. It didn't sound real. It couldn't be real. There was no way it could be real…but how was she supposed to tell him that? She hadn't been there to see what it was exactly that Liam saw. Maybe Dr. Hyde had a severe nosebleed and it got all over Ronald and Liam thought it was something that it wasn't. Even as she thought it, she knew it wasn't true. All she did know was that Liam's version couldn't be true either.

Liam Scott slowly moved his head to focus his tear soaked eyes on his fiancée. "I've killed us all," he said, low and steady. "I should have stopped them when I had the chance."

"Please, stop, Liam. You're scaring me."

"I should have killed them. Why did I run away like that? I've killed everyone."

They both stared at each other in desperation. The only sound to fill the silence was the whir of the air conditioning that blew from the vents.

All at once, as if a switch went off in his head, Liam snapped out of his daze and grabbed Christine by the shoulders, shaking her as he spoke. "We need to prepare," he said with wild eyes. "We need to stock up on everything we can and barricade ourselves in."

Christine looked back with narrowed eyes and a crinkled nose. She put her hands ontop of his and slowly pushed them from her shoulders. She spoke in a soothing, calm tone. "Liam…it's OK."

"No, it's not OK. Don't you get it? The world as we know it is going to end and we need to be ready!" Liam paced the room, brushing his unruly ginger hair with his hands so it stuck up on its ends.

"What we need to do is call the police."

"Already called. They're probably at the university now, getting their faces ripped apart by..." He trailed off, unable to bring himself to say their names. "We need to go to a supercenter of some kind."

Christine looked up at Liam with a furrowed brow, unable to follow his train of thought.

"Yeah, we need to go and buy everything we can and get back here. Let's go. Right now."

It was all too much for Christine. She rolled her eyes and sighed. Was she supposed to call the police on him? Was he crazy? Was he dangerous? Deep down, a loud voice shouted that it was Liam, the same man who nursed a fallen bird with a broken wing for weeks until it could fly again. *Something* had happened. Liam believed his boss and his friend had died infront of him and rose up again to try to eat him, for some reason. Was he having a breakdown? Was the pressure of working tirelessly to create a flu vaccine getting to him? Her shoulders relaxed as she closed her eyes. When she opened them she was staring into Liam's pleading face just inches from hers. She flinched back involuntarily.

"So, you think this is what? The zombie apocalypse?" she asked, hoping he would laugh and say he was joking the entire time. Anything was better than him actually believing in what he said.

He nodded his head, face steady, lips pursed, and eyes more serious than ever.

"O…K…" Her voice was drawn out and skeptical, her head tilted to the side. "Let's say we go and buy the place up, stock up our tiny apartment with thousands of dollars' worth of supplies. What happens if you're wrong?" He opened his mouth to protest, but she knew what he was going to say and held her hand up to cut him off. "*Or* you're right, but they put a stop to it before it can ever spread further than Ronnie and Dr. Hyde."

Liam flinched at the sound of their names.

Christine softened her glare, but still shrugged her shoulders with her hands in the air. "What do we do then?" Her shoulders fell and her hands slapped against her jean covered thighs.

Liam's face was unfaltering. "We keep the receipts and take it all back. Walmart will take anything back. Remember when we returned those used tenny-shoes because you said they squeezed your pinky toe too hard?"

She let out a breathy laugh and looked up at the ceiling. "Yeah, I went power walking in them for a week straight, too."

"We won't use any of what we buy until we absolutely have to," he assured her.

Still unconvinced, but unable to say no, Christine sighed. "All right. Let's go, then."

They raided the Walmart next door to their apartment complex. Five hours, eight shopping carts, two trips in Liam's Jeep and Christine's BMW, thousands of dollars on the Capital One credit card, and countless times hauling bags up to the second floor to their apartment, they were finally done. The place looked like it belonged to one of those people from the TV show *Hoarders*.

"And this is just a month's supply?" Christine asked after she collapsed onto the only small portion of the couch not covered in bags and boxes. "I don't think we could use all of this in a year let alone a month." The adrenaline rush from spending an excessive amount of money and then the following exercise of carrying it up the stairs made Christine forget all about why they raided the store in the first place. She no longer had the energy to wonder if her fiancé was insane.

She watched as Liam took to organizing all they had bought in order to make more room in their five hundred square foot apartment. He was no longer in a panic. His eyes weren't wide and wild anymore. If she wasn't mistaken, he seemed at peace, or was it relief? She let her head fall back against the couch and closed her eyes.

Once the initial scare was over in a day or two and Liam realized there was no end approaching, she would convince him to go talk to someone—a shrink or a therapist. But at that moment, she couldn't even get off the couch to help him put stuff away. She huffed out an exhausted laugh, but Liam was halfway immersed in a box full of canned foods and didn't notice. If it *was* the zombie apocalypse then she was fucked, because she was obviously out of shape.

Liam dug around another box with tools and pulled out the battery powered drill. He set to work on installing the extra deadbolts on their front door and patio door.

VI.

Christine stared at the television as the newscaster wept, trying to get out what she had to say about the horrifying attacks around town. As she continually sniffed back her tears, she rambled on about the outbreak that had taken over the entire northwest Indiana in twenty-four hours. Mascara dripped from her eyes like the black blood of the infected.

Liam had been right.

Christine dialed her parents' number again, but there was still no answer. Each time she got their voicemail her stomach sank and she thought she would be sick. She'd been trying to call them since they got back from shopping the day before, but even then there was no answer. Her eyes burned from sleeplessness.

She let the phone drop from her hands to the floor where she sat with her back rested against the couch, her knees curled up to her chest. The woman on the news was hysterical. She cried into her cell phone and then the screen turned to snow.

Somewhere in the apartment, Liam dug through more boxes. He stayed up all night to organize everything. At eight in the morning he was only halfway done and the living room was the one place where they could walk through or sit.

Christine stared ahead at the fuzzy screen in a daze. It felt best to feel nothing at all, to check out for a minute and turn her brain off completely. She jumped when the phone rang by her feet. Her hands grabbed for it in a panic and she fell over trying to reach where it lay. Her long blonde hair fell over her face and into her mouth. She spat it out.

"Hello!" she yelled desperately, "hello?" Everything inside her hoped the sound of her mother's voice would greet her from the other end as she brushed her messy hair back.

"I see how it is," a woman said. "The plague breaks out and you can't even bother to show up for work."

Christine let her body slump against the couch again. "Oh, hey, Allison. I'm surprised there's anyone even at the firm today."

"You know Shale. He wouldn't close the doors if his own wife was on her deathbed," Allison Murphy said with bitterness.

"What are *you* doing there?" Christine felt more like herself with the distraction of Allison's call. It felt good to talk to someone who wasn't panicking.

"I don't know. Things seem pretty normal over here. There's only been like a few cases of this thing in the city so far so I figured why not? Get out of the empty house. My husband's out of town for the next two days anyway," she said as she sat at her desk, legs propped up and crossed at the ankles, her black high heels clicking together. She twirled a strand of her short, brown bob around her finger as she threw her head back and stared at the ceiling. "There's only ten of us here in the office total. It's like a ghost town. When Shale calls the first meeting it will just be me, Calvin, Maria and that weird new lawyer."

Christine listened without interruption. It was a great escape. She tuned out the sounds of Liam shuffling things around in the bedroom.

"I should just leave. Go to the gym or something. Buy a huge tub of ice cream and watch chick flicks all day in my pajamas."

Christine actually laughed. When the sound escaped her lips she stopped in disbelief that she was even still capable. Maybe things weren't as bad as she thought. Maybe the media was blowing things out of proportion. Wouldn't be the first time.

"So, what's going on with you?" Allison asked as Maria Sanchez walked by her door, peeking in only to point a finger gun to her head and pull the trigger before walking on to her own office next door.

"I'm held up in the apartment right now," Christine said with a sigh. "Liam won't let anyone in or out. He's put like a hundred extra locks on both doors and is getting ready to board up the windows if necessary."

"When would that ever be necessary?" Allison chuckled, letting her legs fall to the floor when someone's office door slammed shut. There was yelling next door.

"I don't know…"Christine trailed off. "I don't know that I want to know. This is all so surreal. I still can't get ahold of my parents. I'm really starting to freak out, cooped up in here. We had this huge fight last night because I wanted to drive to their house to make sure they were OK and Liam went on this rant about how if we left the apartment we would die. He actually said that. We would *die* if we left." Christine huffed from her nostrils.

"Wow. I told you he was nuts," Allison said as she stood up and walked over to her closed door.

There were multiple people yelling and their shouts rose high in panic. She placed her hand on the doorknob and let it rest there, deciding whether she should open it or not.

"What's that?" Christine asked, the faint screams echoing through the phone.

"I don't know," Allison replied. "Let me find out. Maybe someone finally went crazy and tried to murder Shale, not like we all haven't thought about it."

Christine let out a breathy laugh. She remembered all the times she wished she could've kill the senior partner. But all at once her face tightened as she realized what her friend was about to do. "No!" she yelled as her back stiffened. "Stay there!"

Allison was already in the hall though and Christine heard the shrill cry of her friend. Reflex told her to pull the phone away from her ear before the drum burst, but she couldn't move. Her body was rigid.

"Allison!" she cried out, her voice high and shrill.

Liam came running from the bedroom. He tripped over a box and caught himself on the counter that separated the kitchen from the living room. When he saw Christine on the floor with the phone to her ear, tears streamed down her cheeks, he didn't say anything. He rest a hand on his hip, turned on the spot, and ran his other hand through his unkempt hair.

Christine sobbed, choking on her every breath. "Allison?"

There was no answer.

She hung up the phone and threw it to the floor. Her shoulders shook as she bawled into her hands.

Liam paced in a circle before he doubled over, hands on his knees, to catch his breath. He removed his red-rimmed glasses and wiped at his face. *Pull it together*, he told himself in his head. *Your fiancé needs you.* He walked over and bent down into a squat to wrap his arms around her. He let her cry into his chest as he stroked her hair.

"We have to go…we have to go to…my parents'…" Christine said in between sobs, her words muffled by his navy blue t-shirt.

Liam continued to pet her hair, squeezing her to him. "We can't," he said in a steady voice. "I'm sorry. We can't." He held onto Christine as her body jarred violently.

It was the first time his accent didn't make her swoon. She wanted to punch him. Her best friend was dead. She thought about the last time she saw Allison at work and her eyes burned with tears.

VII.

Christine Moore sat at her desk and watched the minutes tick by on her watch. She held her breath as she waited for the last one to fall away, hoping Mr. Shale didn't call everyone into the conference room for another emergency meeting. The further the pension fund smuggler's case progressed, the nuttier her boss was over it. This lead to them working long nights and very little time with Liam. That's why she planned a special night for him and, so far, the stars had aligned and everything was going as planned. Step one was to leave the office on time.

Only twenty seconds left until six o'clock.

She listened to the sounds of her fellow lawyers and their assistants as they shuffled around the office. She dreaded seeing one of their faces pop up in her doorway to call her away.

Ten seconds left.

Purse in hand, she poised herself to spring up from her chair when the big hand hit the twelve.

Five seconds.

"Oh there you are," Allison's voice called as she leaned against Christine's doorway with her arms folded.

Christine's shoulders sank as she settled back into her chair. "If you're here to tell me there's another meeting I'll kill you with my bare hands and stuff your body into one of the drawers in my desk."

Allison gave a girlish laugh. "My fat ass wouldn't fit."

"I'll make you fit," Christine said with a sober expression.

Allison threw her head back and gave in to full laughter. "You're dark. I like that." She walked in and sat down on the edge of the desk. "No, I just came in to say hi and wish you a happy birthday and weekend."

Christine exhaled a sigh. "In that case," she said and grabbed her purse again as she jumped up from her leather chair. "I will." She made for the door, but stopped short and turned on her heel back to Allison. "And you're not fat."

Allison let her head fall softly to the side as she looked at Christine with loving eyes.

"You're just old."

Allison's face tightened as she glared. "You can go now, bitch."

VIII.

Christine sat on the bay window seat and looked out at the darkened, empty parking lot. All the cars, along with their owners, had cleared out before nightfall. The trees blew back and forth in a breeze that didn't cool, but only pushed the hot air around. She'd been locked in their apartment for thirty-six hours. It felt like weeks as Liam constantly rearranged things from box to box, never settling in one place for too long. Christine hadn't picked herself up to move or help at all. Allison was gone. Her parents were likely gone, too. She wondered if her sister was alive, wherever she was.

"Can I at least go outside for a quick walk or something?" she yelled, her head craned up so her voice carried to the bathroom where Liam was finding room for all the toilet paper he'd bought.

"No," was all he said.

"Just for a minute. I can't breathe in here."

"No," he said in the same, quick, solid voice.

Christine sighed and turned to look out the window again. "It's not like anyone's even going to be up at four thirty in the morning to attack me. I'll be really careful. I'll even take one of those knives you bought if it'd make you feel better."

"No."

She wanted to scream. He wasn't the boss of her. They were a team. She was his fiancée, not his prisoner. The outburst boiled and rose inside her, and then simmered and dissipated until it was entirely gone. She remembered the agonizing screams from Allison she'd heard from the safety of her apartment, the one Liam had stocked with over ten thousand dollars' worth of supplies for them. Something moved in between the abandoned cars left in the parking lot and caught her eye. She didn't tell Liam.

A knock on the door made Christine jump. It was loud, like multiple fists were pounding in furry. Liam ran from the bathroom. The banging grew more desperate. Liam and Christine looked at each other with wide eyes, but neither went to open the door. Suddenly, Christine was thankful for all the locks that kept them inside and whatever was outside out.

"Please, open up!" a familiar woman's voice traveled through the door. "My son needs help! Please, he's hurt badly. Please, help!"

Christine got up from the window seat and started to walk over to the door. Her path was blocked by Liam before she could extend her hand to start the tedious task of unlocking the deadbolts.

"It's just Mrs. Ramiren," Christine said, matter-of-factly with her chin jutted out. "Her son's hurt."

Liam didn't move. His eyes fixated on Christine as he towered over her with his lanky body. She saw her reflection in his glasses. Her eyes were squinted and her brow was furrowed together. Could he really be denying someone help? That wasn't the Liam she knew.

He stood like a stone statue with his arms extended in both directions to grip either side of the small entryway walls.

"You're seriously not going to help them?" Christine asked as she moved to get around Liam.

He gripped her upper arms and held her back. She struggled against him, throwing herself around wildly to break free from his grip.

"Let me go!" she yelled. "We have to help them!"

"Yes, please, help us!" Mrs. Ramiren said from the other side of the door. The sound of her rapid pounding fists kept in time with Christine's racing heartbeat.

Liam gripped her harder and shook her. She stared at the brown and green swirls in his hazel eyes. The water collecting in them gave the allusion that the colors were moving and mixing with each other.

"The only way we're letting them in is if you're prepared to put a bullet in that kid's head!" he yelled, his fingers wrapped completely around her small biceps.

Christine's shoulders were scrunched up to her neck. She leaned backwards, held upright by Liam's strength alone. She pursed her lips to fight back the tears. She didn't want to appear weak. She was a lawyer, dammit. She should have been able to argue her way into making him open the door. But her lips stayed tightly shut while her eyes bore through him.

She wrenched her shoulders free, but didn't walk away. She matched Liam, stare for stare. The pounding at the door finally subsided as they continued to glare at each other, though it still rang in Christine's ears.

She tried to calm herself to sit back down on the window seat, but immediately bounced back up. "I babysat Ahmed before. Do you remember that?" She thrust a pointed finger at the closed door.

Liam looked at the floor with his hands on his hips. He didn't answer.

"And now we're just supposed to let them die?" Her voice border lined on shrill.

"Yes," Liam said quietly. He couldn't raise his eyes to look at her. He hated the way things were. "If we let them in then we're all dead." He finally raised his head. "It's us or them."

Christine was left to stand alone in the living room as Liam walked into the bedroom. He shut the door behind him.

IX.

"Ralph, you need to go get my mother," Sally Sherman said as their daughter, Lilly, balanced on her hip in the kitchen.

Ralph Sherman groaned over his cup of coffee at the sound of his name. They'd only been together for two years, but he knew his wife exclusively used it when she was irritated with him. He sipped at the steaming medium roast in his DirecTV mug.

The Northwest Times sat unopened on the counter. The front page was riddled with stories about the outbreak, most claiming the new strand of flu was to blame. He was sick of hearing about it already.

Work had called that morning to tell him not to come in. He couldn't afford to take an entire day off. His boss assured him he'd get paid for the day, but he knew it was going to come out of his vacation time. When everything blew over there was going to be a shit ton of cable and internet to fix, that was for sure. Maybe he could make up the lost hours with overtime.

"She can't stay down there all by herself, Ralph!" Sally said, the annoyance turned on in her all at once like a light switch. "You heard the panic in those peoples' voices last night, the ones begging for help. She needs to be up here with us, at least until this all dies down. Now, go get her."

Ralph gave another loud groan as he set down his coffee mug. "And you expect me to go out there with sick people running around the building? Doesn't matter if I get attacked right? People are dying, Sally. I'm not risking our lives to go get your mother from downstairs."

Sally stared at him as their daughter reached for the hand that held her bottle. She sucked on it, oblivious to the argument going on around her. Sally didn't say anything. She didn't even looked surprised, but Ralph knew he'd hurt his wife.

"Just call your mom and tell her to lock her doors and stay inside. When things quiet down and those people stop panicking over nothing, I'll go and get her, OK?"

Sally sat Lilly down on the couch and let her hold the warm bottle herself. She grabbed her phone from the counter and shut herself in their bedroom. Lilly cooed as she kicked her feet and drank her milk. Ralph looked at her, but his mind was elsewhere. Nearby gun shots brought him back.

Screams echoed outside as everyone ran to their balconies. Ralph and Sally joined, leaning over the railing to peer into the darkness. Multiple bodies shuffled slowly toward one spot in the parking lot, where several more bodies were bent over. The gargled cries told Ralph what it was they hovered over on the ground as their hands ripped back to shove bits of something into their mouths.

He heard Christine Moore yell from the balcony on the other side of the stairway. "Oh, God. Liam…the Goldsteins! Liam!"

Sally Sherman covered her face with her hands and wept, turning to burry herself in Ralph's arms. He squinted his eyes to see through the darkness. The bodies shambled away from two unmoving lumps on the ground. With the sun breaking the horizon, transforming the sky from a deep, navy blue to a lighter indigo, Ralph finally saw the bloodied, mangled bodies of the Goldsteins.

He continued to stare, not wanting to look but unable to turn his eyes away. That's when he saw it. Sylvia's hand moved. Then her arm. Ben's legs were shifting back and forth as he lay on his back.

"They're alive!" Christine Moore yelled from her balcony. "Somebody help them!"

The Goldsteins fumbled slowly to their feet. Sylvia's legs shook as she tried to steady herself on her tall heels. She fell back down to her knees, but relentlessly got up again to try to stand on her wobbly legs.

Ralph gaped. There was no way either of them could be alive. Ben's throat was torn to shreds. Sylvia's arm was hanging on by a thread of carnage and her stomach was ripped open. Her entrails dangled down to her knees as she moved in sharp, jagged motions.

Another gunshot rang out from a first floor balcony and Ben Goldstein was blown back, his face unrecognizable as he fell to the pavement. Screams rang out from the building as everyone watched in horror. Another blast and Sylvia's hanging arm dropped to the ground. Black ooze dripped from the gaping hole in her torso. She let out a sound none of the people watching had ever heard before. It was a shriek mixed with a hissing growl. An echoing bang rang out again and Sylvia was thrown back. She crumpled to the ground next to her husband.

Sally was sobbing hysterically by then. Her body shook as she kept her face tightly pressed to Ralph's chest. They'd left the patio door open and he heard Lilly wailing from inside the house. He released Sally and ran inside, scooping Lilly up in his arms and holding her head to his shoulder as he bounced on the balls of his feet, shushing her.

"It's OK, baby, it's OK," he said over and over again. "Everything's OK."

Sally shut the patio door and collapsed to her knees onto the carpet. She wept into her hands, choking on her sobs as she struggled to breathe.

"Shh," Ralph hissed through his teeth to Lilly. "Everything's going to be OK."

X.

Carolyn Bock sat on her zebra striped bedspread as she painted her toenails a neon shade of turquoise. She huffed at the TV. She didn't want to watch the news, but no matter what channel she turned to it found a way onto her screen. She gazed up at what was an old rerun of *Buffy the Vampire Slayer* to see a middle aged, balding man in a white button down shirt and a loose, crooked tie talking into a microphone in the lobby of some building in Chicago. The underarms of his shirt were stained yellow. Carolyn rolled her eyes and turned the TV off. She dropped the remote to the bed with a groan.

Work had called early that morning to tell her not to come in until they called again. They didn't specify what it was about or when that would be, only that there was no work. This sent a pained lump of worry down to the pit of her stomach where it sat like a bad piece of sushi.

Business was slow at the steel mill and even though HR had to stay open as long as anyone was working there, if they shut the plant down completely she would be out of a job. And with steel being cheaper overseas, that was entirely possible, a thought that terrified Carolyn. As if that wasn't enough to worry about, the news made a huge deal over some flu virus and also over a few people who had gone crazy in town. Carolyn laughed the day before when she first heard about them biting people. Everyone blamed drugs. That was nothing new.

She didn't understand why it made national news and she didn't care to find out. Instead, she shut it out of her life all together and tried to focus on bettering herself with her day off, in case it became a permanent thing. She started with new polish on her toes and fingers.

She walked to the bathroom on the heels of her feet with her toes turned up so the polish wouldn't smudge. She looked at herself in the mirror. She wore a tiny towel with Velcro that kept it secured around her large breasts. She did a turn, admiring herself, wondering why she couldn't hold onto a man with her curvaceous body. She scrunched her hair in her hands and looked at herself from behind.

If she had a husband, or even a serious boyfriend, she could quit her job and stay at home, her ultimate goal. That was living the dream. On other side of the bathroom wall, a series of screams from the Hansens' apartment scattered her daydreams until they were lost in the depths of her mind again. Her shoulders slumped and she let go of her long, blonde mermaid waves in a huff. She wouldn't allow anything to ruin her day of relaxation.

Carolyn Bock turned on the warm water and let it fill the tub. Steam rose and moisture gathered on her upper lip. She dipped a toe in first and then lowered herself slowly, throwing the flowered towel onto the floor. Once she was submerged, she rested her head back against the inflatable pillow attached to the wall.

A pounding in her right temple crept behind her eyes as she closed them. She rubbed the spot, but it did nothing to get rid of it. With every piercing cry from next door, a sharp pain stabbed her head and ran down her neck. She couldn't take it anymore. Colt Hansen and his abusive hands needed to be stopped and she was going to be the one to stop him. Debbie was her friend, sort of, maybe, or maybe Carolyn just felt bad for her. Either way, she felt overcome with the need to help poor Debbie.

When Carolyn rose from the tub, the water cascaded down her body. She wrapped the flowered towel around herself, another around her sopping wet hair, and left the apartment, slamming the door behind her. She hadn't bothered to put on shoes since she planned to get back in the tub immediately after she told Colt off. Her wet, bare feet slapped at the cement of the open hallway as she marched next door.

Carolyn banged her tight fist against the door and held nothing back as she yelled obscenities at the man inside. "You better open this door right now motherfucker or I'm going to call the police and you'll be in a lot of fucking trouble when they haul your ass off to jail. You know what they do to wife beaters there, you piece of shit?" She paused.

No one answered, but there was another scream from the inside that tapered off into a high squeal like a wounded pig. It faded out until there was nothing but silence. Carolyn stared at the door with wide eyes, her fist frozen in the air mid-knock. What if he'd done it this time? What if he actually killed Debbie? All Carolyn could do was stare at the gold numbers on the door as she breathed heavily through her parted pink lips. She couldn't let Debbie die.

Carolyn turned the doorknob carefully. It was unlocked. She pushed the door open gently so it wouldn't make any noise. It didn't seem smart to go in guns blazing anymore, no matter how much she wanted to karate chop Cold Hansen in the throat. She didn't know what he was armed with, if he was armed at all. He could have killed

Debbie with his bare hands. He was six-three and had at least a hundred and fifty pounds on his stick-thin, sickly-looking wife.

The door was cracked open just enough for Carolyn to peer through. When she caught sight of the two bodies in the living room, she took a stumbling step back. It was worse than she thought.

Debbie Hansen leaned over her husband, his face a bloody mess with claw marks across his forehead and cheeks, exposing torn pieces of muscle underneath. One of his eyeballs was pulled loose from the socket and sat, trying to balance, on his carved out, hallow cheek. There was a look of terror petrified onto his face as his mouth gaped with his final scream.

Debbie didn't notice that her neighbor was watching as she dug into her husband's stomach and pulled out his intestines like a horrifying clown trick. She stuffed entrails into her mouth with urgency, gnashing at them with her teeth until they could slide down her throat. Her chartreuse eyes rolled into the back of her head as she sucked the blood off the coils of insides.

Bile rose from Carolyn's stomach. She covered her mouth to muffle the sound of her gagging. She reached her hand out to close the door, but stopped. If Debbie heard her, would she come after Carolyn too? Could Debbie even open a door in her state? She looked demented, like she'd ripped out her own hair out of her head and tore away the skin on her own arms and legs before she attacked her husband. Her mouth was stained a deep red and the skin around her eyes were sagging and shadowed. Maybe Debbie had finally lost control after all the abuse she'd endured over years.

Carolyn Bock took a guarded step away from the horror in front of her. She wanted to run back to her apartment, but was too afraid to move in front of the crack in the Hansens' door. She bumped into the door of the empty apartment across the hall. Her head banged against it with a dull thud.

Debbie Hansen looked up at the sound, able to just barely peer through the doorway where Carolyn stood in plain sight.

Carolyn whimpered into the hand that was still pressed over her mouth. Her first instinct was to run back to her apartment, lock the door behind her, and shove her dresser in front of it for good measure, but she didn't. Instead she reached out and grabbed ahold of the Hansens' doorknob.

Debbie was there before she could close it all the way, her arms stretched outward through the small crack. Carolyn yelped, pulled hard, and smashed the door against Debbie's arms. She heard the sickening sound of bones cracking which made her want to let go immediately to spare her friend the pain, but she held tight. Debbie's graying fingers frantically grasped for anything they could reach.

Carolyn had to do something or she would be stuck holding the door forever. Why didn't anyone come to help her? Knowing her neighbors, they never would. What a bunch of assholes…

She took a deep breath. She knew what she had to do. She released her hold on the door. Debbie lunged forward with her mouth open, but Carolyn was prepared. She drove her bare foot into Debbie's thin, porous chest.

The blow threw her back into the apartment. She stumbled over her dead husband's body and fell drunkenly to the ground. Carolyn slammed the door shut and took a few jarring steps away from it. She heard Debbie throw herself against the door, clawing at the white paint to leave deep brown scratch marks in the wood.

Debbie, or the thing that used to be Debbie, gave an ear-splitting cry, but Carolyn couldn't make out any words. It was nothing more than incoherent shrieks, wails, and moans. Her chest rose and fell in deep breaths. Her legs started to shake the longer she stood still, her eyes trained on the door as her brain tried to process what she'd just seen. She didn't know if Debbie could get out or not. She couldn't stay there.

She ran to Luke Benson's apartment across the hall from her own. She pounded on his door in a frenzy and begged him to open up.

Luke was still in his sweatpants and no shirt, his dark brown, hairless chest exposed. He'd been enjoying a rare day of sleeping in since the library he ran was closed. A librarian's job was never finished, so even on his days off he usually found himself planning events for the children or filling out orders for new books. But the library was closed...indefinitely, at least that's what he was told and he planned to take advantage of the unexpected vacation. He rubbed his eyes as he shuffled to the front door.

It wasn't a shock to hear Carolyn Bock banging on his door at such an early hour, even if it did sound urgent. She was always trying something new to get him to let her inside and into his bedroom. He scoffed at the sound of her begging. Even this seemed a little desperate for her.

He opened the door, keeping his hand on it so she couldn't come in right away. "What do you want, Carolyn?"

She didn't say anything when she pushed past him and used all her body weight to slam the door shut again. Luke's first instinct was to be angry and upset. This woman had gotten him in trouble with his ex-wife, almost caused him to miss a weekend with his daughter, because she just couldn't seem to stay away from him, especially when she was drunk. He wasn't in any mood to do her any favors. He looked at her with a stone cold glare, arms folded across his bare chest.

"Oh my God, thank you!" she exhaled all in one breath. She pounced on him and wrapped her arms around his neck in a tight embrace.

He didn't hug her back. His arms hung loose like a ragdoll's at his sides.

Carolyn squeezed Luke tighter as tears started to cascade down her tanned cheeks. The image of Debbie devouring her husband's entrails flashed in her mind and the light tears turned to uncontrollable sobs. Luke tried to lean back to get a look at her face, but she resisted. She pawed at him to pull him closer as she buried her face into his neck. He felt the hot tears trickle down his chest.

"Hey…hey. It's OK," he said, finally raising his arms to place one lightly on her back and the other to pat her gently on her head. "What's going on?"

"I don't know," she said, finally pulling back and wiping her face.

Luke wanted to roll his eyes, but he stopped himself.

"I heard the Hansens arguing. Or at least I thought they were arguing. I guess I really never heard Debbie. Only Colt," she said, unraveling the truth in her head as she spoke disconnectedly. "So I went over there. I knocked, but no one answered. No one said anything." More tears fell from her eyes as she stared blankly ahead. "I tried the door and it was open. I was going to go inside, stop Colt from hurting her, threaten him with the police again, but…" she broke down and covered her face with her hands as she sobbed.

"But what?" Luke asked. "What happened? Did he hurt her? Is she alright? Should we call the police?"

Carolyn looked over the tops of her freshly painted fingers and whispered into her palms. "He's dead."

Luke scrutinized her with narrowed eyes, unsure that he'd heard her correctly. "He killed her?"

Carolyn shook her head. "*She* killed *him*…she was *eating* him." She let her hands fall to hug herself around the waist.

"What?" Luke barked. "What? She was *eating* him? What does that mean? Like she *ate* him? I don't…" He paced in circles as he rubbed at his buzzed black hair.

"Can I stay here?" Carolyn asked meekly as she continued to hold herself. "I can't go back to my place. I can't listen to whatever's going on next door. I can't…" she heaved rapid, shallow breaths. Her chest clenched. She couldn't breathe.

"OK," Luke said and placed his hand on her back as he led her over to the couch. "It's all right. Just breathe. Everything's gonna be OK."

"My neighbor just fucking ate her husband!" she screamed, shaking her head so her wet hair slapped Luke across the face. "How is anything going to be OK?"

Luke wiped the water droplets from his cheeks. "I don't know. That's just what people tend to say in bad situations."

Carolyn doubled over and cried into her lap. Luke watched her. He wanted to feel sorry for her, knew he should, but he couldn't. If what she said was true, then they were all in some serious shit. The virus was worse than he thought. Fuck Carolyn. What was he going to do?

Luke pretended to comfort her. He let her cry it out in silence as he patted her shoulders gently. His eyes roamed her bare, smooth back and her tanned, toned arms. Why did so much crazy have to be wrapped up in such a tempting package? He let his eyes wonder down her bronzed legs until they stopped dead in their tracks on her ankle where there was a fresh, deep scratch. Droplets of blood dripped down to her foot and ran off onto the beige carpet.

Luke had watched the news for hours late into the night. It warned people to not go near anyone who had been bitten or scratched by people who were likely infected with some sort of rabid disease or virus, and there one sat in his living room. His hand pulled away from her with a quick jerk.

"How about I walk you back over to your place, check it out, make sure everything's safe, I'll call the police? Before you know it, this whole thing will be over." he said, reaching out to console her, but he pulled back as his eyes settled on the bloody gash again.

"Can't I stay here?" she sobbed and looked up at him from her lap. Black mascara and eyeliner was smeared under her wet eyes.

His mind raced. He licked at his full, dark lips. "I have to go pick up my daughter."

Carolyn took a few calming breaths as she sat up straight and nodded. "OK."

Luke walked Carolyn back to her apartment across the hall. He never took his eyes off the Hansens' door, which shook as Debbie relentlessly pounded on it like a wild animal. He pulled out his phone to call the police as Carolyn opened her door. She stepped inside, but Luke stopped in the doorway. Who knew how long she had until she was as crazy as Debbie. He wasn't going to take any chances. The phone rang and rang, but no one answered at the police station.

Carolyn turned to look at Luke as panic crept up into her blue eyes. Why weren't they answering?

Just as the tears were about to spill over the brim of her eyes, Luke started talking. "Yes, hello. We need an ambulance here at the Dune Ridge apartments off highway twelve. A woman has killed her husband and she seems to be a bit…well, crazy. She's locked inside her apartment at the moment, but she could get out. Please hurry. Yes. Yes. Thank you." Luke hung up the phone. "They said they'll be here ASAP."

Carolyn let out a deep sigh. "Oh thank God."

"Yeah," Luke said, his eyes fixated on the ground. "Well, everything seems to be OK for now. Just lock your door and I'm sure the police will come by to ask you some questions once they get here."

"Thank you, Luke," she said, wrapping her arms around herself again as she stood alone in the entryway. "You're a good man."

The corners of Luke's lips pulled back quickly into a strained smile and then he turned to leave, shutting her door behind him. He looked down at the phone in his hand and shook his head. If the police weren't answering then things were worse than bad. Their little lakeside town had gone to shit. Had the outbreak really spread that quickly? It seemed implausible, but then again he filed books for a living. He had no idea how an outbreak started. He walked back to his apartment, shut the door, and locked both the deadbolts.

Luke Benson paced his living room and kitchen, opened the fridge and closed it without taking anything. He opened the pantry and shut it, looked out the window, and then circled back to the kitchen. Carolyn was infected. She had to be. They said the infection or disease or whatever it was spread through bites and scratches. Blood to blood contact and it sounded like Debbie had blood all over her when she got Carolyn's ankle with her nails. Carolyn was going to become just like Debbie—wild, crazed, murderous, a cannibal. The entire building was in danger. There'd be two of those things and eventually they'd find a way out of their apartments. It was just him and them on the third floor. He had to protect himself.

Luke ran to the storage closet out on the patio and rummaged through his bag of tools. He remembered buying rope a while back, unable to pinpoint why exactly, but that didn't matter. Tools, old DVDs, and boxes of books were tossed out onto the concrete patio as he searched frantically.

He pulled back and clapped his hands together. A grin took over his face as he pulled out a thick, long rope. He ran back inside and to his front door, unlocked it, and stuck his head out to look around.

No one was above his floor so that meant no one would come down the stairs and see what he was about to do. Realistically, no one had any reason to be up on the third floor at all now that Colt was dead, Debbie was trapped, and Carolyn was next to go. Luke hadn't ever seen anyone visit the Hansens' before. Sometimes Carolyn's dopey friends came around, but with the state of things, the disease running rampant, he suspected no one would come to visit her either. He emerged into the hallway once he was sure the coast was clear.

Keeping a vigilant watch on the staircases on either end of the hallway, he walked lightly over to the Hansens' apartment, which had fallen silent. He tied the rope around the doorknob nimbly so as not to make any noise and alert Debbie to the fresh meat on the other side.

He walked the rope out as he approached the door opposite the Hansens' and tied it around that doorknob as well, pulling the rope tight so there wasn't any slack. He flicked the rope and watched it vibrate from the tension. A smile flashed across his face.

"Let's see you get out of that one, you crazy old bitch," he said as he smiled and rubbed his hand together. "Onto the next one."

Carolyn's apartment had to be handled differently. He couldn't tie a rope to his own door. He went inside his apartment again and grabbed one of the metal bistro chairs from his two person dining set and walked it over to Carolyn's. He held the chair firmly in his hands and leaned his head against her door. Nothing. Carolyn was most likely held up in the bathroom, cleaning her wound. Luke pictured her sitting on the toilet, using a cloth to wipe the blood away as she bandaged her ankle, her face slowly stiffening as the realization that her life was over finally came. He shook his head to wipe away the image.

Luke shoved the chair under the doorknob and shook it to make sure it was wedged in there good.

XI.

Christine slept on the couch while Liam had the king size bed all to himself. The decision had been hers, punishment after another fight about her going out onto the patio ended with a stern 'no', but she blamed him anyway for her sleeping arrangements. She looked at her phone, which hadn't rang once in four days, and checked the time. Liam closed all the blinds and hung light resistant curtains so the apartment was constantly cloaked in darkness. Day ran into night and disoriented Christine. She barely slept.

Thoughts about the night gun shots rang out, killing what used to be Sylvia and Ben Goldstein, fogged her mind. She tried to push them away as she rolled over onto her side to bury her face in the back of the couch. She wondered if

Liam had gone crazy. She knew things were dangerous, but not on their second story patio. What would be able to get her that high up? All she wanted was to go outside. The apartment was stifling.

She pulled the lightweight sheet up to her chin. It was only nine thirty at night, but she closed her eyes anyway, wishing the day was over. Sleep wouldn't come, though. Her mind continued to turn, like a rat's wheel. She rolled onto her back again and flopped her arm over her forehead. What was the point of trying to go to sleep? It wasn't like tomorrow was going to be any better. She huffed out at the ceiling. It was quieter than it'd been the night before, when she heard the constant sound of cars starting and tires squealing as the last people fled the complex. As far as she knew, they were the only ones left.

Morning finally came and Liam and Christine ate in silence at the counter. Christine's feet dangled over the floor as she sat rigid on the bar stool, stabbing at the eggs Liam made for her. She didn't put a single bite into her mouth. Liam, on the other hand, shoveled it in like it was his last meal.

Christine looked at him and wrinkled her nose. "How can you eat?" she spat at him.

"What do you mean?" he asked without a hint of bitterness in his voice.

It angered Christine more that he was pretending nothing had happened. "I mean, how can you eat when you basically sent the Ramirens to their death?"

Liam wasn't taken aback by what she said. It wasn't the first time she'd said something about the Ramirens. He didn't flinch at all, though the words stabbed at his heart.

When he didn't respond, Christine threw her fork onto her plate and shoved off from the counter. She went to the bedroom and shut the door behind her.

Liam finished the last bites of his eggs and then reached over to grab Christine's plate, eating hers too. The Ramirens were all Christine had talked about whenever she was distracted from the desire to breathe fresh air from out on the patio. The Ramirens were also all Liam could think about.

Christine was right. He'd sent them to their death. But by not opening that door, he saved her life and his own. He kept telling himself that over and over again, but it never did any good. He still had a gnawing feeling in the pit of his stomach every time he pictured their faces. He couldn't even remember the last time he'd seen them, but he knew he would continue see them forever.

XII.

There was a loud banging at the door. Liam jumped up from the bar stool. He stood with his legs slightly spread and knees bent, his fists were up in the air in an attack pose. When he realized what he was doing he lowered his hands and stood up straight. Christine ran from the bedroom to glare at him. Her eyes were perfect circles, overtaken by fear. *And she wanted to go outside*, Liam thought.

A familiar voice cried out to them. "Please, open up, Liam! Please! They're coming! Please, open up!"

Christine walked over to where Liam stood in the living room. She displayed her hands at the door as if to say "you regret what you did to the Ramirens? Well here's your chance to do right. Open the door." But he found he still couldn't. His friend was on the other side and he couldn't open it and endanger himself and the woman he loved.

"This is ridiculous," Christine barked as she walked over to the door.

It took her half a minute to undo all the extra locks Liam had installed. He didn't stop her, but he couldn't bring himself help either. It was a bad idea. The cries on the other side of the door escalated in panic.

"God, please! Help me! Open up!"

Christine fumbled with the last lock. Liam stood with his hands on his hips, trying to control his breathing as it became shallow and rapid.

"They're coming! Please!"

She ripped the door from its seal and Zack Kran rushed into the apartment.

He slammed the door behind him and stood up straight. He walked past Christine to stand next to Liam and dropped both his hands onto his friend's shoulders. "You never open the door. *Never*," he said with a stern face. "I don't care who it is—family, friends, anyone. You don't open that door."

Christine's mouth fell open as she stared at Zack.

"I've been telling her this all week," Liam said, looking at Christine as if Zack was proper validation for his theory of survival.

The blood rushed to her face and burned her cheeks a hot red. She clenched her jaw shut, her teeth applying so much pressure on each other that they hurt. She ground them together in an attempt to gain control of herself again.

Liam and Zack looked at her in silence. Zack had a spreading smile that took over his face, while Liam's gaze fell to the floor. He'd really messed up this time. It wasn't his idea to have Zack come over like he did. He hadn't even know if Zack was still alive. It was his policy to assume everyone was dead so there'd be no disappointment when he learned the truth. But he certainly shouldn't have agreed with Zack like he did. He should have been as outraged as Christine clearly was. He knew he would get the full force of her wrath even though Zack was the one who pulled the stupid prank.

"You were *faking?*" Christine hissed through her teeth.

Zack couldn't help it as he broke out into laughter. "You should have seen your faces," he said. "It was—"

Christine punched him so hard that he couldn't finish his sentence. His dark, wooly beard did nothing to soften the blow. He looked at her hand to see if she was wearing brass knuckles as she shook it wildly through the air. Groans and curses escaped his lips as he rubbed his already swelling jaw.

"God dammit," he said, bent over. "It was a joke. A test!"

"Well, it wasn't fucking funny!" Christine yelled at him as she breezed by him. She shut herself in the bedroom again.

Zack straightened himself up and moved his jaw in a slow, circular motion. Liam wanted to smile. Somehow he'd avoided the blame. Instead he simply shrugged his shoulders when Zack eyed him.

"It was barking mad what you just did, scaring her like that," Liam said loud enough for Christine to hear through the wall. "Life's been hard enough without us having to think these things are at our doorstep."

"Kind of the reason I came by, actually," Zack said as he gave his jaw one last massage before he moved on from the incident. "I think we should do a sweep of the building to see who's still alive and we should 'clear out' the infected ones." He used air quotes, but the meaning was obvious.

Liam nodded his head. Why hadn't he thought of it? He had been completely obsessed with cutting themselves off from everything that he didn't even stop to think that the apartment would be safer if it were free of the infection all together. He didn't allow himself to think of how they would go about it. His upper lip sweat as he drummed his fingers over his thin lips. He wiped it away with a quick flick. "Ok. Good. Yeah. Let's clean this place up a bit. Make it safe again."

Zack's adrenaline rushed. He clapped his hands together and hopped in place. "Yes! Let's do this!"

Liam's eyebrows pulled together as he held his hands out in front of him. "Woah. We can't charge out of here without a plan."

Zack stared at him unblinkingly as he rubbed his hands together and shifted his weight between his feet. He leaned forward slightly, as if he were literally hanging on Liam's next words.

"We'll think on it and meet back here in the morning, weapons in hand. Got it?"

Zack nodded as a joker grin took over his face, his eyes wrinkled until they were almost completely shut. "Good idea. OK, I'm going to get out of here before Rocky comes out here again. I'll see you tomorrow at eight." He opened the door, looked both ways, and then ran next door to his own apartment.

Liam shook his head and chuckled. Zack was insane, but it was just the right level of crazy they needed to make it alive. He walked to the door and started the process of securing themselves in again when he heard the bedroom door open. He stopped and turned.

"You're not really going to kill them, are you?" Christine asked softly as she held onto the door frame. Her large, blue eyes pleaded with him.

"We have to," Liam said. "You know what they're capable of."

Christine closed her eyes and pictured Sylvia and Ben Goldstein, two people she hadn't liked very much when they were alive, but no matter how much she detested them she wouldn't have wished them to die the brutal way they did— ripped apart, eaten alive, and then gunned down. It was inhumane. She didn't want anyone else to suffer that way. Giving the people who were too far gone some peace was the least they could do.

"I want to come."

"No," Liam said quickly. "No way."

"I want to help," Christine urged as she stepped out from the bedroom.

"No," he said again. "I can't risk you getting infected."

She opened her mouth to argue, but shut it again. She was the only family he had left. He was all she had as well. "Fine," she said to the floor. "I'll stay."

XIII.

Luke Benson tossed and turned in his bed. The light of morning crept in through the gaps in the blinds. He rubbed his eyes and looked at the clock. It was already eight. He rolled over and closed his eyes again, but he knew if sleep had avoided him all night, then it wasn't going to come now that it was morning. He huffed and threw the covers off. "Fuck," he grumbled as he stood up.

The image of Carolyn's scratched ankle had plagued his thoughts every time he closed his eyes. It kept him up all night wondering how long it took for someone to change once they were infected. How long did Carolyn have until she was trying to eat people like the others? Would she die in her apartment, the one he'd locked her inside of? Would it be his fault? Could he have saved her, helped her in any way? His mind had raced all night with unanswerable questions.

He got out of bed and dragged his feet across the room and looked at himself in the bathroom mirror. His brown eyes had puffy, dark bags under them. His stomach wound tightly into knots when he glimpsed his aged and tired face. Carolyn was probably dead because he was too much of a coward to try and help her. He couldn't look at himself any longer. He turned away and walked to the kitchen.

Luke poured himself a bowl of cereal. The spoon made it to his lips, but his mouth remained closed. All the "what ifs" and "maybes" had piled down on him in a matter of seconds and threatened to crush him to death.

He had to know for sure if Carolyn was still herself or one of those flesh eating monsters. If she was all right, then maybe there was still time to help her, drive her to the hospital, something, anything.

He dropped the spoon into the bowl and rushed out the front door and into the warm, shaded hallway. There was no forgiving summer breeze. The air hung thick with humidity and the rotten, putrid stench of death. Sweat collected on Luke's forehead and upper lip. He walked to Carolyn's door and leaned in close.

Silence.

He rested his fingers on the chair he'd wedged under the doorknob. The black metal was warm to the touch. A relaxing sensation ran from his hands, through his stomach, and down to his toes. *Maybe everything was OK*, he thought. *Maybe Carolyn was sleeping, perfectly healthy and fine in her bed.* He turned away to go back inside as he shook his head with a smile, but was pulled back immediately. "No more maybes," he said aloud.

Just as Luke was about to remove the chair, he heard voices carry up from the floor below him. Two guys—one overly excited and the other calm and British—were discussing plans for something. Luke knew it had to be Liam Scott and Zack Kran. Liam was the only British person that lived in the building and Zack was always by his side.

Luke heard a few distinct words travel though the hallways, but most were lost in the distorting echo—something about the building, every apartment, blow to the head, the brain. The last words "don't get bit" were clear as day.

Luke's burgeoning curiosity pulled him from Carolyn's door. He couldn't be sure, but it sounded like the two men were going to take out the infected people in the building. If that was true then he wouldn't have to go into Carolyn's apartment alone. It was possible he wouldn't have to go in at all. The two of them could do it for him.

He walked down the stairs to the second floor and stopped on the last step. He felt sick at the thought of where his mind had just leapt to. They were talking about killing people down there. That wasn't something to take lightly, and yet Luke went straight there with relief.

Zack Kran and Liam Scott were standing in the middle of the hallway on the second floor, an equal distance from each of the four doors. Zack was bouncing up and down, a black paintball mask covering his face and a shiny replica sword clenched firmly in both his hands, ready to strike. His elbows and knees had bulky pads strapped to them and his chest was covered with a bullet proof vest. He looked like he was ready for battle.

The sword was made of flawless steel with a wooden hilt and antique brass handle parts. Luke recognized it from when he attended one of Zack's infamous game nights at the comic book store. It was a *Games of Thrones* replica, or was it *Lord of the Rings*? He couldn't remember exactly, but he knew it was the same one that had been on display behind the cash register, its own set of spotlights shone down proudly upon it.

Liam Scott, on the other hand, appeared his normal self—khakis, a beige and orange striped t-shirt, messy ginger hair, and dark red-rimmed, rectangular glasses. The only thing that seemed out of place was the quiver of arrows on his back and the handcrafted wooden longbow clutched in one of his hands.

Luke shook his head as he looked on at the two men. Those nerds were going to get themselves killed and it made him chuckle to himself. Then, the overpowering urge to watch them open each door and slay the hungry creatures inside, if they could, overcame him. He cleared his throat and the heads of the two men snapped to attention. Their eyes inspected every inch of Luke as he stood awkwardly on the last step, one of his house slippered feet continually kicked at the edge.

"What are you two doing?" he said as another chuckle escaped.

"We're clearing this place out." Zack pounded a fist into the wood siding of the exposed hallway wall. He shook his hand to disperse the pain.

"You're...getting rid of the sick people?" Luke thrust his hands into the pockets of his gray sweatpants, his dark chest muscles flexed tight.

"That's right," Liam said, though his face failed to mirror Zack's enthusiasm. "This infection, or flu, or whatever it is, is taking over the country. There have been reports of it as far as Idaho and Connecticut. We need a safe place to live, to survive in. I don't know about you, but I'd like that to be our home."

Luke nodded. "Mind if I tag along?"

Zack and Liam looked at each other, unprepared for anyone else to volunteer to join them. They spoke silently with a quick exchange of a few loaded glances. It was Liam, with his wide hazel eyes and brows turned upward in the center, who spoke first. "Do you have any sort of weapon? Something that will damage the brain like a bat or a long knife?"

Luke fought the urge to let his jaw drop open. Instead, his brown eyes bulged and his stomach gave a revolting lurch upward. Sweat dripped down the side of his round face. "I have a nine iron in my golf bag."

"That'll do it!" Zack said with a smile. "Go get it. We'll wait here for you." He couldn't stand still. If he wasn't pacing around, smacking the walls or his own head, which sat safely under a hard helmet, then he tapped his foot.

Luke returned two minutes later with his golf club.

"Time to nut up or shut up," Zack said with a maniacal grimace.

Liam's eyes shifted rapidly. He reached for an arrow from his back. "Maybe we should start up on the top floor and make our way down." His voice cracked, but no one seemed to notice or they were kind enough to spare him the embarrassment of pointing it out.

Luke looked at Liam and took him in when Liam's eyes averted to the stairs. The kid was scared. Liam's fingers trembled as he gripped his arrow. Luke would never admit it to anyone, but he was terrified as well. He didn't want to die. He wanted to see his daughter, hug her close, and tell her that he loved her one more time. He wanted to kiss his ex-wife and tell her he was sorry for everything. He wanted to keep his insides inside him and not watch some monster eat them as he faded away. He licked his thick lips and pushed the image from his mind. His eyes blinked rapidly.

"Right," Liam said with an exhale that deflated his puffed out cheeks. "Here we go."

They climbed the stairs in a single file line, weapons clenched in their sweaty hands, ready for whatever awaited them behind the closed doors of the third floor.

XIV.

Zack Kran and Liam Scott eyed the rope that held the Hansens' door closed. They walked over to Carolyn Bock's first.

Luke Benson's eyes shifted between her door and his. He was the only one who knew there was a chair missing from underneath her doorknob, which was safely placed back under his table in his own apartment. He hadn't wanted them to know he trapped her in there when she was still human. He wasn't sure which would make him feel worse; if she was alive and fine and he'd chaired her in for no reason, or if she was a hungry, walking corpse. Neither was good. So, why'd he do it, then?

The three men looked at each other and each gave a nod of encouragement. Without saying a word, Zack pulled the crowbar out from his backpack. He wedged it into the jam and pushed hard three times before the door flung open with a bang.

Zack took a few steps in with Liam at his heels. His sword was raised over his head, ready to be brought down on a dead and vicious Carolyn, should they find one, but she wasn't in the living room or the kitchen. The group inched forward as they each tuned their ears to listen for any sound of movement.

Zack glanced from Liam to the closed bathroom door and nodded his head. Liam placed a hand on the doorknob and waited for Zack to do the same with the bedroom door. They bobbed their heads three times in sync and threw the doors wide open.

When they both came back out into the living room empty handed, Liam shrugged his shoulders while Zack's face was riddled with disappointment.

His eyes narrowed. "Where the hell is Luke?" he barked as he spun in a circle.

Liam frowned and scanned the empty apartment. "Must still be outside."

Zack marched across the room to the open doorway like a bull charging a matador. He was positive Luke ran off on them until he saw his round, sweaty face through the open doorway.

"Onto the next one, then," Liam said as he followed.

When Zack saw Luke leaned against the wall as he inhaled heavy breaths he whistled and waved him inward to the Hansens' apartment. He pried the door open with more ease than Carolyn's.

It was only a split second that everyone froze to take Debbie Hansen in—the deep slashes across her grayish, mottled skin, her sunken, marble eyes that only hinted at life when blood touched her leathery, black tongue. She was the first infected person any of them had seen up close. When the Goldstein's went down it was in the dark and from across the parking lot. Debbie was no more than fifteen feet away. Her putrescent stench made their eyes sting. Over a gallon of fresh blood was slopped across the carpet, walls, and furniture like Jackson Pollock had just stopped by for an impromptu paint session.

Zack charged in with a warrior cry, his collectible sword raised above his head. Debbie took a few sluggish steps towards him, her arms poised to grab. He jumped and brought the sword down with the weight of his entire body. It cracked the thing's head open as easily as an egg and sank a few inches down. Zack pulled it free and panted with his sword at his side, thick murky blood dripped down the blade. His eyes were locked on the lifeless body crumpled on the floor, brain matter scattered around the opening of its cranium.

Zack's body felt electric. His hands shook as he white knuckled the hilt of his sword. The look on the two faces that stared at him didn't match his own smile. He let out a howling laugh that turned into a whooping yell of victory.

"Holy shit!" he roared. "Holy fucking shit!"

Luke disappeared into the hallway again. Hunched over with his hands on the railing by the stairs, he dry-heaved until it felt like he'd done two hundred sit-ups. No one came to check on him.

Zack continued to laugh in a frenzy as he tried to get a rise out of Liam. His laughter tapered off with several small coughs when Liam looked up from the blood-spattered ground with heavy eyes, the third floor left in silence. Zack wiped his sword off on a cloth from his bag and gave an accomplished nod, the excitement of the first kill already dying down.

Liam tried to remember the last time he saw Debbie Hansen. At first he thought it was at Christine's birthday party, but then he remembered he saw her walking to her car in her waitress uniform the morning he went to meet Dr. Hyde at the university…the day it all started.

Although, he couldn't know for sure that everything had started with his boss, it had for him. He was sure the flu was to blame and the first case of that had been in New York City a couple of weeks ago. It could have started somewhere else in the country, in the world even, and spread so quickly that he only heard about it after the incident with Dr. Hyde and Ronnie.

That one quick thought of Ronald Conrad brought all his regrets rushing back. He should have stopped them. He should have laid his friend to rest.

"Whose place do we have to check on the second floor?" Zack asked, all business and ready to get to it. "'Cause we know mine is clean and yours is clean." He looked to Liam.

"Uh," Liam stammered, trying to remember anyone else besides his undead colleague and friend. "There's the Ramirens and Ralph Sherman and his family." His voice was slow and distant.

"OK, then," Zack said as he clapped his hands together once. "Let's get on with it!"

Luke walked with Liam and Zack to the edge of the stairs and then stopped. He didn't want to go any further. All he had wanted was to know what happened to Carolyn, and now that she was missing all he wanted to do was curl up in his warm, cozy bed and try to forget what he'd just seen. But Zack wouldn't allow it.

He turned to where Luke was frozen and called out for him to follow. Luke walked a few paces behind the two blood-stained men as he contemplated running back home the second they busted open the next door. It wasn't like he was helping them anyway.

There was no surprise in the Ramirens' apartment. Liam knew what their fate had been days ago. Mr. and Mrs. Ramiren shuffled around the house, parts of their faces torn away, complete chunks missing in a hallowed out, bloody mess. Little Ahmed hissed and growled as he snapped his teeth, untouched except for a single bite on his left arm.

Liam felt a sting in his eyes and a dryness in his throat. They'd suffered horrific, slow, painful deaths. Three quick shots of his arrows and the family was on the ground and finally at peace. Liam took a deep breath through his nose as he gripped his longbow in one hand. Another apartment cleared.

The door to the Shermans' apartment opened slowly. Ralph walked out and locked the door with his key behind him.

"Oh, hey guys," he said and then stopped once he looked up at Liam, Zack, and Luke. He took a moment to digest the sight of the three men, armed with a sword, a bow, and a golf club, wet blood staining the clothes of two of them. Ralph's eyes lingered on Zack and all his make-shift riot gear. "What's going on?" he asked with a shaky laugh.

"We're clearing out the apartments, y'know, so it's safe for everyone left," Zack said while he smacked the side of his sword against the palm of his hand like some grand punisher.

Ralph nodded slowly with wide eyes. "O...K..." he said in a reassuring voice, like he would use if he were talking to a child. "I'm just going to get my mother-in-law from downstairs."

"Is everyone all right in your place?" Liam asked as he lowered his bow to hold it behind his legs in hopes of easing the concerned look on Ralph's face. The last thing they needed to deal with on top of everything else was a panic.

"All right?"

"Yeah. All right." Zack answered with bite. "Everyone alive and well in there? No one's been bit or scratched or turned into a flesh-eating zombie or nothing like that?" He wanted to get back to clearing the apartments out. It was almost impossible for him to stand still with the adrenaline that coursed through his body, so he swayed on his feet while his finger felt ran along the edge of his sword's blade.

"Oh, yeah. Everyone's good."

Liam gave a constrained smile and the group of three walked on towards the stairs.

Ralph shook his head and laughed to himself, but didn't move to go downstairs. He pictured walking into his mother-in-law's apartment to find her dead, or worse…dead and hungry. His eyes shifted down both ends of the airy hallway and the hairs on the back of his neck prickled. He had an undeniable feeling that someone was watching him, but as far as he could tell he was alone.

"Hey, guys, wait up!" he called and jogged down the stairs to the first floor. He ran right into Luke's short, solid frame.

Luke gyrated awkwardly with his golf club raised halfway.

"Shh," Liam hushed as he stretched out his lanky arms to prevent anyone from stepping down. All four looked at each other, brows furrowed and dripping wet with sweat.

"Jerry?" Liam called out.

He was met with an eerie silence after the echo of his voice dispersed. A breeze rushed through the hallway and broke up the thickness in the air.

"Yup," a rough voice answered.

Liam lowered his arms and gave a feeble smile. "All right, Jer?" he called out as he hopped off the bottom step.

"Can't complain," Jerry Middleton said from his patio, where he sat in a plastic chair with a loaded Remington 870 Express Pistol Grip lying in his lap.

"We're going to be entering the apartments to see if anyone is infected, so if you hear anything odd, it's just us." Liam hoped he sounded reassuring, because inside he felt like he was on the verge of having a panic attack. He struggled to keep his voice steady.

Once again there was silence.

The group of four men looked at one another. Zack shrugged his shoulders and then turned to face a door with the number 614 on it.

Jerry emerged from his apartment and gave a nod to each of them. Liam gave a weak, distracted smiles in return. Luke reserved all his concentration for keeping the contents of his stomach down, so he only raised his hand as he took heavy breaths. Jerry hiked up his baggy sweatpants, his white tank top tucked in tight.

Jerry shifted his shotgun from one hand to the other. "Well, my place is clear," he said. There was no emotion on his aged, wrinkled face.

"And we know the Goldsteins aren't in theirs," Ralph Sherman said as he eyed Jerry. He waited for any sign that Jerry was either proud or ashamed of gunning the couple down, but the old man's face was stone cold and still.

"Do you want to check in on your mum first?" Liam asked Ralph, but Ralph shook his head, his eyes still locked on Jerry.

"Let's do hers last." He wanted to put off facing whatever was behind her door for as long as he could. If she was dead, Sally would never forgive him. He didn't know if he would ever be able to forgive himself either.

"That just leaves our fraternity brethren." Zack pointed his crowbar at apartment 614.

"Wait. Does anyone know their names?" Liam asked, finally removing his bow from behind his legs.

"Nuh-uh."

"Nope."

"What does it matter?"

Silence from Jerry.

"It's just," Liam started. "I can't just..." He couldn't finish his thought.

Zack looked at Liam with wild, crazy eyes that said he was ready to kill again. Luke stared as fear overtook his round, dark eyes. Ralph stood with his hands in the pocket of his plaid pajama bottoms to conceal the fact that they were shaking. Jerry couldn't be read.

"Ralph needs a weapon," Liam finally pulled himself together to say.

"Oh, shit, right." Zack handed Ralph the crowbar. "Would you like to do the honors?"

Ralph took the long metal tool in his hands and examined it. The hooked end looked menacing, like its one purpose in life was to bury itself deep into a skull. He placed it in the door jam and applied a small amount of pressure to it.

Was everyone expecting him to be the one to kill the two college boys? Sweat ran down his face and into his eyes. They were only two years younger than Ralph. He knew because they'd once asked him to buy them beer and when he said no they asked him what was the difference if they waited another six months or not? Ralph had tossed each of them a beer from his fridge and told them to find someone else if they wanted more.

"Just do it already," Zack exhaled.

"We're right here," Liam said. "Just open and step out of the way."

Ralph nodded. Open and step out of the way. Got it. He could do that. The feeling of the door popping opening from his own force was foreign and a little thrilling. A quick smile took over his face, but it didn't have a chance to stay for long.

XV.

Fifteen disparate, changed faces—fifteen college students with various majors and diverse backgrounds from all over the country gawked at the five men with glazed over, yellowing eyes and gnashed red teeth. A few turned away to devour the bloodied entrails that splayed out from the mangled corpse on the floor, but the majority staggered to rise to their feet as they trained their bloodshot eyes on the sacks of fresh meat at the door.

"Holy Christ," Luke whispered from the back of the group.

They were the last words spoken before the men charged into the two bedroom apartment.

Zack Kran was like an apocalyptic warrior as he charged ahead of the rest to start the harrowing battle against the risen dead. He wielded his sword like a trained knight. Each slice happened in slow motion, as if time itself wanted him to savor the victory of another zombie back in its rightful place. He imagined himself as the son of a Greek God, his monumental skills inborn. He would never admit, even to himself, that he acquired them from hours of practice in front of the full length mirror in the back of his comic book store when it was empty of customers.

A few paces behind, Liam Scott shut down his mind and let his instincts take over. It was the only way he knew how to get out of the zombie infested apartment alive. And he had to make it back to Christine. Their apartment was directly above. She had no idea the degree of horror that lie below her feet. Her porcelain face, with its cute dimples that pinched at the corners of her mouth when she gave a little, coy smile, blazed in Liam's mind as he pulled an arrow from the head of a fallen corpse and turned around on his knee to pierce the skull of another before it could grasp his t-shirt to drag him into its red-stained mouth.

Liam shot one arrow after another as he moved with the precision he'd perfected with over two decades of training. The lightness of his weapon was an unnatural contrast to the heavy bodies that collapsed to the floor moments after his arrow penetrated their skulls to hit their brains.

Next to Liam, Ralph Sherman swung the thin crowbar like a bat. It struck a young female with one arm and a shredded leg in the temple. There was a moment of exhilaration as the sound of her skull crunched from the sharp blow of his own sheer force. As the weight of the body dropped, it pulled the crowbar from Ralph's fingers. His stomach dove with it. He reached down to yank the weapon loose, but it barely moved. Suppressing the urge to panic, he placed his slipper covered foot on the female's head and applied all one hundred and forty-two pounds of his weight.

The head felt porous and spongey, giving slightly with each small bounce of his foot. He gripped the crowbar and yanked it back, the way he used to when he started up the lawn mower when he was a teenager. It didn't work, just like it hadn't then. The crowbar's hook was still lodged in the skull. Ralph readjusted his grip on the bar and jiggled it back and forth to loosen it. He looked over his shoulder just in time to see the ravage eyes of a large male in a football jersey as it opened its mouth inches from Ralph's face.

There was a loud bang and the enclosing zombie's head exploded, a spray of thick blood camouflaged Ralph's face and chest. Broken teeth and skull bone shot out like shrapnel. Ralph exhaled as he doubled over from simultaneous shock, disgust, and relief.

His soft brown eyes met Jerry Middleton's for a brief moment. He hoped they conveyed how thankful he was to him for saving his life. If that college frat boy turned monstrous cannibal had gotten ahold of him it would have been all over for Sally and Lilly. They couldn't survive without him. The thought made his heart want to race right out of his chest.

The sound of Jerry's pistol grip shotgun boomed again and again as it obliterated four standing targets. He stood in the center of the apartment to get a view of the entire living room and kitchen. There was no way one of those things was going to get past him to infect any of the survivors in the building. Over his dead body would he allow it.

Hot breath beat against the back of Jerry's neck. He spun around and shoved the barrel of his 12 gauge into a hardened stomach. Luke raised his arms in the air and squeezed his eyes shut. When he breathed out, flecks of spit flew from his lips.

Jerry turned back to the room, which was almost cleared except for two stragglers that wouldn't go down without a fight. He blew the head off one and hit the other in the leg, giving Ralph enough time to swing his crowbar and hit it in the temple. Jerry turned back to face Luke, who lowered his arms slowly and took quick shallow breaths. He snorted at the pathetic, sniveling man in front of him and shook his head. "Coward," Jerry grumbled as he moved out of the way so the others could vacate the apartment.

The white walls were painted red with the blood of the dead. Luke stared off into the room long after the others had moved on to stand in front of Ralph's mother-in-law's apartment door, the last one to be checked.

He wasn't a coward. He was protecting himself, preserving himself, so he could see his family again. That's what a good man would do. A good man would be there for his family, like Liam was. All at once, Luke realized he had to get to his ex-wife and daughter before it was too late. He closed the door to 614 and joined the others. He kept his distance and averted his eyes in case Jerry tried to shame him again for tapping into his basic human instincts of survival.

Ralph tried to swallow as he stared at Marianne Dunbar's door, but it felt like there was a rock wedged in his throat. "Let's get this over with." He meant to say it as normally as possible, but it came out in a raspy whisper.

There was no doubt in his mind what he would find behind that door. Marianne was dead. He was sure of it. There was no way she could have survived everything, especially with what he just saw in the apartment diagonal to hers.

Jerry cleared his throat loudly and shifted on his feet.

Ralph was pulled from his vision of Marianne as a rotting, walking corpse and, instead, thought about the last time he'd seen her alive.

XVI.

"What is that old man doing now?" Ralph Sherman asked as he rolled over in bed.

"I don't know, but he's going to wake up the baby if he doesn't shut up," Sally answered with pique and discontent.

She'd been up half the night with Lilly because of the partying college boys downstairs and now she was up at the crack of dawn because some old geezer couldn't wait a few hours to nail something to his door. Right on cue, she heard the baby cry out for attention and a bottle. Sally rolled her eyes, not at the needs of her child but at the man who woke her up.

Ralph stayed in bed. He rolled over to face away from Sally.

"Oh, no," she said as she poked him in the back. "If I have to get up with the baby, then you have to go downstairs and check on my mother."

"Why do I have to check on her? She's *your* mother," he said into his pillow.

"Fine, but then you have to get the baby, change her diaper, and feed her, but just a fair warning, her morning diaper is usually a poopy one so have fun with that."

"OK, all right, I'll go check on your mom," Ralph huffed as he threw the covers off.

Sally was pleased. If she'd have had to go downstairs she would have felt compelled to change out of her warm, cozy pajamas and do something with the matted, long mess of red and blonde hair that sat in a bun on top of her head.

Ralph pulled on the pair of green plaid pajama pants he found on the floor and gave a dramatic sigh of exasperation. He looked over at Sally, who stared back at him. His eyes begged for her to do all the work while he went back to sleep.

"No," was all she said as she pointed towards the door. When she saw his fallen face she softened and picked up the babbling baby in the crib next to their bed. "I'll make some biscuits and gravy when you get back!' she called after him.

Ralph scuffed up his dishwater blond hair and shuffled in his camoflauge house slippers down the flight of stairs and over to Marianne's door. He passed by Jerry Middleton, who nodded in his direction. As irritated as Ralph was with Jerry for waking him up, he didn't give him a piece of his mind about it. Something about Jerry reminded Ralph of his dad back in California. It made him not want to say anything to him at all.

He hadn't seen his dad since the big fight right before he left for Navy boot camp after high school. He thought about going back home when his four years were up to try to make things right again, but he met Sally through a group of sailors on another ship and after six months together they were married and she was pregnant.

Before they even became a family, Ralph felt closer to Sally than he ever had with his own and knew how important it was for her to go back to Indiana to help her mother after her dad died. It made no sense to deny his wife time spent with her own family just because he didn't care to see his. So after they were discharged from the Navy, Ralph and a seven months pregnant Sally drove from Norfolk, Virginia to Chesterton, Indiana, and that's what brought Ralph to Sally's mother's doorstep at least once a day to make sure she was still alive and breathing.

Ralph knocked and waited for Marianne to hobble over to the door and answer it. He heard her approach as the rubber soles of her slipper-covered feet scraped at the fake wood linoleum. Her hands pressed on the door as she straightened her slightly hunched back to look through the peep hole. Even though Ralph couldn't see any of this as it happened, he knew it was Marianne's routine before she opened for anyone, per her daughter's request. One time Marianne hadn't adhered to the rules and got a long lecture from Sally on why it was important to not open the door for strangers at her age.—a phrase Marianne hated.

"Hello, Ralph," Marianne said and then turned back into her apartment to leave him in the hallway. "Sally send you?"

"Of course. She wanted to make sure Jerry wasn't beating you to death with his hammer."

Marianne snorted and then went to the kitchen to make tea in the new Keurig machine Sally got for her. It was the first time Ralph laid eyes on it and he immediately wondered how much it had cost him, and also why he was making his coffee in an ancient Mr. Coffee machine while Marianne got a brand new one that she couldn't figure out how to use. He walked over and helped her put the K-cup into the holder and shut it.

"Oh, thank you, dear," she said with a wrinkled smile. Her thin, silver, curled hair stuck up in all directions. She pushed her wire-rimmed glasses up on her button nose as she tried to work the machine again to make Ralph a cup of tea as well.

It amazed Ralph that he could show her how to use something so simple and not two seconds later, she'd forgotten how to use it again. He put the second cup in and closed the lid before he pressed the painfully large start button. One, two, three.

"I don't want any tea, though," Ralph said. Marianne glared at him with dull, tiny eyes. "Maybe Jerry would like a cup." Ralph smiled at her and waggled his eyebrows.

"You stop that," she said as she swatted at him. She carefully walked over to her round, bistro table for two and sat down.

"I see the way he looks at you," Ralph teased as he continued to stand by the counter.

Marianne looked down at her cup and Ralph saw the slightest hint of blush on her liver-spotted cheeks. Suddenly, the vision of his mother-in-law and Jerry together in a sagging, wrinkled tangle popped into his mind and caused him to shudder. He averted his eyes to the floor and ran a hand through his short hair.

"Well, I better get back upstairs. The baby's awake and Sally promised me breakfast," he said and shot straight for the door.

"OK, dear!"

Jerry was still in the hallway making a raucous. His eye caught Ralph's at the last second. He smiled, but Ralph turned away and jogged up the stairs to his apartment, taking two steps at a time.

"I think your mom and Jerry are having an affair," Ralph said once he was inside. He heaved heavy breaths.

"It's not an affair if both their spouses are dead," Sally laughed. She was in the kitchen stirring the gravy while the biscuits baked warm and golden in the oven. The smell of sausage wafted up Ralph's nostrils and perked him up again.

"Well they're doing something hideous and unnatural, then," he spat as he filled a mug with dark roast from his shitty coffee maker.

XVII.

With one push of the crowbar, Marianne Dunbar's door swung open. The apartment was sunny and light, hot like the air outside. Ralph Sherman stepped into his mother-in-law's apartment with his toes first and then lowered his foot slowly and quietly as he made his way further in. It only took three steps to make it past the entryway and into the living room.

A long, gauzy curtain billowed up and out. Everyone snapped their heads, raised their weapons, and waited for something hideous to pop out from behind it. Another breeze blew and pushed the curtain into the room again to do its ghostly dance. The patio door was open.

Without hesitation, Ralph ran over and threw the curtain behind him. He stopped on the other side, the curtain stuck to his back like a leech. His breath was caught in his lungs. He thought he had prepared himself for the worst, but what he saw out on the patio was more horrible than he could have imagined.

Liam craned his neck and saw, lying on the concrete, bare, liver-spotted legs and one foamy sandal on an unmoving foot. He lowered himself back down and looked over his shoulder to the others behind him. He shook his head as his eyes softened, his brow pulled together.

Luke rubbed the sides of his head with both hands and spun around, as if he'd been expecting to go in there and find the old woman knitting happily on the sofa. He tried to contain himself, but the sounds of soft weeping escaped his lips.

Zack slowly lowered his sword to let it hang at his side as the tip grazed the fluffy, light carpet.

Jerry stared in silence with his free hand shoved in his pocket, his shotgun rested on his shoulder.

Ralph's upper body shook as he lowered himself down to one knee and lightly touched Marianne's arm. He said her name, but she didn't move. He knew she wouldn't. The back of her head had been blown away, nothing left but tender, red meat and brains that spilled out onto the hot surface. An overturned watering can lay next to her.

XVIII.

Back at the apartment, Christine sat at the window seat. She read a book she forgot she owned as she soaked in the sun's warm rays through the glass. The only locked deadbolt clicked and the front door opened. She kept her eyes on the yellowed page until she was finished with the sentence she was reading.

"How'd it go?" she asked with the casualty she might have used when asking "how was work".

Liam had stopped off at Zack's apartment before he returned home to wash away the blood that streaked his face and hands, though there was no removing of the thick, dark blood that splattered his shirt and pants.

When Christine looked up from her book and saw his clothes, she stood up and made her way to him with wide eyes.

"Oh my God. What happened?" she asked frantically. The tears were already welling in her big, blue eyes. "Are you OK? Are you hurt?" Her bottom lip trembled.

Liam nodded his head and leaned his bow and quiver up against the coat closet. "I'm all right." His voice was drawn out and exhausted. He blinked and forced a meager smile for Christine's sake.

She exhaled and smiled back, oblivious to the pain just beneath the surface of his sparkling eyes. "Well, let me wash those clothes. I'll see if I can save them."

Her choice of words made Liam's eyes sting profusely. His throat clenched shut. He hadn't been able to save anyone that day. He peeled off his shirt, dropped his pants, and handed them over to his fiancée. As their hands met, his eyes looked past the side of Christine's head, unable to focus on her. He was afraid that if she looked him in the eyes she might be able to see what he'd done, see all the people he murdered and the bodies that had fallen under his arrows.

"Excuse me. I'm just going to wash up," he said softly.

Liam shut himself in the bathroom and rested his hands on the counter. Each breath he took was a stab to his lungs, quick and sharp. His vision blurred as he looked up at the mirror. A wave of heat rose through him and burned his face. His cheeks matched the color of his ginger hair. He couldn't keep it inside any longer.

His shoulders shook while he sobbed, as quietly as he could, over the sink. The tears dripped from his chin and fell onto the porcelain before they slid down the deep, dark abyss of the drain.

When emerged from the bathroom, Christine was rearranging the pillows on the couch—picking them up, fluffing them, and then setting them back down just so. She looked up at him with a smile that said she hadn't heard a thing.

He loved her even more for pretending that.

Part Two

"As far as he could discover, there were no signs of spring. The decay that covered the surface of the mottled ground was not the kind in which life generates."

– Nathanael West

I.

A young woman walked through the woods of the Dunes State Park with her head constantly turning to keep watch. In the twenty-eight hours since Anita fled her dad's house, she came in contact with three different monsters hungry for her flesh. Luckily, she was quick and was able to make a run for it before they could grasp her in their cold, hard hands. During the last escape she had to climb a tree and wait for the thing to lose interest and move on. She waited up there for fourteen hours. Her mouth had been so dry that she thought she was going to die of thirst in the summer heat as the sun beat down and burnt her skin.

"I need to find somewhere to hide. I need shelter," she said to herself as she walked with awkward footsteps in red high heels along one of the dirt trails. "I need…other people."

Her legs felt like cooked spaghetti noodles and her knees buckled at random. When she fell it was a struggle to pick herself up again. Her arms shook as her hands pressed into the dirt and twigs. She wanted to cry, but she didn't have it in her. She smacked her ruby red lips together. Her tongue clicked on the parched roof of her mouth. She ripped the blue bandanna from her pinned up retro hairdo and dabbed at her drenched face, her liquid liner ran down her cheeks like black rivers.

"Where is everybody?" she asked aloud. "They can't all be dead. I can't be the only one left."

The woods were silent and dark. Anita couldn't see two inches in front of her nose for the first few hours. Eventually, her eyes adjusted to the lack of light and she was, at the very least, able to navigate around the trees with her arms outstretched like one of the infected. She couldn't continue that way and survive. She had to find somewhere safe to lay low, even if it was only for a few hours.

She took her heels off and attempted to tread lightly in her bare feet. She clutched the red shoes in her hands with the heels pointed outward, the best weapon she had on her. "Thank God it's summer," she whispered as softly as she could. The sound of her own voice was comforting against the chirping of crickets and the rustling of the trees.

The animals didn't seem to notice that the world was at its end. A raccoon walked lazily across the trail at Anita's feet. When she felt the fur brush against her skin she jumped. The raccoon stopped for a second to sniff her toes before it moved on. She let out a burst of air from her nostrils, a quick and quiet laugh. In all the times she'd hiked the Dunes trails with her dad, never once had she seen an animal up close like that, let alone have one sniff her and decide she wasn't worth their time.

"Bye, Mr. Raccoon," she said with a small wave of her fingers.

The fat raccoon walked off and disappeared into the brush on the other side of the trail.

Anita was alone again, but the silence that once weighed on her shoulders heavily didn't seem so ominous anymore. The brief interaction with the raccoon had given her hope. She wasn't the last survivor. She couldn't be.

She stood on the trail and stared blankly ahead, letting her ears tune in to the world around her to give her strained eyes a break. Her lids were heavy. But the minute she let her eyes close, her dad's face flashed before her. His arms reached for her longingly, his teeth ready to tear the colorful tattooed flesh from her thin arms. Her eyes burst open as her heart thumped loudly.

"Come on!" a voice echoed from somewhere in the darkness.

Anita blinked a few times as she stood perfectly still. Did she really just hear someone or was she going crazy? She'd only been alone for one day. "I can't be going crazy already," she mouthed silently.

"It's this way," another voice whined. She squinted her eyes and saw a tiny white dot of light up ahead.

People! They were really there! The whites of her eyes were visible as her mouth split into a toothy grin. She broke out into a run, as if her life depended on it. Her feet made almost no sound as they barely touched the soft ground.

Suddenly, all her exhaustion was gone.

Suddenly, hope had been restored and she could breathe again.

Suddenly, she wasn't alone anymore.

She slowed to a walk once she could make out the two figures in the dark. They both held flashlights and were approaching an abandoned park building. Anita had been there before. It was the visitor's center. She used to watch the birds from the glass room while her dad read all the plaques on the walls.

"Shh," the fatter of the two men hissed as he whirled around and shined the flashlight in Anita's direction, but she was concealed by a large, leafy bush where she crouched and observed.

"I didn't hear nothin'," the other man said in his normal, slightly loud volume. "Let's go already. I'm tired and I'd like to give this to my old lady." He held something up for a quick second and then lowered it to his side again.

It was too dark for Anita to see what it was that he held loosely in his hand—something round, like bowling ball.

The two men turned towards the building again. The fat man reached out for the door while the taller, older man stood waiting to disappear inside. They were leaving.

Anita's breathing sped up. She had to make a decision. Sweat ran down her face. Was she going to approach them, maybe find shelter with them, or was she going to hide in the bushes like a wild animal and live alone for the rest of her short, miserable life?

She stepped out from behind the bush and stood in the middle of the open trail.

The two men whipped around at the sound of movement. They both had long knives gripped in their hands, raised and ready to stab whatever lacked the common sense to sneak up on them. "I told ya I heard somethin'," the rotund man who held the door said with a sneer. He released his grip on the handle and let it shut slowly and softly behind him.

"Please," Anita begged. "I need somewhere to sleep."

The two men smirked at each other. They holstered their knives in the sheaths on their belts and walked toward Anita casually. As they approached, her heart pounded in her ears. The overweight man in overalls and a flannel shirt let out a low laugh through his crooked teeth.

Anita wanted to run away, but she couldn't. She couldn't abandon the thought of civilization, of coexisting with other people. She needed them, no matter what they were like. What kind of life would she have without them? Even if they made her feel uncomfortable. She wouldn't last long out there by herself.

With the way they looked at her she expected them to flirt with her, kiss her, touch her, demand sex in exchange for shelter. She already had it made up in her mind that she would do whatever it took to receive shelter.

She never saw the first punch coming.

Once she was down on the ground, the two men kicked at her with no direction or precision. Anywhere their feet made contact was a win for them. Anita's body demanded she cough and gasp for air, but every time she tried another foot found its way into her chest or kidneys. She felt like she was drowning as her mouth opened and closed fruitlessly.

"I'll take those, thank ya very much" The older of the two men said as he snatched Anita's high heels from the ground next to her. He turned them over in his hand. "Mary Beth will love 'em!" he said, his stained teeth the only part of his face visible from underneath his dirty, old baseball cap.

"Let's go," his swollen hick friend said with a laugh. "Nightie night!" he called over his shoulder as he raised his hand and waved. "Sleep tight. Don't let them dead fuckers bite."

They both laughed heartily together as they went inside.

Finally able to take in any sort of breath with them gone, Anita pushed herself up onto all fours. Her ribs felt like the bones had been pulverized to dust. Her face didn't feel like it was hers anymore, or she wished it wasn't with how badly it throbbed and stung. She started to sob, but each intake of air felt like it was ripping apart the muscles inside her stomach. Spit and blood fell from her mouth onto the dirt trail. Slowly, she raised herself to her feet, but was unable to stand upright.

Hunched and holding her waist, she shuffled back into the woods before the men returned with reenforcement. She dropped to her knees in a cluster of thick bushes about a half a mile away. Edging her way in so the braches didn't scratch her already bruised and beaten body, she immersed herself and then collapsed to the ground. Everything went dark.

When the sun shone through the trees and onto her face, Anita awoke with a start. She sat up. Immediately, her head pounded something fierce, as if she had been beating it against a tree trunk all night. She took in a sharp breath through her teeth and raised a hand to her head. It hovered over her muddied, strawberry-blonde hair rather than touch it directly.

The rhythmic thumping of footsteps in the distance made its way closer to where Anita sat. When the sound finally separated itself from the pounding of her head, Anita held her breath. Her lungs ached the longer she kept it in. Was it an animal? Was it one of the infected? Or was it more people? That last thought made tears rush to her eyes. She choked them back before she broke into a full on sob again. Her ribs wouldn't be able to handle it.

She could distinguish multiple footsteps and heard faint voices talking to each other. It was people. Her stomach dropped. They were practically on top of her, just a few short feet away as they walked the trail. She lowered her hand from her head to slowly cover her mouth. Coated in dirt, she pressed it against her busted lip which gave a sharp sting. She winced. With enormous eyes, she watched through the leaves as a group of six walked past her. They were too busy arguing to notice she was there. Anita shrank back further into the bushes.

II.

Four guys and two women walked together in a loosely knit group along the trail. The sun was fully in the sky and it brought the relentless heat of an Indiana summer. Before the outbreak, the news had reported it as one of the hottest summers in forty-three years, and it was only the end of June.

Lonnie Lands carried a Colt AR-15 semi-automatic assault rifle in both of his thick, small hands, the barrel pointed out in front of him. He kept his stocky body crouched, knees bent, as he swept the woods. "I'm just sayin'," he said loud enough to echo off the trees. "Every group needs a leader and it should be me. I'm in the Army and I know how to take apart and reassemble this rifle with my eyes closed in under a minute. Everything I did for the Army is top secret, so I can't really talk about it, in case they actually clean this shit storm up and I return to…well I can't say, but I can say that I've seen some shit and done some shit and it ain't pretty."

Gale Lewis rolled her narrow brown eyes. She was a few paces behind the majority of the group and with every step they took they got further away from her, but she didn't mind. She couldn't listen to Lonnie go on about his supposed job in the Army. It was all bullshit. The way he was holding his gun made Gale laugh, like he was Rambo.

When Gale walked she leaned side to side, unable to put too much pressure on either foot since they both throbbed from endless walking. It was Lonnie's idea not to stay in one place too long and as a result she'd only sat down collectively for thirty minutes in the last twenty-four hours. Never mind that she was approaching her mid-fifties while he was barely the legal drinking age.

"You alive back there, Big Bertha?" Lonnie called to Gale every so often. It was an unclever jab at her weight somehow, but she didn't get it. That didn't subside her desires to punch him in the mouth every time he said it, though. She watched the back of Lonnie's white-blond, wide head turn on what little neck he had. His gun followed his every move.

Rowan Brady followed Lonnie and looked at him like he was a God descended down to Earth. He hung on Lonnie's every instruction on what he believed was the right way to shoot a gun. It made Gale sick to think that a fresh out of boot camp baby was teaching anyone anything. Lonnie should've looked to Rowan in that way.

Rowan Brady was thirteen years older than Lonnie and to say that he was easy on the eyes would have been an understatement. He was downright yummy with his chocolate-brown, flippy hair, high cheek bones, and sultry, stubble-covered, incredibly perfect jaw line. Even though Gale was a proud lesbian, having declared herself so, to her parents' disappointment, when she was only twelve years old, she still appreciated beautiful people no matter what their gender. And there Rowan was, a perfect specimen of the male gender, drooling over Lonnie's bullshit so-called knowledge like a lost puppy dog.

Gale wondered for a moment why she ever asked to follow the group when she stumbled upon them. Then she remembered—her swollen feet, her dry mouth, her growling stomach, those things following her relentlessly. Lonnie had saved her. Whether she liked it or not, she owed him for that night.

III.

Gale Lewis ran through the dark with her feet dragging along the grass. She made her way slowly across an open field to an old, large barn on the other end. She moved only slightly faster than the shadowed bodies that stumbled after her. Her chest wheezed as she pushed forward, not sure how much more she had in her. Before she could reach for the doors to the barn, someone stepped outside.

"Get in," the young man growled at her and gave her a shove.

She fell through the doors and collapsed on the hay-covered floorboards.

"Die, you sons-of-bitches!" she heard him yell before he fired off an array of bullets into the warm, night air.

That wasn't how Gale would have approached the situation had she had an assault rifle, but she wasn't in any position to tell him anything. He was out there saving her life. She didn't want to think about what would have happened had she not found the barn.

There was a rustle in one of the dark corners. Gale scrambled back up to her feet with her fists raised.

An even younger man crawled out from the shadows and stood with a Mossberg 500 shotgun clutched tightly in both his hands. They were shaking. Another man walked out behind him with what looked to be a Beretta .9mm pistol hanging down by his leg. Gale saw a pair of muscular legs and large feet sticking out from behind one of the horse stalls, but they didn't move.

"Fuck you, you people-eatin' motherfuckers!" they heard shouts from outside the barn. The rapid gunshots slowed and then tapered off into silence. The young man came back into the barn and secured the doors behind him.

The three men stared at Gale without saying a word. She looked into each of their eyes and decided she would ask to stay, at least for the night. "Thank you," she said to the man, who was really more boy than man, who'd come to her rescue.

"No problem. Just doin' my job as a United States soldier," he said with his chest puffed out as sweat ran down his thick neck.

She nodded and turned to the others. "I'm Gale."

"I'm Lonnie," the soldier jumped at the chance to speak again. "That's Mitchell," he said as he pointed to the teenager with curly brown hair and an angular, clenched jaw.

"That's my man, Rowan Brady." He pointed the barrel of his gun over at the tall man with the pistol. His expensive-looking jeans were dirty and his designer t-shirt was ripped. "And somewhere hiding over there in the dark like a fucking scaredy-ass-cat is the hulking Lee." The legs that stuck out from the shadows still didn't at the mention of his name.

Gale had finally caught her breath and forced at smile at all of them. "Do you think I could crash here with you till morning?"

Rowan and Mitchell looked to Lonnie. He stared straight into Gale's gray-blue eyes as the light from the propped up flashlights all around shone lit up her round face and salt and peppered short hair.

The muscles in Lonnie's large arms tightened as he stuck his chest out even further. "Why not? I didn't go through shit just to send you back out there."

Gale's smile turned sincere. She had a place to hide for the night and she wasn't alone. Her face fell when the three men returned to their spots in the hay for the evening. If only Salena had made it there with her.

IV.

Thankfully, Lonnie switched from talking about his various made-up accomplishments in the Army to his dull, black, cliché tattoos. This brought on a whole new slew of eye rolling, but not from Gale, who had successfully tuned him out to listen to the sound of the leaves in the trees whenever they were lucky enough to catch a breeze. Mitchell

Barnes walked directly behind Lonnie and Rowan, which was torture on his ears.

Lonnie had shoved a loaded shotgun into Mitchell's hands the second they met in the abandoned barn just hours before Gale arrived. He'd gone in there to take shelter after his house was overrun with the infected. At first it was a blessing to have someone take charge of the situation and keep him safe, but slowly Mitchell remembered how much he hated people and he especially hated Lonnie, who he assumed was a dumb jock in high school. They were the very people who made fun of Mitchell's curly brown hair and shoved him into the hard metal lockers as he walked down the hall. He despised Lonnie for everything those kids had done to him, but knew that if Lonnie tried anything funny like they had he wouldn't do anything to stop him. He couldn't survive without him.

"Can we stop for a second? My ankle's killing me," Carolyn Bock said as she sat down on a log and bent her foot around to take a look at the deep, bloodied gash. She winced when she touched a finger to it.

Carolyn had found the group as they were leaving the barn earlier that morning after fleeing her apartment. She'd begged them to let her tag along. Lucky for her, none of the men could refuse a sobbing blonde—none of them except Mitchell. Carolyn was the epitome of all the dumb cheerleaders he used to know and loathe.

"I still think we should have checked her out a little better," he said to the others.

"I told you," Carolyn huffed, "I scratched it on the little metal thingy that holds the door shut."

Mitchell gave a quick snort. "OK, even if you *did* scratch it on 'that little metal thingy', what was your foot doing up there in the first place?"

Carolyn looked away and didn't answer him.

"My point exactly. How can we trust her?"

Lonnie stopped walking and looked up at the sky to take a long, deep breath. He turned to Mitchell. "I know that puberty hasn't hit you yet and ya don't really understand the importance of girls, but trust me, you'll want to collect them soon enough like rare comic books, or whatever gave you wet dreams before shit went down."

"I understand the importance of women," Mitchell called after Lonnie, who walked back to the front of the group. "I just don't understand the importance of this one in particular," he added under his breath.

Carolyn glared at him through squinted eyes and heavy makeup. She held up her middle finger as she stood to her feet again.

Bringing up the rear was a wall of a man, who stood about six foot four with broad shoulders and thick calf muscles. He had dark, wavy, shoulder-length hair that brushed against his neck as he walked. No one had heard him say more than seven short words since he joined Lonnie, Rowan, and Mitchell the afternoon before. "I'm a nurse. My name is Lee." That was all he said.

Carolyn and Gale hadn't heard him speak at all, but his presence behind them was comforting. Carolyn liked a man who didn't talk much. Especially one with big, strong arms and deep, brown eyes.

"What was that?" Lonnie whirled his gun around at whatever nonsense he thought he heard, which he did countless times that day.

Rowan stopped on his toes and peered over Lonnie's head. He was a good five inches taller than him. The woods were silent.

Gale and Mitchell exchanged eye rolls, which they also did countless times that day. She shook her head and frowned while he tried not to laugh.

Something moved in the brush ahead of them. Everyone saw it that time. The mood changed and the air thickened. It wouldn't be the first infected person any of them came across since the outbreak, but the fear in each one of them was just as intense as when they saw their very first one. A foot attached to a thin leg in torn black jeans slowly stepped out of the brush and onto the trail.

An array of bullets flailed across the dirt and kicked it up in little fountains where they hit. The group covered their ears as the sound pierced the sky and traveled through the trees. "Cut it out!" Gale yelled at him. "Are you crazy?"

The woods fell silent again.

Lonnie was panting and his eyes were wide. The leg had disappeared and a pair of small hands attached to two colorfully tattooed arms stuck out instead. They waved in surrender.

"Please, don't shoot," a woman's shaky voice pleaded. "I'm not one of those things. I'm just…me." She stepped out onto the trail.

It was the first time Lonnie lowered his gun since he grabbed it from his truck more than a day ago. He stared at the woman, taken in by her thin waist, curvy chest, and plump lips. She wasn't like Carolyn, who was also curvy and beautiful, but dumb and shallow. There was something real about the woman in front of him, a deep connection he hadn't felt in a long time. He had to give his head a good shake to bring him back. There was a protocol to follow for newcomers. "State your name and business," he said with authority as he pointed his black and tan rifle at her again.

She raised her hands higher in the air and took two shaky steps forward. "Um, my name is Gretchen," she said slowly. "And my business is…survival?"

A loud snort came from behind Lonnie.

He quickly whirled around to point the gun at Mitchell, the barrel inches from his face. "You got something to say, nerd?"

"N-no," Mitchell stuttered as he shook his head. His prominent jaw clenched tightly shut afterwards.

"I'm here to protect the group," Lonnie proclaimed to the sky as he moved the gun away from Mitchell. "If anyone has a problem with that, there's the door."

Mitchell tried his hardest not to laugh again, but air escaped his nostrils in bursts.

Lonnie glared at him. He rested his gun on his shoulder like a little toy soldier. His cold, blue eyes dared Mitchell to speak.

"I'm sorry, it's just, where's the door exactly?"

Lonnie's brow furrowed while, simultaneously, his eyes widened to show the whites around the pupils. He could have been clinically insane in that moment. "Shut up," he said flatly.

He turned back to Gretchen and relaxed the muscles in his face. Without a word he raised his thumb and jabbed it at the air behind him to signal Gretchen to fall in line with the others.

"We're not even going to check her out?" Mitchell couldn't resist. "Look at her. She's got scratches, bruises, blood all over her clothes. She could have been bit. She could be infected."

"I was in a car accident up the road," she said in heated defense to Lonnie.

He looked at Gretchen and nodded his head, and then he narrowed his beady eyes at Mitchell before he continued ahead of everyone else.

Gretchen scanned each person individually as they passed her by and then eyed the back of Lonnie with suspicion. She walked carefully over to Gale's side and did her best to muster up a pathetic, soft smile.

Gale returned it with a quick pull of her mouth, but let it immediately fall back down to the miserable, tired frown she'd been wearing all day.

"Welcome to the Wanderers."

V.

Christine Moore opened the door to the patio and stuck her head out cautiously. The humidity in the air was heavy on her face, but it felt fantastic. She couldn't remember a day in her life when she hadn't gone outside, even if it was just to go to and from her car. She took a deep breath. The fresh air filled her stale lungs. It'd only been a week since it all started and she was locked away in the apartment, but with the warm sun on her face she could have sworn it'd been years. Her shoulders relaxed as she closed the door behind her so it was only open a crack.

Liam was still somewhere in the building with Zack and the others checking for infected people, as they did every morning since that first infamous day they were brought together. Some days the building remained infected free overnight and they were home within twenty minutes. Other days they had one or two that wandered in that they had to take out again. Either way Christine had a little bit of time to enjoy the outdoors in peace.

She sat down on one of the plastic chairs with a long, slow sigh. Her eyes closed as she faced up toward the sun. Something moved below in the parking lot and caught her eyes before they were able to close all the way.

"Mr. Alexander?" Christine said to herself when she spotted the elderly man walking towards the Dumpster. The old man lived in the building next to hers, building five.

He took slow, bumbling steps, which wasn't unusual for him. Mr. Alexander was eighty-two years old and had lived in the same one bedroom apartment since his wife died almost twenty years ago. There'd been days when Christine saw him in his pajamas wondering outside on her way to her car in the mornings, too early for the sun to be up let alone anyone else. Every single time, she took him softly by the arm, spoke to him reassuringly, and lead him back to his apartment where the door was always left wide open. She had no idea where his kids were or why he wasn't in a nursing home. It was clear he was in some stage of Alzheimer's.

Christine watched while leaning forward in her chair. He legs told her to stand up and go to him as they bounced up and down, but her head made her stay put. She chewed on her thumbnail as the old man lumbered forward awkwardly.

Mr. Alexander finally made it to the Dumpster, which stood ten feet tall, and let out a raspy exhale as he peered inside the side window-shaped opening at chest height. His large head turned on his frail neck to scan the contents.

Christine considered calling out to him to tell him he should go back to his apartment. It wasn't safe to be outside anymore. The poor man probably hadn't heard about what was going on. But something stopped her. He didn't look right. She ripped off a chunk of her overgrown nail with her teeth and spat it to the patio floor as she continued to watch in silence.

The feeble man leaned inside the opening as he reached down with both hands. One foot left the ground and Christine wondered how the metal wasn't digging into his stomach. What did he see in there that was worth sticking his head in other peoples' garbage? Finally, he reemerged again, clutching something moving in his hands.

Christine's eyes narrowed as she tried to make out what he was holding so dearly. When she saw the long, pink, leathery tail her eyes widened in horror and her mouth parted. She should go help him. He clearly didn't know where he was, let alone that he was holding a giant, hairy rat. It could have rabies. What if it bit him?

"Mr. Alexander!" she called down to him. Her voice carried over the lot.

The old man turned his head slowly to look at her with white eyes.

Christine slapped her hands over her mouth.

The old man's skin was pale and sagging, but it had always been that way. His hair was balding. A few stray white wisps clung for dear life in the breeze, but Christine had never known him with a full set of hair, or even half. But the gaping hole in the side of his face and the skin missing from his jaw that exposed the red tender muscles and stained teeth underneath, that was new.

When his body turned to her she saw that his light blue button up pajama shirt had been ripped open and the white tank top underneath was soaked with old, dark blood. What was left of his crooked, yellow teeth snapped at the air as he gave a low hiss and then he turned back to the rat in his hands. He shoved the poor rodent into his mouth and bit it in half as it squealed in panic.

Christine let out a muffled whimper behind her hands and felt the sudden rise of her breakfast from her stomach. She repeatedly swallowed the spit in her mouth to keep the bile down.

The entrails of the rat spilled out of the open end and fell to the pavement with a splat. Mr. Alexander dropped to his knees and devoured every last bit with a ravenous hunger. Furred skin clung to his cracked, white lips.

Christine lowered one hand to press against the patio door. Her heart was racing, ready to beat right out of her chest. Her breaths came out hard and fast as it flared her nostrils. Tears gathered in her eyes, but they never fell. The sound of the front door opening doubled her rising panic as she imagined Mr. Alexander walking in to devour her next.

Liam shut the door behind him and started the process of locking the dozen deadbolts and chains. His hands were quick, but unsteady.

Christine forced herself to breathe as she lowered her hand. She watched Liam walk over to the couch and sit down slowly. His face was frozen still, his eyes fixed on a random spot on the wall across from him. Her heart raced again as she peered at him. Something was wrong. She needed him to tell her what had happened, but he didn't say anything when she walked back inside.

"I went out on the patio," she blurted out. She expected him to stand up and yell at her, to tell her how stupid that was and that she shouldn't go outside again. At least then she could get the conversation going.

Instead, Liam remained petrified on the couch with his back rigid, hovered a few inches off the cushion.

"Liam?" she asked and took a few careful steps into his line of vision.

"I think I need to go to the university," he said. His stale tone matched the vacant expression on his face.

"What? Are you serious?"

Liam nodded slowly.

"Why?" she asked harsher than she meant to. "I mean, what could you possibly want from there? We have everything we need here."

He shrugged his shoulders up and then let them slump back down.

All Christine could do was scoff at his ridiculous response. He didn't want her to take one step outside, even on the patio two floors up, but he could get in his car and drive to his old place of work for absolutely no reason? What a hypocrite. Then, she remembered Mr. Alexander and how close he was to the entrance of their building. The urge to leave the apartment left her immediately along with her animosity.

"What happened today?"

Liam stood up and walked over to her. He rested one hand on her shoulder and kissed her forehead. "I'll be back later," he said. "We're having people over for dinner." He unlocked the door and walked out.

Christine was left with her face scrunched in disbelief, nose wrinkled, as her eyes clung to the sight of him until he disappeared altogether behind the door.

VI.

Liam didn't return until the sun was low in the sky, ready to vanish beneath the horizon for the night. As far as Christine saw, he didn't return with anything except a tattered leather journal. She wanted to scream at him for being so careless with his life. After all, what was she supposed to do without him if he died, or worse, was bit?

Before she could work up the nerve to tell him off, there was a knock at the front door. The sound seemed alien already, the last time she'd heard it having been when the Ramirens came begging for help a week ago. Christine hung back as Liam opened the door.

"Who wants some wine?" Zack bellowed as he held two bottles in the air. He barged in past Liam.

Behind him, Ralph and his family came in and looked around nervously, as if they expected one of the dead to jump out from the bathroom. Jerry sauntered in after with heavy footsteps followed by Luke Benson. Liam promptly closed the door behind them and locked everyone in.

Christine stared at the group from a distance. She'd never made an effort to get to know her neighbors and only knew Ralph and Luke from her birthday party, which seemed like it'd happened in an alternate universe many years ago, but as she counted in her head it had only been eight days. Jerry hadn't been at the party, but since the night he gunned down the Goldsteins from his porch Christine made the effort to ask Liam all about him. She smiled at each of them, but didn't say a word.

Everyone placed what they brought on the kitchen counter and grabbed paper plates to fill up. They used large water glasses to drink the wine out of, pouring it to the brim. Both bottles were drained dry before they all sat down on the couch, window seat, or floor.

Liam handed Christine a full glass of wine and kept one for himself. Neither felt much like eating after what they'd seen earlier, the horrors they'd witnessed their own little secrets to be kept. Christine wondered if Mr. Alexander was still roaming outside, eating whatever rats he stumbled across.

"Let's get started." Zack Kran said. He leaned his back against the couch.

"What's going on?" Sally Sherman asked as she locked eyes with Christine to see if she'd been informed before her. "Why are we all here?"

"It's the first official meeting of the zombie crew…zombie squad? Zombie corps?" Zack rambled off.

Everyone eyed him with tight lips.

"We'll figure out a name later. What's important right now is the rules."

"Rules for what?" Christine asked with bite. She hated not knowing what was going on in her own house, with her own fiancé.

Liam cut in between them. "We need to keep this building safe if we're going to stay here, or at least as long as we *can* stay here. We've successfully decontaminated the building this week, but more will come. The five of us," he said, waving a hand towards the men in the room, "are going to work together to make sure our home stays *zombie* free." He said zombie as if it were a made up word he'd just invented.

Christine didn't say anything. She looked around the room with narrow eyes to judge whether they were joking or not, even though the image of Mr. Alexander eating the rat was still clear in her mind. They weren't zombies. That was ridiculous. They were sick.

"The first rule, I think, should be that everyone retains their own living quarters," Liam said to get the ball rolling.

"Me too," Zack agreed right away.

"Yup," Jerry mumbled through his food.

Luke looked to Sally. Their eyes both shared the same anxious glare.

Ralph moved his daughter, Lilly, from one arm to the other as she reached out for his plate of food. "Well if everyone is going to be separated, then we should meet in the mornings to make sure we all made it through the night and no one was attacked by one of those…whatever they are."

"People," Christine said in a steady voice. "They're people."

"These things aren't people!" Zack responded wildly. "They don't do anything but walk and eat! They don't even feel anything."

"How do you know they don't feel anything? Did one of them tell you that?" Christine spat over her cup of wine.

Zack rolled his eyes. "'course not. They can't talk. They can't do anything but devour people whole and turn them into walking, eating, rotting corpses! Zombies!"

"That's enough!" Liam yelled, standing to his feet. "We don't need to be arguing amongst ourselves. We can all agree they're dangerous and we're better off without the lot of them. Can we get back to the rules, please?"

Everyone was quiet. They each skillfully avoided eye contact to stare down at their food or take interest in the framed art on the walls.

"Good. Right. We'll meet every morning at eight on the third floor and work our way down. Now what's next?" he said as he sat back down on the couch. He took a large gulp of dry white wine.

"How are you getting rid of these *people*," Christine said as she eyed Zack.

"Good question," Sally chimed in as she took Lilly from her husband's arms. The baby squirmed to get loose, so she could watch her dad eat his food.

"Well, we, um, exterminated the threat," Liam said in a wavering voice. "As of now they remain in their respective flats until we can decide what to do with them."

"Let's just pile them up in the park for now," Zack said, taking the last bite of the vegetables on his paper plate before he tossed it aside.

"Like trash?" Christine said in a huff.

"Are you going to jump all over me every time I speak?"

Zack looked at Liam for support.

Christine did the same.

Liam took a deep breath. "Everyone's opinion is valid here. We have to hear each other out and come up with a solution we can all agree on. This is everyone's home."

Respect was restored, at least for the moment.

"Only until we figure out if putting them in the ground will somehow spoil the dirt or whatever," Zack said in a calm tone as he addressed everyone. "What if we want to grow food out there someday and their rotting infectious body juices seep into our crops or something?

Christine had to admit he made a good point, one which she hadn't considered at all. But she'd never admit Zack was right after his callous take on the sick. She rested back against the couch and raised her glass to her mouth to fill the void from her lack of a comeback.

"Does anyone have a problem collecting the dead and placing them outside until we can come up with something better for them?" Liam asked, calling the rule to a vote.

Sally shrugged her shoulders. "So, does that mean we're going to…put my mom with them?" she asked, forcing back the tears that crept up on her.

No one said anything. They all looked at her with soft, sorry expressions.

She tried to smile as the corners of her mouth turned up slightly and then fell back down to the frown she'd been wearing since she received the news about her mother. She nodded and then turned her attention back to her daughter, who was trying to pull the collar of her shirt into her mouth.

"Let's move on," Liam said. "We've got a meeting time, where we'll live, and how we'll dispose of the bodies. Is there anything else anyone would like to add?"

"Yeah," Ralph said, looking at Jerry. "I think everyone should be responsible for getting their own supplies and food."

Jerry snorted as he rested his fork back onto his plate.

"No, that's a good one," Zack said. "We need to help each other out, but I can see it getting ugly if we try to give each other stuff, playing favorites and what not."

"But we can't just go wandering about by ourselves," Liam said.

"Then, we'll go out in pairs. That way we'll always have back up in case anything happens," Ralph said nonchalantly, as if he were talking about going on a fun hunting trip together.

His wife looked at him like he was crazy. "If it's that dangerous maybe we should all stay indoors." she said, almost pleadingly.

"And what? Starve to death?" Zack said.

"He's right, babe. We need food and supplies or we won't survive. The baby still needs formula, diapers, and other...baby stuff."

Several pairs of eyes drifted around to glare at the stacks of boxes piled up against the walls of the living room. Liam looked to Christine from the corner of his eyes.

"We don't even know how long this is going to last," Christine said, brushing it off. Now that her glass was empty, she had a new found confidence. "The National Guard could come tomorrow and take care of this whole thing."

It was Zack's turn to snort as he shook his head at the floor.

"What?" Christine demanded.

"Wake up, Chris. No one's coming. This is it. This is life now. The sooner you get used to it, the better off you'll be."

"Whatever, Zack, like you know everything—" she started to say, but Liam stopped her from going any further with one look. She raised a hand in surrender and slumped back against the couch.

"It's settled, then," Liam said. "No one goes out alone, not for anything."

With rules finally in place, everyone sipped at their wine with wandering eyes, avoiding eachother like the plague. Liam was the only one who dared to glance into every single face. They were supposed to pull together in order to survive. Instead, they were sitting on the floor, arguing with each other over petty differences.

"Why don't we try to get to know one another a little better?" he broke the silence in hopes of breaking the tension as well. "What did everyone do before...before all this?"

They eyed each other and waited to see who would jump in first. The silence was unbearable.

"I owned the comic book store downtown," Zack said. He couldn't watch his friend be ignored like he was. He'd seen how sensitive Liam could be.

"Corporate lawyer," Christine said, annoyed, still leaning far back and clutching at her wine glass.

"Stay-at-home mom, but before that Ralph and I were in the Navy," Sally said.

"Really?" Christine perked up. "What did you do in the Navy?"

"We were electricians."

Everyone's eyes widened as they nodded their heads, sighing a collective "ahh".

"Won't do us much good, here, though," she added at the sight of their eager expressions. "We can't keep it going. Once it's gone, it's out of our hands."

The silence weighed on them again. How long did they have left in the light until the power went out and enclosed them in eternal darkness?

Liam looked around and took a breath. "I was a scientist."

This brought about a bigger, more intense reaction than electrician had. They all stared at Liam, some with their mouths hanging halfway open.

"You're a *scientist?*" Sally asked, her voice high-pitched and excited. "Can't you fix this then?"

Liam couldn't stop the small laughter that escaped his lips. It tapered off when he saw the hurt look in Sally's almond eyes. "No, sorry, I'm a plant geneticist. The people to figure this out would be biologists, microbiologist."

Her entire body slumped downward as her eyes fell to gaze at the empty paper plate on the floor in front of her.

"What about you Jerry?" Ralph asked coolly.

Jerry took his time chewing the last piece of broccoli in his mouth and swallowed before answering. "Retired."

Ralph's eyebrows pulled together as he stared and waited for the rest. Jerry pounded a fist on his chest until a low, rumbling belch rose from within.

Sally and Christine wrinkled their noses at each other in mutual disgust.

"Retired from what?"

"Crane operator. Steel mill," he answered in as little words as possible.

"All right then, see? I have a feeling we're all going to be great friends," Liam said with a hopeful smile.

When there was nothing left to say, the Shermans stood up first. Sally thanked everyone for dinner and Christine for having them over.

"Yeah, see ya tomorrow," Jerry said to the couple on the way out the door.

"Thank you," Luke said. It was the first thing he uttered since the discussion began.

Christine looked at him like she'd forgotten he was there altogether.

"Bye," he added and walked out briskly.

Zack closed the door and sat back down on the couch beside Christine. "Sorry things got a little heated," he said, giving her a pat on the knee. "No hard feelings?"

She cocked her head and glared at him.

He removed his hand carefully.

A slow smile spread across her face. "Sure. We're fine."

"Something on your mind, mate?" Liam asked as he put the dirty glasses in the sink to be washed.

"I was just thinking…" Zack started to say, but trailed off.

Christine and Liam both waited for him to continue as the air hung with his words.

"I just wonder…do you think Anita made it? Do you think she's…alive?" He winced, the words hurt him as he spoke them.

"Oh, Zack," Christine said and placed a hand on his shoulder. "You barely knew her. She came into the comic book store a few times and what? Only talked to you once?"

"I have to know what happened to her," he said as he stared at his lap and wrung his hands together. "I think I'm going to try to find her."

Liam walked to the couch and stood over him. "That's not a good idea. We need you here."

"I won't leave for like days at a time or anything," he said looking up at his friend. "Just search some places around town during the day after we check the building out. See if I can find her."

Liam rubbed a hand over his face. He shook his head and ran the same hand back over his messy ginger hair. "I'm not sure…"

Zack stood. He was a few inches shorter than Liam and had to look up to stare him directly in the eyes. "I wasn't really asking for your permission."

Liam saw the desperation on his friend's face. It was worse than the one day a month when Zack used to pay the bills at the comic book store. "All right," Liam breathed out. "I'll help you find her."

VII.

Gale Lewis threw her head back and groaned into the white hot rays of the sun. "How much longer are we just going to wander around aimlessly? My ankles are swollen and we've been down this road at least three times now."

They trudged along the scenic route of highway twelve. Tight knit trees lined both sides, but did little in the ways of providing shade since the sun was high in the middle of the sky. Not a single cloud could be seen, leaving no hope for a brief release from the smoldering sunlight. Up ahead the scenery blurred like a mirage from the heat rising off the pavement.

"How 'bout you stop worryin' and shut up?" Lonnie barked without turning to look over his shoulder. He was sick of all the complaining—first Carolyn and her scratched ankle, Mitch the bitch and his incessant worrying about Carolyn's scratched ankle and now Gale and, low and behold, her ankles…When would it end? He should have let those things eat the old woman the night he found her.

Gretchen, the newcomer, glared at the back of Lonnie's wide head wrapped in his wet t-shirt. Sweat dripped down his red neck and white wife-beater tank top. "She's right," she called out with solidity. "We can't keep exhausting ourselves. We need somewhere to go or else what's the point?" She'd been with the group for a few days and had seen Lonnie order them around and march them through the woods and over the highway without the smallest hint of some sort of plan.

Lonnie stopped and turned on his heels. He marched back to Gretchen, his piercing blue eyes locked on her. Rowan and his long legs made it to her first, but Lonnie waved him off.

His faced softened as he leaned his head to one side and smiled sweetly. "You are absolutely right." He reached out to brush a strand of her shoulder-length blonde hair behind one of her ears. God, was she beautiful.

"I thought you said staying in the woods was our best shot?" Rowan turned to him. "The uneven ground slows them down and we can always hear them coming. You said being close to people would get us killed. You said..."

No one was listening to Rowan, especially Lonnie, who was lost in Gretchen's sapphire eyes, her pouty blushed lips, her colorful, tender arms that he wished would wrap around his waist and pull him in close to her.

Gretchen's breath caught in her chest. The young, stocky man stood so close that she could smell the dried, stale sweat that soaked his clothes and hair. She kept her face stern and unflinching, but inside she wanted to scream. Nothing but unnerving concentration kept her eyes from darting away from his, wanting to stand her ground. "We should gather supplies and find a place to rest, at least for a couple of days."

She caught a glimpse of Lee from the corner of her eyes standing with his arms crossed a ways behind Lonnie's shoulder. Why didn't he say something? Anything? He was just standing there like a useless statue. Was there no one in the group who would stand up to the asshole in front of her? She would love nothing more than to see the hulking man pick Lonnie up with one hand and drop him to the pavement like a ragdoll.

Lonnie blinked slowly as he continued to grin. All at once, he snapped out of whatever trance he was in and looked around at his people. "The new girl here,"

"Gretchen."

"Gretchen," he repeated with an echo. "Thinks we should look for supplies and shelter." There was a long pause as he spun in a circle to see everyone individually.

No one responded as they waited for Lonnie to get to the point without all the dramatics of a drill sergeant.

"Well, I think she's right. We're tired, hungry, and damn thirsty. At least I am."

Carolyn and Rowan nodded their heads, willing to agree with anything Lonnie said.

Gale rolled her eyes for the hundredth time that day, but Lonnie didn't notice, just like all the other times.

Lee was silent and still, an onlooker rather than a participant in the going ons of the ragtag group.

Mitchell's eyes darted around nervously.

"Let's head to the lake and then find a store to raid," Lonnie ordered.

Gale's round body perked up. "That idea's shit."

Lonnie threw his arms up and looked at the sky with an exaggerated sigh. "Here we go again. Big Bertha, do you have to argue with me every step of the fucking way?"

"Only when you're wrong."

He collected himself from his borderline fit and puffed out his chest to stroll over to her. "What did you say?" He was inches from her face.

Gale's voice didn't waiver as she spoke. She stood as tall as any other five foot four woman with aching feet could have. "I said it's a dumb idea. There are houses all up and down that lake. You think those people aren't protecting their water? Their *fresh* water? Think they let just any wannabe G.I. Joe kid come waltzing up and take as much as they want?"

"She *does* have a valid point, there," Mitchell agreed.

"Hey!" Rowan barked with his pistol raised. "Lonnie thinks we should go to the lake so that's where we're going!"

"Ya'll don't like it you can find another bunch of assholes to go die with, because I don't plan on dying of thirst when there's a fucking giant-ass lake not even a mile away and dead people walking around trying to eat us!"

"You might want to keep your voice down, then," Mitchell rambled quickly.

"Man, you need to learn when to keep your fucking mouth shut!"

"I think that's exactly what he was just telling *you*," Gretchen chimed in. She stood with one foot planted firmly on the pavement of the winding highway as the other one jutted out in front of her, her hip popped as her hand rested on it.

Lonnie glared, but didn't walk her way again. He looked down at the ground and shook his head with his hands on his hips. His rifle was slung over his back. "You know, you're absolutely right again, Miss Gretchen. I'll try to...*control*...the volume of my voice." The corners of his light blue eyes crinkled from his joker grin.

It was unnerving. Gretchen couldn't hold his gaze any longer and looked away towards Gale, who gave a snort once Lonnie was back at the head of the group. Gretchen walked slowly as the others moved on to follow Lonnie to the lake. She let her feet drag and stayed close by Gale's side. She watched her from her peripherals.

Did Gale not remember meeting her before or was she pretending not to know her now? And for that matter, was Lonnie doing the same? The questions had constantly filled her and clouded her head since she joined the group. She hadn't know them well before everything happened, but she recognized them immediately when she stepped out from behind that bush days ago. How could they not remember her? She'd met them both on the same night, in the same club. She let the thoughts of that night, not long ago, swirl through her mind as she shuffled aimlessly forward.

VIII.

Gretchen locked the door to the photography studio and turned off the lights in the front room. The computer monitor she used to check customers in gave off an eerie glow around her desk. She walked to the back where boxes and crates were piled everywhere, containing cloth backdrops and props for shoots.

Perched on a stack of crates was Gretchen's girlfriend, Charlie. She was hunched over a Nikon camera, twisting the long lenses off as she inspected it with great detail.

Charlie did the same thing every night after closing up shop. Her work was her pride and joy. She'd built her studio up from the ground after she graduated from Columbia College of Chicago. The city had proved to be such a miraculous subject that she never went back to Long Beach.

Gretchen wasn't thrilled about the decision to stay. Chicago was too close to home for comfort. She wanted to go back to California, where the sun shone year round and her judgmental parents were thousands of miles away.

She stood by the door, concealed behind a stack of plastic crates, and watched Charlie for a moment in admiration. Her girlfriend looked effortlessly cool as her short, wispy, dark hair fell into her equally dark eyes. The sleeves of her thin, cotton shirt were pushed up just past her elbows, showcasing her bronzed, flawless skin. Her khaki skinny jeans hugged her narrow legs all the way down to the ankles, where she kicked her feet out and let them fall with a thud against the crate. One of her brown flats threatened to break free from her foot and tumble to the floor as it hung on for dear life.

Gretchen smiled and exhaled the softest breath of laughter.

Charlie's head sprung up with spritely eyes widened in curiosity, her thin lips parted in a smile. "Spying on me from the shadows, you weirdo?"

Gretchen came out of hiding, the light from the long hanging lamp above her illuminated her silky blonde hair. "Just like watching you work."

"Well in that case," Charlie smiled and picked her camera back up to clean it with a Q-Tip. She looked up at her girlfriend with bedroom eyes as she wiped the lens. She couldn't contain her girlish laughter and burst out with her head thrown back. "You about ready to go?"

"I guess." Gretchen meandered around and peeked into random boxes as she passed by them.

"Uh oh. I know what that means. You don't really want to go, do you?"

Gretchen shrugged, unable to lie and say she wanted to go, but also unable to voice that she absolutely did not want to go in fear of hurting her girlfriend's feelings. They had only lived together for ten months, but it still felt new to Gretchen. Charlie was her first girlfriend and her first serious relationship.

"I know you're not completely comfortable there, but we're just going to the gay bar because that's where my aunt and her fiancée are having their bachelorette party," Charlie said as she stood up and carefully put the camera back in its nylon, black case.

Gretchen leaned over the sink by the back door to apply a rosy shade of lipstick and shag up her wavy hair. She ran her fingers over her smooth, tanned cheeks and pulled them back to make them skinnier, then let them fall back into place. She took out a pencil eyeliner from the pocket of her pink and gray plaid shirt. Her mouth hung open as she applied it meticulously.

Charlie waited in the background for Gretchen to say something, anything, to reassure her that she wanted to be in the relationship. It was impossible to ignore the angst in Gretchen's eyes when people on the street stared at their clasped hands. She still wasn't comfortable with her newfound sexuality and it made Charlie writhe with worrisome fear.

"I'm fine with the bar," Gretchen said, distant.

"OK. Good." For being such a tomboy, Charlie's voice was soft and feminine, especially when she had doubts.

Gretchen turned and cocked her head to the side. Her blue eyes softened. She walked over and wrapped her arms around her waist. "Stop worrying," she said in a subdued voice. "I love you."

It was just what Charlie needed to hear. Their lips touched briefly and softly before their fingers intertwined and Charlie dragged Gretchen out the door.

The bar was enormous. A thumping bass vibrated the walls from a hidden source. The lights were dim and the circular bar was placed in the direct center of the floor. The girls opted for a long table off to the side that would seat the entire small bachelorette party once they arrived.

They were the first ones there. Gretchen sat down on a stool next to the wall.

"Want a drink?" Charlie asked as she rested her hands on Gretchen's shoulders and massaged them.

"Yeah, Sam Adams." She reached over to pat Charlie's hand twice, not allowing herself to linger for too long.

Charlie leaned in and kissed her on the cheek. "I know. Just like always."

Gretchen sat alone and looked around the bar, which was slowly filling with more people. She swore she felt their eyes inspecting her, wondering if she was really a lesbian or just some straight girl who wanted to try a new, exotic lifestyle for the night. Some days even she didn't know which one she was.

A stocky boy with short blond hair cut in military fashion came striding up to her with his friend at his heels. His sunburnt arms were covered in a random mixture of flat, black tattoos and white-blonde hair.

"Can I get you a drink?" he asked Gretchen as he leaned his hand on the table, his eyes boring into her.

She could tell he was freshly twenty-one and his friend wasn't much older, too young for Gretchen who was rounding on thirty in the fall.

"Ah, no…I'm good. Thanks."

"I'm Lonnie," he said as he extended his hand out to her.

The nameless friend behind him, who had been sipping on his beer continually since they walked over, raised a hand in silence.

Gretchen took Lonnie's hand in hers and shook it loosely and briefly before she dropped it. She wrung her hands together in her lap and looked around for Charlie. "Gretchen," she said, distracted as she searched.

"Has anyone ever told you you've got a rockin' body, Gretch?" Lonnie asked unabashed.

Her eyes opened wide to show the whites around her pupils before narrowing. She'd been told many times by similarly obnoxious men that she had a voluptuous, scrumptious, provocative body that wouldn't quit. Those men were the reason she was open to trying a relationship with Charlie in the first place. When they met, Charlie didn't make her feel like a pig being judged at the county fair.

"Hello…" Gretchen heard her girlfriend's voice from behind. "Who are you?" There was an edge to it that hadn't been there when she left. She put her arm around Gretchen's shoulder and reeled her in close. "They didn't have Boston Lager. Only Summer Shanty. Sorry, babe."

"That's OK," Gretchen said quickly. She picked up her beer and held it to her mouth as long as she could, taking several large gulps. She didn't want to talk to the boys anymore, but she also didn't want to play into Charlie's jealous tantrum either.

"I told you this was a fag bar," Lonnie said over his shoulder to his friend.

The bored young man stood with his hand in his jeans pocket while the other held his beer. He looked just as out of place as Gretchen felt.

"Yeah, it's a *gay* bar, asshole, and you're hitting on my *gay* girlfriend." Charlie removed her hand from Gretchen and stood just inches from Lonnie, flat chest to flat chest.

It was almost comical to watch. Charlie was five foot three and Lonnie only stood somewhere around five-ten, but he looked like a giant in comparison, towering over a small, angry elf.

"Don't get your panties in a wad, or is it boxers? I can never tell with you butch women," Lonnie spat at her.

Charlie held up her middle finger as he turned and walked away. His friend looked back with apologetic eyes. "Fucking assholes," Charlie muttered after them.

"Not talking about us are you?" an older Hispanic woman said as she strolled up to the table.

Charlie's face lit up. She wrapped her arms around the woman and squealed. "No, auntie, never you!"

Salena Perez squeezed her niece tight to her. The two could have been twins, except Salena had longer, wavy black hair that fell in sheets down her back. Even though she was at least twenty years older than Charlie, she certainly didn't look it. Her brown skin was smooth and firm to match the curves of her body.

Gretchen had no idea how her partner had landed such a gorgeous girlfriend. Gale Lewis was the polar opposite of Salena. She had pale skin with rosy cheeks and her body looked like a pear. Her hair was cut in the same boyishly short style as Charlie's, but hers was salted with gray and white. She wore loose khaki jeans, a denim button down shirt left open with a white t-shirt underneath, and generic tennis shoes. When she walked there was the slightest hint of a waddle as she bounced from side to side. She stood in the background like a lonely gnome on the lawn, keeping watch with her hands in her pockets.

Gretchen gave them both a quick smile and then returned her attention to the half empty bottle of beer in front of her. The night couldn't end fast enough.

IX.

Gretchen blinked a few times to clear the memories from her eyes, which were adjusting to the dimness of the evening. The sun sank down behind Lake Michigan, which changed from blue to various shades of oranges and yellows, as if the water itself were on fire.

The group of wanderers waited on one of a mountainous sand dunes in the shade of scraggly, thin trees. They sat perched in the tall grass away from the rows of three-story houses on stilts that lined the lakefront.

Gretchen made sure to keep her distance from the others as she cornered Gale alone. It was time Gretchen locked down her only, and possibly last, friend in the world.

"We've met before, haven't we?" she asked quietly so the others wouldn't overhear.

Gale laughed under her breath and nodded her head as she picked the grass out of the ground. She crumpled the strands between her fingers before she threw them back down. "Yeah, we have."

Excitement coursed through Gretchen. Her face lit up as she shifted from sitting on her butt to her knees. "I knew it!" she said louder than she intended.

What little neck Lonnie had stretched out to get a look at the two women.

Gretchen shut her lips tightly and stifled her laughter, which came out as a weird gasp caught deep in her throat.

Lonnie turned back to the group.

Rowan sat next to him with one leg tented and the other stretched out in the hot sand.

Lee stood across from them while Mitchell sat Indian-style, his shotgun clenched in his pale, white hands.

Carolyn leaned all the way back on her elbows, her tanned bare legs on display in her short jean shorts for whomever might want a good stare.

Lonnie took the invitation multiple times with no shame. He licked his lips and eyed her barely covered body.

"Why didn't you say anything?" Gretchen whispered when she was sure no one was paying attention.

"The same reason you didn't."

Gretchen stared at her and waited for more of an explanation.

"You're not sure about these people. Just like I'm not sure about them either. You got Lonnie over here, fresh out of Army boot camp thinking he's Sergeant Highway."

Gretchen's face scrunched as she shook her head.

"It's a movie," Gale said waving her hand. "Anyway, then there's this Mitchell kid who has the eyes of a puppy who's been kicked one too many times. So when we're out there fighting these things off, we have to worry about one shooting us in the back." She glared at Lonnie with narrowed eyes. Then, she nodded her head to Mitchell. "And one because he doesn't know the first thing about handling a gun."

Gretchen hung on Gale's every word. She nodded her head as her eyes begged the older woman to continue. Gale had only known the men two days longer than Gretchen, but with how fast the world fell apart, those two days were a lifetime. Her knowledge was valuable to survival.

"Then, there's pretty boy, Rowan," Gale scoffed and broke out into a fit of quiet laughter. Her chin touched her chest as she rocked back and forth. "He's got his head shoved so far up Lonnie's ass I don't know what to think of him…except he's the biggest pussy I've ever met." The laughter stopped and she looked at Gretchen with steel-gray, tired eyes. She sighed. "And Carolyn…she's not much of a threat. Just looking for protection."

"And what about that guy?" Gretchen asked as she looked over her shoulder at the towering man standing watch over everyone else.

"Who? Lee?" Gale laughed again, but with her head thrown back this time. "I wouldn't worry about him."

"Why's that?"

"How many men you know like that become male nurses because they're deranged and dangerous?"

They stared at each other for a good long time before they both broke out into muffled laughter.

"Hey!" Lonnie hissed at them sharply. "Keep it down over there!"

"Yes, sir, sorry, sir," Gale said as she saluted.

The two women chuckled with their heads together as Lonnie turned away and muttered a slew of curses under his breath. "Stupid, fucking, bitch-ass…"

The giggling tapered off as Gretchen leaned back on her hands to look up at the black, cloudless sky. The stars flickered one by one and reminded her of where she grew up, which wasn't too far from where they sat. She'd been to the very spot countless times in her life while hiking with her family, but all she could think of now was if she was going to make it to see daylight again or if the stars would be the last thing she saw in her life. It felt like she was on another strange planet, a dangerous and deadly one. Lonnie cleared his throat and shooed the thoughts from Gretchen's worried mind.

"OK," Lonnie whispered, crouched on his feet with his gun poised. "Let's head out."

They stayed low and moved as fast as they could while crouched. They crept down the sand dune towards the placid water. The air was completely still, which made the lake look like a thick sheet of glass that they could walk out on forever, away from the world of chaos behind them.

Lonnie kept waving everyone forward, but the only one who seemed to pay him any attention was Rowan. He mimicked Lonnie's every move.

Gretchen's heart pounded as they moved out into the openness of the lakefront. The sound of sand and stones crunched under her feet and seemed to echo out for everyone to hear, if there was anyone around to hear.

Lonnie held up his fist and turned to make sure they followed his order. "On three we make a break for the water. Big Bertha," he said as he smiled at Gale. "It was nice knowing ya."

She held up her middle finger and he chuckled.

"One…two…"

Gretchen couldn't breathe. There was a relentless pounding in her head and a queasy turning in her stomach. All at once she didn't want to do this. She didn't care how thirsty she was. She wanted to turn around and run away, from the lake, from the group, from everything. What had she gotten herself into?

She looked over her shoulder and saw three lumbering figures in the dark on the very spot they'd just been sitting. They stumbled as their unresponsive feet got caught in the weight of the sand. She turned back to the black lake with her lips parted, her eyes perfect blue circles.

"Three."

X.

There was a flash of white light. Gretchen couldn't see anything, but she kept running forward to the water's edge as fast as her legs would carry her. It was as bright as day as beams shone down from several of the houses and the surrounding lifeguard towers. The silence of the night was broken by the sounds of gunshot and the beating of Gretchen's racing heart in her ears.

She looked back to see Gale still standing where the tall grass met the sandy beach, hidden from the houses, the three figures growing larger behind her. Someone from the group screamed. Gretchen turned and ran back into the safety of the trees when the fresh water was just several feet in front of her. The rest of the group seemed to have had the same idea as they, one by one, came to a halt next to her heaving through their gaping mouths.

"What the hell was that?" Rowan yelled as he doubled over and tried to catch his breath.

Gale stood with her hands on her hips. "*That* was exactly what I said would happen. That was people defending what they believe is theirs."

Out of nowhere, Lonnie drove into Gale with his hands on her shoulders and pinned her to a large tree trunk. "You were supposed to go out there like the rest of us!" He roared in her face. "Someone could've died!"

Gale didn't squirm or show an ounce of discomfort in her stone-cold face, even though her head throbbed where it slammed into the hard bark. She was grinning. "And you were hoping that someone was me?"

He gave her a good shove as he backed off and scratched at his head. He threw his hands down to his side as he paced in circles, breathing heavily from his nose, his nostril flaring wildly. All at once, Lonnie threw the rifle over his shoulder and aimed it in Gale's direction.

Before anyone could move to put a stop to it, he fired openly.

Gale ducked down and raised her hands to cover the back of her head. Multiple shots whizzed by her and landed with quick thumps as the bullets penetrated something hard. She'd pushed Lonnie too far. The kid was a grad-A jerk, but she never thought he would actually try to murder her. She swore to herself, right then and there, that if she made it out alive, she would rip him apart with her bare hands.

When the gunfire ceased and silence was restored, Gale raised her head slowly. She looked behind her and saw three motionless bodies lying in a heap in the tall grass, black blood oozing from the bullet holes in their heads. Lonnie had saved her…again.

"Well, we need fucking water and we need it right fucking now so what do you suggest, Big Bertha? Since you think you're some kind of apocalyptic survival genius, you tell us where to get our fucking water!"

Small moans and whimpers in the distance broke up the argument. In the openness, Mitchell lie in the sand with Lee by his side. Slowly, as the arguing subsided, everyone turned and gathered to see what was going on with the youngest member of their group.

Mitchell couldn't seem to keep still as he rocked side to side. Lee was trying to unlace his tennis shoe to remove it, but kept losing his grip with every jerky movement.

"Hold still!" Lee grumbled. His face was stiff and his jaw was clenched.

Mitchell took one quick look at the broad man's narrowed, dark eyes and stopped moving instantly. His whimpering changed to sharp outbursts of air from his nostrils as he clamped his mouth shut. His fingers dug into the sand as he moaned.

Lee tossed the shoe aside and removed his white tube sock slowly. There was a circular blood stain on the outer side. When Mitchell's foot was finally exposed, Lee held it close to his face. He tried to inspect the wound, but it was too dark to see. "Gimme a light," he said, holding out his hand.

Rowan reached into his pocket and pulled out his cellphone. With a few taps, brightness beamed from the camera's light on the back. Lee took it and held it close to Mitchell's foot. His nose was just inches from the pinky toe. He made a few approving and disappointing clucks while everyone else huddled around to get a good look.

"Right," Lee said, setting the phone down in his lap. He reached deep into one of the pockets of his khaki cargo shorts. He pulled out a small bottle of Hydrogen Peroxide and a roll of medical gauze. "The bullet just grazed da side of ya foot. You'll need ta keep it clean and covered for a few days. You'll be fine," he said in a thick accent.

Mitchell sat up, his lips neither turned up in gratitude nor turned down in pain. "I didn't know you were Irish." The curls on his head bounced as he gave a few small shakes of his head. He looked to the others as multiple eyes rolled in his direction.

"There's a lot ya don't know." Lee poured a few drops of the Peroxide onto the open wound. It fizzed on contact and Mitchell took a sharp intake of air between his teeth and released it with a long sigh. Lee wrapped his foot quickly and stood up when he was done.

"Thanks," Mitchell said as he pushed himself to sit up. He grabbed for his shoe and put his sock on slowly and carefully. Blood was already starting to show through the layers of white gauze.

"Think you'll make it, Mitch the Bitch?" Lonnie asked. He didn't wait for an answer before he turned away again. "Good. Great. Back to business. What do you suggest we do now, Big Bertha? What's your awesome plan to keep us alive?"

"We find supplies and shelter, like we've been saying." There was less acidity to her voice.

"There's a Walmart not too far from here," Gretchen offered. "I know it'll probably be cleaned out, but I bet we could still find a few things we need that we haven't been able to get from the houses we've been to."

Gale smiled at Gretchen. "Great idea, hon. Good thinking."

Gretchen smiled back with all her teeth and her brilliant blue eyes lit up her face.

Lonnie's gaze shifted between them as he scowled. "Oh no, Big Bertha, don't get any ideas here. You're not turning this one into some rug muncher."

"Actually," Gretchen spoke up. "I *am* gay."

Lonnie's mouth dropped wide open. His head started to spin. It couldn't be true. "You gotta be shittin' me," he said flatly. He couldn't catch a break. "Just my luck, man, another fucking dyke."

Gale took a few bounding steps toward Lonnie with her fists clenched, but Gretchen put a hand to her shoulder to stop her. Lonnie stood rooted with a grin on his face red face.

"It's OK," Gretchen whispered.

Gale fumed. Her shoulders rose and fell with deep breaths. The sight made Lonnie chuckle as he shook his head.

"Well, come on then, Big Bertha, you and your girlfriend are leading the way." He had his gun in his hands and used it to point them in the direction of the trail that lead away from the expansive lake.

"It's already late, everyone's tired and scared, Mitchell is hurt," Gretchen said with a sigh. "Let's just rest and head over in the morning." She looked around at the restless faces of the group instead of Lonnie.

Gale nodded, but no one else made a move. They avoided eye contact with either side.

Lonnie swung his gun around his back again and shrugged his shoulders. "Whatever you want, pretty little lady." He winked at Gretchen and walked further into the trees to find a good place to make camp for the night.

XI.

The small fire Lonnie built smoldered close to the ground while everyone sat scattered around it. With the thick, hot air no one wanted it for its warmth. It was merely a comfort to be able to see in the dark. Lonnie instructed Rowan on how to disassemble his rifle and clean it. Both their fingers fumbled clumsily over the small parts.

Carolyn sat nearby and leaned over to watch them closely. She smiled at Rowan whenever he looked up at her.

Lonnie was too focused on keeping track of the miniscule pieces of his gun to notice their exchange.

Lee sat upright with his back against the trunk of a tree and his eyes closed. No one knew if he was really asleep or only pretending, and no one cared. He was never good for conversation.

Mitchell took to keeping close by Lee. He made a pillow with his bent arm and lay on his side on the warm, hard dirt and leaves. His injured foot lie separate from the rest of him, sticking out awkwardly like a broken tree limb. Every now and again he let out a small whimper in his sleep.

Gale and Gretchen sat close together, further from the fire than the rest. Once again, Gretchen didn't want anyone to overhear their conversation.

"What's Lonnie's deal?" Gretchen asked in a sour tone as she sat on a fallen tree trunk. "He still eyes me like a piece of meat, even though I told him I like girls." As she said it, she snuck a peek through her eyelashes at Lonnie and found him looking up from his gun at her.

He gave a quick smile and wink before returning back to cleaning his gun with the bottom of his stained white t-shirt.

Gretchen couldn't help scrunching her face in disgust. She'd never hated someone so much in her life, even if he did save Gale from those things. Without warning, the image of their grayish arms extended out, ready to clasp Gale with their bloodied fingers flashed in her mind. She shivered.

"Don't worry about him," Gale said with a wave of her hand, as if she were swatting away an annoying bug that buzzed around them. "Boys like that think they are God's gift to women. The minute you told him you were gay, you became the forbidden fruit. It just as easily could have been me."

Gretchen looked at her with crinkled eyes as she smiled big. She let out a few breathy giggles.

Gale laughed along. "Just don't let him get to you. Before you know it, he'll be fighting Rowan over that blonde bimbo, Carolyn."

Gretchen let the laughter die and looked around before she leaned in close to Gale. "I've met Lonnie before, too."

Gale stared at her with a furrowed brow and intense, solid eyes. They urged Gretchen to continue.

"At your bachelorette party. Lonnie was with someone other guy and they came up to me when Charlie left to get drinks. They tried to pick me up. The funny thing is he doesn't even seem to remember. I told him that night I had a girlfriend. He even saw Charlie. They exchanged a few words…"

They both laughed quietly, each individually remembering the feisty fire of jealousy that used to burn inside Charlie, before they tapered off and were silent again.

Gretchen's smile faded away at the mention of her girlfriend's name. Toward the end, she constantly complained about how jealous Charlie used to get when anyone even looked at her with lust in their eyes, let alone talked to her. She would have given anything to hear Charlie tell Lonnie off one more time.

"Can I ask what happened to her?" Gale's face fell into a deep-lined frown.

Gretchen didn't say anything right away. She dug the toe of her designer combat boot into the tightly compacted dirt and broke it apart. Her eyes filled to the brim with tears, but she wouldn't allow them to spill over and run down her cheeks. She sniffed. Her lips pursed so they couldn't tremble.

"It's OK," Gale said. "We don't have to talk about it. I don't even like *thinking* about Salena anymore, to be honest. Hurts too damn much."

Gretchen nodded her head and took another large sniff of hot air to clear her mind.

"Why don't we get some sleep?" Gale suggested as she stood up to walk over to a clearing by the fire.

Gretchen stood as well, but stayed in the shadows. "I think I'm gonna take a quick walk around the camp, just to make sure it's safe."

"Here." Gale tossed her a sheathed Bowie knife. "Just in case."

Gretchen gave a weak smile before she walked off into the trees and was swallowed up by the darkness. No one tried to stop her. Her shoulders relaxed. She needed to be alone to collect herself and stop Charlie's face from haunting her. It wasn't easy to push her from her mind. The last time she saw Charlie plagued her thoughts as she walked through the shadows of the trees.

XII.

Gretchen drove Charlie's beat up, old Toyota Corolla away from the city of Chicago with her fingers intertwined to rest in Charlie's lap. Tall buildings and gridlock traffic gave way to expansive, open highway. Small, run down houses transformed into larger, modern suburban homes once they crossed the state line into Indiana. Charlie looked eagerly out the window at the fenced in backyards and open fields of nothing but green grass.

"I still can't believe I'm finally going to meet your parents," she said as she gripped Gretchen's hand in both of hers and held it to her chest. "What'd they say when you told them?"

Gretchen looked in the rearview mirror, then each of the side mirrors, then the rearview mirror again. "Uh, they said they couldn't wait to meet you."

Charlie squealed with glee and squeezed Gretchen's hand harder. "I'm so freaking excited!"

"Look, there's something I should tell you, but I don't want you to get mad, OK? You can't get mad."

Charlie relaxed her grip on her girlfriend's hand to let it rest in her lap again as her face fell into an apprehensive frown. "Oh, God. What is it now?"

"No big deal or anything. It's just…my parents…they don't exactly know that you're…" Gretchen worked laboriously to spit out the last part, a pained grimace on her face. "…a girl." She bit her bottom lip and waited for the inevitable outburst.

Charlie threw Gretchen's hand back into her own lap. "Are you serious?" she screeched as she tossed her arms up in the air to let them fall with a slap against her thigh. "What the hell, Gretch?"

Gretchen shrugged her shoulders up until her neck disappeared. "I'm sorry. I told them I was dating a Charlie and we were coming home together, so I didn't exactly lie or anything. I just let them come to their own conclusions."

When Charlie didn't yell, scream, or curse her out, Gretchen let her shoulders relax cautiously and looked at her through the corner of one of her eyes.

Charlie didn't say anything. Her head was turned to glare out the window at the scenery passing by. There was a black and white cow grazing in the grass. She wanted to smile about it, but couldn't bring herself to.

"Say something," Gretchen prodded in a docile voice.

"What do you want me to say? There's nothing we can do now. Let's just get there and get this over with."

Gretchen let out an exhale of relief. She'd been expecting more of a scene. Charlie could be so dramatic sometimes, which was the one of the many things about her that bothered Gretchen, about girls in general.

Unable to stand the silence, she turned up the radio. Fall Out Boy blared through the three working speakers and it reminded her of high school when her life started to spiral out of control. A reminiscent smile pulled at the corners of her pink glossy lips, but she did her best to contain it for Charlie's sake.

"We'll talk about this when we get home," Charlie said through her teeth at the window.

Gretchen rolled her eyes. She knew it'd been too easy.

Gretchen pulled into her parents' driveway and turned off the car. The house looked the same as it always had, even when her grandmother was the one who owned it decades ago, with its slightly off white, dingy wood siding and tall grass that hadn't been mowed in months. The two story house loomed over her like a monster from one of her nightmares. She hadn't set foot inside since she left over ten years ago. Charlie had some masterful powers of persuasion. Gretchen's throat was dry and it made it hard for her to swallow her dread.

"Are we going in or what?" Charlie asked with sting. She looked over and saw Gretchen's pale face, hands gripped to the steering wheel so tightly her knuckles were white. The tides changed inside her. Charlie's voice normalized to its comforting, girlish nature. "Baby, it's going to be OK. Don't worry so much."

The car grew hot as it baked in the summer sun. Gretchen pushed up the half sleeves of her light blue t-shirt. Every inch of her arms, from the wrist up, were covered in colorful tattoos, some brand-new and vibrant while others were faded from the harsh years.

"Come on," Charlie said as she rested a reassuring hand on Gretchen's arm.

Gretchen released the breath she'd been holding and pried her fingers from the steering wheel.

They got out of the Toyota and walked up the driveway. The gravel crunched under Gretchen's black leather boots while Charlie moved in silence thanks to her tiny frame and delicate flats.

Charlie looked up and watched the breeze from Lake Michigan blow through the leaves of the trees with a soothing rustle. She'd never been out in the country before, but as she took a deep breath of the fresh air and let the heat from the sun warm her face, she thought maybe when she married Gretchen they would settle down somewhere like that. Maybe even return to Chesterton and work on rebuilding some sort of relationship between her and her family. Hope filled her warm heart.

They stood in front of the large oak door in heavy silence. Neither made a move to announce themselves. After a long minute dragged by, Gretchen raised her hand to knock, but stopped. Her entire face scrunched together as her eyebrows pulled inward and her nose crinkled. She extended a single finger and pushed it against the door, which creaked open a tiny crack. She looked at Charlie, her face still contorted, and then back at the door. Something wasn't right.

She took a step forward to go in, but was stopped by Charlie's wiry arm.

"Don't. What if someone's in there?"

Gretchen nodded. It wasn't normal for her parents to leave their house unlocked, even when they were home. They were close enough to the city to see crime spill over into their middle-class suburbia. Gary, a crowded town that gave birth to the Jackson Five, but had also once held the title of murder capital of the United States, was only a straight shot down highway twelve, the highway Gretchen's parents' lived off of.

"Stay behind me," Charlie whispered as she pushed against the door. With every inch it opened the hinges gave a ghostly groan.

Gretchen remained in the light of the doorway. She bit down on her lip until she drew a small drop of bright red blood.

Charlie inched inside. She craned her neck to look around the corners of the entryway. The house was dark, the blinds still closed from the evening before. There was a wafting scent of dead animal carcass as the breeze from the open windows charged around the room.

Gretchen wrinkled her nose again and wondered if something had died in their backyard. It wouldn't have been the first time, just one of the perks of living in the middle of a wooded state park.

Charlie looked over her shoulder and waved her hands for Gretchen to follow. "Seems empty." But Charlie stopped immediately when she saw Gretchen's face drained of all its color.

"Mom?"

Charlie turned around just in time to see a set of rust-colored teeth clamp down onto her shoulder and tear through the skin. She let out a piercing scream as she reached her free arm out to Gretchen for help.

Gretchen stood fixed in the doorway as her mother dragged her girlfriend down to the wood floor. She begged her trembling legs to move, for her body to do anything besides stand there, but they wouldn't.

The fifty-four year old fresh corpse was dressed in a floral patterned, summer nightgown. The short sleeves displayed a battle field of bite marks and scratches with black blood smeared on her grey, mottled skin. There was a jagged gash along her jaw line as if someone had dug their nails in and dragged them across with ferocity. The leathered skin hung loosely from the bones, discolored and wrinkled.

Gretchen couldn't take her eyes off the thing that used to be her mother. A loud bang came from the dining room as the door swung open and hit the wall. Her brain screamed for her to look, but she couldn't take her eyes away from the massacre in front of her. Her girlfriend was still alive as her dead mother bore her decaying hands down into Charlie's soft gut and ripped out her entrails. The sound of blood bubbling up in her throat was soft, but rang in Gretchen's ears like a siren telling her to run.

Footsteps pounded on the hard floor and echoed throughout the old house. Gretchen moved only her eyes to look. Standing tall on the other side of the couch was her dad. A dark reddish-brown ooze dripped from his mouth over the jean overalls he only wore when he did yard work. His dead, vacant eyes stared her down. Teeth bared, he swayed where he stood as he groaned.

Tears slid down Gretchen's cheeks. "Dad?" she whispered.

The soft exhale of that single word was all it took to turn the focus from Charlie, who lie dead on the floor with her eyes wide and her jaw wretched open in an eternal scream, to Gretchen. She shook fiercely in the open doorway as the dead forms of her parents gazed at her with milky eyes. Her mother struggled to raise up from the ground as her dad lumbered over. Both groaned with the desperation for her flesh.

Gretchen viewed Charlie for the last time. She didn't want to leave her there, but she was out of options. Her girlfriend was gone and she would be too if she attempted to drag her body with her. She still heard Charlie's sweet voice in her ears, saw the gleam in her elfish eyes as she smiled, felt the touch of her fingers as they wrapped around her leg...

Gretchen let out a sharp cry. Her mother's corpse had grabbed onto her leg and was pulling itself closer, using Gretchen to raise itself up.

The primal instinct for survival finally kicked in. Gretchen danced her legs around as she tried to shake off her mom's dead, forceful hands. She screamed wildly. She hoped someone would hear and come to help, but there was no one around. She drove her free foot into her mother's already mangled jaw. There was a loud snap as it jutted to the side. It hung loose and unhinged like a broken cabinet door.

"You're not my mother!" Gretchen screamed over and over again as she kicked out with everything she had in her.

Her mother's face cracked, broke, and finally caved in on itself after a relentless beating.

"You're not my mother!"

The grip on Gretchen's leg released as the cold hands fell to the floor, her father's lifeless body still trying to maneuver its way around the furniture to get to her.

Gretchen ran for the car just as her dad made it to the doorway. She fumbled her way inside and slammed the door behind her.

Instead of pursuing, the large, overall-clad corpse turned around and kneeled over Charlie's mangled body. It lowered its face to devour what little was left of her.

Gretchen put the car in reverse and slammed the gas pedal down to the floor. The tires kicked up a cloud of gravel and dust as she sped down the driveway and back to the two lane highway.

She sobbed uncontrollably as she gripped the steering wheel. Her arms shook violently. She screamed as the images of Charlie's bloody, horrified face tormented her, a single hand reaching out for help. Why didn't she help her?

Gretchen wiped at her face, but the tears were falling too fast. Unable to see, she ran off the road at the first turn and drove head on into a tree.

XIII.

Gretchen walked aimlessly as Charlie's face clouded her mind. Her feet dragged along as she wandered with Gale's large knife held limply in one hand, a flashlight in the other. Charlie was gone and it was all her fault. She didn't think she could ever forgive herself for being such a coward that day.

A twig snapped and brought her back to the dark woods that surrounded her. Sweat dripped down the back of her neck as her hairs stood up on end. What was she thinking going off by herself? She wasn't ready to take on any decomposing, vicious zombies one on one. She'd made that clear back at her parents' house.

Anita watched Gretchen from high up in a tree, crouched on one of the thick braches while she held on to another above her head. For a moment she considered going down to reveal herself once more to another human being, but couldn't. She'd been watching them for days and knew the shoulder-length, blonde-haired woman who walked alone in the dark wasn't really alone, but part of a group Anita wanted nothing to do with. "Gretchen," she whispered, just wanting to say something, anything, to someone else in the world.

Gretchen stopped in her tracks and whirled around in a circle. Her eyes narrowed as she tried to see through the darkness. She didn't want to shine her light out into the trees in case there were dead walking nearby. She kept it pointed at the ground. It made it impossible for her to see the person just twenty feet above her head. "Hello?" Gretchen whispered into the black void.

No one answered.

"Not funny, guys," she whined. She turned to go back to camp, but her body slammed into something hard and cold. A soft wheezing filled her ears.

A female with patchy, dirty blonde hair, red gaping holes where her eyes used to be, and loose strips of meat that hung from her cheeks grabbed onto Gretchen with strong hands.

Gretchen couldn't contain the scream that escaped her lips as she tried to break free from the grip of the monstrous thing's long fingers. Jagged teeth bit the air just inches from her nose. She had to break free. She had to get out of there and get back to the group. She couldn't die there alone.

Her arms shook as she forced her hand with the knife up to the zombie's head. The thing inched forward, its teeth getting closer to Gretchen's supple shoulder with every bite. It leaned forward as Gretchen pushed away, her weapon unable to make its way upward to save her life.

The scraggly, female zombie's head cocked quickly to the side as it went for Gretchen's jugular.

It was a split second when Gretchen's hand was freed to make its final move. She drove the blade into its temple with a sickening crunch just as its teeth were about to clamp around her throat. The grip on her loosened as its body slackened to the ground with a soft thud.

Gretchen heaved deep breaths, completely unaware of the tears that spilled down her cheeks. All around her she heard the rustle of uneven footsteps scraping along the grass, dirt, and dead leaves. She slowly raised the shaking flashlight in her hand. Everywhere, dead bodies were shuffling between the trees. They turned to her when her light passed over them. They moved as a herd, their course changed.

"Oh, God," Gretchen whimpered. Her knees were ready to buckle from fear, but she had to push forward and get back to the group. She had to warn them. She couldn't let them die the way she allowed Charlie die.

Gretchen's body propelled forward on legs she had no control over. Her arms pumped hard as she ran back to the camp. The deep moans grew faint as the distance grew wider, but she knew it wouldn't last long. Those things moved relentlessly with no need to stop until they had flesh between their teeth.

Gretchen approached the camp loudly with pounding footsteps. She attempted to dodge the trees and bushes in the pitch black of night. A few times she tripped over a root and caught herself against a rough tree trunk. Each time she stumbled forward with her eyes trained ahead on the dimly glowing fire of the camp, with its unsuspecting bodies gathered around as they slept.

Lonnie went from dead asleep to alert in mere seconds from the sounds of someone running nearby. He shot up to his feet and aimed his gun into the woods with one eye closed as the others stood behind him.

Gretchen ran into the exact spot where Lonnie had his gun pointed. She dug her heels into the ground to bring herself to a skidding halt, her arms raised in the air. "Whoa, don't shoot! They're coming! A bunch of them! Maybe hundreds! They're headed right for us!" she yelled. Adrenaline coursed through her veins. Her hands and knees shook.

She didn't have to say who the "they" was. Lonnie swept from left to right with his weapon as he searched for the corpses, but he couldn't see anything past the orange ring of the fire. He only heard the faints sounds of moaning, growling, and endless shuffling.

"Grab your shit! Let's go!" he said before he took off in the opposite direction. He didn't wait for the others and he didn't turn around to make sure they were behind him.

Gretchen only had her purse to grab, which she'd pulled out of the car after the accident. She slung it over her shoulder and across her body. It slapped against her thigh as she jogged after Lonnie and Rowan at a pace which Gale, Mitchell, and Carolyn could keep up with.

Lee brought up the rear even though he could've caught up to and surpassed Lonnie and Rowan with his long, muscular legs. There wasn't anything he needed to collect to take with him. What little medical supplies he had bounced in the cargo pockets of his tan shorts as he jogged. And yet, he remained behind the rest.

XIV.

The group followed the faint pattering of Lonnie and Rowan's footsteps up ahead. Luckily, neither could keep quiet as they breathed heavily, swore loudly, and let out whimpering cries of exhaustion. It wasn't hard for the others to keep track of where they ran, though with each passing minute the sounds grew dimmer in their ears.

Gretchen and Mitchell had their flashlights out, but couldn't hold them still to see as they ran. Bursts of light streaked the ground and the tree tops as their arms pumped with desperate effort. The slow, clumsy bodies that walked through the trees lit up quickly and disappeared again, like a disco for the undead.

Mitchell Barnes hobbled as he tried to keep his weight off his wounded foot. He kept turning his head to see how close the ever moving herd was to him. Each time the details of their putrid bodies were more distinguishable through the darkness, but it seemed impossible. They didn't move that fast. How could they catch up? Mitchell's head spun and his legs wobbled. He was going to faint. He could feel it. His foot throbbed with every step.

The din of the dead was all around. The bloodied corpses moved with slow, shuffling feet that scraped along the ground coverings. Gretchen wanted to fall into a crumpled heap and cover her ears. She imagined what it would be like if she did and let the dead overcome her—their hands digging into her, the indescribable pain as their fingers wrapped around her intestines and ripped them out with a quick jerk, the world fading away as she died in agony. She had to keep going.

Gretchen linked her hand in Gale's and forced the older woman to pick up her pace. She wasn't going to let them go down without a fight. She wasn't going to give up. Hungry moans seemed to come at her from behind every tree. How would they ever make it out alive when they were surrounded? She looked over her shoulder and saw that Mitchell had fallen behind.

Lee stopped and bent down in Mitchell's path. With the encasing darkness, blinded by fear, Mitchell ran right into Lee and tumbled head first over him. He scrambled back up to his feet.

Lee Hickey fell forward and caught himself on his large hands. He reached out to Mitchell so he couldn't run off in a panic.

Mitchell jerked away at the touch of a hand on his leg.

"Get on," Lee said.

"What?" Mitchell asked as his eyes adjusted to the blackness around them to see Lee squatted on the ground.

"Get on!"

Mitchell didn't waste any time as he jumped onto Lee's back and held tightly around his neck. His shotgun, still clenched in his hand, hit Lee repeatedly in the chest as he bounded forward to catch them up to Gale, Gretchen, and Carolyn.

A slew of curses echoed out as Lee tried to regain his footing after he stumbled over a tree root that stuck up out of the ground.

"Oh, shit! They're coming!" Mitchell yelled.

A tall male in soiled khakis and a ripped polo shirt reached out as he closed the distance between the two living men. The skin around his jaw had been peeled away from ceaseless consumption to reveal two rows of tall, red teeth.

"Come on!" Mitchell yelled as Lee raised himself up. "Let's go!"

Cold, hard fingers grazed the back of Mitchell's neck as Lee took off again. The grasping, ravenous corpse fell forward from the momentum of trying to grab onto Mitchell's warm flesh. Once the spongey body hit the ground with a revolting splat, it pulled itself forward with weak muscles, like an infant learning to crawl for the first time. Several others tripped over the body as they continued onward after the group. The pile squirmed and writhed as it tried to stand up again as a whole.

"Where are we going?" Gretchen called to Lonnie once she'd caught up to the two men with Gale and Carolyn at her side.

"Anywhere these fucking things aren't!"

Lonnie had no plan, no direction, no clue where to go. All he knew was that if he wanted to live he had to keep his legs moving, and he had to keep them moving faster than the people behind him.

XV.

Zack Kran grabbed Marianne Dunbar's feet while Liam Scott hooked his hands under her arms. They lifted her up and carried her out of her darkened apartment and through the open hallway to the back of the building. The sun shone brightly in the center of the sky and Liam had to squint his eyes as he took small steps backwards. Hers was the last body to be taken outside that day.

They walked along the tan wooden fence that surrounded the perimeter toward a small chain-link fence that encased what was formerly knowns as the "Bark Park". A pile of dead bodies lay on the green grass where dogs used to run and play.

"Wait," Sally Sherman said in a shaky voice as her husband opened the gate for them to bring her mother through.

"Sal, we have to—" he started to say, but she him off.

"I know," she said. "Just…over there." She pointed to a corner away from the already rotting bodies stacked in the middle. "She should be separate from…those things…" Lilly shifted endlessly in Sally's arms as she tried to turn to look up at the expansive tree. The leaves and branches waved in the hot breeze.

Christine rested a hand on Sally's shoulder and guided her back to the picnic table in the shade off to the side. They sat with their backs to the guys, who shifted the bodies around and shut the gate behind them.

Liam walked over and stood in front of the two women and baby. His face was lax with emotional fatigue and there was a sickly green tinge to his pallor. "We're ready." He held out a hand for Christine.

She linked her fingers through his as they walked back to the fence. They stood outside to focus on the bodies of everyone they knew in the building and some they had never met.

"I just want to say," Sally said and then stopped to take a deep breath. "I want to say that I loved my mom very much. Even though she could be stubborn and hard to deal with at times, she was always there for me when I needed her...I just wish I could have been there...when she...needed me." She broke down and handed the baby off to Ralph to hide her face in her hands.

Christine extended an arm and wrapped it around Sally's shoulders so her new friend could cry into her neck. Liam gave her free hand a squeeze.

Everyone waited in silence for Ralph to say his last words. He held Lilly in his arms so she faced over his shoulder, away from the mound of bodies. She bounced and wiggled to get down. Ralph remained silent and nodded his head so lightly that it could have been the pounding of his heart that made it move.

All those times his mother-in-law had made him sit with her in the mornings and sip tea as she talked endlessly about God knows what, he thought he was being tortured. Now that he'd never drink tea with her again, he realized he'd grown to like it somehow. And now that she was gone, he'd miss it forever.

"I'll never drink tea again," he said with a weak laugh.

Zack and Jerry chuckled quietly, as the others let the corners of their mouths twitch upward with benign smiles.

Ralph sniffed and took a few steps away from the fence to stand next to his wife, who turned from Christine to bury her face in his chest. She sobbed harder at the soft touch of her daughter's hand as it patted the top of her head.

"May they rest in peace," Zack said. He backed away from the small, enclosed park as the summer breeze picked up again and the stench from the bodies washed over him.

The smell of rotting, baking flesh overwhelmed his nostrils. He lifted the collar of his shirt over his nose.

Lilly let out a shrieking wail as she flung her body back against her dad's arms, which held her close to him.

On the other side of the fence, several hands reached their fingertips over the top. One gripped down on the wood and tried to pull. There was a loud creak as it bent slightly from the force. It had been going on for days. Each morning there were a few more fingertips grasping for what was on the other side.

"It's not safe out here," Luke Benson said as he shook his head back and forth. He started to walk off back to the apartment building. "We shouldn't be out here."

Zack jogged after him and blocked his way. "Show some respect." He gestured his arm to the dogpile of unmoving corpses. "That was her mother. The fences will hold. They can't get in. Man up for once in your life."

"What's that supposed to mean?" Luke asked. Even though he felt a twinge of guilt, he still had the urge to stand his ground, but Zack towered over his short frame and made him feel two feet tall.

"It means you're a pussy. You run when you should be fighting. Don't think for one second I didn't see you cowering in the hall while the rest of us were in there doing what we had to do to keep this place safe for everyone else!"

"You don't even know me!" Luke yelled as the anger rose inside him.

"I know you."

"Oh yeah? Whaddaya know about me?"

"I know you're living here while some other guy raises your daughter and sleeps with your wife."

There was a collective gasp as the others watched from the shade of the Crabapple tree.

Luke closed the gap between them. His round face turned up to gawk Zack's. His dark eyes glared with an intensity he could never match physically.

They cussed at each other irrationally, their voices rising hirer with each swear.

"Shut up! Both of you!" Sally yelled as her face streaked with tears. She had nothing to follow up with. She only wanted a bit of silence to mourn her mother for a few minutes longer.

The echoes of her voice faded out and deflated the tension. Zack and Luke both turned to her. Her face was scrunched into an ugly mess of tears. Zack sneered at Luke, clucked his tongue, and stalked off to stand next to Liam and Christine.

Luke was left alone in the open grassy area. On one side of the fence the undead beat to get in and on the other side, the building where he took shelter. "We need to leave here," he said in an even tone. He stood with one hand on his hip while the other pointed a finger out to the group.

"We're not leaving," Liam said coolly.

"Yeah. This is our home," Zack agreed. He tightened his eyes on Luke. "We need to protect it and ourselves. Not run away like a bitch with nowhere to go."

Luke laughed at the sky with his hands on his hips. When he was done, he stared down at his loafers and kicked at the ground. He knew he wouldn't stand a chance if it came to a fight. He had the muscles, but Zack had his sword sheathed and slung over his back. It wasn't worth it. Surviving was his number one concern. His daughter and ex-wife were waiting for him. They had to be.

"He's right," Liam said. "Our best chance is here. We can seal it off. It's already gated. That will limit the number of dead that can make their way in. We've already cleaned out our own building so it'll be easier to maintain it, keep it cleared and safe. Eventually we can push out to the other buildings, see if there are any other survivors, and help them to clear out as well. We can make this a thriving community if we don't give up on it." He let go of Christine's hand and took a few steps out to the middle of the group.

"So now we're cleaning everyone else's mess? Saving everyone else's lives while we put our own at risk? Well, you can count me out," Luke said in a fluster. "No way. I did my part. I'm done."

"You'll do what you're told," Zack spat from behind Liam.

Christine and Sally stood closer together. Lilly's arms draped around her mother's neck as she rested her head on her shoulder. Ralph was a few paces in front of them with his arms folded. He looked over his shoulder repeatedly at the bodies behind them.

Jerry avoided looking at everyone all together, his eyes focused on the gray fingers that reached longingly over the fence.

Luke chuckled under his breath again and clapped his hands together. "And who put Prince Charles in charge?"

"Prince Charles?" Liam said with a wrinkled nose. "That's a little insulting. I'm at least a Prince William, or Harry..." his voice trailed off. "Beside the point. We're staying here. We have to. There's too many people freshly turned into these things walking around out there. We'd never make it. We need to work together to keep this place safe. If you want to leave, we can't stop you."

Luke's eyes widened.

"But we'd like you to stay."

Luke tapped his foot, sending his body into a fit of bouncing as he considered the proposal. He looked from Liam to Zack to Sally and her baby and back to Liam. He licked his lips and bit down. "OK. Fine. I'll stay…for now."

Liam nodded his head and clasped his hand with Christine's again. They walked off towards their apartment, ready to forget the entire day. Neither looked back at the heaping mound of exposed dead.

Luke kept his eyes on Zack and Zack glared at Luke. They both walked in the same direction but kept their distance from each other.

"I'll be right up," Ralph said to Sally. He kissed her and Lilly on the forehead and watched them walk through the opening in the hallway. "Wait up," Ralph called to Jerry as he tapped him on the shoulder.

Jerry turned and his large belly almost grazed up against Ralph's. He looked on with wrinkled eyes and an annoyed stare. He didn't ask what Ralph wanted. Instead he gave a small grumble and hiked up the same sweatpants he'd been wearing for days.

"I know you were…involved…with Marianne." Ralph tried to keep his voice intimidating and the disgust from creeping onto his face. "You could have helped her."

Jerry only stared back at Ralph, his face as solid as stone, his thin lips unmoving.

"Why didn't you help her?" Ralph practically shouted.

"I did," Jerry said evenly. When he was sure the kid understood, Jerry walked away to leave Ralph alone with the corpses, some lying motionless on the ground like they were always meant to while others walked freely outside the fence.

Part Three

"I would rather be tied to the soil as a serf ... than be king of all these dead and destroyed."

—Homer, *Odyssey*

I.

Liam Scott and Christine Moore sat on the floor of their apartment together, an empty bottle of wine at their feet and a half empty bottle in Christine's hand. She took a chug and handed it over to Liam. They were laughing. They didn't remember why, but they continued to laugh until the walls were impregnated with it.

The TV was on, but there was no broadcast, only a blank, snowy screen. There hadn't been any in almost a month, but they left it on just in case there was someone out there who wanted to be heard someday. The lamp attached to the end table next to the couch shone dimly and encased the couple in a circle of yellow light. Their heads were thrown back wildly and tears ran from the corners of their eyes.

All at once, the power went out and encased them in darkness. The laughed stopped. They both looked over at the now shadowed lampshade.

"Well, whoever held on this long to provide us with electricity is finally gone…or gave up," Liam said with a push off the floor to stand. He disappeared into the bedroom.

"I'm surprised it lasted a whole month. That's amazing," Christine said. "Whoever they were, they were heroes."

She stayed put in the living room and waited for Liam to get one of the hundreds of candles he bought. She wasn't privy to his organizational system and she didn't want to be until it was absolutely necessary. As the weeks went by, she became content with him handling everything. And if she ignored all the boxes lined up along the walls, her world felt almost normal again, like she'd abandoned her career as a lawyer to become a lonely housewife.

"Longer than that. About a month and a half now," Liam answered from the other room with his head in a box.

As he dug around Christine heard the dull clanking sound of hard wax hitting more hard wax. "Just pick one. I can't see anything."

"We're safe," he assured her like he'd done countless times since it all started.

"I *know* we're safe," she said coolly. "But I still miss being able to see, so come on with the candles already. It's still too hot to light the fireplace yet."

Liam gave a breathy laugh and lit an apple scented candle with a match. He placed it on the end table to fill the lamp's void. He flopped down on the soft, beige couch and let the cushions hug him as he sank in. He patted the seat next to him and Christine smiled. She climbed up from the floor and curled up in his arms.

"You know what I *don't* miss?" he said as he held her close.

"What?" Christine looked up into his face with big, blue eyes.

"Tom Cruise movies."

She giggled and pushed off his chest. The two of them were encased in a dim orange bubble while the rest of the apartment disappeared into blackness.

"Why Tom Cruise?" she laughed.

"I don't know," Liam said with a shrug of his shoulders. He pushed up his glasses with one finger. "I never really liked him. There's something about the man that just...irks me!"

The both laughed again, unable to stop, their heads swimming.

Christine leaned over the edge of the couch and swiped the wine bottle off the floor. She was still laughing through her nose when she took a large sip. "You know what I don't miss?"

"What?" Liam took the bottle and drank from it with a smile plastered on his face.

"The sound of the neighbor above us stomping around like a Clydesdale."

Liam chuckled. "Oo, you're dreadful." Somewhere in the depths of his mind, he remembered that it was Carolyn Bock who lived above them and used to walk with her full weight charging through her feet. He took a sip from the nearly empty bottle, the smile gone from his face. "You know, tomorrow will be the first time that I have to leave the complex with everyone else to get supplies."

"I know," Christine said softly. As if she could forget. It was all she thought about for days.

"We're lucky the food has held out this long."

She nodded her head. "You'll be fine," she said and turned her face up to stare into his eyes. "You have to be."

Liam gave a single nod and steadied his face so he wouldn't give away just how terrified he was. Only a few of the dead had wandered into their building over the weeks, most likely from the other buildings they hadn't gotten around to clearing out. The team took care of them one by one, more bodies to join the pile in the park before they took a day to toss them over the fence. But he knew, somehow, that it would be different out there—more dangerous, more intense, more…real.

"Zack's been going out there every day looking for that Anita girl with Ralph and they've been fine. He says it's not bad." Christine reassured him.

Liam could recall every single stomach churning, gut wrenching story Zack had told him about the state of the world outside the fences and knew his friend had been lying through his teeth when he retold them to Christine. She hadn't noticed the look in Zack's eyes as he lied, the look that said he'd done something horrible that he wanted to forget about, but never would. Liam couldn't miss that look in Zack's normally shining brown eyes if he tried.

"He seems different, though," Christine added. "Quieter, calmer."

"I think he's nervous about finding Anita is all." That was a lie too. Zack *had* changed because of the things he'd seen and done while he searched endlessly for the girl. It tore at Liam's heart to know his best friend was at such a loss. He changed the subject. "Luke drove out to his ex-wife's house last night to see her and his daughter, make sure they're all right. It's over in Whiting, about forty minutes from here…or at least it was. I don't know what the roads are like now." Liam couldn't fathom what it was like beyond the fences anymore.

Christine looked at him with bated breath.

Liam didn't say anything else. His hazel eyes shifted back and forth around the dark room.

"Well?" she said wide-eyed. "Did he find them? Are they OK?"

Liam pushed off the couch and stood up with a sigh. "I guess we'll find out in the morning at the meeting. For now let's get some sleep." He picked up the candle to light the way.

Christine slid into their king size bed after shedding her clothes and cuddled the thin quilt up under her chin. Liam faced her back and watched as her breathing slowed and deepened. Once he was sure she was asleep, he reached into his bedside table's drawer and pulled out the tattered, brown leather journal he'd brought back from his trip to the university.

It was a nightly ritual that quickly turned into an obsession, one that he wasn't ready to share with anyone else. He was finally at the part where he joined the team, mere weeks before Dr. Hyde became one of those things and the world crumbled into madness. He read only one entry.

II.

Dr. Victor Faustus Hyde
June 5, 2020

I've been working around the clock to figure out a proper vaccine for this new strand of flu, the super flu they call it. I've added several new members to my team, including a clever and cunning young Plant Geneticist. (I'll overlook the fact that he's British in order to harvest his brilliance.)

My desires to be the first to create the vaccine is now border lining on obsessive. It's all I can think about, dream about. Many nights it's past midnight before I realize that everyone else has gone home and I'm working in near darkness, like tonight. For my own sanity, I've started this journal and also for those who want to know later on how my team and I have stopped this deadly flu before it wiped out nearly half of mankind.

Dr. Liam Scott is currently working on mutating a few key plants in order to further the third generation of the vaccine. The first two failed, our lab rats dying before the vaccine could rid the bodies of the flu virus. I'm hoping these mutations prove to be the key to developing a working vaccine in the next week. The public needs this. I need this. The world needs us to get this right.

III.

Liam Scott's eyes popped open. The sun shone through the white blinds of the generous bedroom window. He picked up his phone, though he knew what the time would read. He looked at the screen and put it down. Six o'clock on the dot. Tossing back the covers, he sat up and stretched his legs and then his arms over his head.

Christine rolled over and pawed at her eyes as she groaned like one of the dead. Liam rubbed her shoulder with his hands and then stood up to shuffle to the closet. Today was the day. He was going beyond the fence. Navy blue t-shirt, jeans, belt, black socks, boxer briefs, and steel-toed lace up ankle-high boots. He didn't think as he grabbed the items from the drawers and shelves. Once he was dressed he left the bedroom to brush his teeth.

Christine deliberately waited until Liam left the room to rise from the bed. She performed the same monotonous task of getting dressed, her mind lost elsewhere. Tan, loose tank top, skinny jeans, tan socks, bra and underwear, and brown ankle-high boots tucked into her pant legs.

She pulled the kinky blonde mess on her head back and secured it with the ponytail holder around her wrist. There wouldn't be any more straightening her hair sleek with the power out for good. She sighed. Shorter pieces fell down around her face in curls. Maybe she would avoid looking in the mirror from now on.

If they were in the normal world, she would have rolled her eyes and huffed about the stray tendrils that danced in her eyelashes. She would've grabbed a dozen bobby pins to hold them down and then sprayed half a can of hair spray onto her head just to make sure her hair was secured in place. But the world wasn't what it used to be and she could care less about how neat her hair looked when Liam was going out there in a short while.

She stared at herself in the full-length mirror that leaned up against the wall in the darkened closet. Her porcelain skin stood out amongst the shadows. She clenched her jaw to keep her lips from quivering. She was faced with the fact that Liam might not come back. She couldn't swallow.

"Don't cry," she whispered to herself. "Not now. You can't." She wiped at her face and took a deep breath.

"You want Cheerios or Fruit Loops for breakfast?" Liam called from the kitchen.

"Fruit Loops," she called back. They tasted better dry. She walked out and closed the bedroom door behind her.

At eight o'clock everyone who was left in the building gathered outside Liam and Christine's apartment, like every morning, except for Sally and Lilly who stayed behind in their own. No one saw much of them since the dispiriting funeral.

The sun shone through the hallway from one end, lighting it up like a tunnel to heaven. Christine leaned her back against the yellow wood-sided wall next to the opened door to her apartment. She folded her arms, let her head fall back, and closed her eyes for a second as the others joined her. She worried that if they caught of glimpse of what was behind her eyes they'd be able to tell she was scared for Liam's life, unsure if he could handle himself out there or if he'd make it back.

"Anyone seen Luke?" Liam asked as he scanned the hallway and stairs.

Zack was all geared up in his black padding. He'd found a new bullet proof vest that had more pockets and connectors to hang things from while out on his last run. On more than one occasion Christine had suggested he also try to find a razor and trim up his beard. It looked shaggier by the day, like a wooly caveman preparing for winter.

"I got in late last night," he said to Liam.

Jerry just shrugged his bulging shoulders, one hand tucked into his jeans pocket while the other held onto a steaming cup of coffee. He sipped at it. He didn't look too concerned either way.

Ralph leaned on the handle of his upside down axe, the one he'd found two weeks ago when he was out searching for more baby food. Luke's apartment was directly above his and he often heard the comforting sound of footsteps over his head. Last night had been silent. "I haven't heard anything," he said. His face was solid, but grave.

Liam nodded with both hands rested on his hips. "Right, well, let's head out." He gave Christine a kiss. "I'll be back after we sweep the building to say goodbye," he assured her as he cupped her face in his hands. He kissed her again and let it linger before he turned to join the others.

"I'll keep watch," she said with a sense of duty, her chin raised upward and pointed out.

As soon as Liam disappeared to the third floor, she went back inside and locked the door. Her shoulders sagged and her chin sank back to its normal level. Dragging her feet, she went out onto the patio.

The door was left wide open to allow the warm breeze to flow through the apartment. Since the power went out, the air had become stifling inside. Christine had awoken in the middle of the night with sweat soaked into her pillow, gasping for air as if she'd never catch her breath again. As she sat in the plastic lawn chair and kicked her feet up onto the railing, crossed at the ankles, she considered that it could have been from her dream. It was the third night she'd had the same one. Each night, it filled her heart with an ever-deepening dread.

She leaned over the side of the chair and reached for the binoculars that sat of the ground. Christine had taken up on her own the daily job of keeping watch over the parking lot for people, dead or alive. She wanted to feel like a valuable, contributing citizen again, but it was boring to sit in the heat all day alone. It was just another day in her life as she watched nothing happen in her small, small world.

She took a long sip from her water bottle. The thermometer hanging on the storage closet's door handle read eighty-five and it was only eight-ten. It was going to be another hot one. A group of birds flew back and forth, chasing each other through the sky above the lot, singing a song no one had ever heard before. Mr. Alexander walked slowly out from around the side of the building next door and lumbered over to the Dumpster. One of his feet dragged behind him, mangled and squished pancake flat.

"Ah, someone's early today," Christine said to herself.

She'd never told anyone about the dead Mr. Alexander who wandered around the premises. She reasoned that the group was only concerned with what went on in their own building for the time being, not anyone else's and technically Mr. Alexander had never shown an interest in their building. No one else had seen him on their way in or out, either.

Her mind often wondered where Mr. Alexander went when he wasn't Dumpster diving. "Enjoy your breakfast," she laughed and watched as the rotting corpse leaned over the square window-sized opening and rummaged for something alive to much on.

A piece of his torn skin caught on the corner of the metal sliding door. When he reemerged, it decorticated like the peeling of an orange until all the gooey underneath of his entire left side was exposed, neck to hip. The sheet of leathery skin hung down at his knees like a long shirt tied around his waist. Christine gagged and hid her eyes behind her hands.

IV.

The four men of building six stood in a row outside Luke's door. They all clutched their weapons tightly in their hands. Liam remained steady with one of his arrows knocked and ready to release. He hoped he wouldn't have to use it.

Jerry had his pistol grip shotgun pointed at the exact level Luke's head would be if some version of him were in the apartment, ready to spring out the moment the door was opened.

Zack had his sharpened sword raised to the side and behind his neck, eager to roll some heads, almost hoping to see the ravenous corpse of Luke Benson so he could decapitate it with a vengeance.

Ralph held his axe firmly in both hands, his knuckles white from the pressure he applied to keep from shaking. All he could think about was that one story below his feet his wife and baby girl were having a morning cup of coffee and a bottle of milk. There was nowhere else in the world he would've rather been than with them. Sally wasn't the same after her mother died. All hope had been extinguished from her once lively eyes to leave them dull and lifeless, as if she were making the slow, excruciating transformation into one of the dead.

"Right," Liam said softly and cleared his throat, which broke the tension that hung in the air. He leaned forward and knocked three times, then immediately straightened himself back into a readied position.

They all looked at each other after a few seconds went by and the door remained closed.

"Maybe he's asleep," Liam said and knocked again with more force.

They heard a thud from the other side of the door.

"Fuck this," Zack said. He pulled the crowbar from his backpack and jammed it in. He pushed with all his weight and the door flew open with a crash as shards of wood fell to the floor.

A bloodied, disheveled body tumbled forward with its arms stretched out to grab whomever it could get its hardened fingers around. Jerry was the first to jump into action. He charged in, using his gun like a bat, and cracked the thing in the side of the head. It did a one-eighty and slammed, face first, into the wall.

But as the gun swung around, so did Jerry's cylindrical, unsteady body. He fell against the wall and grasped at the lower right side of his back. His face was stretched into a painful grimace.

The decomposing body wasn't fazed at all by what should have been a paralyzing blow. It merely rebounded and continued to come at the group with its red teeth gnashed and its arms out.

Everyone stood frozen as they tried to get a look at it, see if they could recognize any hint of their missing neighbor in its face. Its skin was light and its hair fell around its sickly eyes in brown waves. It was at least six feet in height. It wasn't Luke.

Jerry pushed himself from the wall and charged the corpse again just as its hands were about to claps around the sleeve of Ralph's shirt. The two collided in a jumble into the apartment and fell to the floor, taking an end table and a lamp down with them. Jerry writhed as his back muscles spasmed, enough time for the unidentified rotting corpse to climb onto him and grab to pull Jerry closer to its discolored, oozing mouth.

The smell of its rotting skin was rancid, like old meat left to spoil out in the summer sun. Every time it bit the air its breath rushed over Jerry's face and made him want to throw up. It gurgled the thick fluids stuck deep within its throat. A pink string fell from its cracked lips onto Jerry's cheek as it let out a raspy hiss inches above him.

The shotgun lay over Jerry's chest, grasped tightly in both his hands. He pushed it up and into the vicious dead thing's throat so it couldn't lower itself to bite him. Jerry's aged arms shook as the heavy body sank down lower. Its teeth snapped at the air an inch from Jerry's nose, getting ever closer as his arms gave out. He looked into its glazed over eyes, like those of a great white shark on the hunt.

Like a guardian angel, an arrow shot out from the hallway and landed in the center of the writhing zombie's forehead. Black blood dripped from the hole onto Jerry's neck and chest. He squeezed his eyes and mouth shut tight and inwardly prayed that none of the blood made its way in as he rolled the dead weight off of him. He let out a wounded cry as the pain in his back intensified.

A hand reached down and he grabbed onto it. He heaved himself up with another agonizing groan and stood hunched over as he gripped his back. He wiped his face with the bottom of his white tank top despite the pain it caused to move.

When he opened his eyes again he saw that it was Ralph who had helped him up. He gave him a nod. Ralph smiled back, his hands still shaking as he held onto the axe. They both turned to look back at Liam, but he was gone.

"Let's get this body down with the rest of 'em," Zack said as he slapped the back of his hand against Ralph's chest. "You go home," he pointed at Jerry, who nodded his head and hobbled out of the apartment without any argument. "On three. One. Two. Three." They each gave heaving grumbles as they lifted the limp body off the floor.

V.

Liam Scott leaned over the railing at the back of the building on the second floor. He thought he could make it all the way home without throwing up, but it crept up on him as he bounded down the stairs. He didn't want to heave over the side facing the parking lot, because he knew Christine would hear him. Their patio lie just on the other side of the wall. He didn't want to give Christine a reason to delay him from going out on his first run with everyone else. He was ready, at least he thought he was, before he saw Jerry almost eaten alive.

He wiped his mouth and spat at the ground twenty feet below him. For a few fleeting moments, he stared out over the wooden fence that surrounded the complex. There was a small group of zombies that gathered on the opposite side day and night, their fingers continually extending up to get to the fresh meat that thrived just out of reach.

Liam shook his head and beat the palm of his hand down on the railing. How could he have been so stupid to think everyone would come out of this alive? Luke was missing, probably dead, and Jerry was hurt. Two men instead of four, that's who Liam had to rely on while he was out there. His stomach strangled his insides.

Christine had only locked the deadbolt so Liam could let himself in with his key whenever he was done with the day's sweep. She jumped when she heard the click of the lock so soon after he left. Her legs dropped from the railing and she leaned over in her chair to look inside the opened patio door.

Liam turned several of the deadbolt locks closed once inside before he joined her out on the patio. His bow was still in his hand and his quiver over his shoulder. He set the quiver down to lean against the wall.

"Everything alright?" she asked as she examined him. "Is Luke OK?"

Liam stretched his lips into a grim smile and nodded. He sat in the matching chair next to hers and laid his bow across his lap. "One of *them* was in Luke's flat."

Christine took a sharp breath and sat up straight. "Oh," she exhaled softly. "I'm so sorry."

"It wasn't him. I don't know who it was or how it got in there. The door was closed."

"Did you? I mean...did you have to...?"

Liam nodded again and stared down at his clasped hands.

"I'm sorry," she said again and rested a hand on his shoulder.

"It's fine. Jerry's hurt, but he'll be all right," he said with a sniff. He composed himself and sat upright.

"Do you think someone brought it up there? I mean, from what we've seen, those things can't climb stairs, or at least they haven't tried to yet, and his apartment is on the top floor. Who would do that?" she rambled on as she tried to work it out in her head.

"I have no idea."

Suddenly, Liam's back stiffened and hovered inches above the back of the chair as he looked down. "What do we have here?" he asked as he pointed his bow out into the parking lot.

"Oh, Mr. Alexander," Christine said casually as her voice lifted again to its normal perkiness. "He likes to come out at least once a day and dig through the Dumpster for some reason. Apparently the crumble of civilization also means the rise of the rats. He has no trouble finding them."

She talked about Mr. Alexander as if he were still the old man from the building next door whose mind had started to drift away. As if the zombie state was the inevitable final stage in his advancing Alzheimer's.

"He's getting especially good at finding these little field mice," Christine laughed as the decrepit zombie leaned in at the waist with its legs ready to leave the ground. "I don't know what he'd do if he ever actually fell in there," she chuckled. "Probably take him a week to get out again."

She heard the flick of string and fell silent. When she turned to look, Mr. Alexander was lying still on the ground, face down, with an arrow sticking out from the back of his head.

Liam glared at her. His lips were pursed tight and his eyes flamed with an angry passion. There was a wildness to him that Christine had never seen before. An icy chill ran down her spine. She shivered in the hot, summer air as goosebumps rose from under her fair skin.

"You shouldn't have let him live this long," Liam said as he got up. "If you can even call that living." He stalked off into the house and shut himself in the bedroom.

Through the window, Christine heard the rustle of boxes as Liam stuffed supplies into his backpack. With the way he looked when he got home, almost catatonic, she hadn't been sure if he was still going to go with the others on the run. But after witnessing the seething burn behind his once sweet hazel eyes, she knew there was no stopping him.

It was wrong, but for a moment she had let herself hope that he was in too bad of a mental state to leave her alone for the first time in six weeks. As she listened to him prepare to leave, a twinge constricted her throat. She tried to swallow, but her mouth was dry.

She attempted to keep her eyes averted from Mr. Alexander's body, but they couldn't stay away. Dark, thick blood had pooled around the head and stained the wispy white hairs. She quickly looked away again and bit her bottom lip. There was no reason to feel sad for Mr. Alexander. She knew that. He'd died a long time ago.

Liam came bounding out of the bedroom with his bag packed and a new crossbow clutched in his hand where his longbow had been. He gripped the door frame to the patio as he leaned his head around. "I'm heading out now," he said casually, as if he were going for some take-out dinner.

Christine nodded and stared ahead at the cloudless blue sky. Her mind felt numb. The limbs of her body refused to move.

When she didn't say anything in return, Liam disappeared from the doorway and began unlocking the front door.

"Liam, wait," Christine finally called as she rushed back into the apartment.

He continued to unlock the deadbolts, but stopped before he opened the door. He turned to look over his shoulder with his hand on the doorknob.

"I was thinking…now that you're down a man maybe I could join you guys…out there." Her voice petered off at the end when she saw the intensity of his glare.

"You want to go *out there?*" he asked as he jabbed the menacing black crossbow through the air at the living room window.

She swallowed, let her shoulders drop, and stretched her neck out a bit. "Yes. I want to go out there."

"No." He turned back for the door.

She grabbed him by the shoulders and whirled him around. "You need me," she said through her teeth. "I'm not weak! I can help!"

Liam's eyes grew wider the louder her voice got. He clenched his teeth and ground them slowly as he let out a long, heavy breath. The day he'd feared had finally arrived. He felt like a fool for thinking Christine would've ever been satisfied with a life of being tucked away, safe behind the walls, doors, and locks of their home. He'd hoped. He'd even prayed, though he had no God he believed in anymore.

None of it worked apparently, because there she stood, heaving in a frenzy over going out into the changed world. "We'll start training you tonight."

Christine's heart gave a giant leap, not from the thrill of having Liam agree to let her do something, but from the relief of not having to leave right that minute. There was no way she was ready and she wasn't going to argue otherwise. In fact, the moment she suggested it, she mentally kicked her own ass. She would whoop herself into shape, though, if it meant her days of sitting, bored and sweating, on the patio to watch the leaves rustle in the almost non-existent breeze were over.

Before Christine could thank him, Liam was gone.

VI.

Anita crouched down in front of a thick, green bush with red berries. She plucked one of the spherical fruits off with her thumb and index finger and inspected it, held it close to her eye and then pulled it far away. She stuck her tongue out and licked it, but wasn't able to taste anything. Her eyes narrowed as she scrutinized some more.

"You always said holly berries were poisonous, but do holly berries grow in the summertime? Mom used to make you go buy them for Christmas and I never really see people hanging holly except in the winter, but that doesn't mean it *can't* grow in the heat too, right?" Anita said aloud.

She sat on her knees with her bare, blackened feet sticking out from behind her. The nights had started to cool off and Anita didn't have long to find new clothes. Her tank top and high-waited shorts wouldn't provide her with much warmth in the coming weeks of fall.

Going into town to scavenge for outerwear wasn't an option. It was too big of a risk. She might run into more people and the thought made her entire body rack with fear. Zombies, she could deal with them. They were slow and stupid. More often than not they ignored her completely. She moved among them like a ghost. She assumed because the blood of their own covered her top and shorts, but she couldn't be sure. She couldn't bring herself to care why, either. All that mattered was that she was still alive somehow.

She turned her focus back to the berry she held. It rolled it between her fingers before she brought it up to her nose to sniff. "Like I even know what a holly berry smells like, right, dad?" she laughed.

Anita reached up and scratched at her head, ruffling her already frizzy, dirt-mangled hair. She shrugged her shoulders, popped the berry into her mouth, and chewed a few times before swallowing.

Anita's hands jerked upward to clutch at her throat as she gasped for air. She fell to the ground and rolled violently as her nails clawed at the skin on her throat, the other reached towards the sky.

Her gasps quickly turned to chuckles as she rolled over onto all fours and pushed up off the ground to stand again. "Just kidding, dad," she said. "The berries are fine. You worry too much." She leaned over the plentiful bush and picked one berry after another to toss them into her unfolded blue and white bandana.

A twig snapped. Her head jerked up. There were voices in the distance. She couldn't make out what they were saying, but they grew clearer as they neared. Without a second thought, Anita dropped the bandana containing the berries and jumped up to grab the closest branch. She pulled

herself up, swung her leg over, and turned herself upright to
wait for whoever was approaching.

VII.

"Ooo, look!" Gretchen's voice rang out in a sing-
songy manner. "Berries!" She quickly scooped the pile off
the ground and blew on it, rubbing a few against the
somewhat clean part of her shirt. Her stomach gave a deep,
rumbling growl. Food had been scarce the last few weeks.
Lonnie and Rowan claimed they'd been hunting on many
occasions before everything went down, but had nothing
more than a few squirrels to show for their skills. And
squirrel just wasn't cutting it.

"They're probably poisonous," Lonnie said as he
continued past Gretchen without as much as a glance.

"No," she said sharply. "These are red elder berries.
They're edible. They actually settle your stomach if you're
feeling sick."

Mitchell Barnes took a berry from Gretchen's hand
and looked at it closely, then popped it in his mouth. He
scrunched his face and swallowed. "Tart," he said as facial
muscles clenched involuntarily and then relaxed. "How do
you know about this stuff?"

Gretchen turned a berry between her fingers as a
smile pulled at the corners of her lips. "I grew up around
here. I used to walk the Dunes all the time with my family.

We'd go hiking and camping and fishing…" Her voice trailed off.

An image of the last time she saw her parents flashed through her mind. She dropped the berries to the ground as she took in a sharp breath, caught off guard by the appearance of their decrepit, mutilated faces.

"Are you all right?" Mitchell asked. He bent down to pick up the berries she'd dropped.

"Yeah," she said, distant. "Yeah. I just…gather what you can. We should keep going."

Lonnie, Rowan, and Carolyn were already ahead of the group, as Gale and Lee remained behind with Gretchen and Mitchell.

"My dogs are barking," Gale groaned as she stood up after sitting down for only a few seconds on an overturned tree trunk. "And I think I have the worst case of farmer's tan in the history of farmers."

"Actually it's more of a farmer's burn," Mitchell said in his quick, stammering voice. "See." He stuck a finger to Gale's red arm. It left a white print that slowly faded back to red. "That's a sunburn."

Gale looked at him through a thin slit in her gray eyes. Her mouth was turned down into an aggressive frown, the aged lines in her skin deepening. "Yeah. Thanks for that," she grumbled and started to walk off after the others.

"No problem."

It didn't take long for them to catch up. Lonnie, Rowan, and Carolyn had been moving at a slow pace as their feet dragged along the scorching blacktop of the winding highway. "God, I would kill for some water right now," Lonnie said.

"We have to conserve what we have till we find more," Gale said with the annoyance of someone who had to repeat themselves daily.

"I know, Big Bertha," Lonnie groaned, his voice rising in volume at the end. "I was just saying."

"We should be looking for shelter," Gretchen beat that dead horse with a stick. "If we could find an apartment, or something that's off the ground, we'd be safe for a while. Then, we could gather supplies." There was a smile on her face as she spoke in hopes of building a life again, even if that life involved Lonnie Lands.

"That *does* sound better than wandering around the same ten miles of road for another month," Mitchell agreed softly.

"My feet could sure use the break," Gale said.

Lonnie stopped walking and looked up at the sky to exhale a long sigh, his signature move before an outburst that was normally directed at Gale. But when he finished, he turned and marched straight for Gretchen, who was stopped in the middle of the road with wide eyes.

"You really wanna find someplace to live and settle down in?" he asked her sweetly as she flinched. He rubbed a piece of her blonde hair between his fingers before letting it drop back against her face. His eyes lingered on her smooth skin as he leered.

Gretchen did her best to hide the look of disgust lurking just beneath the surface of her composed face. If it was going to get them shelter, she could pretend to like Lonnie for a little while, a very short little while. "I really do," she said in a breathy, girlish voice. She leaned her face in closer to his as she spoke.

Lonnie's grin spread to expose his small, dingy teeth through a thin part in his mouth. He licked his dry, cracked lips and bit off a piece of flaky skin. With a hacking spat, it came shooting out to land somewhere on the pavement at Gretchen's feet. "Well, let's go find us an apartment then." He winked.

The second he turned to head the group Gretchen exhaled the breath she'd been holding in. She wrinkled her nose as her eyes followed the disgusting little man with asperity.

Gale gave her a pat on the back as they walked together behind the rest. Lee brought up the rear as always, though neither of the women worried any longer about him listening in on their conversations. "Thanks," Gale said. "I know that couldn't have been easy."

"I really do hate him," Gretchen hissed through her teeth.

"Me too," Gale agreed.

"Then why do we keep following him?"

Gale smiled. "Are we following him or is he following us?"

Gretchen looked up as she contemplated Gale's words. She got Lonnie to do what she wanted with a simple bat of her eyelashes. What else could she get him to do? Give up leadership of the group? Was he even in charge anymore? Could there be such a thing as leadership when the world had descended into disarray and chaos? Questions ran through her head as she stared at Lonnie's wide, burnt shoulders, a tattoo of an eagle flying next to the American flag waving with the rippling of his muscles.

She wished Lonnie would turn his attention to Carolyn, who so obviously craved it from anyone willing to give it. Even when Gretchen was into men, he never would have made her cut. By the looks of Carolyn, anyone and everyone was invited to come on in.

"We should check the Walmart up the road again," Lonnie called out.

There was a rustle in the trees alongside them.

"We already went there," Mitchell said.

"That's why I said again, dipshit."

Three lethargic, bent bodies moved sluggishly about twenty yards away.

"Then why go back?" Gretchen spoke up. She felt the need to show Lonnie she still didn't like him. It wasn't worth what he might try to do if he thought she was starting to have feelings for him. "It's not like anyone's been in there to restock the shelves."

Heads turned on their slackened necks and jaws fell open.

"We're going," Lonnie barked back.

So much for him following her. They continued on as the three listless zombies trailed after at a snail's pace. No one in the group looked back at them as they faded into the shadows of the trees.

VIII.

The automatic doors were wide open as the group crept forward into the superstore, their weapons poised to strike down whoever, or whatever, they saw. Gretchen,

Mitchell, and Lee turned right and swept the aisles closest to the doors while Lonnie, Rowan, Carolyn, and Gale went left, a strategy they'd debated and rehearsed previously. After they made a quick lap they met back in the middle at the end of the entryway.

Lonnie lowered his AR-15 to point it at the ground. His walk was loose and casual, almost strut-like, as he rejoined the group with a smirk on his face. "Let's split off into pairs. Me and Gretchen will go this way," he flexed his muscles to raise his gun toward the area he'd just looked over with the others. He gave Gretchen a crooked smile. "Rowan, Carolyn, and Gale will take center. Mitchell and Lee can go thatta way." He swung his gun again.

Lee was already headed in the direction Lonnie had chosen for him. Wherever they went to raid for supplies, Lee always made a dash for the pharmacy to stock up. He'd found a khaki backpack lying in the woods with a couple Band-Aids and Neosporin in it a few weeks ago. When the bag became light, Lee became anxious. It was almost empty and his heart pounded so intensely that it sounded like someone was beating against the drums in his ears.

Lonnie walked close to Gretchen and put his hand on the small of her back to lead her away from the group. His head leaned back to sneak a peek at her firm, round ass. Gale watched him intently.

Gretchen peered over her shoulder to lock eyes with her only friend. The older woman gave her a nod and Gretchen nodded back. They'd been training together in hand-to-hand combat most nights while the others slept.

Lonnie had grown more confident in his chances with Gretchen with each passing day. Her little flirtatious display earlier hadn't helped the situation. "Preferences go out the window when it's the end of the world," he'd said to her one night after she refused to lay with him by the fire. The more persistent he was, the more uncomfortable Gretchen became around him. After telling Gale so, she insisted Gretchen learn to defend herself. The undead were not the only danger anymore.

Mitchell took quick steps once he caught up to Lee to stay in stride with the long-legged man. Lee was on a mission. He'd found a practically untouched supply of invaluable medications the last time they were there and his backpack had almost burst at the seams from it. That was two weeks ago and they'd used almost everything between Mitchell getting shot, Carolyn's scratched ankle on the border line of infection, and Gale's feet swelling every other minute. His heart leapt as he neared the counter. A smile almost crawled across his lips.

"So, did you like being a nurse? When you were one, I mean?" Mitchell stammered out to break the awkward silence.

Lee continued on without looking back or answering.

"Oh right, I forgot. You're the strong silent type. I get that. That's me, too. I don't like people knowing a whole lot about my business either, although there isn't much business to keep secret lately, is there?" He rambled on as Lee hopped over the counter and dropped to his feet inside the pharmacy.

There were rows of trays with letters stuck to the front of them on over a dozen shelves. Little white bags stuck up in perfect rows, like tombstones in the ground. Lee didn't hesitate in rifling through them. Occasionally, he ripped one open and stuffed the orange labeled bottle into his bag.

"Is there anything in particular you want me to look for?" Mitchell asked with his shotgun raised as he turned in circles to maintain a three-hundred-and-sixty viewpoint.

"Antibiotics," was all Lee grumbled through his Irish accent. He disappeared around one of the shelves.

Mitchell walked to the left to start at the beginning of the alphabet and work his way back. As he rounded the corner he saw two feet turned upright sticking out from behind the furthest shelf. He quickly raised the butt of his gun to his shoulder as he held his breath. It slipped. "Shit," he whispered as he fumbled to put it back into position. He took slow, precise steps until he saw the entire body sprawled out on the white tile floor.

The young man wasn't moving. Mitchell tapped him on the arm with his foot and immediately jumped back. His gun rattled from the jerky movement, but the young man still didn't stir. Mitchell couldn't see any bites on his exposed dark skin from where he stood. "Hey, Lee!" he hissed. His hands began to shake. His eyes blinked rapidly as he tried to keep the sweat from dripping into them. "Lee!"

Lee's head appeared from around one of the shelves, but he didn't step out. He stared at Mitchell with several bottles clutched in his hands.

"There's a body here…not a zombie one."

It was one of the only times Mitchell could remember ever seeing anything close to an emotion pass over Lee's face, his eyes widened and his brows raised up an inch.

Lee shoved the bottles he held into his bag and slung it over one of his shoulders as he walked briskly. He didn't think twice before he dropped to his knees next to the unconscious body and felt for a pulse. The man's dark, caramel skin was cool to the touch. Lee lowered his ear to the unmoving lips.

The longer Lee stayed hunched over, his pink flesh dangerously close to a mouth that contained strong, white teeth, the harder it became for Mitchell to take a breath. He waited for Lee to say anything to reassure him they weren't about to be eaten alive by a fresh corpse.

"Go get tha others," Lee ordered. He kept his eyes focused on the unconscious man.

Mitchell ran off immediately. His tennis shoes pattered on the hard floor.

The sound grew fainter in Lee's ears the further Mitchell ran. He scanned over the still body while he waited. The man looked to be about twenty-five years old, fit, healthy as far as he could see. Lee grabbed onto a sturdy shoulders and rolled the man towards him and then away. Three packets of pills were flattened underneath his back, all empty. Lee didn't waste any more time waiting for the others to get there. He swept his finger inside the man's mouth. There were no pills stuck in his throat. He began CPR.

IX.

Lonnie and Gretchen made a b-line to the pharmacy after Mitchell told them about the unconscious man on the floor. The two stopped short of running into Rowan as he rounded one of the aisles, Gale and Carolyn on his heels. Lonnie pushed his shoulder against Gale's chest to move her out of the way and continued to sprint so he'd be the first to arrive. When he finally hopped the counter seamlessly he was brought to a skidding halt.

The unconscious man was no longer unconscious. He stood up with the help of Lee and walked clumsily to where the others had gathered by the counter. His dark jeans and red hoodie hung loosely from his thin frame. Sunken and vacant, his brown eyes looked almost black as he struggled to keep them open. They rolled back into his head. Lee gave the young man a quick jerk and brought him back around. His lids flickered open and then closed halfway. His short, wavy dark hair had dirt and broken pieces of leaves and twigs woven into it.

The others looked at him as if he were one of the undead. Lonnie took a few steps back as Lee dragged him forward. Rowan did a double-take and noticed Lonnie wasn't beside him any longer. He scrambled backward to stand next to him again. His chest puffed out to model Lonnie's once his feet were planted at the kid's side.

Gale, Carolyn, and Gretchen were rooted outside the pharmacy counter. They each inwardly squirmed at the sight of someone new. It had been over two weeks since they'd seen the smallest sign of anyone else alive, the last one a smoldering abandoned fire. A couple times Gretchen thought she saw a woman hiding in the bushes or perched up in the trees, but decided it was nothing when the woman in question never revealed herself.

The thin black man doubled over, his knees buckling, but Lee caught him by his shirt before he hit the ground in a fit of coughing.

"What's wrong with him?" Gretchen asked. She bit her lip and looked on with soft blue eyes and raised, contorted eyebrows.

"He overdosed on sleepin' pills," Lee said as he pushed the halfway comatose man down into a discarded plastic chair.

Gale clucked her tongue and shook her head at her tennis shoes. "Damn shame."

"So, the sorry bastard tried to off himself, is that it?" Lonnie chuckled as he shifted his gun from his left shoulder to his right. The barbed wire tattoo around his bicep waved as his muscles flexed and released.

"Have some compassion," Gretchen snapped at him. "He almost died."

"And we should have let him," Lonnie barked back. "He obviously doesn't wanna live or he wouldn't of downed all those pills. Let's just get back to gathering supplies and get the fuck out of here like we planned."

"We can't just leave him here!" Gretchen said in a shaky voice. "He needs our help."

Something changed in Lonnie. His eyes were overtaken by that wild, crazed look again. "People who *want* to die can't be helped!" he yelled from deep within his chest. It caught everyone off guard as his voice echoed throughout the vast, empty store. "So do yourself a favor and fucking forget about him!"

Gretchen's mouth hung open as she looked at Lonnie, tears gathered in the corners of her eyes. He turned and walked off to leave the group staring in bewilderment. Gretchen looked to Gale, but all Gale did was shrug.

"Wonder what that was all about," Mitchell said in his awkward, fast way of talking that made him stumble over his words.

He said what everyone else had thought silently to themselves and it made Gretchen roll her misty eyes. They'd obviously pushed a button for Lonnie, one of his many, but a deeply rooted and highly sensitive one. Gretchen's mind wandered away from the dark scene in the small enclosure of the Wal-Mart pharmacy and over to the brooding man in the distance, ready to disappear into the shadows of the empty aisles.

For the first time, she thought of Lonnie as more than the asshole who appointed himself God and leader of the group. He wasn't simply put on Earth to take zombies down and boss people around. He had a history before the dead destroyed everything—a life, a home, a family—and for some reason, she desperately wanted to know what it was.

Mitchell spoke again to everyone's dismay. "Is there like a history of suicide in his family or something? Did he know someone or..."

"Just shut up already," Rowan grumbled as his almond eyes narrowed.

"Got it. Sorry," Mitchel stammered and backed away.

Lee knelt down in front of the man in the chair and tipped back a water bottle to his dry lips. Somewhere in the foggy unconscious of the man's mind, he was grateful. Luke warm water dripped down his chin and neck.

The cool sensation seemed to revive him. His dark eyes opened fully and began to dart back and forth. He jumped back, scooting the chair away from the broad, muscle-toned Irishman in front of him. His hazy gratitude quickly transformed into enraged paranoia.

"What the fuck? Who the fuck are you people?" he rambled off, panic-stricken. "I don't have anything, I swear." His breathing sped up until it wheezed in his chest. He coughed intensely.

Lee held out a hand to him, but the man flinched away from it. "It's all right," Lee said, reaching out again. "Nobody is going ta hurt ya."

The man couldn't keep his eyes still for more than a second. When he saw Lonnie double back around with a determined stride and red face, they widened until they were ready to pop out of their sockets.

"What's your name? Where are you from?" Lonnie demanded as he stood over the hunched, frail man.

Wheezing turned to sobbing. The black man lowered his elbows to his knees and rested his head in his hands. He didn't hold back as his entire body shook up and down. Tears and spit covered his palms. He shook his head. "Why didn't you just let me die?" His voice was muffled through his hands. When no one answered he shouted again. "Why didn't you let me die!"

Lonnie bent over at the waist with his hands on his knees, gun slung around his back, so that his face was level with the scared young man's. "What. Is. Your. Name?" Lonnie demanded.

The man peeled himself away from his hands. His red-rimmed eyes looked up at Lonnie as he tried to catch his breath. "Dan…" he said in between sobs. "Anderson…Dan Anderson from Chicago."

X.

The group gathered in one corner of the pharmacy while Dan Anderson sat in the other.

"We should leave him," Lonnie stuck to his guns. "Someone like that is only going to slow us down, drain us of supplies, and get us killed."

"How can you be so heartless?" Gretchen whispered so Dan couldn't hear. "He's obviously been through a lot. He doesn't *really* want to die. No one wants that for themselves. He just thinks he had no other option."

"How can you know that?" Rowan asked with his hands on his hips, his thumb flicking his belt loop. "I mean, he looks pretty miserable to me."

"Look, we're all miserable," Gale said with her hand thrust out, as if to display the sad bunch of misfits, poster children for the definition of wretched, pathetic, and miserable. "But that doesn't mean we should abandon someone when there are so few people left in the world."

"I don't know," Carolyn said slowly. "How'd he get all the way here from Chicago? And why? Just to off himself? It's weird, don't you think?"

Lonnie sighed. He turned away and then turned back again as if he was trying to keep a tally in his head of everyone's misguided votes. He rubbed at the back of his thick neck. So far it was Gretchen and Gale yay, Carolyn and himself nay. Rowan would do whatever he said. Lee probably wouldn't answer either way. He couldn't care less about anything except his medical supplies. If the Irishman wasn't such an intimidating figure who watched the group's back vigilantly, Lonnie would have left him for dead long ago. That meant Mitchell was the only one left to voice his opinion.

"What do you think, dipshit?" Lonnie asked the kid.

"Uh…" Mitchell stalled as he looked around at the group, their faces long and withered from the harshness of their new way of life. "I think you talk a lot about preserving humanity and repopulation and it'd be counter intuitive of you to left him here to die."

Mitchell made a valid point, but something still didn't feel right deep in Lonnie's gut. If the new guy was bad news, he could end up killing someone in the group—multiple people, in fact. *That* would be even more counter intuitive, or whatever Mitchell said. "I still think we should get what we need and go." His face was solid, like his stance, his gunned gripped firmly in his hands.

A collective sigh rose to the ceiling.

"Well, I'm not leaving without him," Gretchen said as she crossed her arms and planted her feet.

Lonnie closed his eyes, turned his face upwards, and took a calming breath. "Gretch, you're killing me," he whined.

When he opened his eyes again she was still standing firmly next to the lip balm and condoms. Her pink lips were puckered together in the cutest pouty face Lonnie had ever seen. "Fine," he gave in quickly. "But I'm not babysitting suicidal Dan, over there. That's going to be your job and fucking Green Giant's. Got it?" His thumb was hitched over his shoulder at Lee, who was leaning against one of the white pharmacy shelves with his arms folded.

Gretchen didn't smile with relief or thank Lonnie for his decision. She didn't even move.

"But the kid's on a fucking trial run," Lonnie called over his shoulder as he walked away. "If he tries anything stupid or attempts to off himself again, we leave him behind. That's it."

"Whatever," Gretchen exhaled.

She relaxed her stance once Lonnie and Rowan disappeared to ransack what was left in the aisles to the right of the pharmacy, which were the over-the-counter drugs, home and garden, and toys. She heard his faint voice ask his companion if Play-Doh was edible and shook her head. "Idiot," she breathed.

"Thanks for that," Dan Anderson spoke out to the blonde woman who vouched for him. He rested his back against the chair with his legs sprawled out.

Gretchen let herself smile as she took a few steps forward. Her stomach felt warm and her heart beat fast, a result of sticking up for herself and getting Dan admitted into the group. They saved a life. But she'd heard what Lonnie said and she knew he'd hold her to it. Dan was her responsibility now.

"But I don't want your help," Dan said as he looked away.

"That's fine," Gretchen said in a sturdy voice. She strode over to him and shoved a black bag into his hands. "*You're* going to help *us* then."

As if summoned for the duty of testing Dan's loyalty, an eroded body shambled out from between two of the seasonal shelves twenty feet away. Its jaw hung open in a perpetual moan as bile seeped out from between its black teeth. It locked its clouded red eyes on Dan and Gretchen who stood concealed behind the pharmacy counter.

"Here," she said as she tossed Dan a compact scout knife from her jeans pocket.

Dan caught it clumsily in his hands and stared down at the small concealed knife that looked more like a child's toy than a weapon. "You're not serious?"

Gretchen looked back at him over her shoulder with her hand on the doorknob. "Better get to it. It's not going to kill itself." She smiled.

Dan narrowed his eyes and stood up. He flicked his wrist and the knife popped out of hiding, the blade not even as long as his middle finger. He marched out after Gretchen.

She felt the hair stand up on the back of her neck as his footsteps neared. Her breath caught in her chest as his thin figure approached and cast a shadow on her back. She squeezed her eyes shut tight.

Dan Anderson continued past Gretchen toward the lowly zombie circling the pool toys. His feet never slowed as he came up, face to face, with the corpse and plunged the knife deep into its left eye socket, slicing the eyeball in half as it drove into the cerebrum.

The zombie's mouth still hung wide open as the fight went out of it. It sagged to the tile floor as thick, black blood ran down its decayed, grayish face. There were no last twitches or spasms as life was extinguished. The thing had never been alive to begin with.

Dan's shoulders rose and sank as he heaved over the unmoving corpse. His hand was drenched in bile and blood. He raised his dark eyes to Gretchen, who stood on the other side of the body in front of him. Her mouth hung open like the dead's, but her eyes swam with emotions only the living experienced—awe and fear.

XI.

When Liam Scott went of his first supply run with Zack Kran, they were lucky enough to find an abandoned, fully stocked home not too far from the apartment complex, one that Zack and Ralph had previously overlooked, but had been a favorite of Liam's since he moved in. It was an old Victorian tucked away behind the trees off a backroad behind a corn farm. They came back with a two week supply of food for everyone. He figured he would need that long to train Christine how to survive out there now that she wanted to go along with them.

"Here," he said, handing her a complicated looking black crossbow, with wires, pulleys, and a scope, but unfortunately no rope cocking aid.

Christine took hold of the hunting equipment and immediately almost dropped it as her small hands struggled to get a good grip, especially since she had no idea how to grip it in the first place. "I don't think this is going to work for me," she said as the crossbow swayed side to side before she let it fall to the ground completely with a thud.

Liam snorted.

"What?" she barked as she shoved it against the wall. "I've never used one of these things before and this one has all this stuff on it that it doesn't need…"

He smirked with his arms crossed. "Whatever you say, love," he said upbeat as he handed her his longbow. "You can use this. Now you do remember what I taught you before, correct?"

"You mean the one time you took me to shoot this thing and you were a condescending jerk? Yeah, I remember that." She cocked her head to the side and tried to keep from smiling, but couldn't.

"Then you'll remember this is a longbow so it's a bit large for you and the muscle required to nock an arrow back may be difficult for someone like…"

Christine glowered at him and pursed her lips, daring him to continue with what he was going to say.

"…someone of your stature," he recovered with a smile. "But you did all right that day and I'm confident you'll do even better today."

He held onto the quiver of arrows as she gripped the sixty-eight inch longbow in one hand. It stood just as tall as she when placed on the cement of the patio. Her arms were already starting to feel flimsy after a few seconds of holding it up, but she'd never admit it. Instead, she would work herself to death before she told Liam she didn't think she was capable of going out to gather supplies with him. He needed an extra set of hands, to carry and to kill. And she needed out of the apartment, which she hadn't left in two months.

They stood and faced the brilliant sun over the parking lot. Garbage and debris of those who left in a hurry scattered the hot blacktop. Liam pointed outward to a small line of trees that clustered around the parking spaces directly in front of them. Tied with pieces of twine at different heights in the branches were crudely made round targets.

"Where did you get the wood for those?" Christine asked as she squinted.

Liam looked down at the ground and shuffled his feet. Both his hands gripped the protruding bones of his hips. He smiled and looked up at her through his light orange lashes. "The seats of the bar stools…" he said with a quick wrinkle of his nose. He waited for Christine to huff and sigh as she complained about him ruining the few nice things they had left.

Her lips twitched upward in a brief smile as she nodded her head. She shrugged. "Whatever, it's fine. Let's just do this."

"Right," he said, relief flooding his face. He stood close behind to correct her stance as she nocked back the first arrow.

It was only two seconds before the desire to release overwhelmed her stringy muscles. The arrow shot forward and took a plundering nosedive straight into the grassy median, nowhere near the trees she'd been aiming for. "These targets are too small," she said as she let the bow drop to her side.

"If they were twenty feet wide you wouldn't have been close," he said with a laugh. She looked at him sharply and he wiped the smile off his face. "Oh, come on. Even you have to admit that wasn't a commendable shot."

She rolled her eyes before she lifted the bow again and snatched another arrow from the quiver, jarring it in his hands.

"Just relax," he said slowly from behind her. "Breathe and hold long as you feel comfortable. Remember, the longer you hold it back the less sturdy your arms will be and the further off you'll be from your target. That's it," he said as she nocked the arrow back and took a deep breath. "Now release the arrow as you exhale."

He barely finished his sentence before her fingers released. She searched the ground with her hand raised to shade her eyes from the bright white rays of the sun. A steady breeze had finally rolled in and was cooling things down for fall, which she was grateful for, but she was also certain that it was the reason her arrows were landing so far from their targets. It had to be.

"Where is it?" She threw her hands up in the air, one still clutched around the bow's limb.

"There," Liam said. He pointed to one of the trees holding a makeshift target. "It's in the trunk." He turned to her with wild laughter that pierced the noon sky.

"OK, I get it," she grit through her teeth. "I'm horrible at this. I shouldn't even be—"

"No," he interrupted, grabbing both her shoulders so she'd look at him. "That was brilliant!"

"You're just saying that because you want to get laid tonight." She gave a disappointed, crooked smile.

Liam kissed her on the forehead. "That was a really *really* excellent shot. Really!"

She shoved him in the chest and they both laughed. "You think you're so slick," she said. "Enough. Let's go again."

She looked out at the arrow that protruded from the thin, twisted tree and grinned. Could she be a natural? After all, she'd only used a bow twice in her life. Maybe a day or two of practice would be enough before she went out with the others.

XII.

Later that night, as Christine lie next to Liam, who was naked under the thin white sheet, she stared up at the unmoving ceiling fan. They'd practiced on and off the entire day and she hadn't hit a single target. The excitement of nailing the tree trunk earlier had left her after her tenth failure to hit anything else. How was she ever going to survive out there? Maybe she shouldn't go. They'd be better off without her. She would only hold them back.

Her mind wandered as she tried to fall asleep. She looked over at Liam, who was on his back with one arm draped to shield his eyes from the inevitable morning light. His breathing was deep, but soft. She watched his chest rise and fall and felt the pit of her stomach twist into a gut-wrenching knot.

Were they even going to bother getting married with everything that had happened? It seemed a little ridiculous given the state of things. But every girl, even Christine, dreamed of their wedding day. A day that, for her, would probably never come. And what about children? Would Liam ever have anyone to carry on the Scott name? She knew that was something he found extremely important, given what happened to his parents, or at least he did before. Would there ever be someone to continue the tradition of shooting arrows on their birthdays? Her heart ached every time one of her questions went unanswered.

She rolled over onto her side and lay her arm across his bare chest, even though the air was warm and thick in the small, stale bedroom. He stirred and took a deep breath as he lifted his head from his pillow for a second. With a groan, he rolled into her and pulled her body toward him so that her head was buried in his soft skin. She took a deep breath despite the fact that they hadn't bathe in days. He smelled of stagnant sweat and faded deodorant. She wondered how many more chances she would get to hold him like that before one of them was dead.

XIII.

It took the entire two weeks of nonstop training on the longbow, crossbow, and even a Bowie knife for day before Liam let Christine go out with them for supplies, still not fully onboard with the idea. He paced around the apartment that morning in a frenzy, rifling through boxes but never pulling anything out, tugging at his orange hair and rubbing the back of his neck.

Seeing Liam like that made Christine's stomach clench until it ached. Sweat had already collected on her forehead. It ran down the side of her face, over her collarbone, and between her small breasts to soak into her bra and shirt. She tried to steady her breathing, but it came out in ragged uneven huffs.

Liam handed her a large, empty backpack and a long Bowie knife. Why had they trained excruciatingly with two separate types of bows if she wasn't even going to use them? She took the knife and stared at it like some alien object, her nose wrinkled. It got tucked away behind her belt loop with the bottom of her shirt pulled down over it.

"Gimmee one second," she said as she ran back to the bedroom, threw the closet door open, and stopped in front of the floor length mirror.

She looked herself over one last time. She had on a gray t-shirt, a black zip-up hoodie, tight dark jeans tucked into her lace-up ankle boots, and a scary-looking knife hung from her waist, the tip peeking out from underneath her clothing menacingly. Her stomach muscles finally relaxed. She looked the part of zombie killer extraordinaire and it made her blue eyes light up like the sky.

"I'm ready!" she called, never more honestly spoken in her life.

Ralph, Zack, and Jerry waited in the hallway. Jerry still in his sweats, as he was every morning since he hurt his back weeks ago, with a steaming cup of coffee in his hand. The morning air had a cool nip to it, which explained the gray hoodie no one had ever seen him wear before. There was a black union symbol on the front above the pocket he had his free hand tucked into.

Ralph leaned on his axe in a dirty pair of Hollister jeans and a forest green, ribbed, long-sleeved shirt. Covering his outgrown dishwater blond hair was a camo fleece beanie with a pair of antlers stitched to the front. He swiftly swung the axe around the back of his head to rest on his shoulders while his hands hung loosely over the handle, as if it were the most normal way to relax and wait for someone.

Zack looked the same as he had every day since the dead started to walk around, armored in padding, his dark, scraggly beard stuck far out from his chin, not quite touching his chest yet. His eyes drooped with deep set bags underneath as he leaned against the wall with his head back. He chimed in on the conversation between Ralph and Jerry whenever his mind was present. He only bothered to lift his head when he heard the familiar click of Liam's door opening.

"Finally," he sighed. "Can we go?"

"It's only eight now," Christine said as if he had accused her of making them late.

He let his head fall to the side to rest on a shoulder pad. "I was up all night…" The pained look in his eyes gathered the sympathy of everyone around him.

"Still nothing?" Liam asked, resting a hand on Zack's shoulder.

Zack shook his head and looked at the ground. Silence. He'd been staying out longer each day to search for Anita. No one had the heart to tell him it was probably a waste of time, that she was already dead. Nobody wanted to see what that would do to him.

The guys turned to head down the stairs and Christine followed behind with a bounce in her step. She sniffed in through her nose and closed her eyes to savor the crisp morning air. Something touched her face and her eyes sprung open.

"Where are *you* going?" Zack asked with his hand held out in front of him. He looked to Liam with his brow furrowed and then to Jerry, as if to ask him if he'd invited Christine to take watch with him.

Jerry sipped his coffee and shrugged his broad shoulders.

"I'm going with you," Christine said. She looked to Liam, but he was looking away at the sky. "You did tell them, didn't you?"

He reluctantly met her increasingly hostile gaze. "I hadn't gotten around to it yet."

"You hadn't gotten around to it?"

"Well, hey, welcome aboard," Zack jumped in. "I think it's badass. Way to go, Chris." He thrust his hand up in the air and she slapped it with a resentful smirk.

"No way," Ralph said, shaking his head. "We can't trust her. She's never been out there before."

Christine wanted to tell him off like she constantly did with Zack, but something held her back. She didn't know Ralph that well. In that moment she realized that Zack was the closest thing she had to a friend with Allison gone. She snorted through her nose at the thought, causing Ralph to glare at her with narrowed eyes. "You're going to get us all killed," he said with disregard.

"We were all new to this at one point," Zack said. "What do you think Jer?"

They all turned to the old man as he lowered the steaming mug from his lips. Ralph waited with a confident grin plastered onto his narrow face. Jerry took a deep breath of contemplation. "I think she can take care of herself."

Ralph's mouth dropped as he let the axe fall from his shoulders to swing back down to the ground. "Oh, come on!" he whined. It was one of the rare times he showed his true, young age. "There's no way you actually believe that!"

"That's the way the world works now, kid. If it makes you feel any better she might get herself killed, maybe Liam, because he'll do anything to protect her, but that's about it." With that, Jerry walked off down the stairs and back to his apartment to sit on the porch with his shotgun and coffee cup.

The air was electric as Ralph glared at the thin blonde. He snorted and shook his head before bounding down the stairs two at a time, his axe clanking against the wrought iron railing.

Christine's face turned red and she struggled to take in a full breath. What if Ralph and Jerry were right? Maybe she shouldn't go. She looked to Liam and, without a word, could tell that he was concerned about the same thing. His face was steady, but his eyes always gave him away. They wouldn't meet hers.

Zack was the only one who wasn't fazed by what Jerry said. He waved the comment off. "Pft," he pushed out from his mouth. "Don't listen to him. You'll be aces."

She took the same steadying breath as when she released an arrow from the longbow, just like she practiced. "We're all going to be fine," she whispered to herself as she exhaled. "We're all going to be fine."

"It's easy for Jerry to say," Ralph came around once the others caught up to him. "I bet his back doesn't even hurt anymore, the lying bastard."

They all forced a chuckle as they walked down the stairs and out of building six. There was a slight overcast that day as billowy gray clouds drifted in front of the sun. The wind kicked up and pushed against the group with blustery force before dying down again. The leaves on the trees clung to the branches for dear life until the next gust of chilled air blew through.

Once her feet touched the pavement of the parking lot, Christine's heart began to race right out of her chest and up into her throat. She looked around in search of the cause for the rapid onset of panic, but there was nothing out of the ordinary. Everything around her was calm and they were alone.

She took a few more steps and all at once she realized what it was that made her heart pound. It was the farthest she'd been away from the apartment in two months. She used to think, when locked in the apartment, that that moment of revelation would uplift her spirits, but instead she cowered at the expansive grounds. It felt unnatural to be outside, exposed and vulnerable. She tried to steady her wobbly knees as she watched the guys walk ahead without her. She shoved her hands into the pockets of her hoodie so no one would see them shake.

Ralph Sherman walked along in a casual manner. He slapped the back of his hand against Zack's bulging shoulder pad. "Hey, man, can we go out again after this? I have to make a run for something I don't think we'll find."

"Sure, but we'll have to go further out this time. Walmart's cleared out and so's the one in Valpo. We might have to take a car if we can get one to start."

They continued their conversation as if they were talking about something as simple as a stop at store on the way home from work. Christine was engrossed by their casual planning over Ralph's mysterious item.

"We're almost completely out," he continued as Christine listened in. "There's not even enough to make it through the night so I have to find more today."

"We'll find it, man. Don't worry. We always do," Zack said, looking at Ralph with a tilt of his head, his brown eyes soft and caring.

"Why don't we all go?" Liam suggested.

Ralph and Zack looked at each other from the corners of their eyes. They'd never gone out at night with Liam before. With how heavily Liam had prepared for the apocalypse, they'd barely gone out with him at all. They were a two man team and Liam saw this in their eyes as they stared at him silently.

Christine noticed too and jogged a few steps to catch up. She nudged her fiancé with her shoulder. "Actually, I have something planned for us tonight."

There was no plan and he knew this. He smiled back at her and nodded with gratitude.

"Here. You should take this," he said to her as he held out his longbow. "I don't want you to have to get close to any of the dead."

"If we see any," she said, hopeful.

Liam didn't say anything. His eyes shifted down to the pavement. The heavy crossbow hung from his back.

Christine took the longbow and shoved several arrows into her empty backpack, the tips showing from the top. She breathed in through her nostrils and out through her mouth. Over and over again, she prayed she wouldn't have to use them.

XIV.

Christine's black boots pinched her feet with every step she took, but she refused to complain. None of the guys complained, but they were all used to it. She should have worn the combat-style boots around the house to break them in more. The leather was stiff and rubbed at her heels. They walked for miles through downtown Chesterton, keeping close to the buildings along the sidewalk.

There was no one else outside, no movement inside any of the abandoned buildings. Windows were busted out of storefronts and blood was smeared across the doors. Christine looked at these familiar buildings and her eyes watered over. It was hard to swallow seeing them in such disarray.

The diner she used to go to on the weekends with her grandmother was burnt to the ground. Ashes and garbage blew in the wind. She tried to picture the details of her grandmother's face as she had so often seen it from across the table, a plate of biscuits and gravy in front of them both. But her face had faded over the years. It'd been ten years since she'd seen her.

Christine's eyes scanned the line of buildings in search of a distraction. Anything would do. They stopped by a dilapidated storefront with a sign hanging crooked over the door. "Isn't that your comic book store?" she called out to Zack.

Ralph spun around and shushed her, his eyes ready to burn her alive.

"Sorry," she whispered bitterly.

Zack kept walking as he mumbled a quick, "Yeah, that's mine."

"Shouldn't we go in, check it out? Or have you guys already done that?" She tiptoed around the subject, unsure where her place was with them. She felt like the odd man out in a close group of friends—the tag along girlfriend who nobody wanted there, not even Liam.

Zack stopped in the middle of the sidewalk. "No, we haven't."

"Well, come on!" Christine said with a grin. They hadn't searched a single place in the hour they'd been walking. What was the point? They were supposed to be collecting supplies, not sight-seeing. If they entered somewhere commonplace it would be a nice transition into the new terrifying world. Maybe they could pop in and pop out again unscathed.

"If I'm lucky it's been trashed and burned," Zack said with a laugh.

He doubled back and opened the thick glass door. The bell above didn't sound as it had for years. He looked up and saw a bloody handprint on the top of the door frame where it had been secured. He rubbed at his beard with the palm of his hand and ran it over his mouth.

His eyes lowered to take in the state of his store as everyone else stood behind him, still on the sidewalk. Shelves were turned over on their side, comic books lay torn and scattered on the dirt covered floor. A pair of legs stuck out from underneath an overturned bookcase along the back wall, a ring of blood around it.

Zack inhaled a sharp breath, but it caught in his chest and the intake was fragmented. He wanted to look over his shoulder to see if the others had noticed, but he didn't.

Instead he moved forward, deeper into the dark, bedraggled store.

His sword hit the counter with a clank as he hoisted himself up to lean over. The register was wide open and had been cleared of all its money, not that that mattered anymore. Still, he felt his stomach drop. What little he had was completely gone. He turned around to look at the wall of video games near the door. His vision blurred as he stared.

"That was where I first saw her," Zack said softly, more to himself than to the others huddled in the doorway. "Anita." He sniffed and released an anguished sigh. It was impossible not to picture her standing there, smiling at him while she pretended to browse the Wii games.

XV.

Zack looked around his bright, empty comic book store and then out the darkened windows to see if it looked like there was anyone headed toward his shop. He thought about closing early. It wasn't like anyone was going to come in anyway and even if they did, they wouldn't buy anything. He walked to the front door with a set of keys connected by a Superman keychain, but the door opened before he could lock it.

He gawked at the woman standing in front of him, keys still held outward. He didn't say a word. Anita was too beautiful to talk to, he'd decided that months ago, with her shoulder-length warm brown hair, her too cute freckles that speckled her nose, and those high waist shorts that made her legs look like they went on for miles. There was no way a girl like that would ever be interested in a comic nerd like Zack, but there she was, smiling at him in the doorway.

"Hi," she said, her cherry red lips contrasted with her snowy white teeth.

Zack tried to talk, but his words got caught in his throat and he made a guttural croak instead. His entire face turned bright red as she tried not to laugh. He cleared his throat and attempted to speak again. "Hi."

She looked around the empty store and back at Zack, who blocked the entrance. "Are you still open?"

Zack had been staring at the many tattoos that littered both Anita's arms. He blinked a few times to bring himself back. "Oh, yeah, I'm open. Sorry. Come on in." He walked quickly back behind the counter and left her to browse in peace.

Anita had come into his store a few times before. She'd meander around, look at the games, toys, and comics before leaving again. She never bought a thing. Her high heeled, red shoes clicked on the tile floor as she strolled around.

Zack picked up a small stack of receipts and shuffled through them. He looked up at her when he thought she wasn't looking. When she whirled around to face him, it caught him off guard. The receipts he held loosely in his hands fluttered down to the floor. He left them there and looked at a spiral notebook on the counter, as if he'd meant to throw the receipts to the ground all along.

"I'm Anita," she said and smiled again as she took a few steps closer to the counter.

"I know. One of the guys who was in here when you came in last week told me. Said you work over at that used bookstore a few blocks away."

"That's right," Anita said. She lifted her head upward. "I'm the manager."

Zack gave a big cheesy grin. "That's great!"

"But really I'm a writer. I just work at the bookstore to pay the bills till someone agrees to publish me," she added as she walked, one ankle crossing slightly in front of the other as she headed in a straight for Zack.

"Really? That's so cool," he said. His face grew redder the closer she got.

"What do you do? I mean, besides work at the comic book store, obviously." She rested her hands on the counter with her hip popped out.

"Actually, I own it." He didn't exude nearly as much pride and confidence as she had over his choice of careers.

Debt weighed on Zack's mind at least a little bit every minute of every day. Even as he talked to Anita, the woman he had hoped would turn around and notice him for months, he also thought about the receipts he dropped and if they would add up to any kind of profit. He doubted it. He ran his fingers through his neatly trimmed beard as he tried to recall numbers and add them up in his head.

He snapped out of it. It wasn't the time for business woes. There was a beautiful woman in front of him and she was grasping at straws to keep a conversation going for some reason. He forced his hands back into his lap and focused his attention on her again.

"I wanted to draw comics when I was little, but like you said. It's hard to pay the bills that way." He wanted to add that opening a comic store wasn't a great way to pay the bills either, but feared he'd come off as self-deprecating and depressing. He was sure pathetic, desperate, broke store owner was not high on her dating list.

Anita smiled, but this time the excitement had faded and all that was left was awkward politeness. She started to turn away, back to the shelves and bins stuffed with Mylar encased comic books. Zack had lost her. He had to get her back.

"Would you like to go for a cup of coffee sometime?" he blurted out before she'd turned her back to him.

She spun around on her heel, her face relaxed, but her eyes turned down to the ground. He never should have opened his mouth. He scolded himself inwardly as he waited in silence for her to answer. She looked back up at him. The brilliance of her eyes knocked the breath right out of his lungs. He cleared his throat.

"Sure. I'd love to," she said with a soft laugh.

Zack exhaled a sigh of relief. "Phew. Good. That would have been awkward if you'd said no."

This made Anita open up again and laugh with her entire body. Zack loved the sound of her laughter. It was loud and echoed off the walls, but still seemed petite and girlish, just like her.

"How about Sunday afternoon? I close up early usually."

Her smile faded and her face fell as she cocked her head to the side. "Oh, I'm sorry. I always go to my dad's on Sundays. It's kind of our little tradition ever since my mom died. I cook us dinner and help him clean up around the house."

"Oh, OK. No problem," Zack said. His mind worked in double-time to figure out if she was telling the truth or trying to get out of hanging out with him. "Some other time, then."

She walked toward the door and smiled at him over her bare shoulder. "Definitely." She disappeared.

Zack picked up a pen and pounded it on the counter a few times, hitting it so the tip disappeared and reappeared with every click. Was Anita telling the truth about going to her dad's, or not? It was a toss-up. On the one hand, she'd seemed sincere and she did agree to have coffee with him before he named a date, but on the other hand she probably would have left after saying yes and never set a date. In fact, that was exactly what she did. Yeah. Zack was sure that was what just happened.

He picked up the keys from the counter and swung them around his finger. He walked to the door with his skateboard tucked under his arm. After locking up, he hopped on the board and rolled down the sidewalk toward his apartment.

XVI.

Christine walked the aisles of the comic book store, focused on her job of gathering supplies, but there was nothing they could use. Her stomach sank as she wondered if the others already saw her as a burden dragging them off course. Her eyes stopped on the long, shining sword on the counter, but she laughed to herself when she realized it was the one Zack had been carrying around for months.

A loud bang made everyone spin. The door to the backroom had been thrown open. A gnarled, decaying man stumbled out at full speed, tripping over his own feet, pushing him forward even faster. Zack was knocked down as the zombie's arms thrust forward.

Ralph was the next closest. He swung his axe, but it hit the doorframe and stuck there when the ravenous corpse fell forward on all fours from the momentum of his lunge, avoiding the blade unsuspectingly.

Christine was frozen no more than fifteen feet away from it. She smelled the rot of decomposing flesh. Its skin was mottled and thin, a strange mixture of green and gray that hung loosely from its bones. Pieces flapped away from the torn muscles of its cheek.

It pushed itself upright again and grabbed ahold of the quiver that was slung over Liam's shoulder. He fell to the ground from the weight of the corpse that tugged at his back. It stood over Liam with a mouth full of jagged, broken teeth, its jaw wide open to clamp down.

"Shoot it!" Christine heard from all ends of the store. "Shoot it!"

She had Liam's longbow clutched in her sweaty hands, but she didn't raise it. All she could do was stare out at the monster before her with wide eyes, horrified to her core. Her lungs felt constricted. It hurt too much to breathe, so much that she considered stopping all together. Soon, her entire body was convulsing in fear as she watched the dead thing's teeth move closer to Liam's throat.

The sound of an arrow piercing soft skull caused the store to fall into a deadly silence. The rotting corpse fell to the ground next to Liam and didn't get back up. Ralph huffed as he stood over it. There was blood on one of his hands, the one that drove the arrow tip into the zombie's porous skull.

He turned to Christine with his fists clenched. "I told you we shouldn't of let her come," he growled to her even though he meant to address Zack and Liam. He took a few strong steps toward her, closing the gap between them so he towered over her. "I'm not killing myself so you can feel like you actually contribute to something around here. I have a wife and baby. Did you ever think about what would happen to them if I wasn't around to take care of them?"

Christine tried to force her lips move, but all that came out was a soft uncontrollable trembling. "I...I..." she stammered and then fell silent.

"Of course you didn't! You run around here in your fake-ass combat boots like you know what you're doing, like you know what's going on outside the walls of your safe, little apartment, but you don't!" his voice rose until he was shouting.

"Hey, come on," Zack said, taking a few steps with his hands out. "Let's just—"

"No!" Ralph shouted over him. "I'm not dying because she's some bored housewife who wants to play warrior princess. It's bullshit!" His arms waved wildly as he yelled.

Zack placed his hands slowly and carefully on Ralph's shoulder and guided him to the door. "Why don't we step outside for a minute, cool off?"

Ralph heaved heavy, angered breaths, but he didn't object. They disappeared outside to leave Christine alone with Liam, who stood next to the body of the zombie that almost ended his life.

Christine's eyes darted between the two of them. Tears spilled out and down her cheeks as her shoulders convulsed. "I'm sorry," she said between sobs. "I'm sorry. I'm sorry," she kept saying whenever she caught her breath.

Liam didn't go to her right away. He stood there as she broke down. The side of his foot rested against the zombie's pliable head as blood oozed around his boot. He could barely hear Christine's apologies. His mind was lost on what had happened. He questioned whether he was really standing or if he had died. There was the overwhelming urge to look down, but the fear of seeing himself lying half eaten on the floor kept him from doing so. His stomach lurched, but he swallowed, forcing the bile back down.

Christine's sobbing grew louder in his head until he was forced to look at her. The realization that he'd survived rushed over him like a tidal wave. He ran to her and pulled her head to his chest. She wrapped her arms tightly around his waist and cried into his shirt, still mumbling a slew of apologies. He shushed her as he held onto her head. "It's all right," he said in a soft voice. "Everything's OK. I'm all right." Her body shook with heaving sobs.

He wondered if he'd just lied to her or if he told the truth. Was he really unharmed? He hadn't had time to check himself over. Maybe he was bit and didn't even know it because of an adrenaline rush, or maybe the bites don't hurt because of some weird toxicity in their saliva. He had no idea what it felt like to be bitten by one of those things and it scared him. Instantly, he wanted to push himself from her and check his entire body. Instead, he clung tighter until her sobbing started to secede.

"Let's go home," he said as he peeled her from him and looked into her drenched face.

She sniffed and wiped the wetness from her cheeks and eyes. With a nod, she released a small, quick laugh. "Yeah. OK. Let's go."

As Liam guided her out of the store, his arm wrapped tightly around her shoulders, he allowed his eyes to wander down to his own body, where he saw that the front of his shirt was stained with fresh, wet blood.

XVII.

Back at the apartment, Liam warmed water in a large pot over the gas stove. Christine sat on the couch with her knees pulled up to her chest as she bit the nail on her thumb. Occasionally, Liam turned to look at her. He wondered if there was anything he could say to ease her guilt. He was still at a loss for words by the time steam rose from the water. He carried the metal pot into the bathroom with both hands and filled the tub with about an inch of water. He closed the door behind him.

Liam Scott stared at himself in the mirror as he peeled off the blood stained clothes that clung to his body. As the shirt came off over his head, he closed his eyes, not ready to see if the blood was his or not. He opened one first and let out a sigh at the sight of his pale skin. There wasn't a single scratch on him. He lowered himself into the warm water and started to wash vigorously with his loofa. He scrubbed so hard his skin turned a bright red.

Outside the bathroom door, Christine got up and paced the living room floor. How could she have been so stupid, so cowardly? Liam could have been killed because she froze when she saw that *thing*. How could she have thought of them as sick people? They weren't people. They were monsters.

It was the first time she'd seen one of them up close. The stench alone was enough to convince her it was no longer a living being, but a walking, rotting, dead corpse that was only capable of one thought—must eat everything and everyone in sight.

She pulled her hair tie out and let her long, blonde hair fall down to her waist. It swung back and forth at her back as she continued her repetitive path from the window to the kitchen counter, blood-stained rotted teeth burned into her brain.

It could have reached out and grabbed her if someone hadn't been there to swoop in and save the day, as Ralph did. He was right. Going out with her was dangerous. Maybe the only thing she was good for was sitting on the porch like Jerry did to watch over things from a safe distance through binoculars.

The thought caused her mood to sink and crash. She didn't want to be that. She didn't want to be useless in the new world. Jerry was watch guard now. She had nothing that was her own to contribute to their survival. After Luke's disappearance, she wasn't sure how long they could rely on Zack, Ralph, or Jerry for support. One day they would be gone too, and she would be all Liam had left to count on.

She marched over to the patio door and wrenched it open, snatching up the crossbow from the floor on her way out.

Liam heard the door shut hard, but he didn't move from the tub. The warmth of the water calmed his nerves. He leaned his head back and sank down to try to submerge as much of his body as he could in the low water. What he wouldn't give for a full tub, just one more time.

Even though he tried to clear his head of any lingering thoughts, all he could see was Christine standing there in the store with a terrified look possessing her normally composed face. When he pushed her from his mind, the zombie that had almost latched onto him replaced her. There was no relaxing.

He stood up and wrapped a towel around his waist and another over his shoulders. When he looked in the mirror again, he thought he saw a bit of who he used to be before everything happened, but the image faded away as quickly as it had appeared. He left to check on Christine.

The cool breeze hit his wet hair immediately and chilled him to the bone. He shivered and pulled the towel on his shoulders down to wrap around his arms and torso. Christine was hunched over the crossbow as she balanced it on the ground and tried to pull back to lock the arrow in place. She grunted, each time getting it a little further before she had to let go and it snapped back.

"God, dammit!" she said, halfway between a yell and a whimper. She pulled back on it again. She gritted her teeth and growled as she used all her strength.

Liam walked over to her and put a hand on her shoulder as the other one reached for the crossbow. She let him take it from her. He leaned it against the wall and sat down in the chair, looking at the other one for her to sit next to him.

She stood up straight. Her face was scrunched in anger, concealing the tears that gathered in her eyes. "Why couldn't I do it?" she blurted out. "Why couldn't I shoot it?"

She looked to Liam, but didn't wait for him to answer.

He didn't know how to answer her, anyhow.

"When I left this morning I was all ready to play the part, be one of you guys, kill one of those things if I had to. I really thought I could do it, but I don't know…" Her voice was rapid and loud as she turned to look over the railing.

Liam let her talk as long as she wanted. She needed to figure out what happened earlier, what caused her to freeze up after all the hours of training she put in. Only then could she work on fixing the problem.

"Maybe I'm not cut out for this world," she said with a shaky voice as she looked down at the darkened parking lot. "Maybe I don't deserve to be here." Tears spilled from her eyes and ran down her rosy cheeks. Her cheeks burned with embarrassment. Why couldn't she stop crying over everything? Why was she so weak?

Liam stood up and wrapped his arms around her. "It's all right, love. You did your best. Nobody was hurt. Everything is all right."

"It was a person once," she said with her head resting against his chest, wiping at the tears on her face. "It was a person like you or me and somehow it turned into this…this ugly, disgusting monster!"

He stroked her hair and rested his chin gently on the top of her head. "I know," he said. "I know. But you can't think like that when one of them in trying to kill you. You can't."

"What if it was me?" she asked as she looked up into his hazel eyes. There were dark circles under them that hadn't been there before. "What if I was one of them? Could you kill me?"

He looked back at her. Her soft, pink lips were slightly parted as she awaited his answer. There was a deep bow in her upper lip that he caught himself staring at on many occasions. He took a shallow breath. "I don't know," he said honestly.

"Do you think they can feel anything anymore?"

His eyes widened as he stared out at the trees swaying in the cool breeze. Leaves scattered through the air before they fell to the ground. He'd hadn't thought about it before. He hadn't allowed himself to. Now the question beat against his brain for a definitive answer.

"Do you think they still have thoughts?"

Liam released his hold on her. He scratched his head, not knowing what else to do. He couldn't answer any of her questions. He considered promising to think about it, but closed his mouth again before he let the words escape. If he wanted to survive he couldn't think about it at all. He couldn't see them for who they used to be. He could only see them for what they were in that moment—already dead.

"Why don't we go inside?" he said, placing his hand on the small of her back.

The rest of the day was spent in silence and solitude. Liam curled up on the floor with his back against the couch as he read through his old boss's journal. Deep down he had hopes that something in Dr. Hyde's writing would inspire him to creating a cure. It was a fool's dream, he knew that. But he couldn't help hoping for it.

The man had been a genius at creating vaccines. The flu that was supposed to wipe out more than half of mankind was stopped because of him. Of course, it was replaced with an even worse condition that the doctor was not around to cure, but Liam still was.

Some nights he lie awake thinking about Dr. Hyde and wondered if he had been the one to get sick, if the doctor would have been able to stop it from spreading and cure the ones infected. Every time he came to the same conclusion— you can't cure death.

Not that it mattered in the end. Liam was alive and the one man he believed could cure anything was dead and all he had was a journal. There had to be *something* in that journal. There just had to be.

XVIII.

Dr. Victor Faustus Hyde
Friday June 12, 2020

I think I've done it! I think we've done it! Earlier this week we developed a vaccine with some of the mutated plants from Dr. Scott's lab. (I knew that Brit would be invaluable!) He hasn't been here long at all and he's already provided us with the answer to preventing this wretched flu from taking over the world.

I tested the vaccine on various lab rats, all with the flu virus given to them. Some were in the advanced stages while others were not showing any symptoms yet. I'll be damned if every single lab rat didn't pull through and rid itself of this God forsaken flu!

I have to get this out to the people. I have to release it before anyone else figures out what we've done here and tries to duplicate it, pass it off as their own. This is my vaccine. Our vaccine. No one will be the face of ending the end of humanity, but me and my team.

Clinical trials are required, but we don't have the time. I'd have to seek out people, gather volunteers, (not that it would be hard to do. Everyone is scared to death of this flu. They'll take anything we say might stop it.), give them the vaccine, watch them, study them, record their every symptom, lack of symptom, and move. I'd have to organize all this information into a lovely cockamamie presentation that proves the vaccine works. This. Vaccine. Works.

So here is the start of my recordings of the clinical trial.

Patient One
June 12, 2020
11:49pm
Age 58
Native of New England, currently residing in the Midwest.
Has not contracted the flu virus yet, but will be injected with it in mere minutes.
Marital Status, Single. Never married. No children. No surviving parents. No family to speak of at all.

11:53pm The flu virus was injected. There was no sensation to speak of aside from the sting of the needle.

June 13, 2020

03:36am I've given sufficient amount of time for the virus to inhabit my body. We're told it acts at an alarmingly fast rate once it enters. Already I am feeling a touch of nausea and warmth in my head. Fascinating when compared to the common influenza which takes 24 to 96 hours to show symptoms. This flu is extremely advanced. Mother Nature must be pissed off.

03:41am The vaccine has been injected. Upon injection there was the sting of the needle and then a dull burn as the liquid entered the body. This faded as the vaccine dispersed.

04:57am Already my rising temperature has begun its decent back to normality. The nausea is also subsiding. I am done for the day as it is Saturday now.

I can't wait for the coming week to see what happens.

XIX.

After practicing her kill techniques all day, Christine Moore gave up, just as Liam had. He didn't instruct her any longer on how she should stand or hold her weapon of choice for the day. Instead, he shut himself inside and read from the frayed leather journal when he wasn't out with the guys. So, Christine sat herself down on the window seat and read the book she could never finish, *Anna Karenina*. She'd started the massive classic five years ago and was still only halfway through it. What else did she have to do now that the world had fallen apart and she wasn't fit to go out in it?

As night fell, she got distracted by her reflection growing more vivid in the window pane. She caught herself glancing over to look into her own face, lost in thought. Even with nothing else to do but read, she wasn't getting through the eight hundred plus pages of miniscule type. She forced her eyes back onto the book, but only a minute passed before she realized she was looking at herself again.

She closed the book and let it fall against her leg as she sat perfectly still. The fireplace gave off a warm, orange glow that spread throughout the darkened living room.

"You know what I don't miss," she finally said as she sat up to cross her legs Indian-style. She leaned forward with a cheeky smile. "Telemarketers calling during dinner. How did they even get our cellphone numbers?"

Liam chuckled despite what he'd just read. He set down the journal and bent his right leg up and rested his elbow on it, bringing his thumb to his lips as he thought. "I don't miss….eBooks," he said, looking straight at Christine. "I'm glad that paperbacks are the reigning king of the book world."

She threw her head back and laughed as she clutched *Anna Karenina* to her chest. "Low blow!" she said through giggles. "This apartment isn't big enough to house every book we own, so I was saving us money by using an eReader. We didn't have to rent out a storage unit to house hundreds of books that we would only read once."

They both laughed fully, their eyes squinted and creased in the corners.

"Speaking of saving money," she said as she tried to control herself. "I don't miss saving all our loose change for a big, expensive vacation that we're never going to take."

"We could've taken one," Liam said through his laughter. It tapered off in his throat.

"Yeah, right! Between your sixty hours a week at the lab and my seventy-five at the firm, when could we have found the time to take a vacation?"

"Well, now we don't have to save our pennies anymore," he said with a smile. "We can go wherever we want whenever we want." He made a sweeping gesture, as if the world was theirs for the taking.

The faint screams of Lilly crying across the hall brought the conversation to a halt. They listened, staring down at their hands. "I guess Ralph's not back with the formula yet." Liam's mouth pulled back into a sad grimace. "Shall we go to bed?" He picked up the journal again and held it to his chest.

Even with the bedroom door closed, tucked under the warm blankets they'd recently dug out of the storage, they could still hear the shrill wails of a starving Lilly. It penetrated their ears and burrowed deep inside their heads.

Christine turned over on her side with her back to Liam. She took long, slow breaths in hopes that he would think she was asleep. The last thing she wanted to do was talk. Ralph and Zack were out there and she wouldn't know until morning if they were alive or dead. Meanwhile, a sweet nine month old baby was wailing her heart out from stomach pains her mother couldn't subside. She thought about going over there to see if she could help in any way, but the fear of running into Ralph kept her tucked in bed.

She closed her eyes and repeated the world "sleep" slowly and quietly, almost making no sound at all, until she drifted off to another place in time.

XX.

A five-year-old Christine stood on the Calumet bike path that ran alongside the train tracks near the Dunes. The hot, summer sun beat against her back. She looked down at the vibrant green grass and searched the wildflowers for the perfect one to pick. She smiled a toothy grin as her tiny hand lunged forward, plucking a purple flower from the overgrown weeds. It was the perfect addition to her boring collection of white daisies and yellow dandelions.

"Grandma, look what I found!" she said, running over to an older woman further up the path.

Her grandmother stood with her back turned to little Christine and her older sister was even further away, squatted in the tall grass as she picked blade after blade and tossed them aside out of boredom.

"Grandma!" Christine said again, but stopped short.

She dropped the flowers in her hand when she heard a slow rattle from deep within her grandmother's chest. The white haired woman turned around slowly. Her feet dragged on the gravel pathway. When Christine saw the mangled face, and entire side completely gone, blood oozing from her missing jaw as she gurgled from deep within her throat, she screamed with everything she had.

"Christine," she heard someone say from a distance. "Christine." She sat upright and she gasped for air. Liam was sitting next to her. "You were having a bad dream."

She panted as sweat dripped down from her forehead and neck.

"All right, love?" Liam asked with his eyes still half closed, also awoken from a deep sleep.

"Yeah, go back to bed. I'm fine." She lowered herself down onto the cool gel pillow and turned her head to look at him, but he was already fast asleep. She took a deep breath. Would she ever dream of anything else again?

As soon as she turned over and tried to fall asleep again, Lilly's cried returned to her canals. She picked up her phone from the bedside table. It was one in the morning. Ralph still wasn't back yet. Or if he was, then he hadn't found any food for the baby. She squeezed her eyes shut tight, and willed herself to sleep. "Fall asleep, fall asleep, fall asleep," she repeated in her head over and over again. When she opened her eyes, the sun was up and the room was silent. Lilly had finally stopped crying.

XXI.

Christine's eyes opened at the same moment Liam's did. She debated rolling over and pretending to go back to sleep while he got up and ready for the morning meeting with everyone. Her face burned with embarrassment as she replayed her failures at the comic book store in her head.

They made it look so easy, shooting something that was once human through the skull. She knew the only way she would get over her fear was to face it. And she would start by facing the group. When she threw the covers off, her body shivered. The morning was even cooler than the previous one, the dreaded one where she showed everyone just how much of a coward she was.

She tossed her legs over the side of the bed and hung her head to stare at the ground. Who was she kidding? She wasn't going to leave the complex ever again. Ralph wouldn't let her. She shook her head and settled on the decision to go to the meeting, collect the walkie-talkie from Jerry, and resume her spot on the patio with her binoculars. The thought made her entire body feel heavy and slow as she shuffled to the darkened bathroom.

With the scrape of a match, she lit the two candles on the back of the toilet and pulled her hair up into a ponytail. It was lopsided and pieces were already falling down, but she didn't care. She didn't bother to change out of her sweatpants either. Instead, she pulled one of Liam's knitted sweaters over her gray t-shirt and stepped into a pair of wooly slipper boots.

"Good morning, beautiful," Liam said cheerfully as he opened a box of cereal and poured it into a bowl for her.

Plain, crunchy wheat. Again. She collapsed onto the one bar stool they had left and looked up at fiancé with droopy eyes.

"Sorry, love, it's all we have for breakfast. Would you like a cup of black tea?"

"Black tea?" she asked as she sat up straight and craned her neck to look over the counter. "No coffee?"

"I'm afraid we're all out of the instant coffee, as well."

She sighed and sunk back down into her chair, giving a weak smile. She let herself drop from the stool without touching her cereal and shuffled to the front door. "Let's get this over with."

"Oh, come on. It won't be that bad," he said with a smile and draped an arm over her shoulder. "I bet they won't even remember." He gave her a wide-tooth, ridiculous grin.

She looked up at him with a stony face and narrow eyes. Inside she wanted to laugh. Outside she was like ice, unwilling to thaw for anyone, even Liam. He unlocked the deadbolts and they stepped into the open hallway where a chilly breeze whipped through like a wind tunnel. Liam pulled down the sleeves of his navy blue ribbed shirt. He folded his arms tightly to his thin body for warmth.

Christine looked at him with her head lolled to the side. She'd been feeling so sorry for herself that it was almost too much trouble to support the weight of her own head now. All she wanted to do was crawl back into bed and hide under the covers. "You should grab your jacket," she said to Liam flatly.

"Right." He snapped his fingers and popped back inside to grab his wool-lined jeans jacket from the coat closet.

Zack came out of his apartment to join them, but he wasn't wearing the usual padded gear anymore. Instead, he had on a heavy zip up camo print jacket, matching pants, and a black beanie hat, no helmet and no paintball mask. Christine eyed him lazily as she leaned against the wall, wondering where or who he got the new outfit from. The image of Zack tearing the clothes off a dead body made her scrunch her face and look away.

Liam came back out with two mugs of hot black tea and handed Christine one. She took it and held it between her hands for warmth. She hated black tea. In the morning she drank coffee. That was her routine for the last ten years. Did the end of the world have to mean the end of every good routine she had? She brought the mug to her face and took a tiny sip. It was disgusting, but she drank it anyway.

Christine didn't notice Jerry as he made his way up the stairs to stand next to her. He held out a black walkie-talkie while his other hand rested in the pocket of his hoodie. He didn't say a word to her. She wondered who had told him about the incident at the comic book store. With a quick snatch, she shoved the handheld radio into her pocket.

"I feel like I should tell you all something," Zack said. Everyone was unprepared for his voice to shatter the silence of the early morning. Liam gave a quick jolt and spilled tea down his chin.

Christine perked up and lowered her mug. "Look, we don't have to talk about it, OK?" she jumped in before Zack could say anything to further humiliate her. "Don't worry. I'm staying home. I don't want to freeze up and get any of you killed so there's really nothing else left to say except I'm sorry, OK? I'm sorry..."

Zack gazed at her, brow furrowed, and shook his head. "No, actually, what I was gonna say..."

Christine's face turned bright red. She lowered her eyes and raised her mug to her mouth again.

"Ralph went out by himself late last night to find formula for Lilly."

"What?" Liam spat, spilling tea on himself for the second time. He wiped at his chin. "Why would you let him go by himself?"

"He snuck out, all right? I'm not the guy's babysitter. Anyway, I don't know if he made it back or not. He never checked in. Lilly stopped crying at about two this morning so she either wore herself out or..." His entire body tensed. He couldn't finish his thought.

"That's our first stop, then," Liam said. He handed Christine his half empty mug.

She set both their cups down on the ground outside the door. "I think I'm going to come with you."

Liam looked at her, but didn't dare say anything to argue her decision, though every ounce of his body wanted to. She saw it in his eyes.

"Just to check on Sally and Lilly. I'm sure they're tired of being cooped up alone all day, every day." She wanted to add the words, "just like me," but stopped herself. There was no reason to make Liam feel bad over her own weaknesses.

He nodded and adjusted the red, rectangular glasses on his face. "Let's go, then."

Liam, Christine, Zack, and Jerry stopped in front of the Sherman's door. The apartment was silent. They waited, each holding their breath as they hoped to hear any indication that everything was all right behind the heavy, white door.

Liam wanted to go inside, but felt like his feet were stuck in quicksand. All he could think about was when they hoped to find Luke and instead found a rotting zombie. Driving an arrow through a stumbling, hungry corpse was the hardest thing he ever had to do in his life. Ralph was going to be worse. Sally was going to be worse. He couldn't even think beyond that. His stomach lurched and he had to close his eyes to steady himself.

"Screw this waiting bullshit," Zack growled as he jammed the crowbar into the door. It popped open and hit the wall, bouncing back at them. He stuck his arm out to catch it before it closed again.

Christine immediately screamed. "God! No!" she cried over and over again. Her face hung long with her mouth open as tears poured out of her eyes. Liam grabbed ahold of her and forced her head into his chest so she wouldn't have to look.

Sally lay strewn across the ottoman in front of the couch with her stomach ripped open, her intestines, guts, and entrails on the floor. There was a look of terror petrified onto her bloodied face. The back of her skull was cracked open. The massive, gaping hole leaked blood and brains onto the beige carpet.

Liam had to look away as well before he wasn't able to hold his stomach any longer. Saliva gathered in his mouth faster than he could swallow it. His head spun and he was sure he was going to pass out. He thanked God he was able to stay upright for Christine. She sobbed hysterically into his shirt, her cries more like shrill screams.

Zack couldn't believe the amount of blood. He'd always thought horror movies over did it, throwing the fake stuff on the floors, walls, even the ceiling. He looked up at the red splatters that dripped from the white ceiling fan. He felt oddly detached as he took it all in.

That's when he realized that Ralph wasn't there. His shoulders sunk with heavy dread. He didn't want to be the one to tell him what happened to his wife while he was gone.

No one asked where Lilly was. They couldn't bring themselves to.

A loud thud came from the bedroom in the back and interrupted his thoughts. The door was cracked open and a shadow passed in front of it.

"Take Christine back," Zack ordered Liam.

"But—"

"Just go!"

The body of Ralph Sherman staggered into the living room. Blood drenched his face and dripped down onto the shirt he'd been wearing when he left the day before. His eyes were marbleized, lifeless, a rotting shade of chartreuse with a white glaze. He slammed into the wall, bounced off, and kept walking while his feet scuffed along the carpet. He opened his mouth and exhaled a wet gurgle. The gap between Zack and Ralph diminished by the second.

Zack's eyes grazed over the room, away from Ralph, away from Sally's mangled, bloodied body, and rested on an empty pink stained blanket on the floor. His eyebrows raised and pressed together as his eyes widened. Tears gathered, making it hard to see Ralph's staggering corpse moving closer, arms outstretched to grab ahold of him. At the last second, Zack backed out of the apartment and slammed the door shut. There was a relentless pounding from the other side.

It was impossible to stand upright any longer. Zack rested his hands on his knees and let the tears fall to the floor as he doubled over. His body racked with agonizing sobs. Every time he tried to take a breath it felt like a knife was being plunged into his lungs.

Jerry put a comforting hand on his back. "If you need me to, I'll do it."

Zack forced a deep breath and released it slowly from his lips. He wiped the wetness from his cheeks and beard before he straightened himself up. His eyes blinked a few times to clear any residual agony from his face. "No, I should do it."

Christine and Liam watched from around the corner of the hallway in silence as Zack opened the door and kicked out his foot. It hit Ralph's putrid body square in the chest and knocked it backward into the apartment again. Zack disappeared. The door shut behind him. Less than a minute later he emerged, wiping oily blood from his sword.

Part Four

"There is no such thing as a residual soil."

— Roger Parsons, 1981

I.

The wind blew through the trees, picking the leaves off one by one until they floated down to rest on the hard, cool dirt of the Dunes State Park. The only heat Lonnie Lands and his group of wanderers felt in the last chilling weeks was from the low burning embers of the fire built only at night. The white crescent moon shone through the branches, but not enough to see if anything was stumbling through the woods for a late night snack.

Lee Hickey leaned his head back against a tree and closed his eyes to fall asleep. Mitchell was curled up next to him with a backpack shoved under his head and his shotgun tucked between his legs. Carolyn sat on a log next to Rowan with her legs crossed and her arms wrapped tightly around her waist for extra warmth.

"Would you lay off, Big Bertha," Lonnie whined as he sharpened a large stick with a hunting knife. "We'll find an apartment when we're ready to find one. I'm not just going to settle in the first shithole I see so that these fucking zombies can eat my face off while I sleep."

"No, of course not. Better to lie out in the open where they can stumble upon you and eat you while you sleep."

He lowered his stick and knife to glare at her. She matched him, her gray, thin eyes never blinking as they bore into his soul. The rest of the group sat back and listened to the conversation with smiled on their faces, like it was a reading of *The Night before Christmas*. Every day since Lonnie agreed to Gretchen's demands for shelter two months ago, Gale had thrown it back in his face when he came up with nothing and they spent another cold night in the woods. It lead to long and heated arguments and entertainment for everyone not involved.

Dan Anderson leaned back on his elbows on a thin bedding of dry leaves and stretched his legs out toward the pathetic fire. The back and forth of Gale and Lonnie had become a comfort, something constant he could always count on in an inconstant world. He pulled out a crumpled cigarette from his pocket and lit it with a small plastic lighter.

"I don't know why ya'll worry about settling down somewhere when you don't even seem care about the big picture here," Lonnie said as he always did when he wanted to end the bickering.

Gale rolled her eyes. She knew where he was going.

"Well, *I'm* not going to make babies with you," Gale said with a wrinkled nose. "And if you go anywhere near Gretchen, I'll kill you."

"Gee, thanks for the love," Carolyn Bock said, but no one paid her any attention.

Lonnie laughed fully with his head thrown back. "Oh yeah, Big Bertha? What are you going to do? Sit on my face?"

"You wish, asshole."

Lonnie stuck out his tongue and faked a dry heave.

Gale stuck up her middle finger. She violently and repeatedly thrust it up into the air.

Rowan Brady sat with his elbows resting on his knees and his hands clasped together as he leaned in for warmth from the fire. He looked into Lonnie's face, the orange flames dancing devilishly in front of him. Even though

Lonnie was laughing there was still something off about him, something careless and alarming, something that made Rowan want to throw in the towel, switch teams, and find permanent shelter. "Maybe finding somewhere to settle wouldn't be the worst idea. We find shelter first and then we can think about the future."

"There is no future if everyone dies," Lonnie retorted. "There's no point in continuing at all. We might as well just kill ourselves now." He looked at Dan. "And if we try to make our home in an empty apartment that's already proven to be a death trap, then we're all dead. If apartments were safe, then people would already be living in them. Come on now. Use your noggins here people."

Dan ignored Lonnie and leaned over to Lee. He hit the Irishman in his large arm with the back of his slim black hand. "Hey, man, you want one?" He held out a bent menthol.

Lee shook his head and turned away. Dan shrugged his shoulders and stuffed the cigarette back into his pocket for later.

Gretchen, who was sitting on Dan's other side, leaned in close to him. "I don't want a whole one, but do you mind if we share?"

Dan grinned and leaned her way, their foreheads almost touching together. He handed her the one from between his lips. She took a long drag and blew the smoke upward. "God, that's good," she sighed.

"Maybe the only good thing left." He took it from her fingers and sucked on it hard.

Lonnie threw the stick he'd been sharpening. It cracked against a tree trunk and fell nosily onto a pile of crunchy red and orange leaves. He stood up and stomped off into the darkness of the woods. "Fucking dyke…stupid-ass… fucking fag…." He grumbled to himself as he left.

"I'm not gay," Dan spoke up even though no one asked. "I just…always enjoyed the company of women better than men. Find their friendship more comforting."

Gretchen smiled and placed a hand on his knee. "And we've found your company extremely comforting as well. You've really come a long way since we found you."

"It's weird, you know, on Halloween I used to go to the clubs and DJ dressed up like one of these…zombies. And this year I'm sitting on the ground, freezing my ass off, hoping one of them doesn't eat me alive," Dan laughed to himself.

"Is it really Halloween?" Gretchen's eyes lit up for a moment, but then the light faded again when she remembered that it didn't matter what day it was. Holidays were meaningless. There was nothing left to celebrate except making it to see another day.

"Um, yeah. I'm pretty sure," Dan said as he pulled out a small notebook from his pocket. He opened it up to reveal a two year calendar. "I…I think it's important, y'know? It's important to remember something like the date or the holidays. If we lose sight of everything completely then we might never get it back."

Gretchen stared at the crackling fire as it sank lower below the feeble sticks. She wrapped the oversized black leather jacket she'd found in a Target tighter around her as a shiver trickled down her spine. "Maybe it's already lost," she said. "And things will never be the same again."

Dan closed his calendar and put it back in the pocket of his loose jeans. "If that's the case, I'll stop after the two years are up."

Gretchen wondered if he was talking about the calendar or life. She didn't dare ask him. She didn't want to know. She let it go and changed the subject. "When you said you dressed up like a zombie," she started to say while still staring into the fire. "Do you think that would work?"

Dan sat upright and looked at her with a furrowed brow. "What do you mean?"

"I mean, if we dressed up like the dead, do you think they'd, I don't know, ignore us?"

He sat in silence as he thought hard about it.

Gale snorted. "I don't know about you, but I'm not smearing guts and blood all over myself for the rest of my miserable life, wandering around these goddamn woods like one of those goddamn zombie pricks. No thanks."

"I don't think it would work anyway," Dan finally answered. He threw the sticks he found on the ground into the dying fire, causing it to pop and grow. "We're alive. Blood flows through our veins. That's why they want us. We're fresh meat. Whether we disguise ourselves or not, I think they'll still be able to detect that in us."

Gretchen lost herself in the orange flames and wood, what little hope she had burning up with it.

A scream came from the darkness behind them. A slew of curses carried through the cool breeze and became clearer as Lonnie approached. Everyone jumped to their feet within seconds, their weapons gripped tightly in their hands.

Lonnie Lands reappeared from the trees with a girl stumbling behind him. He dragged her by her long, brown hair as she cussed him out with every horrible word known to man and a few she invented. When he tossed her to the ground at his feet, her hardened face was illuminated by the fire.

Gretchen stared with her mouth open. Gale lowered her fists. Mitchel gave a long exhale as he let his shotgun rest at his side. Dan fumbled in his pocket for the crumpled cigarette. Rowan patted his hip for the small nine-millimeter pistol he usually kept holstered on him at all times, but it wasn't there. He'd given it to Lonnie to clean and he got it back. Lee was the only one who hadn't bothered to stand, still sitting on the ground with his back against the tree.

"Found this one skulking right outside our camp, casing the place."

The girl looked up at Lonnie. Her hands rubbed the back of her head where he had tugged on her hair. "No! I wasn't!" she yelled.

"Shut up!" Lonnie growled. There was a rustling in a nearby bush. Everyone snapped to look. Seconds went by without another sound and the focus slowly shifted back to the teenage girl. "She was probably gonna run back to her own group and tell 'em about us so they could come and take everything we have."

Gale chuckled and lowered herself back down on the log. "Like what? We don't have anything."

"And that's somehow my fucking fault, right?" Lonnie boomed. His voice bounced off the trees and back to the group staring at him.

"Would you shut up?" Gretchen hissed. "They're going to come if you keep it up."

Lonnie took a deep breath and closed his eyes. When he opened them again, he stared straight into the teenage girl's scrunched, red face. "Who are you and what are you doing here?"

She continued to look around without answering. Her eyes met Gretchen's and they burned with searing hatred.

Gretchen took a step back and felt compelled to look away.

"What do we do with her?" Rowan asked from across the fire.

"I can think of a few things." Lonnie walked over to her and pulled her up by the arm. He leaned in close to her neck and smelled her hair, rubbing it between his fingers. "What do you say, sweetheart? Want to save mankind tonight?" He laughed and looked to Rowan, who chuckled weakly.

She clamped her mouth shut and clenched her jaw as she turned away from him.

"Knock it off," Gale said casually with a wave of her hand. Lonnie was all talk and no follow through, and everyone knew it.

"Leave the poor girl alone. It looks like she's been through enough," Gretchen added.

"You had your chance," Lonnie as he pointed at her.

The barrel of a small, black gun stared Gretchen in the face. She shut her mouth and balled her fists at her side. A shiver ran down her spine and into her loins as she fought the urge to pee.

Lonnie turned back to the girl and ran the side of the gun down her bronzed cheek. She squeezed her eyes shut.

"Let her go," a low, voice growled from the outer edges of the camp.

Lonnie looked up from the girl's bare neck to see Lee standing, his fists clenched. He loosened his grip on her arm, but didn't back away. The small chuckles that escaped his lips filled the formidable silence. "Yeah?" Lonnie waved the gun around in front of him. "And what are *you* going to do about it, Nurse Lee?"

Without a moment's hesitation, Lee advanced on Lonnie with the determined glide of a quarterback. Lonnie pushed the girl at him, but the hulking man sidestepped with ease as she fell to the ground.

Lonnie had his hands raised by the time Lee reached him, but they did nothing to help him. A hard fist drove into the side of Lonnie's wide head, knocking him to the ground. He was out cold.

With a bull-like snort, Lee stomped back to the tree he'd been leaning against and plopped back down on the dirt.

The young girl pushed herself off the ground and brushed the dirt from her hands and burgundy track pants. She turned to scan the group and stopped when she saw the tall, muscular man who'd saved her.

"Lee?" she called softly. "Lee Hickey?"

He didn't say anything.

She ran to him and threw herself into his lap, burring her face in his neck as she squeezed him to her. She was sobbing and laughing, which unnerved everyone who stood and watched in confused silence.

The girl pulled away and gazed at him. Her swirling brown eyes swam with tears, her freckled face was smooth and tanned, and her straight brown hair fell down to the middle of her back. "Do you remember me? From the ER?"

He continued to look into her eyes without saying a word.

"Olivia Darling," she said.

The slightest twitch in the corners of his eyes gave him away as they glossed over.

She threw herself onto him again and wrapped her arms around his neck. "I can't believe it's really you!"

II.

Lonnie Lands groaned on the ground as he held his head. He threw his arms in a fit around him and rolled onto all fours before he pushed himself up. "You're going to regret that, you stupid Irish fuck!" He marched with heavy footsteps over the where Lee and the girl sat. "She's mine! I found her!"

Before Lonnie knew what happened he was down on the ground again, this time with his arm pinned behind his back and a heavy weight resting on his spine, ready to snap it in two.

"What the fuck?" he spattered, trying to turn over to see who was on him. "Get the fuck off me!" With enough wriggling he was able to catch a quick glimpse of his assailant. "I said get the fuck off me, Big Bertha, you bitch!"

Gale tightened the grip on his arm and pulled it back even further, causing him to scream and writhe in pain. "You might want to keep quiet unless you want me to feed you to one of those dead things walking around out there. Don't think I won't." Her voice was quiet, calm, and terrifying. "I'd be more than happy to do it. And it's *Colonel* Big Bertha bitch of the United States Marine Corp, you stupid prick."

Everyone stared in awe across the smoldering fire. They had never seen Gale move so fast before. There hadn't been a single day where she hadn't waddled behind everyone, complaining about her swollen ankles, aching back, and anything else she could come up with. None of those things seemed to bother her as she sat on Lonnie's back, pinning him down with the ease of a well-trained Marine.

"Yeah, right," Lonnie said, but was cut off when she twisted his arm again. He howled, but quickly clamped his mouth shut when he remembered her threat. His nostrils flared as he tried to breathe through the pain.

"I've been wanting to do this for a long time." She jumped up and stood with her fists raised. "Come on."

Lonnie staggered to his feet as he cradled his sore arm. If it'd been bent back any further, his shoulder would have dislocated. He glared at Gale who beckoned him forward with her hands.

"Let's go, baby boot camper. Let's see if your eight weeks of training is any match for my twenty-five years."

Lonnie tried to stand up straight, but his body ached too much to allow it. Heat rose and flushed his rounded face. He wanted to attack with everything he had. How did she know he'd only just graduated from Army boot camp before everything went down?

"I don't need this," he said, wiping the blood off his lips, where it had scraped the hard dirt on his way down. "I don't need any of you." He turned and took a few steps away from the light of the fire and then turned back around. "Come on, Mitch. Let's go."

Mitchell Barnes looked to the group with large eyes. He didn't move his feet. "Why me?" he asked as he clutched his shotgun in both hands.

"I'm going to show you how a real man takes care of things and survives."

Mitchell's dark eyes drifted around questioningly. What did Lonnie mean by that? Was he going to finally find them someplace safe for them to live with more food, water, and supplies? His body swayed towards Lonnie and then away as he considered his options.

"Are you coming or not?" The stocky blond didn't wait for an answer before he stalked off into the trees.

Gretchen placed a hand on Mitchell's shoulder. "You don't have to go if you don't want to. You don't owe him anything."

"I know. But I should go...try to talk him into coming back before he gets too far."

"Good riddance," Gale snorted. She lowered herself back down onto the wood log by the fire. There was a new air about her as she sat with both legs bent at the knee and her back stiffened straight. She rested both her hands down on the rough bark and cocked her head to the side, relaxed and grinning.

Gretchen looked back to Mitchell, but it was clear his mind was made up to go with Lonnie. Her stomach sank into a massive pit that made her want to scream some sense into the boy, but she held her tongue as tears gathered. Mitchell was only nineteen. Gretchen had grown to see him as a younger brother, sharing the same defiance against Lonnie and the same level-headed way of thinking that kept them from being killed. But his history caught up with him and now he was a bullied kid who had finally been picked first for the team.

"Just because he's an asshole to all of us doesn't mean he deserves to die out there alone. I'd never forgive myself if one of us didn't try to stop him."

Gretchen's chin trembled as she removed her hand and watched Mitchell run off after Lonnie into the night. His tightly curled, brown hair bounced as he disappeared altogether.

III.

Anita ran full speed away from the faction she'd been following, watching them from behind one of the trees lining their camp. Lonnie had walked right past without seeing her. Mitchell ran by a few seconds later, but she was already gone. Her cold, bare feet barely made a sound as they gracefully touched the dying grass and leaves. She only stopped when she was at the edge of the tree line, looking out at the black, still water of Lake Michigan.

Her head swept from left to right like a watchful owl. "We can do this, dad," she whispered, breathing in and out. "We've done it a million times before." She didn't wait for her father's voice to answer inside her head. She knew what he would say.

"Go get 'em, kid."

Anita pumped her arms as she ran through the cool sand towards the water. She breathed in through her mouth and out through her nose steadily. By the time the bright white lights of the surrounding houses turned on to illuminate their intruder, the only clue to her existence was a growing ripple in the placid water. Shots were fired regardless. They hit the water and sent little geysers shooting up where they hit.

"You can't catch me," she sang in a whisper. "I'm the gingerbread man!" She chuckled as she watched from the buoy.

She held on and hid behind it as the cold water seeped into her clothes and chilled her to the bones until she shivered uncontrollably. She lowered her head under the water to cover her lips, and let the cool liquid wash over her tongue and throat. Taking in as much as she could, she waited behind the buoy until the shots ceased and the lights shut off, encasing her in darkness once again.

She thought about the movie *Jaws* and pictured a massive shark swimming underneath her kicking legs as she hugged the bobbing object. It was uncanny to the beginning of the flick that gave her nightmares as a child. "There's no sharks in lakes. There's no sharks lakes."

"That's not true," she heard her father's voice ring from the back of her mind. "Remember that episode of Shark Week we watched where they found one swimming up the fresh water river. It attacked someone once it found its way to the lake?"

She narrowed her eyes. "Thanks, dad," she said and sank back below the water.

She dove under and didn't stop until she felt the bottom. With a quick jerk, she pulled up on the slimy water weeds stuck between the rocks. As she reemerged, she threw her head back so her hair slapped the water and stuffed the wet greens into her mouth. She chewed and chewed and chewed some more. "Mm," she moaned as she let the mashed up bits slide down her throat. "Not bad." She sank back under the water to grab more.

IV.

Christine Moore was home alone once again after witnessing the horror of Sally's mangled body and Ralph, who ate her. The light of the fireplace flickered against the blackened room. It was only Liam and Zack left to gather supplies. They let her know before they left that they'd be gone most of the day and half the night and that it could stay that way if they don't find more people soon.

She sat down on the window seat and opened her massive book and then closed it again. With a sigh she stood up and walked over to the kitchen. It was incredible how quickly her eyes adjusted to being in the dark. Candlelight was usually more than enough. She opened the pantry door and browsed the few cans left on the shelf.

She looked down at the walkie-talkie on her hip and checked to make sure it was still on and charged. It'd been silent all day. Jerry didn't use it often, not since she almost got everyone killed. He barely spoke to her at all and when he was in her presence his eyes avoided her. He thought she was unfit to survive and he was right. She had no business going out beyond the complex walls and she hadn't since.

The little green light on the radio blinked. She unclipped it and set it down on the kitchen counter by the dust-covered coffee machine. No point in wearing it around if she wasn't even going to use it.

For a moment she considered going out to the patio. If she leaned over the railing and craned her neck just right, sometimes she could see Jerry's feet propped up on his railing below her and across the stairway. He'd taken to kicking his feet up and napping with his pistol grip in his lap. No one complained. He always got the job done.

Christine couldn't remember the last time she saw one of those dead, rotting things wandering around the grounds. However long, it'd been even longer since she saw a real human. If there were any survivors in the other nine buildings spread out around them, they were keeping to themselves. No new people had found their way in either. Liam took down the sign out by the street for the apartments. The road that lead back through the woods was long, windy, and lined with thick woods. If anyone had passed by, they must have thought whatever was at the end of the road wasn't worth the risk.

Christine often sat on the patio, watching the unsuspecting animals go about their day without a care in the world, and wondered what it would be like if new people came there looking for shelter. She'd been limited to her group of survivors for months and their numbers were only getting smaller. Having more people to rely on would be nice for Liam, so most of the burden to provide for the community of four wasn't weighing down on him. It had started to take its toll, in the heaviness of his dull eyes shadowed by circles, in his wiry, ginger beard and shaggy hair that fell below his ears, in his newly roughened voice that growled monosyllabic answers back at her.

But then again, if a group of strangers came waltzing up to her door, she didn't know if she'd be able to let them in. It felt bizarre to think about expanding the group and meeting new people. There was a veil of mistrust over her eyes that she couldn't shake. It was best if no one new came in until she could figure out how to get rid of the winding sensation in her stomach that constricted her insides like a boa every time she thought about it.

Christine collapsed onto the couch in a huff with a can of tuna. With little food for days on end, her stomach shrank and the small can she held in her hand was actually enough to almost satisfy her. Each time Liam and Zack went out for more, they had to travel further away from Chesterton and into the neighboring towns. Last week they had to take Liam's beat-up Jeep Cherokee, even though it had less than an eighth of a tank of gas. Right before they reached the rural limits of Morgan Township, the old clunker gave out and the boys had to trek it the whole way home, leaving more than half of the food behind. Christine had wanted to drive her fist into the drywall when she heard the story from Liam, not because of her grumbling, aching stomach, but because if she'd been there with them they would have been able to bring more back.

When she'd devoured the wet lump of tuna in four bites, she rolled her eyes and threw her head back against the billowy couch. But sitting still and relaxing wasn't an option, not while Liam was out there. She didn't know if he was still alive or dead or hurt or worse.

She raised her head again and looked out the blackened window, trying to remember how long it'd been dark to figure out what time it was. Long ago, she'd given up on trying to remember to charge her phone with that solar charger Liam bought years ago. They had no working clock for her to reference. Occasionally, she'd message down to Jerry from the other end of the walkie-talkie. It gave her an excuse to talk to him when things were too quiet.

Her eyes fell on the radio on the kitchen counter and she let her head fall back again, deciding it was too far away for her to get up and grab it. Time was illusory. Whatever it felt like, that was what it was. There probably wasn't a single clock in the world that had it right.

Christine heard the familiar sounds of two sets of feet, one heavy while the other was quick and light, pounding up the stairs. Her heart raced with joy. She jumped off the couch with a colossal grin and unlocked the multiple deadbolts for Liam. The desire to throw her arms around his neck and kiss him hard flooded her senses as she bounced on the balls of her feet.

With the last chain on the door unhooked, she couldn't contain her excitement and let out a smalls squeal, but the chain remained pinched between her fingers. The last thing she wanted was another earful from Liam about not being safe to kill the moment. She hooked it back just as the handle on the doorknob turned. Her smile spread from ear to ear as she clasped her hands at her chest. The door opened hard and snapped the chain tight. There was only a small crack to see through. The eyes looking in at Christine weren't familiar. They weren't Liam's.

Christine Moore pushed with all her weight against the door. One of the men on the other side gave a hardened yell. She released a warrior cry as she dug her slippered feet into the faux-wood linoleum flooring as she pushed, but her efforts were insufficient once again.

A hearty slam and the door flew open. The chain broke. Little links of metal sprayed out and landed on the soft carpet. Christine was knocked back. A short, blonde man with a stocky build and pistol raised entered the apartment and stood over her, looking down with a leering gaze.

"Well, hello, there."

Another man stood in the hallway, hidden by the black of the night. All Christine could see was a shadow that rocked back and forth with a long gun in its hands. She locked her wide eyes back onto the man in the apartment. She backed away on her hands and feet until she was pressed up against the couch. He sauntered forward until the gap between them was closed. Christine squeezed her eyes shut and raised her arms to shield her face.

"Shut the door," he called out to the shadowed man.

Christine's heart raced as the young man walked in and shut the door quietly behind him. It would be that much harder to wake Jerry up with her screams. How long would it be before anyone realized she was dead? Would anyone besides Liam even care?

"I don't know, Lonnie," the kid who entered said. "We should get out of here."

"Would you stop being Mitch the little bitch," the man named Lonnie said with a sigh and turned to look at the guy he deemed Mitch the bitch.

"We don't have much left, but you can take whatever you want," Christine said with a shaky, unrecognizable voice. She tried to steady herself, but her muscles were weak with fear.

"Oh, we'll take what we want. We're going to take the whole world back." The sturdy man said as he smiled maniacally upward, his face turned to the unmoving ceiling fan.

Now was her chance.

Christine sprang up from the floor and threw herself at the kitchen counter. She frantically patted for the knife she'd placed next to the radio. Her hands pawed for something, anything to grab. Lonnie was on her before her shaky fingers could wrap around anything useful and grabbed her hard enough to deeply bruise her porcelain skin. She grunted and kicked as he forced her back with his thick hands wrapped around her upper arms.

"Watch out!" he yelled at Mitch as Christine kicked her legs wildly through the air. "This one's a fighter!" He threw her down hard like a sack of spoiled potatoes.

Christine gasped for the air that had been knocked out of her lungs. She continued in her attempts to kick Lonnie, but he rolled her onto her back and pinned them down with both hands. His muscular, burnt arms gripped her calves tightly, the fingers pressing all the way down to the bone. She felt like the weight was going to snap them in two.

Tears rolled down her face as she pleaded. "Please, don't do this! Please, don't. Please, don't." The urgency of her pleas faded away as Lonnie tightened his grip. She continued in pained whispers.

"Get her arms," he ordered to the shadowed man cowering in the corner of the room.

The dark figure name Mitch shook his head. "No," he said with an air of defiance.

"How 'bout this? You hold her arms down or I shoot you in the face?" Lonnie clicked back the hammer of the pistol and pointed it at his partner's face.

Mitchell Barnes stared at the two figures on the ground. The young woman's face was turned away. All he could see of her was a river of golden-blonde hair. His eyes darted back and forth as he bit his lip. What were the chances that Lonnie would actually shoot him if he ran? He'd seen Lonnie attempt to take down a large buck before with his rifle. A buck was much larger than Mitchell and not a single bullet had hit it. Lonnie had blamed the sun in his eyes. That was bullshit. The ex-jarhead simply couldn't shoot.

Mitchell eyed the distance between Lonnie and the door. He came to the conclusion that even a terrible shot with a nine-millimeter like Lonnie had could hit him square in the back from such a close range. "Fine," he said softly.

He swung his shotgun over his shoulder and knelt down on his knees beside the sobbing woman's head. He placed his hands on her wrists and held them over her head. His eyes stung and the corners twitched as tears welled up. He had to look away.

"What a li'l bitch," Lonnie laughed.

He wasn't sure if Lonnie was talking about him or the poor woman they were holding down against her will. He didn't care if it was him. He let the tears fall as he tried to wipe them on the shoulder of his hoodie.

The woman finally turned her head to look up into his blotchy face. She blinked rapidly when one of his tears fell close to her red rimmed eyes. He didn't want to look at her, but he was compelled to. Slowly, he moved his head down until his chin was against his chest and his soft brown eyes met her wet blue ones.

"Mitchell? Mitchell Barnes?" Christine said, her face screwed up to stare at the curly-haired teenage boy in utter disbelief.

The muscles in her body released ever so slightly at the sight of his familiar face, which stared down at her wide-eyed and jaw clenched. She wanted to reach out and wipe the tears from his well-defined face, but his long, thin fingers were still secured around her wrists.

"Mitchell? Do you remember me? Christine. Liam's fiancé," she said, hopeful, as her eyes cleared enough for her to see him clearly.

There was a sharp twist on her ankle that shot a searing pain up through her leg. "You two know each other?" the blonde man holding her down below the waist growled, his eyes locked on Mitchell.

Christine flinched. How could she be so stupid? She should have kept her mouth shut.

"How do you two know each other?" he demanded through his small, yellowed teeth.

Mitchell sat petrified with his face frozen in panic. He opened his mouth, but no sound came out. He involuntarily loosened his grip around Christine's arms.

Things were escalating quickly. Christine lifted her head off the carpet to look at the man by her feet. "Not well at all, we barely know each other, I swear," she lied. "He worked at GameStop and I saw him there a couple times. That's it. If it wasn't for his tag I wouldn't even know his name."

The man's face tightened together. His eyes flickered over to Mitchell and back to her.

Christine's pupils dilated and her heart sped up like a racehorse at the track. She'd seen Mitchell so many times in the last two years since she met him, it was sad for a woman who didn't even play video games. They engaged in small chit-chat at his work while she browsed new games for Liam, they laughed over stories of college life while everyone else played Dungeons and Dragons at Zack's game night in the comic books store, they even shared Mitchell's first beer together there. The last time she'd seen him was awkward, but it would never top the discomfort she felt around him now.

V.

Christine walked into GameStop with a smile on her face, Allison Murphy at her heels. "Hey, Mitchell," she said to the young man working the counter. "You still have any left?"

Mitchell Barnes looked up from the magazine he thumbed through and into Christine's grand sapphire eyes. He dropped the last issue of *Game Pro* from his lap. When he bent down to pick it up his head banged on the underneath of the counter.

Christine tightened her lips and tried not to laugh.

"Yeah I have one more left. I put it in the back in case you came in," he said. "I figured Liam would want this one."

Christine smiled at him warmly. "Thanks. You're the best."

Mitchell exhaled a breath of laughter through his nostrils before he went to the back to retrieve the Xbox game for Christine.

Allison Murphy's eyes followed him until he disappeared behind a set of double doors. "He's not bad for a nerd," she said, still looking for when he came back out. "How come I've never seen him before?"

"Ew, he's nineteen," Christine said with a scrunched face. "And you're married."

Allison turned back to her friend and rolled her eyes. "I'm just looking," she said, exasperated. "Besides, his curly, brown hair and sharp features remind me of my husband when he was a teenager…so long ago."

"It wasn't *that* long," Christine said absently as she browsed the shelves.

"Twelve years is a long time, Christine. Just wait till you've been married for over a decade. You'll be looking at all the cute young boys, too." Allison craned her neck again to see if the young man reminiscent of her husband in better days was headed back yet.

Mitchell Barnes came through the doors and handed Christine the brand new game still wrapped in cellophane. Their fingers touched and his cheeks flushed a bright red. Eyes burned on the back of his neck.

He turned to see Christine's older friend staring at him with what he deemed hungry eyes. He'd never gotten that look from a woman before, but he'd seen it often enough in the horny teenagers throughout high school and his first year at DeVry.

His smooth cheeks burned even brighter and he turned away. Why couldn't Christine ever look at him that way? He glanced at her friend from the corner of his eye and decided she wasn't bad looking for someone twice his age. Her dark hair was meticulously styled in a short, highlighted bob that made her look older, but sophisticated. Her blunt bangs sat on her arched brows and cut them off at the top.

Allison caught Mitchell eyeing her and she gave him a flirty smile. He immediately turned away and walked back behind the counter, stumbling over his own feet. Christine couldn't help laughing softly to herself. Mitchell had a crush. It was cute.

"A bit odd, though, isn't he?" Allison whispered to Christine as they stood close together, as women did when they gossiped.

"Yeah, but he's a good kid," Christine whispered back. "And I think he likes you!"

Allison's brown eyes lit up. She looked over her shoulder at the wiry kid standing behind the counter and gave him her best smoldering, sexy eyes.

"Bye, Mitchell!" Christine called as they left the store. She looked back with her expansive blue eyes and saw Mitchell take a sharp breath of air when they met his.

"Bye, Christine," he said just above a whisper.

VI.

"Mitchell, please don't do this, please," Christine begged softly. Her voice was steady now, but desperate.

Mitchell looked down at her. His vision blurred as more tears collected and then spilled over the brim. He, too, remembered perfectly the last time he saw Christine. She'd looked so pretty that day in her suit, nothing like the tear-streaked woman on the floor. His grip loosened on her wrists again, but he didn't let go. If they did, Lonnie would shoot him. There was no doubt in his mind.

His stomach tightened as a wave of sickness washed over him. Why had he gone with Lonnie? Why didn't he just stay behind with the others, like Gretchen told him to? His grip involuntarily loosened more. Why would he ever go anywhere with a psychopath like him? He should have known it would only lead to something horrible. He never imagined anything like this.

"Please, Mitchell. You don't want to do this. You can walk away still. You can."

Mitchell's hands sprang open. His breathing was ragged as he sat up straight, away from Christine.

"What the fuck are you doing?" Lonnie barked. His gun was tucked away into the back of his pants so his hands were free to hold Christine's legs down.

"I can't," Mitchell whispered as he raised his hands further away from her. "I can't do this. It's not right."

An arrow flew from the darkness of the doorway and pierced Mitchell between the eyes. Christine screamed. She lay still on the floor in shock. Tears spilled from the sides of her eyes and ran down onto the carpet.

She felt the grip on her legs loosen while she watched Mitchell's body slumped back against the couch. The other man was dead, too. Strong, rough hands reached down to force her up by her shoulders.

Liam had her pressed against him before she realized what was happening. Her faced turned to stare into Mitchell's lifeless honey eyes, a few freshly formed tears running down his pale cheeks. She was only able to take in sharp, shallow breaths. Liam killed Mitchell. He must not have known it was him, otherwise he never would have done it. Liam loved Mitchell like a younger brother. Some distant part of her expected Mitchell to rise up as if nothing happened, but he would never rise again as himself or anything else. Her entire body shook in Liam's arms.

"It's all right," Liam said as he stroked the back of her head. He didn't take a single glance at the men as they lay dead on the floor at his feet. "It's all right. They won't hurt you. They can't hurt you anymore."

Christine sobbed harder. She would go through it all again—the fear, the pain, the humiliation, all of it—if she could save Mitchell.

VII.

"Look," Christine said. Her eyes settled on the teenager's motionless body, slumped back against the couch with an arrow sticking out from his forehead. Bright red blood poured from the wound. Her shaking had subsided, but the sickness in her stomach grew more overwhelming. "It's Mitchell."

"What?" Liam said as he released her and whipped himself around. He wiped at his mouth as he felt saliva gather inside. "God," he said over and over again. "Oh, God!" He paced back and forth in front of the body. He groaned and grabbed his shaggy ginger hair, clutching it in his hands and pulling. "What have I done?" He heaved great breaths as his feet carried him aimlessly around the living room. "What have I done?" His eyes flickered over Mitchell's face, the kid's mouth open in shock or maybe even betrayal.

Christine saw that Liam was dangerously close to crossing over into a full-on panic attack. "Liam, Liam!" she said, stepping into his view so he'd look at her instead of the dead bodies slumped over on the floor. "Honey, it's OK." She stroked his arms hoping the repetitive motion would soothe his racking nerves.

"How is this OK, Christine?" he screamed, his voice breaking in the middle as he gave a hysterical, quick laugh. "I killed him! I killed Mitchell!"

Christine's hands fall back to her side. There was nothing she could do to stop his rising hysterics.

"He was this incredibly smart, amazing kid!" he shouted louder. "He helped Zack bring business to his store by designing fliers in his graphics class. He was one of the only people who consistently showed up for game nights. He drove me to work once when my car wouldn't start."

Liam bent over and rested his hands on his knees as the memories of Mitchell washed over him. His face was level with his dead friend's. He stole quick glances into his lifeless eyes. Deep heavy breaths were the only thing that kept him from throwing up where he stood. Tears fell from his eyes and streamed down his face in waterfalls.

"He was so…young…" he said softly.

Christine could do nothing, but watch as Liam descended. Should she comfort him? Should she give him his space to process? Picking the wrong one could set him off, and possibly send him from the apartment again in a blind rage. People did stupid things when they were upset, when they were scared. She couldn't let him leave, even though the apartment was the last place either of them wanted to be.

She took a few steps toward her sobbing fiancé and placed a hand gently on his back. He flinched. With caution, she placed another hand on his back and closed the gap between them to rest her head against him. There was nothing she could say to make it any better. He'd not only killed two people, people who minutes ago had been the only other two left on the Earth as far as they knew, but he'd killed a good friend.

"They were trying to…why would Mitchell…?" Words failed him.

"The other guy made him," Christine quickly said before the memory of Mitchell could be tarnished. "He threatened to shoot him if he didn't hold me down." She spoke with detachment, like she hadn't been the one helpless on the ground moments ago.

Liam took a few ragged breaths. He wiped his mouth with the hand he held there and then let it fall to his side. He reached down and closed Mitchell's eyes with two of his fingers. "Rest in peace, mate," he whispered before turning to Christine. "We'll wait for Zack to get back before we remove the bodies."

The thought made Christine want to run from the apartment and never return. Too much had happened there for it to ever feel like home again. Maybe Liam wasn't the one who was a flight risk. She nodded her head as she tucked her bottom lip in to bite it so she wouldn't cry again. She needed to be strong for Liam.

VIII.

The weather-beaten couple sat out on the patio together as they waited for Zack to return from his search. Their last bottle of wine sat on the floor between the two chairs. Every few minutes Liam reached down and poured more into his mouth before he offered it to Christine.

She declined with a wave of her hand. One of them had to be alert and she was certain it wasn't going to be him. To break the heavy silence, she pressed down and held the button on the black walkie-talkie in her lap.

The desire to bitterly ask Jerry if he was awake after all the screaming burned through her, but civility won. She was too emotionally exhausted to be bitter with anyone. "Jerry, are you there?"

She waited for the familiar beep, but there was only silence. Just as she was about to get up and lean over the railing to see if she could spot his feet, a gruff voice patched through.

"Yup," he said, drawn out and lazy.

"Just checking in."

"Yup."

"Yup," she said mockingly as she set the radio down on the ground with an annoyed sigh.

She hoped that the awkward interaction might've sparked a small chuckle from Liam, but when she looked over he was staring out into the night with a vacant, solid face.

She couldn't stand to see him that way. It was so unlike Liam, but she understood. If she had killed someone, for any reason, she'd be a wreck too, even more than she already was from witnessing it. She would have cried hysterically and broke everything he could get her hands on in the apartment.

Liam was keeping it together well in comparison, even if it scared her to death. She turned to look out at the parking lot. Her back stiffened when she saw something move across the empty spaces in front of their building.

"He's never going to find her," Liam said as he looked out unblinkingly at the figure walking slowly across the lot. "She's probably dead. He's going to die, too, if he doesn't quit chasing after a bloody ghost."

The old Liam would've had hope. He used to believe that love conquered everything. He didn't believe in anything anymore.

The figure stepped out from the shadow of a large red maple tree, allowing Christine to just barely make out Zack's rugged features. He disappeared beneath her into the open hallway below. She heard the pounding of his heavy boots on the stairs as he climbed to the second floor. Her stomach dropped from déjà vu. She reassured herself it was definitely Zack who she saw, but her mind played tricks on her.

Another figure emerged from the trees that lined the spaces in the lot. It moved sluggishly, dragging one of its feet behind it as it shuffled after Zack. They heard the familiar low moan and blood-coated gurgles as it moved relentlessly forward. Black liquid poured from the stumps where its hands used to be.

"Do you think Zack did that? Christine asked, but Liam didn't answer. "Why wouldn't he just kill it?"

She stood up to grab Liam's bow and quiver from inside the patio door. It would be her first moving target practice. Again her stomach plummeted before rocketing back up, this time from excitement. But before her hand could turn the knob to go inside and retrieve her weapon, a single shot boomed from below and the zombie crumpled to the pavement with a sickening, moist thud.

"Shoot," Christine sighed as she sat back down. "I really wanted try to get it."

The corners of Liam's lips pulled upward ever so slightly as he looked over at Christine.

She blinked a few times and then smiled dolefully. "Happy Halloween."

Liam stood up and went back inside. Christine hadn't given up. She needed to learn how to defend herself, especially after what happened with Mitchell and that scumbag. He wasn't always going to be around to save her. If he'd been even a few minutes later that evening, who knew what they would've done to her. His fists involuntarily clenched as his heartbeat thumped in his ears.

He stood up and went back inside and didn't stop until he was out the front door.

Christine remained in her seat and looked up at the stars as she wrapped her arms around herself, snuggling deeper into Liam's oversized, knitted hoodie. The air was still, but cold. The thermometer read forty-two degrees. She threw her head back and downed what was left of the dry white wine.

She called out to Jerry, the walkie-talkie on the floor next to her foot. "I'd invite you up, Jer, but we're fresh out of booze." Just like every other time she'd tried to reach out to him, there was no answer. "Yup, happy Halloween."

She trudged back inside and double checked all the deadbolts to make sure they were locked.

Part Five

"If a healthy soil is full of death, it is also full of life...Given only the health of the soil, nothing that dies is dead for very long."

—Wendell Berry,
The Unsettling of America

I.

Billowy flakes of snow fell from the sky and landed on the tip of Anita's nose. She stuck her tongue out and waited for the ice crystals to fall into her mouth as she spun around in circles. Her bare feet numb to the freezing, hard ground.

When she was a kid she used to curse the sky because the snow came later each winter. One year it didn't show its face until late on Christmas Eve night and she almost went to bed in tears. But with people forced from the comfort of their heated homes to live out in the woods like animals, the snow decided to arrive early, on the first day of December.

Once Anita had collected enough snowflakes to wet the inside of her mouth, she moved on to walk the snow covered trails of the Dunes. She skipped and kicked the snow up with her icicle toes.

"Oo, look!" she stopped and exclaimed. "I knew we'd find one soon!"

She ran over to a body lying several dozen feet away on the ground. It was blanketed with a fresh coat of powdery white. She dropped to her knees beside the frozen corpse. Its skin was a dark grayish, black. Its eyes were still and completely glazed over white. She could only see the slightest hint of a pupil left when she moved her face in closer. Its torso had been slashed deeply and was only connected to its lower half by a few threads of skin and muscle at the back.

Its jaw was frozen shut, but the muscles still worked to snap its teeth.

"It's OK," she said sweetly, as if talking to an old friend. "I just want your shoes. Is that all right?" She smiled down at the mangled, bloodied face as it craned its neck toward her. With a strained growl, its head fell back down the measly inch to hard ground. "Thanks, pally!"

She brushed the snow away from its feet to reveal large, brown leather work boots. She slipped them off as the weak muscles in its ravaged legs attempted to kick. Once she got them off, she turned the boots upside down and gave them each a good shake to see if anything would fall out, like a toe or a loose piece of skin. Luckily, there was nothing and that put a smile on Anita's face. The butt of her loose baggy jeans, which she'd found off another dead body, grew wet as she sat on the ground to put on the boots. Her feet slid right in since the steel-toes were at least three sizes too big.

"It'll have to do for now," she said as she stood up. Her toes had plenty of room to wiggle. They could have been clown shoes on her.

She tried to lift one foot up off the ground, but the boot fell to the ground, leaving her foot cold and exposed. Scraping her feet along the ground so she wouldn't lose one again was a better idea. It wouldn't be ideal for when she needed to run or climb, but she'd find a good place to hide them when those moment snuck up on her. For now, she was glad her feet had somewhere warm to thaw.

She waved goodbye to the moaning frozen body on the ground. "See ya around!"

Wandering aimlessly around the woods gave Anita countless hours to think about the last time she had someone real to talk to. She pretended it was her dad and the exchange had been filled with loving last words, but in the back of her mind, buried deep down, she knew the last time she'd spoken to another human being was the night she was beaten up for her shoes. That was five months ago. She shook her head violently to clear their leering faces from her head.

"Of course, I still have you, dad, so they don't even count. It didn't even happen, really. And it won't happen again...I mean, ever." She giggled to herself like a child caught in a silly lie before she let out a sigh and looked up at the gray sky. "You always loved this time of year. I can't even count how many times you dragged me out to the woods at the crack of dawn to hunt."

The echo of a twig snapping sliced her reminiscent thoughts in two. "Shh!" she shushed herself sharply as she looked over her shoulder. Every time she did this, she expected to see her dad standing there, but he never was.

She crept forward as quietly as she could with her new boots dragging along the ground. The snow made a crunching sound with each swipe of her feet. A large doe nudged the ground with its nose in front of her. Slowly, she took off the boots and leaned them against the tree she was crouched behind. "So cute," she whispered. "Look at its fluffy little brown and white tail, like a bunny."

She tread lightly as she neared closer. The peaceful creature didn't seem to notice her as it continued to forage for something to eat. Before long, Anita was able to reach her hand out to pet it. The fur tickled the tips of her fingers.

Her knife plunged deep into the doe's neck. The animal let out a high cry as it hopped and kicked, its vibrant blood splattering the white snow. Anita charged the doe again with her knife raised above her head. With an angry cry she thrust it down to the hilt into the deer's chest over and over again. A geyser of blood sprayed splashed face and clothes. The grunts and moans of the dying animal faded until it lie motionless in Anita's arms, its head cradled like an infant. She looked down at its black, marble eyes as blood ran down her face.

Quickly, she dropped the head and moved to the doe's hindquarters to start cutting away the meat from the bones, the ruffled fur still attached. Once her arms were stocked full of blood-soaked meat she ran back to her boots, jumped into them with ease, and shuffled away.

It wouldn't be long before the dead came, the agonizing sounds of the dying doe beckoning them from their path. There was always the alternative, too. One that made Anita's skin crawl with goosebumps—living people would come. She wasn't going to take that chance again. When she looked over her shoulder she saw bodies moving slowly through the trees headed for the downed deer.

She didn't stop again until she found a heavily wooded area with fresh snow absent of track marks of any kind. She tossed the deer meat into a pile and searched nearby for wood to make a fire. Her heart raced and her lips parted into a toothy grin as she envisioned the feast she would have that afternoon. She couldn't wait to sink her teeth into the fresh kill.

II.

The group of wanderers was finally able to catch a break in the densest part of the woods, well off the beaten trail. The dead didn't seem to be bothered at all by the plummeting temperatures, which were well below freezing. It did, however, slow the group down. They sat in a tight-knit circle around a roaring fire for warmth. With Lonnie not there to tell them what to do, they made the fire as big as they could. There was no longer any worry of anyone else seeing the smoke through the trees.

"We can't keep going like this," Gretchen said through chattering teeth. "We don't have the winter wear to survive out here. We need shelter now. And not just these random building we find in the park that we can stay in for about a week before they're unsafe again. A real home."

Rowan stared into the crackling fire as the flames danced in his unblinking eyes. When Lonnie got back with Mitchell, he was going to take over again and then Rowan wouldn't have to worry about keeping everyone safe anymore. The weight would lift from his sagging shoulders and he could return to a life of following blindly, no questions asked. He longed for those days.

Even though it'd been a month since Lonnie and Mitchell disappeared into the darkness of the woods, never to be seen again, Rowan still had hope. He wasn't going to give up on his dream of being unburdened. Gretchen's sharp voice drifted in his closed off ears and woke him up from his miserable stupor.

"Hello in there? Are you listening?"

He moved his eyes slowly to gaze at her from across the fire.

"We need to find somewhere to stay. These things are getting closer every day. It's not safe out here in the open like this. If we don't get eaten alive, we'll die of hypothermia."

Rowan sucked on his teeth as he thought about the hardships the group had faced in the last few weeks with Lonnie gone. There was the realization that they were down two men when the number of dead roaming the Earth seemed to have doubled. And the fact that all the people left in the group, besides him, were virtually useless. Not to mention, he wasn't a leader. Sure, he looked the part, but when it came down to it, he didn't have the balls. None of them did.

The girls were more than Rowan could take. Carolyn was a babbling bimbo who hadn't once touched a weapon in all the time Rowan knew her. Gale still complained every step of the way about her feet, her back, the cold, her clothes, her shoes, the clouds, anything she could think of. Gretchen's sole purpose in life was to butt heads with whoever was in charge without offering up any solutions of her own.

Sadly, his two accompanying men weren't any better. Dan was still lost in his la-la-land of near suicide, only surfacing to speak to Gretchen in the dim light of night. Rowan wasn't sure if Dan was coming to grips with what had almost happened to him or if he was planning his next attempt. Either way, he didn't care. He never liked the guy, not after Lonnie suggested they leave him behind. Plus he smoked like a chimney and it irritated Rowan's eyes.

Lee was a silent shadow forever behind the group. He held his own when the shit hit the fan, which Rowan should have seen as a blessing, but he hated silence and therefore hated Lee for bringing it upon them.

And then there was Olivia Darling, the new girl, the outsider. She was only seventeen and already tougher than every single one of those sad saps, including Rowan. But there was something off about her. The state of the world didn't faze her like it did everyone else. She seemed content and that sent a warning off in Rowan's head. He didn't trust anyone who smiled when they smashed in a skull, even if it was a zombie's.

As he sat in contemplation, Rowan narrowed his eyes to glare at Gale as she picked the burnt squirrel meat from between her teeth with her fingernail. A seething burn rose within his chest, filling him with hatred. She was the reason Lonnie never came back. She humiliated him in front of everyone, made him seem weak and pathetic, and that's why he took off. Wherever he was, Rowan wished he was with him instead of the useless group in front of him.

And why had Lonnie asked that squirmy little Mitchell kid to go with him? Rowan was his number two, his right hand. He imagined them off somewhere with an entirely different and better group, laughing over the ragtag misfits he was left to deal with.

"Excuse me!" Gretchen hissed as she waved her hands in front of Rowan's face. She was standing up, looking down at him with her hands on her hips.

He blinked a few times and sat up straighter. His back muscles tightened and ached from being hunched over for too long. He let his head loll to the side to look up at the seething woman. "Yes. We'll find somewhere to stay." His voice was void of any emotion.

Snow crunched somewhere off in the darkness. Each person around the fire tensed up and snapped their heads to look around like startled gazelle at the watering hole. They couldn't see anything beyond the small circle of orange glow from the fire. From all sides, sounds of movement met their finely tuned ears. They were surrounded by several clusters of hungry dead coming together.

Rowan's head spun side to side as the distant moaning grew closer. What would Lonnie do? What would Lonnie do? Everything in Rowan told him to run, climb a tree, get the fuck out of there any way possible and screw the rest of the group. But Lonnie wouldn't do that.

Lonnie was good. He wanted everyone to survive, not just himself. He did everything in his power to keep those people alive, even though on more than one occasion he told Rowan how much he hated each and every person in the group for one reason or another. Still, he never gave up on them and until Lonnie returned, Rowan wouldn't give up on them either.

"Shh…" Rowan held a single finger up to his bowed, rosy lips as his eyes widened to look at everyone. They were frozen where they stood, like headstones in a graveyard. "OK," he whispered to the frightened bunch. "Let's grab our stuff quietly and—"

He was cut off by a loud, shrieking scream.

Carolyn was on the ground in a matter of milliseconds, a writhing, snapping corpse on top of her. It tugged at her hair as it tried to pull her into its mouth to sink its rotten, blackened teeth into her tender flesh. The only thing that kept Carolyn alive was the way she extended her arms and locked her elbows to keep the hungry monster at bay, its broken teeth just inches from her face. She turned her head to the side, pressing her cheek into snow and dirt, and screamed again.

Rowan and Lee both made their move at the same time. Lee charged the thing that had once been a middle-aged man with thick, black hair and a strong build. He drove his foot into its stomach, sending it flying off Carolyn and rolling several feet.

While Lee kicked, Rowan grabbed his gun from the ground. By the time he spun around with it raised and ready to fire, the thing was swallowed up by the darkness surrounding them and Carolyn was hiding her face in Gretchen's neck as she cried hysterically.

With the determination of a starved lion, the dead thing lunged back into the circle of light with its mouth open and arms outstretched. One shaky blast from the AR-15 Lonnie left behind and the zombie was lying face down on the ground, its arms raised above its head. One down.

"Let's get moving!"

Rowan didn't bother to whisper. He could hear the dead all around them, moaning and stumbling over their own feet as they zeroed in on the spot where Rowan fired the gun.

III.

"In here!" Rowan ushered the group into a darkened park building.

"I'm not going in there," Gale said with her arms folded.

"What? What not?" Rowan asked in panicked irritation. They'd been trying to avoid a massive herd of zombies that followed them for days, but they couldn't shake them.

"We don't know what's in there. What if it's more dead people?"

"Or worse, living people," Olivia added.

Rowan looked at her and furrowed his brow, then shook his head. How could living people possibly be worse than what was chasing them? "Will everyone just shut up and get inside?"

They complied, only because there was nowhere else to go and the herd had been gaining on them in the last hour. As they ran, with temperatures nearing twenty degrees, the simple act forced the chilled air down their lungs and stung like a swarm of bees. Their limbs were stiff and sore.

Whenever the group slowed down out of necessity, the shuffling corpses maintained a lethargic pace and gained on the group, closing the gap they'd worked so hard to create.

Once everyone was inside the building, Lee stayed by the glass doors while the others searched for objects to barricade themselves in. They hoped that if they were quiet enough, the herd would move past without noticing them.

Rowan ran through the second set of doors and into the lobby first. He skidded to a halt and stared out at the darkened room. The floor was littered with bodies.

Carolyn slammed into his back. "Watch it!" she barked at him.

Gale stepped to the front and rested her hands on her hips. When Rowan saw this he stood by her side and did the same.

"It doesn't look like any of them were bitten," she said as she knelt down over a man with a handlebar mustache and a crushed skull.

"Be careful," Rowan hissed. He didn't follow her any further.

Gale poked the chest of the mustachioed man with the tip of her finger. He didn't move. "It's safe," she said, standing back up. "They're dead...dead, dead, that is."

She went over to the information center and opened the door to search behind it. She found a three hole puncher, a crowbar, and a fire extinguisher. She carried her items back out to Lee.

"We can use this ta shove between the handles," Lee said, picking up the crowbar. "Hold onto this." He shoved the extinguisher back into Gale's arms. With his free hands he mimed a bashing. "And this...is basically useless." He tossed aside the three hole puncher.

"Ah, gotcha," Gale said with a smile. "Thanks, buddy."

Lee nodded and turned to watch the parking lot again.

Rowan wandered further into the back of the building to the displays that featured stuffed animals, their marble eyes staring out at him, almost like they were following his every movement.

Carolyn gave a grotesque groan next to him. "Disgusting."

Rowan laughed and poked one in the face. "You never been hunting before?"

"No," she said, distracted by a row of ten gallon habitats in the back wall. "My family didn't do a lot together."

"What about your boyfriend?" he asked as all thoughts of finding supplies flew from his mind.

"Nope. No boyfriend." There was a gleam in her eyes.

He gave a crooked smile as he looked down at her.

Carolyn leaned in closer to look at the contents of the tanks. "Should we be worried that these things are empty?" She tapped on the glass with her index finger to see if anything moved.

"I don't think so," he said as he read the plaques. "Looks like it was just some snakes, spiders, and scorpions."

Her eyes widened to show the whites around her light pupils. "What!"

Rowan rushed his hand to cover her full lips while his other arm wrapped around her shoulders. He looked around, forgetting for a moment that they were safe indoors for the time being. He moved his hand away slowly as she stared up into his almond-shaped, honey-colored eyes. The corners wrinkled as he smiled. "Sorry, habit."

Her eyes grazed over to his other hand that was still rested around her shoulder, one side of her body pressed against his chest and abdomen.

"Just to be safe we should probably keep it down though." He removed his arm and took a step back from her.

Her smile faded. She turned to peer into the empty tanks again.

Meanwhile, in a room with floor-to-ceiling windows for walls, Gretchen and Dan looked out at the snowy dune hills and trees. They didn't see anything moving close by yet, but they both knew what was coming.

"Back in the regular world, this would have been a beautiful winter night," Gretchen said with a forlorn, distant gaze as she reminisced.

"This is the regular world," Dan said flatly. He was staring out the same window, but seemed to see a completely different view. "And a night like this can get you killed."

Comments like that were normal from Dan for as long as she'd known him, but what about before then? Was he always so cynical, so hopeless? "How're you doing?" she asked.

He furrowed his brow as the corners of his lips pulled upward for a quick second before they fell again. "Why?"

"It's just, you haven't really gotten a chance to talk about what happened since we found you and I want to make sure—"

"You want to know if I'm going to try to kill myself again?" he finished for her, shoving his hands into the pockets of his jeans.

She didn't want to answer yes in fear that he would close off and never tell her what he was thinking again, but she couldn't bring herself to say no either, because it would have been a lie. "I've just..." she chose her words carefully. "...grown to care about you in the last, what is it?" she counted off the months in her head, but lost track.

"Four months, three days."

"Wow," she said, her eyes wide. "Four months. That's a long time to keep going without letting anyone in."

She let that sink in as she watched the woods outside stand perfectly still. "Anyway, like I was saying…I've come to really care for you and I just want to make sure you're doing OK."

Dan nodded and gave her question some deep thought. He knew what she wanted to hear—that what he did was stupid and he regretted it, he didn't know what he was thinking trying to kill himself and he'd never try it ever again. That was a promise he couldn't make. He didn't want to lie to her. She'd saved him, though most days he wished she hadn't.

"I'm doing all right today," was all he could honestly tell her.

"Well if you ever want to talk, y'know, about what happened…I'm here." With that she let it be.

Dan continued to stare out the windows. The minute Gretchen was gone from the room, his eyes welled up with crocodile tears as his mom's face clouded his mind.

V.

After the doors were secured and the dead bodies had been piled in the back room in front of the empty tanks in the wall, everyone found their place to try and get some sleep. Rowan declared that he would take the first watch and stood by the glass doors in the small entryway room.

Gretchen and Dan sat huddled together, their backs leaning against the lobby desk as they talked in whispers, occasionally laughing.

Lee sat straight with his back against a brick wall with his head leaned back and his eyes closed. Olivia lay on his jacket on the floor, curled into a little ball with her head in Lee's lap. She clutched a worn-out baseball bat in her hands, cuddled to her close like a teddy bear. Without opening his eyes, Lee rested a hand on her straight, brown hair. He tried to pull it back out of her face, but it kept falling forward. He gave up and went to sleep.

Carolyn had hoped Rowan would sit with her, but it was like just like him to stand up and take the first watch. With Lonnie gone, Rowan was next in line. That power only made her want him more. She sat huddled alone with a clear view of the glass box room. She wrapped her arms around herself. Her long, wavy blond hair covered her exposed cleavage and kept her warm. All the while, Rowan never took his eyes from the view outside. What dedication. She finally zipped her down jacket up to her chin and let her head rest against the fur-trimmed hood.

Gale was the only one not satisfied with closing her eyes. She searched the office behind the lobby desk, but it was empty aside from another small desk, an overturned chair, a broken lamp, and a few framed generic inspirational pictures that hung crooked on the wall. She had hoped to find food stashed away in one of the desk drawers, but she should have known better. Those people who were dead in the back room would have found all the food in the place first.

She left the office and walked further past to check out the bathrooms. In a pinch, the tiny windows they sometimes installed near the ceilings were perfect for a quick escape. If she had to she could shove Olivia, Dan, and Gretchen through one of them. The rest would have to find a bigger way out. She considered if Carolyn could fit, but decided there was no way. Her ass was too big. She laughed to herself with a snort. She'd always liked a nice, round ass to grab onto. Salena's had been perfect.

The bathroom had two stalls and two sinks. The smell was overwhelming. Gale pulled her dirtied t-shirt over her nose. Even though it reeked of stale sweat, it smelled infinitely better than her surroundings. She kicked open the first stall with her knife at the ready. It was empty. The water in the toilet was thick and brown, smelling of old shit. She wrinkled her nose and held her breath as she kicked open the second door.

There on the toilet was a woman. She was leaned all the way back against the tiled wall and slumped over to the side with her face pressed against the stall. Despite the bloody, smashed side of her head, Gale's eyes were drawn to the middle-aged woman's feet. She had on red high heeled pumps.

Gale was taken aback. Who in their right mind would choose to wear heels for the zombie apocalypse? No wonder they died. But she couldn't tear her eyes away from the shoes. Salena had been wearing an identical pair the day she died. Suddenly, it was all she could think about as she crumpled to sit on the dirty bathroom floor.

VI.

Dan fumbled through his pocket as Gretchen fell asleep on the floor next to him. Her arm was curled up under her head for a pillow and her mouth was parted as she breathed deeply. He stopped for a second to watch. Why was that single small act, the one that allowed a human being to continue living, so incredibly hard to maintain? So fragile and easy to cut off? His fingers found what they were looking for and stood up to make his way over to the front doors.

"Where do you think you're going?" Rowan's voiced called out.

Dan held up the crumpled cigarette between his two fingers, ready to put it in his mouth and start puffing away.

"I don't think so. Get back in there."

"I just need a quick smoke, guy. I'll be fine."

"I don't care if you think you'll be fine or not. I care about you making noise out there and drawing those things over to us…and don't call me fucking guy," Rowan said in a boorish voice that closely resembled Lonnie's misguided confidence.

Dan clucked his tongue and shook his head. "Are you serious right now?"

"Why don't you just go have a smoke in the john?" Rowan turned his back to Dan and looked out through the doors.

"I feel a little claustrophobic, all cooped up in here. I need some fresh air." Dan bounced on the balls of his feet as he spoke.

It was Rowan's turn to scoff.

"This is ridiculous, man. I'm going." Dan pushed past Rowan and grabbed ahold of the crowbar to yank it out from between the handles.

Rowan shoved Dan in the chest with both hands. "Get back." His volume was normal, but his tone was not. "Maybe it's time for you to quit." He grabbed the cigarette from Dan's fingers and smashed it in his hand. Flakes of tobacco fell to the floor like brown snow.

"You motherfucking…" Dan charged Rowan, slamming him against the entryway glass walls with his body.

Dan was half Rowan's size, but he knew how to fight. The anger coursed through him and made it impossible to think rationally. His mother's face still lingered in his mind and that last cigarette had been his only option for a release from the pain inside. What he failed to consider when he threw himself onto Rowan was that the tall, scared man was armed with Lonnie's AR-15 still. Dan hit the ground hard when the butt of the gun rammed into the side of his temple.

Everything went black. He was aware he was drifting in and out of consciousness on the cold ground. In his mind he kicked and screamed and got back up to his feet, because he knew he should be awake, alert, and ready for whatever might happen next. Who knew what that Rowan guy was capable of doing to him… he could still be beating him with his gun for all he knew. His thoughts faded like a dream.

"Get off him!" Dan heard Gretchen shout in some far off place. As he came to, her voice became stronger as well as the stabbing in his head.

"He tried to leave the building!" Rowan yelled as he pointed down at Dan. The gun hung loosely to the floor in his other hand.

"Who cares," she yelled back. "He's a big boy. He can take care of himself."

"I just…wanted to have…a smoke," Dan groaned as he rolled on the floor, the pain in his head overwhelming him until he thought he would lay down and die. "I didn't…want to smoke…where ya'll slept…"

Gretchen's heart strings felt a tug as she looked down at Dan's bloodied, beaten face. "See! He wasn't running off, you lunatic."

"I wasn't worried about him leaving and not coming back. If that were the case, I would've opened the door and gave him a handshake on his way out. I was more concerned with him drawing those things to us." Rowan's voice kept raising and lowering as he made an effort to control himself.

"Draw them with what? The soft sounds of him breathing out smoke?" You're insane!" Gretchen scowled up at him as she tried to help Dan to his feet. "You realize he's hurt now, right? That means we have to stay here, take care of him…he could have a concussion. Are you really as stupid as you look?" She was on a rant that she couldn't stop. Her eyes flickered briefly to the gun in his hand, but the fear that he'd use it on her wasn't there.

"You came to *us* looking for help and protection, remember?" His voice was raised again. "I'm just trying to keep everything together till Lonnie gets back with that Mitchell kid."

Gretchen laughed heartily and it echoed throughout the silent building. "Wake up, Rowan. Lonnie's not coming back. It's been weeks. He's dead."

"Shut up, you stupid bit—"

"What's going on?" Gale's sighed lazily from behind them.

"Look what he did to Dan," Gretchen turned, her voice was no longer angry, but fawning with concern. "Look what he did to his face."

Gale looked down at Dan and then over to Rowan. She ran a hand through her short salt and pepper hair and rolled her eyes. "I know you think you're the big kahuna around here now that Lonnie's dead, and believe me, that stupid prick is dead and gone, never to return."

Rowan huffed through his nose. He opened his mouth to retaliate, but Gale held up a hand and stopped him with wild eyes and a tight-mouthed scowl. "Don't speak. You listen to me, Rowan Brady." She held her finger up so close to his face he could have bit it off. "You will not hurt one of your own...ever! Or you'll answer to me. Do you understand?"

Rowan's breathing steadied as he stared past Gale's left ear. His shoulders hunched slightly as he swung his gun around so the strap pulled against his chest. Gale widened her eyes. She didn't blink, didn't look away, until he said what she wanted to hear.

"Yes."

"OK. Good. We can all move on, then." She turned to Gretchen and looked her in the eyes.

"Right. All's good. I'll just take Dan over here and attempt to patch up his head. Thank God he wasn't hit somewhere important." She got the crumpled young man to his feet and they stumbled off together to the lobby desk.

Gale turned back to Rowan. "I want you to go check the perimeter, see if you find anything."

"Like what? What do you expect me to find out there? It's the middle of the night and freezing," Rowan said in a way that resembled a teenager about to throw a fit when their mom asked them to do a simple chore.

"Stop talking and go. I don't want to see you back here till you've found something that can help us. You owe Dan something good," she said quiet enough to not form an echo.

"How about I leave and never come back?" Rowan growled. He leaned in close to Gale's face as if what he said was some sort of threat to her. "See how long you last without me."

Gale didn't flinch. Nothing in her face revealed how she felt, except maybe boredom. "There's the door," she answered. "Go through it and it's up to you if you want to come back. We'll be here."

He turned and threw the crowbar to the tile ground with a loud clank. "I'm serious, Gale. I'll go."

"Say hi to Lonnie for me, then," she said with her hands in the pockets of her black sweatpants.

He wrenched the doors open and stalked out into the snowy night. "At least Lonnie had a plan," he said, turning back around when he was a few steps out. "At least he thought about the future. All you want to do is sit around and wait to die." He walked another few steps and shoved his hands into the pocket of his jacket.

"Oh, and, Rowan…"

He didn't want to give her the satisfaction of turning around once again, but he couldn't stop himself.

"We're doing just fine without Lonnie and we'd be just fine without you, too."

Rowan stalked off into the darkened parking lot alone. The same panic rose through his stomach as the last time he found himself walking alone through the zombie-ridden world. Only this time, he knew Lonnie wouldn't be there to save him.

VII.

Gale went to secure the doors again after Rowan disappeared into the trees, but she went outside instead and found a marble bench in the middle of a dead garden, full of weeds and twigs and cold, hard mulch. She brushed the snow off with her bare hands and sat down, legs crossed at the ankles, as she looked up into the black sky. The door opened again. She didn't look to see who it was. She already knew.

"That was crazy," Gretchen said as she brushed the spot next to Gale on the bench and sat down.

She held her hands together in her lap and shoved them between her legs for warmth. No one had been lucky enough to find gloves yet, but then again, it had been the middle of summer when it all started. What little winter wear stores had in stock people snatched up immediately.

"Do you think he's right?" Gretchen asked as she stared down at her lap.

Gale finally tore her eyes away from the darkness above her and looked to Gretchen. "Right about what?"

Gretchen let her head fall to the side as her eyes darted away from Gale's. She forced them to look at her again before she spoke. "About the whole future thing. Are we just waiting to die? Should we be, I don't know, building a home, a community…families? I mean, what happens when this is all over and these things are gone? We're going to want to start over. To rebuild...repopulate, right?"

Gale licked her lips. She had the sneaking suspicion the "we" Gretchen referred to was not all of humanity, but them specifically. She chewed on her dry bottom lip.

"Here," Gretchen said. She pulled out a small Chapstick from her pocket and handed it over.

Gale's eyes lit up as she took it delicately, grasping it between two thick fingers. "Where'd you get this?"

Gretchen hushed her and looked over her shoulder to see if anyone was watching at the door. "I found it on the ground, believe it or not. Don't tell anyone, OK? It'll be gone in a day if everyone starts using it."

"You secret's safe with me," Gale said, distorted as she puckered her lips. The creamy substance felt like heaven. "Much better." She handed it back.

"Now *I'm* going to let *you* in on a little secret." Gale readjusted herself on the bench.

Gretchen leaned forward.

"There is no end to this. This is it. Forever and ever until we all die."

Gretchen sat back and pursed her lips. "You're the second person to tell me that today. You don't really believe that, do you?"

"There is no cure. There is no way out. And there's no reason to settle down into a place that's just going to get taken away from you again." Her voice growled low as irritation boiled up inside her. "There's no reason to throw your sense of self away, because you feel it's your duty as a woman to bring a child into this goddamn mess of a world."

"I didn't mean, I mean...I wasn't," Gretchen stumbled as her cheeks burned.

"Are you even a lesbian? I mean, really?" Gale asked. She leaned her arm on her knee and glared at Gretchen with scrutiny.

"Yes. No. I think so," she stammered, shaking her head.

"Well, which is it, girl? Either you are or you aren't."

"Charlie was the first girl I'd ever been with," she blurted out and then her eyes filled with tears. "I don't really know who I am without her, I guess," she said as they fell down her cheek.

Gale sat back up and took a deep breath. "Look. Let me put it to you the only way I know how. I'm from Oklahoma, a tiny little town I'm sure you've never heard of called Sweetwater, and my daddy was a farmer, just like his daddy before him and his daddy before him and so on and so forth. Anyway, one summer when I was sixteen he took me out to one of the fields. The entire crop, acres and acres, was ruined. Dead. It never even had a chance. When I asked him what happened he said it was the soil.

"See, there's all kinds of things that can get into the soil, things smaller than the eye can see. No one knows they're coming, either. There's no signs, nothing to give them away, whatever they are. In the blink of an eye, everything you've worked so hard to grow is obliterated. That's exactly what happened to us that year and that's exactly what's happening to us right now.

"I asked my daddy if he was going to start over, plant again, and see if anything grew, but he said no. There was nothing that would grow out of that soil, for whatever reason. It was dead soil, just like now. Humanity will never grow again here. It's gone."

"Then, what's the point?" Gretchen asked after a long pause, her eyebrows pushed together.

Gale shrugged her shoulders and scraped at the ground with the toe of one of her tennis shoes. "Are you ready to check out just yet?"

"No," Gretchen said immediately.

"Then, I guess that's the point."

Gretchen nodded. She stood up to go back inside.

"Don't lose sight of who you really are just because of what's going on around you," Gale said as Gretchen turned and went through the double glass doors.

Gale stood alone in the freezing cold as the snow began to fall again.

VIII.

Rowan ran as fast as he could to the front doors of the building his group was secured in.

"Let me in! Come on, let me in!" he screamed as he yanked on the doors relentlessly. They didn't budge.

Everyone inside jumped to their feet in a matter of seconds; even Dan, though his head felt like it'd been split in two. He waivered on the spot and raised a hand to where it throbbed the hardest.

"Well, someone let him in!" Gretchen screeched, but didn't move to do it herself.

Gale walked quickly to the doors and opened one. Rowan pushed past her in a hurry and closed it behind him, pressing his entire body against it in a panicked huff.

"Secure the doors!" he yelled at Gale.

"What's going on?"

Gale didn't move fast enough as she bent down to pick up the crowbar. Rowan grabbed it from her violently. "There was a bunch of them all over this dead deer." He spoke so quickly it was hard for anyone to understand him. "I tried to back away to leave. I didn't want them to see me. I didn't mean for them to see me, but they did and now they're headed this way!" Despite the freezing temperatures, his face was beat red and drenched with sweat.

"Goddammit!" Gale said to him. "What the hell did you lead them back here for?"

"I didn't know where else to go. They were right behind me." Once the doors were secured he backed away from them slowly with his hands displayed out in front of him.

"How many were there?" Gretchen asked from the lobby desk.

"I don't know. Twenty. Thirty. Fifty. I don't know!"

"Fifty?" Gale yelled. "Why didn't you lead them away so we could have a chance?"

Rowan whirled around to face her. "You? What about me? I had nowhere else to go! They would have eaten me alive!"

"Ok, enough!" Carolyn said, surprising everyone. "We're wasting time fighting with each other."

"She's right," Olivia Darling agreed with the weathered bat clenched in both her hands. "We need a plan. Grab your weapons."

Everyone did as she said without question.

Before Olivia spoke her next order, Gale's tactical training took over. "I want you and you to search this place for another way out," she said, pointing to Dan and Gretchen. "There has to be one. Go!"

They ran off to the back of the building. They opened every door that wasn't locked, but only found closets full of useless junk and cleaning supplies.

"There's nothing here," Gretchen reported back out of breath.

"No window in the bathroom either. I checked. Dammit. Do we have time to make it out the front and circle around?"

Rowan stared at her with his eyes wide and mouth open as his brain worked double time. "Maybe? I don't know if more heard me running. There could be others coming from other directions."

"Were you running around, flailing your arms in the air and screaming like an idiot or something?" Gale snapped at him.

"I thought I was going to die! You don't know what that's like!" he yelled back. "We've been taking care of you while you took it easy ever since you joined this group and come to find you're some fucking Marine officer!"

"They're here," Olivia said with a finger pointed at the doors. The room fell silent.

Emerging from the darkness were moaning, walking, hungry corpses, one after another like moths drawn to a light as they headed for the park building. There were at least forty in the vast, open lot and more trickled out to join them every second. Rowan had called it right. While some came directly at them from the right side where he ran out from, others trickled from the left, the parking lot directly in front of them, and even a few from around back. There were more than fifty.

"Maybe if we open just one door we can take them out one by one, control how many come in at a time," Gale thought out loud as she gripped a long knife in her hand.

"Yeah right!" Rowan said, his voice breaking. "We're not letting those things in here. They'll rip us apart!"

"It's either we let them in on our terms and try to thin the herd for a getaway, or they let themselves in, full force, and we die."

"Lee should be on the door," Olivia chimed in again. "He's the strongest, so he'll be able to hold it closed and he'll also be protected between the door and wall. That leaves the rest of us to kill the zombies." Olivia smiled. She raised her bat to rest on her shoulder. "It's the best plan we've got."

The bodies ambled forward automatically as their horrifying features grew clearer in the darkness. Bloody messes of gore moaned in the freezing night air, their jaws wrenched open, or in some cases torn open, to reveal rows of black, jagged teeth ready to pierce the skin of the warm flesh on the other side of the glass doors.

All the color drained from Gretchen's face. She held tightly onto the pistol she found a few days ago with both hands. When she opened it there were only three bullets left inside. One of her hands moved to her waist to rest on the Bowie knife that hung from her belt. It'd proven itself time and time again.

Dan swayed from side to side as he shook his head. The bloodied wound didn't hurt as much. Maybe the fear stifled the pain. He bounced up and down and shook out his hands, taking deep breaths before he reached into the back of his pants for the matching pistol to Gretchen's.

On the last run they made to someone's abandoned house they found each of the pistols in the hands of a dead man. He was in bed, his ribs pried open to reveal a hollow chest. There was a single small hole in his forehead. They figured he tried to defend himself against the dead with the two nine-millimeters and once he was bit, he knew it was over so he shot himself.

"Oh, and you know those doors have floor and ceiling locks right?" Olivia said, breaking up the electricity in the air. She pointed to the holes.

"Why the hell didn't you tell us that before?" Gale demanded.

"I wanted to see how long it took you all to find them. You're even slower than my last group."

Lee walked over to the door, calm as could be, as if he were waiting for friends to join him for dinner at his house. He secured one door with the bolt locks, removed the crowbar, and put it through his belt loop.

"You," Gale said, pointing at Rowan, "Stand on this side. "You, here." She moved Gretchen to stand next to him. "And you, here. We'll form an arch. That way we have full coverage. Back up a little. Give them enough room to come in so Lee can close the door."

Everyone stood in position with their weapons ready.

"On my count, Lee," she said. Stifling panic wrapped around her lungs and constricted them. "One…"

Gretchen's hands shook as she clutched her pistol. Her eyes darted from the herd of dead bodies approaching outside to the knife on her belt.

"Two…"

Olivia's bat was raised and pulled back behind her, eager to crack some heads open. She tried to stay focused, but Dan's bouncing kept catching her eye.

"Three. Open it!"

IX.

The dead moved forward, shoving into each other as Lee opened one door a tiny crack. It took everything he had to not let them knock the door all the way back to flood in and overwhelm the group. Four got through before he wedged his foot into where the floor and wall met. With every ounce of muscle he had, he kept the rest at bay behind the glass door.

A female with torn, sagging, bloody skin, half her jaw missing to expose ragged muscles and tendons, lurched forward. Three loud shots rang out. Two hit the shoulder and one landed in the head. The body fell face first to the floor at Gretchen's feet, its hand on her boot.

"Whoa," Gretchen exhaled between heavy breaths.

"Your knife!" Rowan yelled next to her.

Gretchen threw the gun to the floor and pulled for her knife at her belt. It was stuck on something. She tugged at it a few times before it loosened. Her arm pulled back forcefully to punch a robust corpse in dirtied flannel square in the chest. He felt spongey, like her hand would be absorbed into him if she didn't pull it away quickly. She sliced its decayed neck, which hung by a few red threads. Blood rushed out like a river. Its head hung to the side and down to look at the floor. That didn't stop it from snapping its broken teeth as it continued to advance on Gretchen.

Olivia looked over. "Go ahead," she urged as her face lifted.

Gretchen drove her knife into the thing's soft head and remained there. It took a few good jerks to break it free. The putrid body collapsed to the floor in a jumbled heap.

"It'll take some getting used to!" she yelled over the moans as Dan and Rowan took out the last two.

Carolyn was backed up against the glass wall with her face turned to the side and her eyes closed. Her knife was on the floor.

"Ya ready?" Lee shouted.

The multitude of hands banging on the glass to get it was maddening.

"Yeah," Rowan said.

"Yup," Olivia yelled.

"Go for it," Dan called back.

Gretchen stood with her knife in her hand. Her chest hurt every time she took a breath, but she couldn't stop from heaving. She stared unblinking at the dead hands on the door and pictured them ripping into her as they devoured her alive.

"Hey!" Lee yelled as he struggled to hold the door closed. "Ready?"

She blinked a few times. "Yeah, ready." She tightened her grip on the handle of her knife.

Lee didn't wait for Carolyn to respond as she sobbed in the corner. He opened the door as a few more pushed to get in and shoved the door closed behind them. One by one the group dropped them all to the floor in a clumsy, unskilled manner. Lee's arms shook as his large muscles tired from the constant pressure. He let out a growling cry as it became harder to keep the door sealed. The ravenous bodies piled against it, smashing the ones in the front up against the glass. The heads of the ones in front crunched as blood oozed from their eyes, nose, and mouths.

"We can't go on like this," Gretchen said in a high-pitched voice. "We've only killed seven and twenty more have shown up since!"

"Barricade the door again," Olivia said. "I have a better idea."

Rowan and Dan helped Lee push the door all the way closed as Gretchen and Olivia secured the floor and ceiling deadbolts. They shoved the crowbar back through the handles for good measure.

"That won't last long so we better hurry," Olivia said as she ran back into the lobby. She waved everyone through and then secured the second set of doors.

"What's the plan?" Rowan asked with wide eyes.

"We bust out through the bird watching room."

They all looked at her like she was crazy.

"Hell no," Gale said. "They'll hear it and come after us."

"Yeah, but we're quicker than they are. We can get away." There wasn't an ounce of doubt in her mind that she'd be able to escape unscathed.

Gretchen shook her head. "I don't know…it sounds insane."

"It's either this, or we stay here and wait to die."

The words rang through Gretchen's head. It was exactly what she feared, exactly what Rowan said they were doing. She had to break the cycle. They had to survive. "OK. Let's try. I mean, we have to try, right?" She looked around to everyone else.

They didn't seem as eager to give it a go, but they all followed as the teenager made her way to the room off the lobby. She crept in. Her movements were slow and low to the ground. She peered out through the windows to assess how many were nearby and how long it would take for them to get to her.

"Rowan," she said and turned to him. In any other life she would have fawned over how gorgeous his eyes were and how perfectly his brown hair fell into them. But in this life she saw him as a coward. It was time he proved himself to her. "Unload on that window." She pointed at the one facing the back of the building, farthest from the side with the dead beating to get in.

"What?" Rowan gave a hysterical laugh.

Olivia rolled her eyes and cocked her head to the side. She sighed and waited for an excuse.

"It's not going to work. It'll take too long to break. It—"

"Give me the gun, then," she demanded, holding her hand out.

Rowan didn't give it to her. His hands clutched at the cold metal. There was a clanking noise at the front of the building as the crowbar fell to the floor. The doors seemed to breathe in and out as the pressure of the dead beat against them.

"Clock's ticking. Let's go. Do it or I will."

Rowan wanted to make the call on his own, to prove that he could be the leader of the group. He wanted to stand his ground and go with his gut feeling on this one. But his eyes drifted to the others to read what they thought about the plan.

"Just do it, you pussy," Olivia growled when his eyes fell back onto hers.

His head jerked back as his face screwed up. Did he talk like that when he was seventeen? He tightened his lips and stood up straight. "Fine," he said. "Stand back." With a deep breath, he counted down in his head while everyone stood huddled behind him.

There was a loud crash from the front as the first set of doors fell from their hinges. The dead stumbled over the broken glass, tearing up the loose skin of their feet. They had no reaction to what should have been excruciating pain as they pushed forward to the next set of doors. They pounded relentlessly, as they'd done with the first set. Their moans grew louder, more excited and urgent. The beating of hands against glass echoed throughout the building. A crack appeared between the two doors as they pushed against them. Several gray, grotesque fingers wriggled through to reach out for the flesh of the survivors inside.

Rowan looked back and decided they were at their last second of safety. He pulled back on the trigger and let the rifle do the work as he swept it back and forth. The glass shattered and fell to the ground outside, mixing in with the white snow.

"Go, go, go," Olivia yelled. She pushed everyone through. Lee gave her a shove on the back to get her out before him.

They ran as fast as they could with Lee bringing up the rear. Gale kept up with surprising ease. Maybe she wasn't as out of shape as she let herself believe. She didn't dare agree with what Rowan said about taking advantage of the group. She'd been saving her energy for this very moment. Her arms pumped like they never had before.

Stragglers appeared out of the darkness alongside her, snapping their jaws and reaching out their bruised and beaten arms as she flew by without a pause to end their miserable existence. She side-stepped and dodged the dead hands like she was in the world's most dangerous obstacle course.

The group ran strong until Gale's lungs started to feel a sharp stab from the freezing air. Every deep breath she took felt like little, sharp needles jabbing in her chest. She slowed down to a jog and then doubled over as she tried to relieve the pain. The rest stopped with her and scanned the woods in a three hundred and sixty degree circle.

"Come on," Rowan urged as he bounced on his feet. "Let's get outta here."

"There's one," Gretchen said, squinting into the darkness a few yards away.

"Got it," Olivia answered. She swung her bat before she took off after it.

All anyone heard was the sticky sound of wood as it smashed in a skull. They stared at her as she walked back with a bounce in her step, shaking the black blood from her weapon.

"What?" she asked. She was taken aback by their judgmental faces, after all the times she'd saved their asses— in the last hour, no less.

Gretchen avoided eye contact. Rowan stared and then looked away when Olivia scrunched her face at him. Dan searched his pockets frantically for a cigarette, but all he found was loose tobacco and his notebook and pen. Carolyn stood with her arms wrapped over each other, her knife tucked in one hand. Tears ran down her tanned face. Gale was still concentrating on standing upright as she fought the urge to be sick. She hadn't run that hard since Afghanistan.

"So, can we start looking for a safe place to settle in now?" Gretchen asked as she threw her hands up and let them slap against her thighs.

Rowan saw the chance to reclaim the group as his own. He took a step forward and straightened his back so that he was almost matching Lee in height. "Yes," he said steady with his chin thrust slightly forward. "We're going to find ourselves a home."

X.

Zack left early without stopping at Liam's to check over the apartments in their building. He didn't see the point. They hadn't found a single body, dead or alive, since Ralph and his wife weeks ago. He spent more time out on his own, searching for Anita and supplies rather than in the comfort of his own apartment.

The place wasn't a home anymore. It was a prison, keeping him closed off from the world and from ever finding the one person he wanted so desperately by his side through it all. He walked the woods with his sword in his hand and his heavy canvas jacket zipped up tight. He wore fingerless gloves so he wouldn't lose his grip in the middle of an inevitable upcoming battle with the growing numbers of the undead. The hood of his jacket hung low over his head to shield his eyes. Christine had made him laugh the other day when she warned him against wearing it like that.

"It's impairing your vision. What if you don't see one coming?" she'd said in her motherly voice.

"Where are they hiding? In the trees?"

It was the last time he saw Christine.

As he walked aimlessly, everything exposed in the whiteness of the snow-covered ground and trees, he thought about Anita—about what she looked like. He didn't have a picture of her so the only time he was able to remember her face, picturing the littlest details, was when he was completely alone. He didn't want to forget her in case he never found her. The very thought drove him mad. He whacked his sword against a tree trunk as he passed by it, the only sound to penetrate the silence of the woods besides his lumbering footsteps. He turned back to his thoughts and tried to focus on the good.

He remembered the way Anita would come into the store, meandering around, picking up games and comics and putting them back down, never buying a single thing. He laughed to himself as he thought about how she always found a way to bring up a conversation so naturally with him. One time they'd even talked about breadsticks for fifteen minutes. Breadsticks! He laughed again to himself. That was the kind of hold she had on him.

He pictured the way she pinned her brown hair up into a retro fifties style, secured by the blue bandana around her head. And the outfits she wore. He let out a pleasurable sigh as he imagined her long legs in those tall red heels. The ones that matched her cherry-red, full lips. He *had* to find her. That was all there was to it. He had to.

For the first time, he let his mind think about what they would do once he actually found her. The plan was always to bring her back to the apartment to live, but how long would they be able to live there? Every day it seemed like there were less people on the Earth and more undead to take their places. The feeble wooden fences wouldn't hold them out forever. Eventually, they would get in. And if they didn't, then that meant they had something good and someone else would seek to take it.

He forgot about his snowy surroundings completely as he got lost in thought. Maybe they would leave Indiana all together and try somewhere new, somewhere warm where he wouldn't have to deal with dead people while also trying to survive through a negative ten degree wind-chill. He pictured himself lying on a beach, the waves lapping at his feet, and Anita next to him in a tiny red and white bikini. His heart raced as he smiled. It was settled. They'd go to the beach. But which one? Long Beach or Miami?

A quick snap pulled him from his dreamy state back to the cold woods. He stopped dead in his tracks and raised his sword. His lungs skipped a breath. A dirty-covered, bloodied woman stood fifteen feet in front of him. He hadn't seen her coming. He didn't know why his heart was ready to burst from his chest as it beat against his ribcage. Killing zombies was almost second nature to him. He'd done it countless times.

The woman took several shuffling steps forward, dragging her boots along the inches of white snow to mix with the dirt underneath. He raised his sword even higher, ready to bring it down on her head once she got close enough. She stopped. Her mouth was parted and her eyes were unblinking. Her dark, shoulder-length hair was caked with mud. Her light skin was smeared with blood and guts. Zack swore he saw her eyes grow wet as she reached a hand out to him, still ten feet away.

"Zack?"

He heard the whisper escape her cracked lips, unsure if it was real. His sword was still raised over his head. He lowered it slowly as he tried to control his heavy breathing. When he saw tears fall, leaving streaks in the carnage on her face, he let his sword slip from his fingers and fall to the ground.

"Anita?" he said, more to himself than as a call to her.

He tried to move his feet, but they felt too heavy to lift. His vision blurred. Was what he saw real or was it all in his head? Had he wanted so desperately to find her that he was starting to imagine her, see her before him?

She moved forward again at a slow pace, her feet still dragging along the ground. Her arms reached forward as she closed the gap between them. Zack waited to feel the embrace he'd dreamt about for countless nights before the world fell apart and after. He'd waited so long for her.

A loud crack echoed and Anita crumpled to her knees. Halfway hidden behind one of the trees was a young man with a pistol that shook in his hands. Zack's eyes darted back and forth between the gun and Anita until he couldn't see through the wetness any longer. He dropped to his knees at her side and rolled her over to cradle her in his arms.

She took a slow, ragged breath as her body began to shake. "Zack," she strained softly.

"I'm here," he sobbed as the tears ran down his face and onto hers. "I'm here now. You can't leave. I've been looking for you. I have. Every day. I finally found you. You can't leave me now!" His voice escalated as her eyes grew distant.

He felt the full weight of her body slump against him as her head fell back onto his arm. "No, no, please, no," he begged, pulling her closer to him.

Bright red blood stained the white snow underneath her as a pool quickly spread. Zack held her face close to his and cried into her neck. Snow crunched ahead as someone approached.

"Oh, God," Zack heard a man gasp under his breath. He didn't raise his face to look at him. He was afraid that if he did he would lose control and kill whoever it was that took his Anita away. "Are you...?" the man started to say as he stood over Zack.

With a gentle hand, Zack brushed Anita's hair back from her face.

"Oh, God!" the man said again, louder. "Anita?"

Zack snapped his head up to look him in the face.

Dan Anderson stared down at Anita's unmoving body. His lips trembled. He dropped the pistol on the ground and raised his hands to his head. No, no, no," he repeated over and over again as he turned frantically. "No!"

Tears streamed down his dark face as he squeezed his eyes shut. "She was my friend!" he shouted. "She was my friend and I…" He broke down and collapsed to his knees, his shoulders heaving up and down as he sobbed.

Zack gently laid Anita on the ground and closed her eyes. He kissed his fingertips and placed them on her lips for a moment, sniffing back his tears to regain some semblance of control over himself. He slowly stood and looked down at the hysterical man on the ground beneath him. Deep, steady breaths seemed to work against him as they built up a roaring hatred in his heart. He clenched his jaw and ground his teeth together. His vision shook. He was going to do it. He was going to kill him.

Five other people raced forward from the trees at full speed.

"Come on! We have to get out of here," one of them called, a tall man in a leather jacket who was leading the way. "They're headed right for us!"

No one else waited for Dan to get up and join the group, or took the time to wonder who the other man was and what happened with the woman on the ground, except Gretchen. She came to a halt in front of them and kneeled down, placing a hand on Dan's back. He was bent in half at the waist, his hands covering his face.

"Dan, we have to go," she said and tugged on his arm.

He shook her off. Gretchen's eyes darted to Zack and then back. "Dan, are you OK?" she asked, more panicked than before.

"I killed her," she heard him whisper from behind his palms.

The anger boiled up in Zack. He couldn't stand it any longer. He took two bounding steps toward Gretchen and Dan with his fists clenched tightly at his side.

"No!" she yelled as she sprang to her feet and shoved at his chest. "We have to go now! Please!" She yanked on Dan's arm as he rose slowly, who put little effort in getting himself back up to his feet.

Before Gretchen stood upright again she snatched the fallen gun from the ground and tucked it into her pants next to its sister. "Let's go!" She huffed as she dragged Dan to follow the group. His feet were lazy and clumsy causing him to stumble forward. He collapsed again and refused to get up.

Gretchen turned back to Zack and her face softened when their eyes met. She looked down at Anita "I'm sorry," she said softly. "Please, come with us."

Zack looked down at Anita's streaked face, her body lying in a circle of blood as her hand rested on her still chest. He heard distant moans and feet dragging on the ground. His face scrunched and he turned towards the sky to exhale a loaded sigh. The man and woman took off together. Zack bent down, picked up his sword, and jogged after them. He didn't allow himself to look back at Anita one last time, though every ounce of his body begged him to.

XI.

The group ran for over a mile with Zack in the lead. He had burst past to the front in hopes of passing them completely, not wanting them to know where he was headed. Pushed to the breaking point, the group trailed after relentlessly. Zack would have preferred the dead.

How were these people able to keep up when they had an older, overweight woman and the man who killed Anita still crying hysterically? Even Zack had shed all the tears he could for the moment. A herd of ravenous zombies at your back will wipe your eyes bone dry real fast. When his lungs couldn't take the strain anymore he slowed down, but didn't stop to rest with the others, who were hunched over here and there trying to catch their breaths. He walked on.

"Where are you going?" Gretchen called out to him.

He didn't turn around or answer her. He didn't know what he'd do if he did. The tears might've subsided, but the rage hadn't.

"Do you have a place to stay?" she called louder. "Maybe we can come back with you?"

He stopped, facing the way towards home with his shoulders square. They rose and fell with heaving breaths, the cold air blowing from his mouth like smoke. The seething burn was rising in him again. He rounded back and came within inches of her face before anyone could stop him. He could have killed her, easily, if he had wanted to. "I don't even know you. One of your people murdered my…"

he didn't know how to finish. "Why would I want you to come with me?"

Everyone stood staggered around as they waited for Gretchen to answer him. Her eyes never left his. She opened her mouth and then closed it again and bit her bottom lip. All she could do was toss her arms up in the air and let out a sigh. "Because you're a good man."

Zack laughed with his head thrown back.

"You just lost someone and you're hurt and pissed off, but you're still a good guy. I can tell. You could have killed me and Dan back there before the rest came, but you didn't. You didn't even raise a fist to him."

"My mistake," Zack growled.

Her head lolled to the side. "I don't buy it."

Zack stared down at the trampled, muddy snow. "You don't know me or what I've done to survive."

She took a step closer and he finally looked into her eyes. They were a swirling light blue and they pierced through him like two sharp icicles. It took his breath away, not because they were stunning, which they were, but because they brought about an overwhelming sense of déja vu, like he'd already looked into those eyes, but he'd never met the woman before in his life.

He stood with his hands on his hips, kicking at the snow as he looked down at the ground again. His brown eyes turned up to scan the group of people standing in front of him. He tapped his foot. It was just him, Liam, Christine, and Jerry back at the apartments. Christine couldn't fight and Jerry's back made him useless as hell. Eventually they'd need more people to survive. The question was, were these the right people? How was he supposed to live with that kid after he killed Anita?

But apparently he was a "good man". He shook his head and scoffed when his eyes met Gretchen's again. "This way."

XII.

Apartment 624 was dark and still. Zack had been out all day looking for Anita. Liam didn't know how he went out alone like he did, with no one to have his back. He himself had been holding off on going for supplies just one more day until his friend returned to go with him, even though he only had one can of peaches to split between himself and Christine.

His body thanked him for the day off as he sat lazily on the couch. It ached from hunger, shooting arrows, and swinging Ralph's axe endlessly when the two men were out together with the dead. The things had grown in numbers the last few weeks, multiplying like bunny rabbits in springtime.

"Do you think they're coming from the city?" Christine asked as they sat and shared the peached. Liam had found two cans of cola on his run the day before and she sipped at hers, wanting to make it last as long as she could. Who knew when they'd get another sweet treat like that. "Do you think they could be trying to get away from something that's happening in Chicago?"

"Like what?" Liam asked muffled while fruit hung from his mouth.

"I don't know. Something." Her voice was distant as she wondered to herself. "Maybe there's a lot of survivors in the city and they're fighting back."

Liam didn't say anything in response.

Christine took that as a sign. He wasn't convinced "Or maybe they've found some sort of bioweapon to destroy them…or a cure." Her voice was hopeful now.

Liam let his fork fall against the ceramic bowl with a clank. "There is no cure," he said. "We've been over this."

Every time he said those words she tried to brush off like what he said wasn't a big deal, but it gnawed at her insides and made her feel sick to her stomach. She ate the last peach and grabbed the bowl from Liam's hands to put it in the sink, smiling at him all the while.

When she returned she sat on the floor between his feet and leaned her head against his knee. "Why don't you read some of Dr. Hyde's journal out loud this time?" He looked down at her and she leaned her head back all the way against the seat of the couch to look up at him. "Just to pass the time."

With little else to do and Liam reading his journal privately, the curiosity had built up in her and hit its peak. She had to know what Liam had been doing in his last days of civilization. She couldn't explain it. It was a craving she had, to know what they were studying, what plants Liam worked with and why, what they mixed them with.

His scientific and technical work used to bore her to death. She laughed under her breath as she thought about how much had changed since then. She moved up to the couch and sat close to him, her knees bent so her feet were tucked under her. Her fingers ran through his shaggy ginger hair as he opened the journal to where he last left off.

"You really need to clean this up," she said, tugging at the ends so his newly grown out beard stood up at odd angels.

"You know what I don't miss?" he said with a crooked grin.

She smiled back as she leaned her head so far to the side it almost rested on her shoulder. "What?"

"Shaving."

They both laughed, Christine burying her face into her arm that stretched out on the back of the couch. "But you have razors! You could at least clean it up so you don't look so wild and grizzly..."

"No thank you," he declared. "The beard is here to stay. I've grown quite fond of it. Now it's your turn."

"OK, um..." she said, her eyes turned up toward the ceiling. "I don't miss...trying on suit after suit to find the perfect one for work and then no one even notices."

"And I don't miss having to watch you try them on," Liam said, pulling the trigger to the finger gun he held to his temple. They laughed again.

"Well apparently you'll never have to go through that awfulness again."

The laughter died out.

Liam sniffed and adjusted his glasses. "Right." He turned back to the journal. "Shall we? We're up to the day before he died."

XIII.

Dr. Victor Faustus Hyde
Saturday June 20, 2020
07:13pm

I don't know what went wrong. The vaccine worked. It got rid of the flu. I felt amazing for a few days after it was administered. My fever broke, the aches in my body disappeared, the nausea…gone. I had several days of health like I'd never had before. There was not one thing wrong with me. Even my back felt better, which I haven't felt the absence of the pinching in my sciatic nerve in almost five years.

Then came the descent. My breathing became labored at first. Activities, like climbing the stairs at the University, a task which at my age wasn't the easiest to begin with, now feels impossible. I wheeze, I clutch my chest. There's no making it in one go. Several stops are needed. As of yesterday, there is a constant rattling with every intake of breath.

All I want to do is sleep. It's a battle every day to get work and stay awake to accomplish anything. I used to welcome the night, thinking of it as my irresistible and mysterious muse who brought out the best in my geniusness. Now she is a haggard woman beckoning me to bed.

The blood is circulating slower throughout my body. My temperature, no longer feverish, has gone in the opposite direction, plummeting, making me cold to the touch…cold all the time. Even though it's summer I am wearing a large sweater under my lab coat. No one has said anything, but then again, who's going to question their boss about his wardrobe choices?

A few members of my team have inquired about my health, no doubt concerned about my pale pallor and sunken face, another effect of slower blood circulation. My skin is mottled, discolored with blotches of different reds and blues.

I look like death walking. Thank God there's no one in the labs today. They would be frightened of my appearance. I don't know how much longer I have. I would hate to have one of my doctors find me, slumped over my desk.

I can't stop, though. Not now. We've tested on a small group of people who contracted the flu naturally. They're going to experience the same symptoms as me in a few short days. When they get better from the drug, everyone will be relieved. They'll think the world will be saved. I need to make the necessary changes to the vaccine before it's released to the public. I can't tell them what I've done. I just need to fix it. These people will just have to pass in silence for the greater good of the rest of humanity.

XIV.

Liam closed the journal slowly as his mouth hung open, horrified.

Christine sat up straight and looked at him with wide, nervous eyes.

"It's all my fault," he whispered, clutching the leather-bound journal tightly in his hands. "It's all my fault. This is my fault. I did this," his voice started to escalate as what he read hit him like a bag of bricks. "I started this! I've killed everyone!" He whipped the journal at the wall. It hit above the desk and landed on the computer monitor, knocking it over on its screen.

Christine's heart raced. Instinct made her run over to make sure it wasn't broken, but then she remembered that it didn't matter. She turned her attention back to Liam, whose face was growing redder by the second. Random thoughts on how to fix what was happening raced through her mind, each one more ineffective than the last. There was nothing she could say to make it better for him. He was right. He had started the end of the world.

Then, it hit her, all at once like a bright ray of sunshine. "If you created it, then maybe you can figure out a way to stop it."

Liam quit pacing the floor and turned to her, his hazel eyes wild looking. "Even if I had a safe place to study what we did, what I did, I wouldn't have the resources to stop it."

"We have to try," she said, standing up. "Liam, you can stop this." She grabbed his arms so he'd stand still and look at her, really hear what she was saying.

He took a deep, steadying breath. His eyes blinked slowly as he debated inwardly, but then he shook his head and stepped out of her grip. "No, it's too dangerous. We'd have to go too far out to find another lab. The university's was trashed. We can't leave. This is our home. We're safe here. *You're* safe here."

"Who cares?" she said, throwing her hands up. "I would die if it meant saving everyone left, Liam. You'd be saving the world."

"If I even know how!" he rounded on her, talking just inches from her face. "There's no guarantee. We could get there and I could have no clue how to stop it or we could both die trying. I won't lose you like that."

"You're just scared."

"You're damn right I'm bloody scared," he yelled. "You've been out there, what? Once? I've been out there every day, fighting and killing to save our lives." His arms waved wildly through the air as he spoke. "Me. And if you die then it would have been all for nothing and I would die too." His voice was starting to tremble. "I would die without you, Chris."

She threw herself into his arms and squeezed him tightly around the waist. His body shook against hers as he hunched over and cried onto her shoulder.

It was best to let it go for now, but when the time was right she'd bring it up again. She had to. The chance to revive civilization wasn't something she could let go of, not yet.

XV.

There was a loud beep and Jerry's voice rang out from the walkie-talkie on the kitchen counter.

"You better get down here, now!" His voice was fast, unlike his normal lazy way of grumbling.

Liam grabbed his bow and quiver and handed Christine Ralph's axe. "Let's go."

They ran out the door and down the stairs. Jerry was standing on his patio, leaning over the waist-high railing to stare out into the darkness. Cold rain drizzled down from the black sky. It washed the snow away to reveal thick, brown mud beneath. The dampness made Christine shiver in her knitted sweater. She pulled the hood up.

"What is it, Jer?" Liam said as they approached him.

Jerry pointed out toward the fence that ran along the side of the building next to them. The lightening was still too far away to provide enough flashes for them to see clearly, but they had no trouble hearing it—the sound of hundreds of hands and bodies beating against the fence, trying to get in.

"It's already leaning," Jerry said with his pistol grip shotgun in his hands. "It won't hold much longer."

"Do we know if there's anyone else left in the other buildings?" Liam asked quickly.

"I haven't been in to check. Zack said you two were supposed to go."

"Shit!" Liam yelled as a louder crack of thunder boomed. He wiped at his glasses furiously as the rain and sleet picked up. "We have to do something!"

"What can we do?" Christine asked. "We can't take them all on, just the three of us!"

"Where the fuck is Zack?" Liam asked, but no one answered. They all knew where Zack was and they all knew him being there wouldn't have made a lick of difference. "If the fence comes down and he comes back, he'll die trying to find us."

Christine's hands started to shake. She wasn't sure if it was from the freezing rain or from being terrified. Her mind raced through ideas. "What about the storage apartments we have?" she yelled as another loud crack echoed through the sky.

The lightening lit everything up like a strobe light for a few seconds and they saw the countless fingers grasping at the top of the fence as it leaned further in.

"Zack told me he used one for wood he found while you two were out, two by fours and stuff like that."

"Brilliant!" Liam said with a snap of his finger. He pointed the way. "Down here."

Jerry went back into his apartment and met them in the hallway at his front door. The wind blew harder and sharp beads of rain stung at the backs of their necks. "It's in the Goldsteins' old apartment," Liam said as he raced down the hall. He pounded on the door with his fist when he got there. "Zack has the key!"

"Get back!" Christine raised the axe over her head. She brought it down on the door, but it only left a long, deep scratch in the wood.

Liam stepped closer to her to take it, but she brought it down again before he could near the doorknob. She chopped away, over and over. The loud banging of the axe mixed with the continual thunder and the door broke open.

"Good job, kid," Jerry said as he passed her to go in. He slapped her on the back a few times and smiled at her warmly. She'd never seen him look at someone that way before—with pride.

They searched blindly in the dark, grabbing at whatever they could that felt long enough to be a support beam for the fence. Liam whistled to Jerry when he'd found one big enough.

"You keep looking," he said to Christine. "We'll take this one out there and come back once we've got it up."

Liam held one end while Jerry lifted the other, his face strained from the weight as his back knotted and pulled. They grunted as they took small, quick steps out to the fence. The rain beat down against them and soaked through their clothes.

Liam couldn't see a thing as the water ran over his lenses. "OK, set it down here," he hollered once they reached the fence.

Back at the apartment, Christine had found all the long wooden beams, but they were too heavy to lift by herself. She stepped out of the apartment and into the hallway to stand at the edge. Her neck craned to try to watch them put up the first beam, but the rain fell in thick sheets.

She straightened up and folded her arms. She had to bounce on her feet to keep warm. What was taking them so long? She bit her thumbnail and stretched her neck again to see if she could spot them through the heavy rain.

"We have to wedge this side in the ground and this side up under the fence. Then, we should be able to push it back up," Liam said. He didn't know if it would work, but they had to try. Liam grunted blindly as he maneuvered the heavy beam on his own.

"Watch out!" Jerry called out.

Wood creaked as the weight of the dead piled onto the fence. The further it leaned, the more the two men could make out of what was waiting for them on the other side— long, boney fingers, bloodied, savaged arms, and torn faces with gnashed teeth.

"Go back!" Liam yelled as he turned to run.

The fence gave way to the cold, muddy ground.

Liam pumped his arms as the rain beat against his face. He didn't look back, he couldn't. He didn't want to know how close the hoard of dead was to him or how many there were. "Christine!" He shouted.

She stepped out into the rain with the axe in her hands.

Liam was only halfway back to the building. "Go back! Go!"

It was hard to hear what he said, but when another white flash of light burst through the sky she saw the mass of bodies streaming in through the fallen part of the fence. The dead expanded outward like a growing pool of blood once inside. The first ones through spotted Liam and Jerry immediately and hounded after them, while others wandered around the grounds, some behind the buildings, hidden away.

"Jerry, come on!" Christine yelled as she jumped up and down to wave him in.

Jerry ran as fast as his legs could carry him. His back sent a sharp, fiery pain down the lower half of his body with every step he took. He looked over his shoulder to see three zombies about ten feet behind him.

His heart beat rapidly in his chest. He swore it was beating against his ribcage. He couldn't swallow. His throat felt constricted as the cold air and rain rushed down it. He pushed himself to run faster than he thought possible, but his back couldn't handle it. With an excruciatingly tight pinch, his left leg stiffened and he fell hard to the muddy ground.

"No!" Christine yelled as she rushed out with the axe.

Liam caught Christine around the waist before she could make it to where Jerry laid writhing in pain.

"What are you doing? We have to help him!" she cried out as she tried to push her fiancé off with her elbows.

The dead fell over Jerry as he rolled over onto his back. His screams echoed through the grounds as hands dug into his abdomen to rip out his innards. Red mouths ate away at him with fervor. Blood and carnage dripped from their chins.

Christine crumpled as her tears mixed with the rain on her face. Liam still had her around the waist and held her up from the ground as she sobbed and screamed.

Jerry, still alive, yelled out as rows of teeth sank into his neck and shoulder, ripping away the flesh to expose the tender muscle underneath. As another set tore at his throat, his screaming turned to blood-filled gurgles and then he was silent.

Several bodies made their way slowly to where Liam and Christine stood, bypassing the crowded mass devouring the lifeless body on the ground.

"Go!" Liam yelled as he shoved Christine ahead of him.

XVI.

Christine Moore ran up the stairs of building six with the axe swinging at her side. She heard an agonizing scream from behind her and almost fell. She turned with both hands clutched on the railings.

Liam held on as he was pulled back by ragged hands that gripped at his ankle. One of the mangled dead was on the ground beneath the stairs, blood dripping from its teeth as it snapped at the air. If he let go of the railing, the rotting corpse would drag him down and devour him. If he didn't do something soon, the rest would come to finish him off.

Christine raced back down the steps to him. With her axe raised high above her head, she took a breath and swung it down to sever the hands from their arms. The thing that was had once been a woman didn't recoil or writhe from the pain. It didn't bleed out or even give up. It snapped its jaws and tried to pull itself forward on its two bleeding stumps.

Christine grabbed Liam's arm and pulled him forward and up the stairs. Once inside their apartment, she slammed the door and locked every single lock while Liam let himself fall onto the couch.

When Christine was done with the door she turned to him. "Are you OK? Are you hurt? Did it bite you? Are you bleeding?" She asked question after question as she touched his head, arms, and torso, working her way down. When she got to his lower legs he stopped her and placed his hand over hers.

Tears filled her large eyes.

XVII.

The muscles in Christine's face pulled downward as she closed her eyes and lowered her head. Her shoulders shook as she cried hunched over at Liam's feet. She threw herself onto his knees and buried her face in her arms.

Liam reached a hand out to her shoulder and pushed her back away from him. The hopeless look in her swimming eyes made his throat tighten as he tried to keep himself together. "You shouldn't get too close."

"Liam," she breathed out.

She reached for him again, but he leaned further back into the couch. It was like a knife to the heart.

"I should go. It's not safe for you. You shouldn't be near me," he said as he tried to stand up. When he put weight on his right leg it buckled and he fell back again with a groan.

"You can't go," Christine sobbed. "You can't leave me now."

He leaned forward and lifted her head up so she would look at him. "You could die if I stay here with you."

She took a few ragged breaths and her bottom lip sucked in. She tried to stable herself before she spun out of control. How could this have happened? Why hadn't they reinforced the fence long ago before those things multiplied so tremendously? A shiver ran down her back as her cold, drenched clothes clung to her thin frame.

They'd been living in a false sense of security. She looked around at their apartment, a dim glow from the two logs in the fireplace was the only light source they had. Other than the lack of electricity, everything looked completely normal. It was untouched by the outside world. She'd even gotten the blood stains out of the carpet. Their supplies had dwindled to the bare minimum, so boxes no longer stacked against the wall, but were broken down and placed out of sight in the walk in closet in the bedroom. Anyone who walked in would have thought it was a safe place, that they were back in the normal world. But it wasn't safe and there was nothing normal about it.

She turned to Liam again and forced herself to take deep breaths as she closed her eyes. It worked. Her heart rate slowed a bit and her hands steadied as best they could. She wiped at her wet face as she sniffed. "I don't..." she sniffed again. "I can't live without you, Liam. I can't."

"You have to," Liam said urgently. "You have to survive this and you have to stop me from coming back."

She shook her head as the tears reemerged. Her blonde ponytail whipped at her back.

"You have to do it, Christine. Right in the head. I don't want this to turn out like it did for Sally. You have to stop me before I come back as one of those things." He reached out a hand to her. It was as cold as ice.

"I can't do it," Christine said. "I'm not going to kill you."

"You don't have a choice! Please. Promise me you'll do it."

She looked into his frantic eyes as they stared back at hers, begging for her to say she would end his life.

He was already going to die. She knew it and he knew it. They didn't have much longer together. Maybe a day, maybe a few hours, maybe less. Neither had any idea how long it took for the bite to infect a person and kill them off. They'd never seen it happen.

Christine thought about Jerry and wondered if he'd gotten back up, if he walked around looking for them so he could devour their flesh and brains. Liam's eyes urged her again and she gave in. She didn't want to spend their last moment arguing.

"OK," she said as more tears fell down her cheek. "I'll do it."

XVIII.

Christine helped Liam to the bed and lifted his leg. She was careful not to touch where it'd been bitten. "I should take a look," she said as her fingers neared the hem of his jeans. It was hard to see what was what through all the blood soaked material.

Liam breathed heavily as he leaned back on his elbows with his leg outstretched. He gave the slightest nod and squeezed his eyes shut. Off came his black sock slowly. It was saturated in blood.

Christine stopped herself from crying, but her heart continued to beat rapidly against her chest. Her thin fingers worked the pant leg carefully upward. Liam's light leg hairs were matted and tangled.

He sucked in a sharp breath of air and gave a small groan as she raised the jeans over the tender wound. Christine winced when she saw his pained face. "Sorry," she said with a matching grimace. Once his wound was exposed, she sat back and stared, trying to conceal the horror she felt.

Liam's eyes were averted to the ceiling as his breathing deepened even more. He couldn't bring himself to see how bad it was. It didn't matter. He would die either way.

The flesh had been torn away completely, leaving a hole with ripped strands of muscle hanging out. The brightest blood Christine had ever seen flowed out and onto the white sheets. "Oh, God," she breathed as she got up and ran to the bathroom. She searched the cabinets in a blind panic.

When she came back seconds later she had one of their first aid kits clenched in her hands. Her fingertips were white from the pressure of her hold.

"There's no point in wasting anything on it," Liam said, still looking at the ceiling. "Just wrap it up and leave it."

She sat on the edge of the bed and unrolled the gauze.

Liam yelled out when it touched the shred of flesh and gaping hole in his leg. With every wrap he lifted himself from the bed and winced. The pain was worse than anything he could have ever imagined. When she was done, Christine climbed onto the bed to lay next to him. He leaned his head back onto the pillow and turned his head to face her. Sweat ran down into his eyes.

"You're so strong, love." His voice was soft and strained.

Christine let out a throaty laugh as more tears fell to soak the pillow. "No, I'm not."

"Yes, you are and you're going to survive this. I know you are." Her head turned down and her eyes shut tight. "Hey," he said sharply. She looked up at him again though her long lashes. "You're *going* to *make it*."

She nodded her head and let her eyes close again as she tried to sniff back the tears. "If I do, then I'll be just like one of them…" Her eyes flickered over the black windowpane. "Dead inside."

Liam coughed into his hands. It racked his entire body and rattled in his chest. Christine reached a hand out to his forehead.

"You're warm," she said, sitting upright.

"Really? I feel so bloody cold."

She hopped off the bed and stood next to him. They worked together to get him under the thick, gray blanket, which he pulled up to his chin and clutched in his hands. Christine wondered which would take him first, the infection or the loss of blood. She looked down at him and brushed the hair from his eyes. Something was missing.

"Where's your glasses?" she asked.

"They fell off when I bent down to set the beam on the ground," he said with a huffy laugh. "Probably why I didn't see that one crawling by the stairs. Blind as a bat, you know."

Something so simple, so small, something they never even considered as lifesaving lay somewhere in the mud, trampled on by the relentless shuffling of the dead.

XIX.

As the sun slowly rose over the horizon, it lit up the apartment grounds. The bloodied dead and carnage that strewn the mud and grass basked in the warm orange glow. A robin chirped in the tree right outside the bedroom window. Christine looked over as Liam, who groaned on the bed. He'd tossed and turned all night, sweating under the covers as his fever rose. He constantly shook with chills.

Christine hadn't left his side for a minute, worried that if she did he would slip away and died alone. She didn't want to let that happen. She needed him to know she was with him to the very end, just as they'd promised when she said yes in the university library, when he got down on one knee and handed her a small diamond ring. They were as good as married in her mind and she wouldn't abandon her husband.

As he tried to sleep throughout the night she drifted in and out of consciousness, distracted by thoughts about what to do when Liam was gone. It seemed almost heartless to think about herself while he lie there helpless, but she couldn't stop. No matter what she tried to focus her mind on to fall asleep, it always wandered back to how she would end his suffering. It was rapidly approaching and she had to be ready for it.

Though she'd told Liam she would stop him before he turned, she was tempted to let it happen. If he became one of them and bit her, then she would be one of them too. They would both be dead and unaware of everything, but they'd be together again. The thought enticed her as she sat in the darkness on the edge of the bed.

By the time he woke up, she'd made her decision. She was going to do it. All she had to do was ease him into death and let him take her with him. She wasn't fit to survive without him. There was no point in trying. She didn't want to spend her last days in lonely misery without the man she loved.

"Christine," he called out for her in a coarse, weak voice.

"I'm here." She scooted closer to him and took his sweaty, cold hand in hers.

He coughed and rolled over to his side so his mouth was covered by the pillow. His chest wheezed and rattled. When he was done he faced upright again. The wheezing continued. All the color had drained from his face. He could barely open his heavy-lidded eyes as they watered continually. His lips were white and cracked. Christine looked over and saw droplets of blood splattered on the pillowcase.

"I want you…to tie me…to the bed," he said.

She looked at him with her eyebrows scrunched together and her lips pursed.

"Just in case…anything…goes…wrong…when you…"

Sticking to her promise not to argue with him as he wasted away in front of her, she forced a thin smile and nodded her head. Her blue eyes softened as they looked into his, which were no longer the brilliant, lively green and brown she'd looked into lovingly over the last few years. They'd turned a light, grayish color as they started to glaze over white.

She went to the closet and dug out several fashionable scarves in various colors and patterns. Once she'd sat him up, she tied a scarf around each of his wrists and then tied the other end to one of the bars on the wrought iron headboard. He tugged weakly at them to make sure they'd hold. His chin fell to his chest as he took labored breaths from the exertion.

"It'll have…to do." When he coughed again blood splattered onto Christine's jeans and tan long-sleeved shirt.

It caught her off guard and she flinched. She looked down at herself and took a steadying breath. When she looked back at him, she smiled softly.

His eyes were wide in horror. "I'm sorry...I didn't...oh, God. I'm sorry—"

"It's OK," she said and grabbed one of his tied up hands in both of hers.

He leaned all the way back and looked up as he tried to breathe normally. Each intake felt like knives in his lungs. Blood started to fill them slowly. He gasped for air like a fish out of water, unable to take enough in. His eyelids drooped as his head started to spin. It couldn't be the end already. There was so much left he wanted to do, so much he wanted to say to Christine.

She started to cry as she squeezed his hand tighter in hers. "You can't die, Liam," she said softly. "You were going to save everyone." She eyed the old journal on his nightstand.

As he coughed, she heard wet gurgles bubble up in his throat. His body made small, jerking movements as he choked on the blood. She stood up and covered her mouth with her hands. She wanted to look away, but she couldn't. Her muffled cries pierced the air as she watched him suffer violently on the bed. She ran back over to him and squeezed his hand in hers again as she knelt down beside the bed.

"I love you," she cried over and over again.

The gurgling became less frequent and his movements slowed until they stopped all together. Blood dripped from the side of his mouth as it hung open. His white, hazy eyes still bulged from his head. All of his limbs were spread out to lay awkwardly, tangled in the sheets.

Christine lowered her head to his chest and gave in to the rush of sadness. Her body ached with grief and exhaustion. They'd promised themselves to each other forever. The fact that he was gone stabbed at her and ripped her heart open. Why did he have to get bitten? It should have been her. She buried her head into his sweater. She was weak. Liam was stronger than her, smarter than her. He could have stopped it if he'd lived.

The covers on the bed shook as Liam's foot moved again. Christine opened her eyes and raised her head slowly. She wiped the tears from her cheek.

His white eyes were wide open. Large red vessels ran through them. He opened and closed his mouth, like an infant taking its first breath. Blood covered his lips and chin. He growled when his eyes settled on her and snapped his teeth. She sat upright on her knees and stared at the monster in front of her. *It was now or never*, she thought. She moved her arm closer as the click of his teeth filled her ears.

XX.

Zack and the group that followed him had finally made their way to the Dune Ridge apartment complex. They walked stealthily through the grounds once they climbed over the front gate.

"It's all the way in the back," he whispered. "Watch it!"

Two of the dead slowly sauntered out from one of the open hallways. They goes guttural moans and redirected themselves to the fresh meat standing ten yards away.

"Oo, can I?" Olivia asked as she smacked her bat against her hand. There was a faded signature scrawled across the middle portion.

"We both will," Zack said.

She was just a child. He couldn't let her do it alone. If Dan had volunteered, then maybe he would have let him and even given him a good push toward the putrid flesh bags. But it wouldn't be right with a young girl, like Olivia.

They charged the two rotting male corpses together. With one swing of the bat, the larger of the two was down on the ground. The side of its head was caved in and leaked brain matter and blood onto the slush-covered pavement.

"Yes!" she cheered herself on.

Zack drove his sword between the eyes of the second one and drew it out quickly. It fell to the ground with a thud. Silence followed as they started forward again, closely knit together with their weapons raised.

They came up to where the fence had been trampled down the night before. Several corpses lay on the ground with their heads smashed to mush, their arms and legs broken and bent in different directions. Zack followed the trail of mangled bodies to where they'd been headed and stopped at a section of the pavement that was stained with a ring of dark blood. There were pieces of flesh and carnage scattered, but no body.

Zack's stomach sank. He knew what a fresh kill looked like. He'd seen those things take down a guy in the woods not too long ago on one of his searches for...

Anita's face popped into his head. He gave a quick shake until it dissipated.

"Not now," he told himself.

"What?" Olivia asked from behind him.

"Nothing. It's that one right there." He pointed to building six.

"And there's three of them you said?" Rowan asked from the back of the group.

"Should be."

More dead loitered around the parking lot, barely moving their feet as they swayed back and forth. But when they spotted the group, they snapped out of their catatonic state and closed in from all sides. Their frenzied moans called more out of hiding as others limped and staggered out of the buildings.

"Everyone, get ready," Zack ordered. "Form a circle and be quick. And don't shoot. It'll only draw more out. Hit them in the temple with your gun if you have to." He took a deep breath as the gap between him and the two dead shambling forward grew smaller.

Olivia jumped up and down. She tossed her elbows out to make sure there was enough room between her and Lee on her right and Gretchen on her left.

Rowan looked over at Zack, who stood readily next to him, and tried to emulate his poised stance. He turned his gun backwards so he would be able to thrust it into the first head that came close to him.

Three more putrid corpses, two bulky males and one petite female, picked up their pace the closer they got, grabbing at the air for momentum to pull them forward quicker.

Gale tried to ignore everyone else around her as she zeroed in on the two males closest to her. She played out in her mind how she was going to take them down with her knife.

The gaps had been closed and the zombies were practically on top of the group. "Now!" Zack yelled. Everyone lunged forward and away from each other.

Gretchen cringed as the sounds of multiple skulls being smashed in hit her ears. She drove her Bowie knife into the ear of the decaying female that reached out for her neck. It fell to the ground at her feet, creating a small obstacle for the others.

The largest of the corpses that headed her way tripped over the body on the ground and lunged forward, grasping one of Gretchen's arms in its hands. It pulled closer to its mouth, already working its jaw into a frantic chewing motion.

Zack brought his sword down on the back of the thing's neck and then quickly turned again to his own target in a matter of seconds. Its neck was severed so deeply that the head hung forward against its chest, its red teeth still snapping. Gretchen gave it a quick shove to the ground and then squatted down over it. She drove her knife through the temple.

Within minutes the relentless undead were nothing more than a pile of disfigured bodies in the parking lot. The group stepped over them carefully and continued toward building six. In the far off distance, more glazed eyes turned from the sound of pattering feet.

Zack stopped at Jerry's place and turned the doorknob to see if it was unlocked. It was and that made his stomach twist into knots and then sink down into a bottomless black pit inside him. The one bedroom apartment was silent and dark. He called out, but no one answered. Jerry wasn't out on his patio either. He closed the door and banged on it with both his fists. They hung in the air as the image of the large bloodstain he'd seen flashed in his mind.

"Come on," he said as he ran for the stairs. "I need to check on my friends."

He ran up, taking two steps at a time as his arms pumped vigorously. He stopped in front of apartment 624. His hand was on the doorknob, but he stopped. He held his breath as he turned it. When the door opened his stomach gave a lurch. He swallowed the lump in his dry throat and stuck one foot out into the apartment.

There was no one in the kitchen or the living room. Zack moved further in and craned his neck to look around and make sure there wasn't anything, or anyone, hidden in the corners of the rooms. Everything was silent.

"Sit here," he whispered to the others as he pointed to the couch.

With his sword clutched in his hand, he crept over to the bedroom door. He took a quick peek inside the darkened bathroom adjacent to it. He pulled back the shower curtain. The tub was also empty. He stood in front of the closed bedroom door and took a deep breath in through his nose and let the air exhale out through his mouth.

The group of wanderers watched him from a few feet away. Gretchen held her breath as he reached for the knob. He turned it and rushed inside, disappearing behind the doorframe. And then there was silence.

XXI.

Christine Moore sat on the edge of the bed, her hands clasped together and her head turned down. She looked up when the door opened, but that was the only movement she made. Tears streaked her cheeks and neck.

"Zack?" she said softly as her eyes opened wide.

His gaze drifted to Liam, who was tied to the bed with his head slumped over. Blood oozed from where he'd been stabbed. Zack's eyes clouded over. He squeezed his eyes shut and let the tears run down his face. He was too late.

Zack ran to Christine and threw his arms around her as he knelt down at her feet. He cried into her lap as she let her arm drape loosely around the back of his neck.

In the next room, the others listened in. "I'm going to see what's going on," Gretchen said as she stood up.

"Just let him be," Dan said. "Obviously something bad happened."

"Yeah, if he needed help he would have hollered," Olivia said as she ran a cloth from her back pocket over her bat to clean it.

"I don't care," Gretchen said. "I'm going to make sure he's OK." She walked over to the bedroom and stopped in the doorway as her hand rested on the frame.

Christine looked up and removed her hands slowly from Zack. He sniffed and wiped at his face and then turned around on his knee to see what she was looking at.

"Gretchen?" Christine said with her face scrunched in disbelief.

Gretchen's hand fell away from the doorframe. As her eyes widened, her mouth parted slowly. "Christine!" Tears filled her eyes as she ran to embrace her.

"You know her?" Zack's eyes shifted from one to the other. He hadn't noticed when he saw Gretchen alone, but now that they stood closely together, he saw the resemblance.

Christine pulled away from Gretchen and looked over her shoulder at him. "She's my sister."

Gretchen laughed as the tears ran down her face. She squeezed Christine tightly. Soon, everyone was crowded in the doorway to see what was going on. Gretchen turned to the group and wiped the wetness from under her eyes. "This is my sister!" she introduced with tearful enthusiasm. "This is the group I've been with," she said to Christine. "That's Dan, Lee, Rowan, Gale, Olivia…"

"Oh my God!" Christine yelled. "Carolyn! Luke told us you were dead, that you'd been bitten!"

Carolyn Bock puffed air out from her mouth and rolled her eyes. "That stupid dick chaired me into my apartment when he saw a little scratch on my ankle. But I got out," she smiled with a sense of pride. "I would've loved to have seen the look on his face when he found the place empty. Where is the bastard?"

"Probably dead," Christine said with a tight, unsympathetic voice. "He left and never came back."

Carolyn blinked slowly as she stared. Revenge had been served. She should've been happy. Her back slackened as she bit her lip. Something heavy grew in her stomach and weighed it down.

"Holy shit," Rowan said under his breath. It snapped Carolyn back from her thoughts.

Gale grinned ear to ear and clapped her hands together once loudly. "Well, I'll be damned! Little Gretchen's sister! I didn't even know you had a sister."

"Yup," Gretchen said as she turned back to Christine with the biggest grin any of them had ever seen on her face. "My sister's alive!"

XXII.

They all left the bedroom and Christine closed the door shut quietly behind them. She didn't know why she handled the door with such delicacy. She didn't have to worry about waking Liam up anymore. He was dead, gone forever.

She walked over to the bay window, but her legs wouldn't bend to sit down. There was too much energy that coursed through her veins. Gretchen stood close by her side, unable to stop looking at her and smiling. Christine eyed her and then looked away.

"What happened?" Zack asked.

Christine looked down at the ground. She wasn't sure how she was supposed to talk about it when she'd come so close to letting Liam bite her. She looked at Zack with her head rested to the side and gave in to a morbid grin. "The fence came down when they were trying to prop it up. They ran, but Jerry…" She sighed and closed her eyes. When she opened them again, she continued. "Liam was bit on the leg," she said quickly and left it at that.

Zack let out a grief stricken sigh. "I should have been here."

Christine shook her head. "It wouldn't have mattered. There were so many. We were overrun."

Silence filled the room and hung heavily in the air. Christine replayed in her head what she'd done to Liam only moments ago. The tears started to well up in her eyes again. She shook them off as she remembered something. She disappeared into the bedroom and returned with a brown leather journal, which she handed to Zack. He turned it over in his hands.

"It's Dr. Hyde's journal, Liam's boss. He started this. He created the virus, accidentally, in his lab," she said, talking excitedly as she gestured wildly to the journal. She tapped her finger on the cover as Zack grasped onto it. "He wrote everything down in here!" She looked up at him with her large, blue eyes wide with hope.

Zack opened the journal and saw the small scribblings. "Did Liam know what he was doing?" He didn't want to think his friend had helped someone destroy the world. Liam wouldn't have done that.

"Of course not," Christine said, pulling her eyebrows together. "Dr. Hyde didn't even know what he was doing. They were working together to try and stop that horrible flu, remember?"

Zack's memory jogged back and he nodded his head. "Right. I forgot about that."

Christine tapped the journal again to keep his attention focused. "If we can get this in the right hands," she said looking up into his heavily bearded face, "they might be able to stop this."

Zack lowered the journal and gazed at her. Everyone else in the room stood perfectly still. Christine took a few steps back so she could see them all at once. They waited, ready to cling for dear life to her next words.

"We need to take this to a lab, or someone who can put an end to this."

Olivia was the first to roll her eyes and look away. "And where exactly is this fantasy lab?"

Zack whipped around and tightened his lips. Olivia straightened up and snapped her mouth shut.

"Chris...I haven't found a single place out there with living people in it, let alone a fully functioning lab with scientists and a team. I don't think it's out there."

"Oh, it's out there," Christine said through her teeth. "And we're going to find it. We have to."

"Where should we start looking?" Gretchen asked as she placed a soft hand on her sister's arm.

Christine recoiled. "Chicago."

There was a grumble from several people in the room.

"That's almost forty miles away," Carolyn whined as her shoulders slumped.

"Why Chicago?" Olivia asked with a wrinkled nose.

"I remember a while back, Liam had to go to this huge research facility there for some test. He said it was the biggest lab he'd ever seen. It's our best shot." As Christine looked out at the group, one by one their eyes turned away.

"Or we could just wait here to die," Christine said in a matter-of-fact tone. "Because those are our options right now. Attempt to get this journal into the right hands and possibly save the world, or die." She let the words sink in before she spoke again. "I don't know about you, but I still think this world is worth saving."

"My sister's right. We should at least try." Gretchen smiled at Christine.

Everyone else in the room looked to Zack, as if he had the final say. He shrugged his shoulders. "I mean, what else do we have to do?"

"I'm in," Gale said.

Olivia picked up her bat and swung it around to rest on her shoulders as her arms draped lazily over it. "Well, Chicago can't be any worse than here."

Everyone turned to look at Rowan, who leaned against the patio door. He had one ankle crossed over the other as he rested his head back. He felt the pressure of their eyes on him as they waited for him to join in on their mission. He pushed off the door and stood tall. "Fine. Let's do this. Let's go to Chicago."

Christine's eyes lit up briefly before they clouded over with tears. She hugged Zack. Even though Liam was dead, she would carry on. She would be the one to save the world, if it was at all possible. She stepped forward to talk with the others, ready to start making a plan for the best way to get into the city. Chatter filled the room as they talked it over with each other.

Zack looked down at the journal in his hands and gave it a squeeze. A smile spread across his weary face. They might not have the key to ending the zombie plague. There was no guarantee they would even make it to Chicago. Some of them could die trying to get there. They could all die. But they going to try.

Look for

Dead Beginnings: Lonnie Lands

The first in a series of short novellas from the *Dead Soil* world that reveal what the characters were doing when the plague took over and how they survived their first night in a zombie infested world.

Coming December 2015